A WILD CARDS MOSAIC NOVEL

FULL
HOUSE

The Wild Cards Universe

A WILD CARDS MOSAIC NOVEL

FULL HOUSE

Edited by
George R. R. Martin

Written by

Daniel Abraham

Victor Milán

Caroline Spector

Carrie Vaughn

David D. Levine

Paul Cornell

Melinda M. Snodgrass

Stephen Leigh

Walter Jon Williams

Marko Kloos

TOR

TOR PUBLISHING GROUP

New York

FULL HOUSE

A Tor Book
Published by Tom Doherty Associates / Tor Publishing Group
120 Broadway
New York, NY 10271

www.tor-forge.com

Tor® is a registered trademark of Macmillan Publishing Group, LLC.

The Library of Congress has cataloged the hardcover edition as follows:

Names: Martin, George R. R., editor.
Title: Full house / edited by George R. R. Martin.
Description: First edition. | New York : Tor, 2022. | Series: Wild cards ; 30 |
"A Tom Doherty Associates book"
Identifiers: LCCN 2022008266 (print) | LCCN 2022008267 (ebook) |
ISBN 9781250167958 (hardcover) | ISBN 9781250167972 (ebook)
Subjects: LCSH: Science fiction, American. | Short stories, American. |
LCGFT: Science fiction. | Short stories.
Classification: LCC PS648.S3 F84 2022 (print) | LCC PS648.S3 (ebook) |
DDC 813'.0876208—dc23/eng/20220310
LC record available at https://lccn.loc.gov/2022008266
LC ebook record available at https://lccn.loc.gov/2022008267

ISBN 978-1-250-16796-5 (trade paperback)

Our books may be purchased in bulk for promotional, educational, or
business use. Please contact your local bookseller or the Macmillan Corporate
and Premium Sales Department at 1-800-221-7945, extension 5442, or by
email at MacmillanSpecialMarkets@macmillan.com.

First Tor Paperback Edition: 2023

Printed in the United States of America

0   9   8   7   6   5   4   3   2   1

to Amy, master minion,
thanks for holding down the fort

and to Jack-Jack, a star of the future,
keep writing, keep drawing, keep dreaming

A WILD CARDS MOSAIC NOVEL

FULL
HOUSE

When We Were Heroes

by Daniel Abraham

MANHATTAN SMELLS LIKE RAIN. The last drops fall from the sky or else the rooftops, drifting down through the high air. With every step, her dress shoes throw out splashes from the thin, oily puddles. It's ruining the leather, and she doesn't care. Her fingers, wrapped around her smartphone, ache, and she wants to throw it, to feel the power flow through her arm, down out along the flat, fast trajectory, and then detonate like a hand grenade. She could do it. It's her wild card power. She's not in the outfit she uses at the exhibitions and fund-raisers. She doesn't look like a hero now. She doesn't feel like one.

The brownstone huddles between two larger buildings, and she stops, checking the address. The east side, north of Gramercy Park, but walking distance. She always forgets that he comes from money.

The steps leading to the vestibule are worn with time and dark green with the slime of decomposed leaves. An advertisement for a new season of *American Hero* covers the side of a bus with the soft-core come-ons of half a dozen young men and women. Sex sells. She walks up the steps and finds the apartment number.

Jonathan Tipton-Clarke, handwritten in fading green ink. When he's being an ace, he calls himself Jonathan Hive. No one else does. Everyone calls him Bugsy. She stabs in the code on the intercom's worn steel keypad.

For a moment, she thinks he'll pretend he's not there, and she wonders how far she'll go. Rage and betrayal and embarrassment flow through her. Breaking down his door would be illegal. It would only make things worse. But still . . .

"Hey, Kate," Bugsy says from the intercom.

"Are you looking at me right now?"

"Yeah. I've got one on the wall. Just to your left."

A tiny, acid-green wasp stares at her. Its black eyes are empty as a camera. Its wings shift, catching the morning light. Jonathan Hive, who can turn his body into a swarm of wasps. Jonathan Hive, who was there when they stopped the genocide in Egypt. Who fought the Radical in Paris and then again during the final battle in the Congo. Kate lifts her brows at the wasp, and Bugsy's sigh comes from the intercom. The buzzer sounds resigned; the bolt clicks open. She pulls the door open, pauses, and flicks a tiny wad of pocket lint from between her fingers. It speeds to the wall and detonates like a firecracker. She can't tell whether the wasp escaped.

His apartment is on the fourth floor, and she takes the stairs three at a time. When she gets there, she's not even winded. He's waiting for her, the apartment door standing open. Hair wild from the pillow. Lichenous stubble. Bloodshot eyes. His bathrobe was white, is gray. Wasps shift under his skin the way they do when he's nervous.

"Come on in. I'll make you some coffee."

She holds out her phone, and he takes it. The web browser is at the mobile site for *Aces!* magazine. In the image, she is standing on the street by a small park, kissing a man. His face is hard to make out. Hers is unmistakable. The headline is DANGEROUS CURVES.

Underneath it, the byline is his name. And then the first few lines of text:

There's nothing more American than baseball, explosions, and first date hookups. Well, lock up your sons, New York. Everyone's sweetheart is on the town, and she's looking for some man action!

"What the hell is this?" she asks.

"The end of a good night?" he says, and hands it back.

♣

Twelve hours earlier, she'd stepped out of an off-off-Broadway theater onto the Sixth Avenue sidewalk. Traffic was stopped on Spring Street and backed up for more than a block, the air filled with braying horns and the stink of exhaust. Clouds hung over the city so low, it seemed like someone on the Chrysler building could reach out a hand and scratch them. Above her, the marquee read MARAT/SADE, black letters on glowing white, then underneath it, NYC's ONLY ALL-JOKER CAST! She paused on the sidewalk, her hands in the pockets of her jeans, cleared her throat. Outrage and disbelief warred in her mind, until she shook her head and started laughing.

"It's always kind of a confrontational play," a man's voice said. She'd been aware of someone coming out to the street behind her but hadn't particularly taken notice of him. Middle twenties. Dark hair that looked good unruly. Friendly smile.

"Confrontational," she said, laughing around the word.

"Not always *that* confrontational. This production was a little . . . yeah."

Curveball pointed at the theater.

"Did I miss something," she said, "or were they actually throwing *shit* at us?"

The man looked pained and amused at the same time.

"Cow pats. I think that technically makes it manure," he said. "It's always rough when you're trying to out-Brecht Brecht."

Tomorrow was her exhibition show, the last one on this leg of the tour. She'd been planning to go out with Ana as her local guide, but her friend had been called out of town on business at the last minute and wouldn't be back until morning. Kate had decided to make it an adventure. Grab a cheap ticket from the same-day kiosk on Water Street, take herself out to dinner someplace, spend an evening on the town. She had enough money to splurge a little, and she wasn't in Manhattan often enough anymore for it to seem normal. The title *Marat/Sade* had seemed interesting, probably because of the slash. She hadn't known anything about it, going in. Then the lights had gone up, and things got weird fast. For instance, the Sade half was actually the Marquis de Sade.

And it was a musical.

"Was there a point to that?" Kate asked, leaning against the streetlamp.

"The cow pats in particular?"

"*Any* of it?"

"Sure, if you look at the script," he said. "Marat's heading up the Terror after the French Revolution. De Sade's . . . well, de Sade. They're kind of the worst of political life and the worst of private life put together for comparison. I actually wrote a paper on Peter Weiss back in college."

"And the shit-flinging?"

"The deeper structural message can be lost, yes," he said with a grin.

From down the block, a young black man in a sand-colored shirt waved. "Tyler!"

The dark-haired man turned and held up a finger in a just-a-minute gesture. Tyler. His smile was all apology.

"I've got to go," he said, and Curveball lifted a hand, half permission, half farewell. Tyler paused. She felt a moment's tightness and the giddiness

faded. She knew what came next. *I'm a big fan. Can I get a picture with you?*
She'd say yes, because she always did because it was polite.

"Some of us are heading over to Myko's for drinks and cheap souvlaki,"
Tyler said. "If you want to come hang out, you'd be welcome."

"Um."

"They don't throw manure. That I've noticed."

Do you know who I am? slid to the back of her tongue and stopped there.
He didn't. Tyler's friend called for him again.

"Sure," she said. "Why not?"

♠

Bugsy's apartment smells stale. She wants to make the scent into old laundry or unwashed dishes, but it isn't that. It's air that has been still for too
long. The kitchen is in the uncomfortable place between dirty and clean. A
radio in a back room is tuned to NPR. In the main room, there are piles of
books on the coffee table. Murder mysteries, crossword puzzles. The DVD
of a ten-year-old romantic comedy perches on the armrest of the couch,
neither box nor sleeve in sight. He starts a coffee grinder, and the high
whining of hard beans being ripped apart makes speech impossible for a
few seconds. The silence rushes in.

"You're working for *Aces!*," she says, even though they both already
know it.

"I am. Reporting to the public at large which of their heroes are going
commando to the Emmys. Keeping the world safe for amateur celebrity
gynecologists."

"Does the Committee know?"

The coffee machine burbles and steams. Bugsy grins.

"You mean the Great and Glorious Committee to Save Everyone and
Fix Everything? I kind of stepped back from that."

There is a pause. *Just like you did* hangs in the air like an accusation, but
he doesn't push it.

"What happened?"

She means *What happened to you?* but he seems to take it as *What happened to your job?* Maybe they're the same question. He pours coffee into
a black mug with the gold-embossed logo of a bank on the side and hands
it to her. She takes it by reflex.

"Well, there was this thing. It was about six months after we took out
the Radical," he says. "Lohengrin called me and a few other guys in for
this sensitive Committee operation at this little pit outside Assab."

"I don't know where Assab is," she says. The coffee warms her hands.

"So you get the general idea," he says, leaning against the counter. His fingernails are dirty. She's known him for years, but she can't remember if it's normal for him. "Idea was to get some kind of industrial base going. Fight poverty by getting someone a job. You wouldn't think there'd be a lot of pushback on that, but there was. So essentially what you've got is this textile plant out in the middle of the desert with maybe two hundred guys working there, and five aces set up to do security until the locals can figure out what a police force would look like. I was half of the surveillance team."

"Was this the fire?" she asks.

He smiles, happy that she's heard of it.

"It made the news a couple of times, yeah. No one much noticed. It happened the same week Senator Lorring got caught sending pictures of his dick to that guy in Idaho, so there were more important things going on."

"I saw it," she says. "Someone died."

"Bunch of folks died, but most of them were African, so who gives a shit, right? The only reason we got a headline at all was Charlie. An ace goes down, that's news. Nats kill him, even better."

Her phone vibrates. She looks at it with a sense of dread, but the call is from Ana's number. Relieved, she lets it drop to voice mail.

"They had us in this crappy little compound," Bugsy says. "Seriously, this apartment? *Way* bigger. The place was all cinder blocks and avocado green carpet. Ass ugly, but we were only there for a couple months. Charlie was a nice kid. Post-colonial studies major from Berkeley, so thank God he was an ace or he'd never have gotten a job, right? Mostly, he hung around playing Xbox. He was all about hearing. Seriously, that guy could hear a wasp fart from a mile away."

"Wasps fart?" she says, smiling despite herself. He always does this, hiding behind comedy and vulgarity. Usually, it works.

"If I drink too much beer. Or soda, really. Anything carbonated. Anyway, Charlie was my backup. My shift, I'd send out wasps, keep an eye on things. His, he'd sit outside with this straw cowboy hat down over his eyes and he'd listen. Anything interesting happened, and we'd send out the goon squad to take care of it. We had Snowblind and a couple of new guys. Stone Rockford and Bone Dancer."

"Stone Rockford?"

"Yeah, well. Be gentle with the new kids, right? All the cool names are taken. Anyway, first three days, there were five attacks. Usually, they'd aim for right around shift change when there were a lot of guys going in or coming out. Then two and a half weeks of nothing. Just East African weather, energy from a generator, and a crappy Internet connection. We figured we had it made. Bad guys had been driven back by the aces, they'd just stay low and act casual until the police force was online and hope they were a softer target.

"I was the senior guy. Been there since the Committee got started. Since before. Charlie gave me a lot of shit about that. How I was all hooked in at the United Nations. Big mover and shaker. And, you know, I think I kind of believed it, right? I mean it's not just anyone can go into Lohengrin's office and steal his pens. I was out there making the world a better place. Doing something. Saving people. Boo-yah, and God bless.

"You know what they sent us to eat? Sausages and popcorn. We had like fifty cans of those little sausages that look like someone made fake baby fingers out of Silly Putty and about a case of microwave popcorn. I mean seriously, how are you going to strike a blow for freedom and right when you're fueling up on popcorn and processed chicken lips, right?"

She drinks the coffee, surprised by how bad it is. Bright and bitter. She expects him to distract her from the picture of her kiss with the tragedy in Africa, so it surprises her when he's the one to go back to it. Maybe he's trying to distract her from what happened in Africa. Maybe he's distracting himself.

"It's not actionable," he says, nodding to her phone. "You can ask any lawyer anywhere. You were in public. There's no legal expectation of privacy."

"Do you think that's the point?"

He looks away, shrugs. "I'm just saying it was legal."

She leans against the wall, unfinished red brick scratching her shoulder. She thinks of the cinder block in the compound and the exposed ductwork at Myko's, the thick, muddy coffee she drank the night before and the one in her hand now.

"Were you following me?" she asks.

"You think? Of course I was following you."

"Why?"

He almost laughs at her. It's like she's asking where the sun will rise tomorrow, if he's breathing, whether summer is colder than winter. Anything self-evident.

"Because you're in town. I mean the whole point is to get stories about aces. We're public figures. Most weeks, I have to find something to say about the people who are in the city. There's only so many issues in a row that the readers are going to care about whether Peregrine's hit menopause. Someone new comes in, I'd be stupid not to check up, see if anything's interesting. I was thinking I'd just write up the exhibition thing this afternoon. The fund-raiser. But this is *way* better."

When the anger comes back, she notices it has died down a little. She tries not to think what Tyler will say about the article. How he'll react. The fear and embarrassment throw gasoline on the fire.

"When I'm at work," she says, forming each word separately, "you can come to work. This is my private life, and you stay out of it."

"Wrong, friend. That's not how it is," Bugsy says. The sureness in his voice surprises her. "Everyone knows who we are. They look up to us or they hate us or whatever. You're not doing these exhibition things because people just love seeing stuff blow up. They can blow stuff up without you any day of the week. They come to see *you*. They pay to see *you*. You don't get to tell them they care about you one minute and not the next. It's their pick whether they pay any attention to you at all, and you make your money asking them to. So don't tell me that here's your personal you and here's your public you and that you get to make those rules. You don't get to tell people what they think. You don't even get to tell people whether they *admire* you."

With every sentence, his finger jabs the air. The buzz in his voice sounds like a swarm. Tiny green bullets buzz around them both, curving though the air. His chin juts, inviting violence. She can see how it would happen: the toss of the mug, his body scattering into thousands of insects, the detonation. Her own anger reaches toward it, wants it. The only thing that holds her back is how badly he wants it too. He's trying to change the subject.

She laughs. "Hey, Bugsy. You know what the sadist said to the masochist?" He blinks. His mouth twitches. He doesn't rise to the bait, so she acts as if he had. She leans forward. "*No*," she says.

"I don't get it."

"We're aces, so everybody knows us. We don't get to pick how they feel. We're still talking about Charlie, aren't we?"

◆

Myko's was a small place with a dozen tables smashed into enough space for half that number. Posters of Aegean-blue seas hung from the walls by Scotch-taped corners. The walls were white up to the six-and-a-half-foot mark where the drop ceiling had been ripped out, exposed ductwork and wires above it. Crisp-skinned chicken and hot oregano thickened the air and made the wind picking up outside look pleasantly cool.

"I don't know why the hell I let you talk me into these things," Tyler's friend said. She hadn't asked his name, and hadn't offered hers. The other two at the table were a Lebanese-looking woman named Salome and a joker guy in a tracksuit that they all called Boss. He wasn't really that bad looking, for a joker. All the flesh was gone from one of his arms, and his skin was a labyrinthine knotwork of scars. He could almost have been just someone who'd survived a really horrific burn.

"Did I talk you into something?" Tyler said.

"You did say it was a cool play," Boss said.

"It is a cool play," Tyler said. "It's just a lousy production."

Everyone at the table except her and Tyler laughed, and his glance thanked her for her tacit support.

"You are the only person I know who'd make that distinction," Salome said. "When you say 'this is a cool play,' I think you mean, 'it would be cool to go to this play.' What was that whole whipping him with her hair thing about?"

"They took that from the movie," Tyler said.

"There's a *movie*?" Tyler's nameless friend said, his eyes going wide.

"Look, I understand that it's kind of an assault on the senses," Tyler said. "That's part of the point. Weiss wanted to break through the usual barrier between the audience and the actors. Not just break the fourth wall, but burn it down and piss on the ashes."

"*That* sounds like the play I just watched," Boss said.

The waiter swooped in on her left, piling the ruins of their dinner on one arm and unloading demitasses of dangerous-looking coffee and plain, bread-colored cookies from the other. His hip pressed against her shoulder in a way that would have been intimate in any other setting and didn't mean anything here.

"I don't know," she said. "I can understand the idea of trying to shake up people's expectations, but then I sort of feel like you have to do something with them. Sure, the actors did stuff actors don't usually do."

"I think one of them went through my purse," Salome said.

"But," Kate went on, holding up her finger, "wait a minute. Then what? Is it just breaking barriers for the fun of breaking them? That seems dumb. If someone sneaks into my house, it breaks a bunch of usual barriers too. It's what you do after that matters. If you keep on assaulting people after that, it's almost normal."

"At least it's not unexpected," the nameless friend said, nodding.

Boss laughed. "Now you get the actors to come home with me and paint my bathroom, then you'll defy expectation."

She sipped the coffee. It was thick as mud and honey-sweet. Something buzzed next to her ear. She waved her hand absently and it went away.

"I can see Carol's point," Tyler said, "but that gets back to the production choices."

"Who's Carol?" Tyler's friend asked.

Tyler's brow wrinkled and he nodded toward Kate. "Carol. You know. Siri's roommate from Red House."

The quiet that fell over the table was unmistakable.

"I don't know anyone named Siri," she said, smiling to pull the punch. "My name's Kate."

Tyler's mouth went slack and a blush started crawling up his neck. Salome's giggle sounded a little cruel.

"Well," Tyler said. "That's . . . um . . . Yeah."

"I thought you were playing it awfully smooth," Tyler's friend said, and then to her, "My boy here isn't a world-renowned pick-up artist. I wondered what gave him the nerve to break the ice with you."

"I'm sure Carol will be very flattered," Kate said. "And for what it's worth, I thought it was pretty smooth."

"Thank you," Tyler said, blushing. "I hadn't actually meant it as a pick-up thing."

"Or you would have cocked it up," his friend said.

"Isn't Carol the one with the big teeth?" Salome said. "She doesn't look anything like her."

"Carol's teeth aren't that big," Boss said. "You just didn't take to her."

"Regardless," Tyler said, turning to her, "Kate. I'm really glad you came with us, even if it was only to see me make a jackass out of myself in front of my friends."

She waved the comment away. A gust of wind blew the door open a few inches, the smell of rain cutting through the air. Salome and Boss exchanged a glance she couldn't parse. Dread bloomed in her belly.

"It's just you looked really familiar," he said, "and I thought—"

"I get that a lot," she said, a little too quickly. The moment started to fishtail.

"I guess . . . I mean, I guess maybe we ran into each other around the city somewhere. Do you ever hang out at McLeod and Lange? Or—"

Boss's laughter buzz-sawed. The joker shook his head. "Jesus Christ, Tyler. Of course she looks familiar. You're hitting on *Curveball*."

In the press and noise of the restaurant, the pause wasn't silent or still, but it felt that way. She saw him see her, recognize her. Know. His face paled, and she lifted a hand, waving at him as if from a distance. The regret in her throat was like dropping something precious and watching it fall.

♥

"Oh please," he says. "I'm talking about *anyone*. Charlie. You. Me. Hell, I'm talking about Golden Boy. He's been around so long, he's lapped himself. He was saving America from evil, then he was a useless sonofabitch who ratted out his friends, then he was nobody, and now he's so retro-cool he's putting out an album of pop music covers. You think he had control over any of that? It just happens. It just . . ."

He shakes his head, but she isn't convinced. She's known him too long.

"You know all of us," she says. "Michael. Ana. Wally. Not Drummer Boy and Earth Witch and Rustbelt. You know *us*."

"Yeah, that's part of why *Aces!* hired me on. You know, apart from the—" He makes a buzzing sound and shakes one of his hands, a fast vibration like an insect's wing. "I know where all the bodies are buried. Or a lot of them, anyway. I know the stories."

"You know the *people*."

"For all the good it does," he says, shrugging. "Lohengrin was pretty pissed off when I handed in my two weeks. Not that it was really two weeks. Two weeks at the UN is barely enough time to get a cup of coffee. Bureaucracy at its finest. Say what you will about the failings of tabloid journalism, it's got a great response time."

From the street, a siren wails and then a chorus of car horns rises. She has the visceral memory of being nine years old and listening to a flock of low-flying geese heading south for the winter. It's a small memory she hasn't told anyone about. It's a thing of no particular significance. He drinks from his coffee cup. A bright green wasp crawls out of his skin, and then back in.

"Bugsy . . ." she says, and then, "Jonathan."

He sits on his couch, pushing the books on the coffee table away with the heel of his foot.

"The glory days are gone anyway. The whole thing where a bunch of us see something wrong and we go fix it? Stop the genocide, save the world, like that? It's over. Everything goes through channels now. Everyone answers to somebody. The Committee? Yeah, it's a freaking committee. No joke. They don't need me. People come in and out all the time. Join up for a mission or three, make some contacts, and go work for some multinational corporation's internal security division for eight times the money. I'm not doing this whole thing for *Aces!* for the cash. I could get a hell of a lot more."

"Labor of love?" she says. The sarcasm drips.

"Why not?" he says. "There are worse things to love. Your boy, for instance, seems nice. I mean in that clean-cut upwardly mobile natworking-for-the-Man kind of way. The bazooka line was great, by the way. I thought that was really a good one."

He's goading her again, pushing her back toward her anger, and it works a little. She wonders for a moment how much the little green wasps have seen and heard. The sense of invasion is deep. Powerful. She's embarrassed and insulted, and she imagines Tyler feeling the same way. If it were only her Bugsy'd held up for public judgment, it wouldn't have been so bad. She wonders if Bugsy knows that.

He is soothing her and pricking at her, pushing her away and asking her in. He's asking for help, she thinks. His bloodshot eyes meet hers and then turn away. He wants to tell her, and he doesn't. He wants to have a fight so he can get out of a conflict. She's not going to let him.

"That isn't what happened to Charlie," she says. "He didn't get the job with a big corporation and get out."

"No," he says with a sigh. "That isn't what happened."

Watching his face change is fascinating. The smirk fades, the joking and the fear. The bad hair and the terrible stubble lose their clownish aspect. When he's calm, he could almost be handsome. Despair looks good on him. Worse, it looks authentic.

"You were the senior guy," she says, prompting him.

"I was the senior guy." The words are slower. "I liked it. It wasn't like having some kid in the crowd come up and ask for an autograph. This was Charlie. He was someone I knew. Someone I hung out with. I'd tell stories about the old days, and he'd actually listen. And he was a funny kid. He pulled his card when he was twelve. Got a fever and bled from the ears.

His sister took him to the emergency room because their mom was working and they couldn't get through to her. He thought he was going crazy. He was hearing people's voices from half a mile away. He was hearing the blood in the nurse's veins. By the time they figured out it was the wild card, there wasn't anything for the doctors to do but shrug and move on. He was still walking around with these sound-killing earphones until he was seventeen. The way he talked about it, it seemed funny, but that stuff's never funny at the time. Anyway, he went to college. Started getting seriously into the African experience, to the degree that you can do that from California. Dropped out of college, signed up to work for the Committee."

She sips her coffee. She expects it to be cold, but it's still warm enough. A man's voice raised in complaint comes from down the hall, and she wonders whether they closed the apartment door. By reflex, she wants to go check, but she holds herself back. There's something fragile in the moment that she doesn't want to lose.

"Charlie just signed up?" she says, and Bugsy shrugs.

"He's an ace, right? That's what we're looking for. The extraordinarily enabled set to achieve tasks that might otherwise be impossible. I got that from a press release. You like it?"

"Was your thing his first time out?" she asks, not letting him deflect her.

"No. He'd done something with tracking illegal water networks in Brazil. Listening for buried pipes. He talked about it some. The supervisor on that one was a nat, though. This was the first time he'd had other aces to work with. Those first few days when we were stopping the attacks? They were amazing. I mean, it was scary because there were guys with machine guns driving around in jeeps trying to kill the people we were there to protect, and if we screwed it up, bad things were going to happen. But we were winning. The textile plant kept running. The folks working there didn't get killed. We were big damn heroes, and it was great."

"Even with the lousy food."

"Hell yes," Bugsy says. "Even with the lousy food. Even with the shitty Internet connection. We had three games on the Xbox, and a crappy little thirteen-inch screen to play them on. The beds were like the mats they give you at the airport when your flight's cancelled and you're going to be on the floor all night, and we were all so jazzed and happy, we didn't even bitch about it. It was great. We were happy just to be there. And then it was quiet for a while.

"At first, we were still tense. Waiting for the other shoe to drop, right?

And then after a couple weeks, we were all thinking that this was it. It was over. It was another month before the local police were going to take over, and we were all figuring that we were looking at another four weeks of sitting around doing nothing much. But I got sick. Not *sick* sick. Just stay-home-from-school stuff. Sore throat. Fever. Felt like I needed a nap every third minute. It sucked, but it wasn't a big deal, and Charlie was up for covering me. Except he needed to sleep too sometimes. So I set up this plan. Sheer elegance in its simplicity. Charlie'd work his shift like usual. I'd do a half shift because I could stand that much, and then in the middle of the night when there wasn't anything going on anyway, the other three—the goon squad, we called them—could head out to the plant and just keep an eye on things while I got a little extra shut-eye. A couple days of that, I'd get my feet back under me, and we'd go back to the usual thing. It wasn't like there was anything happening anyhow."

His gaze is fixed on nothing now, looking past her, through her. A wasp flies through the air, lands on the wall beside them, and folds tiny, iridescent wings. Its stinger curls in toward its own belly.

"No one pushed back," he says. "We were all best buds by then. If Charlie'd been sick, we'd have covered for him. Or if one of the goon squad guys had come down with something, I'd have gone out in his place. I'm not bad in a fight, most of the time. It was just an obvious thing. Someone feels under the weather, you take on a little more. Something you do for your friends."

"Sure," she says.

"Sure."

He swallows. There are no tears in his eyes, but she expects them so powerfully that for a moment she sees them anyway. He shakes his head.

"It was a textile plant," he says. "They were making cheap T-shirts to sell in Europe. It gave a couple hundred African guys some folding money that they could spend in town. It put a little extra juice in the local economy. It's not like we were going in there and burning down the churches or something. And the guys on the jeeps? The ones who didn't like it? They didn't even talk to us. All their preaching and outreach was in the city. We were just a part of the plant to them. There's the building, and the guys that worked there, and the cloth going in and the shirts coming out, and then the aces that kept you from breaking all the rest of it. If they could have busted up the machines, they'd have done it and been just as happy. They didn't even hate us. They hated something that we represented, and I don't even have the framework to understand what it is."

"Western imperialism," she says.

"Maybe. Maybe not. Maybe I've got the whole damn thing wrong. For all I know, the guys in those jeeps were all born in Detroit. We were out there trying to do something good. They were trying to do something else. It was all about international trade and local autonomy and religion and nationalism. None of it was about what kind of people we were. Probably if we'd invited the bastards in, they'd have had a blast playing our video games, right? Sat around eating our nasty little sausages and shooting zombies."

"But that's not what happened."

"No," he says, and hunches forward. He sighs. "No, it isn't. There was this one night, Charlie took his shift, put in his earplugs—he had these amazing industrial foam things that let him sleep—and hit the bunk. I spread out from just before sundown to almost midnight, then gathered back up, sucked down some NyQuil, and called it a night. The others headed out to the plant. Just like we planned."

He lapses into silence, his eyes flickering back and forth like he's reading letters in the empty air. She has known him for years. She's wanted to like him more than she has. He doesn't make it easy. She glances at her phone. The browser is up. DANGEROUS CURVES. She wonders whether feeling betrayed by him means that she does think of him as a friend. Or did, anyway.

"What happened?" she asks, annoyed with herself for the gentleness in her voice.

"It all went to hell."

♣

"Oh. My. God," Salome said, laughter bubbling up with the words. "You really are, aren't you? You're Curveball?"

"I am," she said.

Boss smiled at her, rolling his eyes like the two of them were in on a joke. He'd known it was her all along. It was these other rubes who hadn't seen it. Tyler stared at the saltshaker and wouldn't meet her eyes.

"Did you really date Drummer Boy?" Salome asked, leaning her elbows against the table. There was a hunger in her expression that hadn't been there earlier, like she was seeing Kate for the first time that evening.

"Not exactly."

"What's he like?" Salome asked.

Kate smiled the way she did at public events, the way she did when someone asked for an autograph or a picture.

"He's just like he seems," she said. It was the same answer she always gave, one of the stock phrases she always kept at the ready. Salome laughed, just the way people usually did.

All the conversation shifted to her, the play forgotten, the meal forgotten. What was she in New York for? She was doing an exhibition show tomorrow at the park in support of a fund that was building schools in developing nations. Did she get to New York often? A couple times a year, sometimes more. It depended on the situation. The questions were familiar territory. The diplomacies and evasions and jokes that she'd used at a hundred photo ops.

Boss kept needling Tyler for not having recognized her, and Tyler grew quieter and more distant. In the end, he was the one who called for the check, totaled up what everyone owed, and said his goodnights. The others seemed perfectly willing to let him go. He nodded to her when he stood, but didn't keep eye contact. When he walked out the door, a cool draught of air slipped in past him, smelling of rain.

"Well, you know, when I pulled *my* wild card—" Boss said, one scarred and misshapen finger tracing the air.

"Actually," Kate said, "could you just . . . I mean. Excuse me."

The sidewalk was shoulder-to-shoulder full. A wide curve of cloud looped between the skyscrapers, the lights of the windows turning misty as it passed. She caught a glimpse of Tyler's dark hair, stopped at the corner, heading north. She hopped down to the gutter and scooted along, the taxis whizzing by her, inches away. When she called his name, he turned. Chagrin paled his face.

"Hey," she said. "I just wanted to say thanks. For letting me tag along."

The light changed, and the press of bodies surged around them. He glanced at the white symbol of a man walking, then back to her. Someone bumped against his back.

"Always pleased to have a few more at the ritual humiliation," he said. There was no bitterness in his humor and only a little sorrow. "It was really great to meet you. And coming along with us was something I'm sure my immediate circle of friends will be bringing up for the rest of my natural life in order to tease me. But it was really cool of you."

"Yeah," Kate said. Behind him, the signal changed to a series of red numbers, counting slowly down. The pedestrian traffic thinned for a moment. A truck lumbered around the corner. She pulled back her hair, anxious and embarrassed to be anxious.

The red numbers crept toward zero.

"Do you want to go get a drink?" she said, rushing the words a little. "Or something?"

"You don't have to do that," Tyler said. "I mean, thank you, that's really cool, but I'll be just fine. I'm just going to head home and bury my head under a pillow for a couple days and resume my normal life as if I hadn't made an idiot of myself. You don't need to try and . . . You just don't need to."

"Oh. Okay, then. All right," she said, nodding. She felt like someone had punched her sternum. And then, "But do you want to go get a drink or something?"

His smile was pretty, gentle and amused and melancholy. He had the kind of smile men got after the world bruised them a few times. The light changed, the flow of traffic shifted, pushing her a half step closer to him.

"I'm not that guy," he said. "You hang out with aces and rock stars and politicians. I hang out with Boss and Salome. I'm nobody, you know? I'm just this nat guy trying to make rent in Brooklyn Heights and commuting into the city. You're Curveball."

"Kate, actually," she said. "My name's Kate. And I'm not whatever you think I am just because I'm an ace."

An older black man with gray temples looked over at her, eyebrows raised, but he didn't pause or try to ask for an autograph.

"But—" Tyler began.

"I'm Kate. My father's Barney. My mother's Elizabeth. I read Heinlein when I was a kid and stayed up late so I could watch *Twin Peaks* even though it gave me nightmares and I didn't understand half of it. And I'm wandering around New York by myself because all my friends were busy, and I met this guy I kind of like, only I think he may be blowing me off," she said, watching his eyebrows hoist themselves toward his hairline. "Drawing an ace isn't that impressive. It's just something that happens to people."

"I just—"

"I don't do anything that anybody else couldn't do," she said, and then a beat later, "I mean, if you gave them a bazooka."

He laughed, and the sound untied something in her throat. He shook his head just as a wide, fat drop of rain patted onto the cement at their feet.

"Well, when you put it like *that*," he said.

"What do you do? Your day job."

He raised his hands in something like surrender.

"I work at a tech start-up that's using social media to address inefficiencies in medical laboratory tests," he said. "Honest to God."

"Really?" she said. The light changed again. An insect buzzed past her ear. A police siren rose up somewhere not too far away. "I would have guessed something about theater."

"I was a theater major when I was in college, but it didn't end well."

"No?"

"No," he said, ruefully. "I got in a fight with my advisor. A real fight. He hit me."

"Sounds serious," she said, smiling. "What were you fighting about?"

"Tennessee Williams. We had different interpretations of *The Glass Menagerie*."

"Is that the 'always relied on the kindness of strangers' one?"

"No, that's *A Streetcar Named Desire*," he said, and the rain began like someone turning on a faucet. Hard, wide drops falling through the air. Thunder muttered, even though she hadn't seen any lightning. Tyler grinned. "Why don't we go someplace dry. I'll tell you the whole story."

♠

"We didn't hear them coming," Bugsy says. "I was sick and drugged. Charlie was asleep. It was the middle of the night, and we were complacent. Who in their right minds attacks a compound of aces, right? We're the guys who can shoot laser beams out of our fingers or lift tanks or whatever. If you come at us, it's with a bomb or something. Something fast. You don't get a bunch of kids on bicycles with bottles of gasoline. C'mon. Fucking *gasoline?*"

He looks up at her, a goofy smile stretching his lips, false as a mask. A wasp crawls out of his tangle of hair and buzzes away. He shakes his head, looks down. She can tell that he wants her to say something, to divert the words spilling out of his mouth before the pebbles turn into a landslide, but it's too late. He fidgets with the puzzle book on the coffee table. When he speaks again, the reluctance in his voice hurts to hear.

"You figure it all out later, right? I mean, we've got the tracks, and it was all little mountain bike snake trails. And the plastic jugs. They were like milk jugs. They poured it all around the outside of the building. And you know what's weird? I can absolutely see them doing it. I mean, I can see them leaning their bikes against the wall. I can hear the gas making that *glurp-glurp* sound it does when you're pouring everything out of one of them. I can smell it. I can smell the fumes coming off it even before they light the damn stuff. I was asleep. I didn't see any of it, but I remember it just like I was there.

"First real thing I knew, Charlie was shaking me awake. He was wearing a Joker Plague t-shirt. How's that for insult to injury? He was shaking me awake and telling me there was a fire and we had to get out, and Drummer Boy was on his chest looking like some kind of rock-and-roll god. It took me a little while to figure out what he was talking about, and then we were running around the compound—and it was like ten steps any direction, the place was that small. Everything outside was burning. It was like they'd dropped us in hell while we were sleeping. We closed the windows, and I tried to use the cell phone. I got through to the goon squad even, but the fire was so loud we almost couldn't hear each other. Charlie was dancing around like a kid who needs to pee. I told them what was going on, but they were six miles away. They came as fast as they could."

He rubs his fingers together, the roughness of his fingerprints sounding like the hiss of a book's pages turning. A wasp appears in his fingers, conjured from his flesh. He looks at it like Hamlet staring at Yorick's skull.

"They're small," he says, holding the insect out to her. Exhibit A. "When I bug out, really all the way out, I've got all this surface area. Can't thermoregulate for shit. Get cold fast. Or I cook off. Seriously, too much heat, and I'm like popcorn."

"You took off," she says. "You left him."

"I stayed as long as I could," he says. "I couldn't get him out. I couldn't lift him. The fire was baking the place, and I had to go. I knew I had to go, but I couldn't just leave him."

"Except you did."

"Except I did. Went out through the vent over the oven. Lost six percent of my body mass to bugs dying in the fire, and I just got out and flew straight up until I hit cold air. They were gone by then. The guys on the bikes? They were gone. I saw the goon squad's jeeps booking it for the compound. I thought maybe they'd make it in time. Maybe they'd get him out."

Bugsy sighs.

"He didn't burn," he says. "The fire ate up all the oxygen, and he asphyxiated. They found him curled up on that nasty-ass little couch like he was asleep. He had a cover over him. He was in the middle of a fire, and he went and got a blanket? Why would you do that? What's that even about?"

He takes a huge breath, lets it flow out from between his teeth.

"The attack was a diversion," she says.

"You think? They had a second team ready. Torched the factory. Burned it to the foundations. Shot about a dozen maintenance guys. Huge embarrassment for the United Nations. Maybe half a billion in hard capital and trade agreements. Lohengrin had to give me a letter of formal reprimand. You could see it killed him to do it, but the secretary-general needed to blame someone, and they picked me."

"I'm sorry," she says.

"It's all right. I had it coming."

He stands. The floor creaks as he walks across it to the window. The insects in the room are silent, then one buzzes for a moment, like someone in the next room clearing their throat. The siren is gone. The car horns mutter at the low, constant mutter of the city.

"You know how many kids are living on the street in New York?" Bugsy asks. "Want to guess? Sixteen thousand. Just in New York City, center of the civilized world. And I can't fix that. You know the climate's changing, right? The Arctic's melting, and it turns out there's this freaking plume of methane coming up out of all the melting permafrost. I can't fix it. There are a bunch of parents out there who aren't getting their kids immunized because they'd rather watch little Timmy die of polio than do a little basic research. Can't fix them. Most of Africa is hosed beyond belief, but what're you gonna do, right?"

"We have to try."

"Do we? I mean do we *have* to? You remember *American Hero*? That first season? Bunch of young aces trying to out-macho one another. King Cobalt, dead. Simoon, dead a couple of times. Gardener, dead. Hardhat. We were trying to make the world better, and it killed us. You were one of the first ones to bail on the Committee, you know? And I think you were right."

"I just needed some time off," she says.

"Yeah, well," he says. "Don't go back."

She doesn't know how to reply. The anger is gone, and there's a sense of shame. And sorrow. Maybe he means there to be, but it doesn't matter. He walks back across the room, disappears into his bedroom, and reemerges with a tablet computer in his hand. On the screen, a dozen thumbnail photographs glow. They are all of her and Tyler. In one, they are going into the little neon-lit bar. In another, they're coming out of it, huddling together under the cheap black umbrella they bought from a street vendor. His arm is around her shoulders. One of them is Tyler hailing a taxi. One is the kiss. She takes the tablet from him. She's still angry, but without the headlines, without the joke about her ace nickname and the gossip column banter, it's kind of a pretty picture. A man and a woman, kissing. If it were something private, it could be beautiful.

"I want to care about something that doesn't matter," Bugsy says. "I want to tell the world about which movie star got drunk with which ace. I want to debate whether *American Hero* should have another season and laugh about who had a wardrobe malfunction when they were meeting the president. I want to care about things I don't care about."

"Like me?" she asks, handing back the tablet.

He takes it. Looks at the pictures.

"Yeah, like you. Your love life, anyway," he says, gently. He raises the tablet. He lifts his arms out, fingers reaching for the walls. He looks like a mocking image of Christ, crucified on the air.

"I'm done saving the world. I tried. It didn't work. Now I want to live a small, petty life doing things I'm good at where if it goes south, no one dies."

She crosses her arms. She isn't sure whether the thickness in her throat is contempt or grief.

"No one's going to stop you," she says.

"It was nice, watching you. I mean not in a stalkery creepy number-one-fan kind of way. Just you and your boy out together. It was nice. It was . . ."

"It was?"

"It's what's supposed to balance out the shit, right? I don't mean to get all ooey-gooey, but it's the beginning of love. Or it could be, if you don't screw it up. That's the kind of thing that's supposed to make all the sacrifices worthwhile. Make the world worth living in."

He chuckles, and there's amusement in the sound, but also disappointment. Bugsy had wanted something from her—forgiveness, maybe, or courage—and she doesn't have it to give. He considers the tablet and taps at the picture.

"It probably doesn't matter to you," he says, "but I had them run the one where you can't see his face."

◆

The worst of the storm passed while they were in the bar, but there was still enough rain to justify standing close to each other under the umbrella. Kate felt warm and a little freer than usual, but not tipsy. Tyler's cheeks looked redder than when they'd started. Behind them, a small park sat, not even a half block deep, with skyscrapers on all sides, rising up into the clouds. The rain that still fell was cold, but soft. Across the street, the hotel rose up like a wonder of the world, the golden light from the lobby spilling out onto the wet, black street. Taxis whizzed by, throwing off spray. Men and women hurried by in black raincoats. Kate looked at the little green niche and thought how incredibly improbable it was to have a small bit of grass and ivy in all this concrete and asphalt.

When she turned, Tyler was looking at her. He had the look in his eyes—regret and hope and the small, unmistakable glimmer of a masculine animal. It was the end of the night. Neither of them wanted it to be, but the evening had a shape, and this was where that curve met the earth.

"I know you told me not to," he said, "but really, thank you for not letting me go back to the apartment with my tail between my legs."

"It wasn't charity," she said, laughing. "I had a good time. I don't actually meet new people very much."

"I'd never really considered the problem, but I can see how it would be difficult separating the Kate from the Curveball. I guess that's why some aces have secret identities. Just so they can go get some groceries or hang out at the bar."

"That's part of it," she said, pushing her hair back from her face. "Or to have room to be who they are. Not spend their whole lives filling the roles that people expect of them."

"That's not just aces, though. That's the whole world."

They were talking without saying anything, each syllable another tacit, doomed wish that the moment not end. Another taxi sped by, the black sludge spattering against the curb. A squirrel loped across the grass and took up a perch on the back of a green metal park bench. Everything smelled of fresh rain and car exhaust.

"So I should probably go," he said. "I'm supposed to go into the office tomorrow, and they like me to show up on time."

"Yeah," she said. "And I've got the exhibition show. Be better if I went in rested."

"Yeah."

The rain tapped the sidewalk by their feet.

"It was really great meeting you, Kate. I'm glad I totally didn't recognize you."

"I'm glad you totally didn't recognize me too," she said.

"Do you want to keep the umbrella?"

"I'm just going across the street."

"Right. Right."

He squared his shoulders, steeled himself.

"If you're going to be in town for a while," he said, "I'd . . . Boy this is harder than it should be. I'd like to do this again."

"You're asking me out," she said.

"I am. On a date. Because that's just the kind of mad, reckless, carefree guy I am."

"I'd love to," she said.

"Oh, thank God," he said. "I feel much better now."

The squirrel jumped away into the darkness. They didn't speak. They didn't move.

"If this were a normal evening," he said, "out with a normal girl, this would be the time that I kissed her."

"It would," she said.

He lowered the umbrella. His lips were warmer than she'd expected.

♥

She walks over to the window, looking out at the city. Dread and embarrassment tap against her ribs like wasps against a windowpane, but not rage. The rage is gone. Manhattan is damp and shining as a river stone. The city is a symbol of the greatest powers of the world and of its darkness. The aces were born here, and the jokers. Shakespeare in the Park, and the terrible production of *Marat/Sade*. It is the city at the heart of the American century, and the target of all the tribes and nations that resent it. And what is it, really, but a few million private lives rubbing shoulders? For a second, the view through the glass shifts like an optical illusion, great unified city becoming a massive chaos of individuals and then flipping back as fast as a vase becoming faces.

She opens the window. A cool breeze stirs the air.

"We're done, Bugsy," she says. "This doesn't happen again."

"Of course it does," he says. "You're a public figure. You're an ace. If it isn't me, then—"

"It's never you. And you *never* do it to him."

"Tyler, you mean?"

"Tyler, I mean."

He runs his hands through his hair. The cool air drives the free wasps back into him. She didn't realize until now how much larger they make him. As they crawl back under his skin, he literally gets larger, but also seems to shrink.

"It was all legal. I didn't do anything wrong," he says petulantly. She doesn't answer. He nods. "All right, but the boss won't like it. If it's not okay with you, pretty soon it won't be okay with anyone, and then I'm out of a job."

"You'll find a way," she says.

"Always do."

Her phone buzzes again. Ana's number. She ignores it. On her way past the couch, she puts her hand on his shoulder.

"Get some rest," she says.

"Will. Don't fuck it up, okay?"

In the street, she turns north, walking in the shadow of the buildings. A block down, a coffee shop presses out, white plastic tables and chairs impinging on the sidewalk. The closest they have to real brewed coffee is called a double americano, so she gets that. Her shoes are still wet from last night and this morning. She looks at the two messages from Ana, her friend. She wants to call back, but when she does, she'll have to tell the story of what happened, and she still doesn't know the end.

A taxi carries her back to the hotel. The exhibition is in five hours. She needs to be in prep in three. The hotel waits for her. The world docs. She crosses four lanes of Manhattan traffic to get back to the little park. In the light, it looks smaller than it did at night. She sits on the green bench and takes out her phone, starts writing a text message, then deletes it and actually calls. He answers on the second ring.

"Hey," Tyler says.

"Hey."

"Did you know we're on the *Aces!* website?"

She leans forward. She's less than ten feet from where they kissed. She's on a different world.

"Yeah, I just got finished kicking the reporter's ass," she says.

"I'm just glad he didn't write it as a review," he says. "It's a little disconcerting to see my private life in the news."

"It's probably not the last time it'll happen," she says. *If it's too hard, I understand* waits at the back of her throat, but the words won't come out.

Somewhere in Brooklyn, Tyler groans. She's faced armies. She's had people with guns trying to kill her. This little sound from a distant throat scares her.

"Well," he says, "this is going to take a little getting used to."

"We're still on, though?"

She's afraid he'll say no. She's more afraid he'll say *Are you kidding? This is great.* Across the street, the hotel staff is telling a beggar to move on.

She can see into the lobby, where a television is tuned to a news channel, footage of fire and running bodies. She closes her eyes.

"I am if you are," he says. "And . . . you are, right?"

"Like the world depends on it," she says.

Evernight

by Victor Milán

CANDACE WALKED BETWEEN WALLS of stacked bones and skulls, and was afraid.

It wasn't the darkness that scared her. Though it was the total darkness of a place light never touches, her eyes saw clearly, if in tones of gray. She could see even through her own Darkness, as nothing else on Earth could unless she temporarily shared the gift. Darkness was, if not her friend, her intimate and tool.

It wasn't the bones that scared her, either. She put out a hand and let her fingertips trail along knobbled walls of crania and condyles, and felt nothing: they were stones to her. She knew death too well. Through her actions, if not directly by her hand, she'd left a few rooms' worth of bones to bleach beneath the African sun, herself.

For five years Candace had known her brother was dead. Then last night, in a dive bar in Atlanta where she was doing a job for the Miami Mob, she'd seen his grown-up face on CNN, wanted for a terrorist attack in Paris.

Getting an entrance visa and a ticket on such a crash basis had blown much of the roll she'd been saving to buy her way out of that employment, which she'd entered unwittingly. But she wasn't thinking of that now.

She feared for Marcel. She feared the unknown she was walking into. She feared what the children of perpetual night might be doing to Marcel—and what he might do to them. Because she knew from her own experience the rage that bubbled within him.

It was that fear that drew her irresistibly on, through the domain of the dead.

Chill water sloshed around the ankles of her hiking boots. She stayed out of it as much as she could. She told herself it was leakage from the city above, not seepage from the sewers that laced Paris's underside even more completely than the ancient limestone mines and the ossuaries which took up a small part of them did. But the smell suggested that wasn't the whole truth, sadly.

She also smelled death. It had been too long since the Catacombs' mute, dismembered occupants had come here for even that persistent stink to linger. But Candace knew her death-smells, of every stage of decay. Death *was* here. Recent death. Probably of a rat or cat. But death, all the same.

She smelled mildew and mold and rat turds. She smelled stale human grease and dirt, and the rot that afflicts people who are still alive, if often in such an existence as not to merit the term *living*. And all of it—the smells, the closeness of the walls, the unfamiliar sensation of uncountable tonnes of soil and cement and stone hanging almost on top of her—conspired to give Candace Sessou, The Darkness, internationally wanted terrorist ace, a raging case of the creeps.

The Catacombs of Paris was a tourist destination long popular because of the macabre overload induced by the spectacle of hundreds upon hundreds of meters of walls made from the dried skulls and bones of literally millions of the dead. The walls had a special name: *ossements*.

But this wasn't the underworld's tame tourist district. Candace wasn't here to sightsee. And she was well aware that she was entering a domain claimed by a being of a power so fierce and expansive that it terrified not just the civil authorities, but the Corsican Mafia—and their rivals, the atrocity-loving, erstwhile secret police and terrorist Leopard Men.

"Okay, this is actually kind of cool," she said out loud in English, which she'd gotten used to speaking every day, as she hugged a façade of faces void of eyes and flesh, trying to skip over a wide spot in the stream and succeeding somewhat.

Something stung her left ankle, above her hiking boots and thermal socks, inside the leg of her pants.

She jumped and failed to entirely stifle a most un-terrorist-ace-like squeak of startled terror. *Do they have scorpions down here? Venomous spiders?* Before coming down here she would have ridiculed the very idea that Paris, the ultra-civilized heart of sophisticated and homogenized Europe, could possibly harbor creepy-crawling horrors to compete with what she was accustomed to finding even in the well-manicured and prosperous Kinshasa suburb where she'd grown up.

The sting had forcibly reminded her that *almost literally anything* could be living down here among the dead.

She caught herself thinking, *Well, I might and I might not.* Followed at once by, *Where the Hell did* that *come from?* She looked around uneasily. She saw nothing but bone walls and the water flowing along the limestone floor. She was actually tempted, briefly, to whip out her burner iPhone and use its flashlight app to look to see if her darkness-piercing vision was missing any nasty bugs.

Was that a ripple in the water? She squelched an urge to hop away. *Just your imagination. You're letting the stress get to you.*

But the stress was real. She had no idea why her brother had defied the Leopard Men's current policy of avoiding overt terrorism in favor of pursuing lucrative, conventional crime. If he'd even been behind the midnight bombing of an empty bus kiosk, which seemed pretty pointless any way she looked at it.

Marcel's likely mental state worried her too. As a child he'd always been afraid of the dark, with a touch of claustrophobia. She'd never been—until now. This place was enough to get to even an ace-powered nyctophile.

And who was hunting him, to make him desperate enough to seek refuge in a realm called Evernight? She knew why to fear the Leopard Men: they'd stolen her from her childhood and tortured her until she either died or became an ace. What Paris's African refugee community had told her about the antiterrorism unit GIGN didn't make them seem much kinder.

She started moving forward again, staying as close to the ossement on her left as possible, and avoiding the water as best she could. She also feared what he'd found down here. Or what had found him.

A thing which she knew was trying to find her own way *towards*. No pressure.

Navigating by touch, keeping her eyes on what she hoped was the naturally rippling stream, she made her way toward the Queen of the Underworld's likely seat of power.

She had lost six hours already to the need to sleep. She'd also eaten up precious time to use her phone for some research, followed by some tentative connection. Two groups defiantly explored the Parisian underworld's hundreds of kilometers of Catacombs, mines, and sewers forbidden to the public. The Urban Experiment—*les UX*—considered themselves cultural vigilantes, restoring lost and neglected areas of the great city above ground as well as below. As paranoid as the UX abbreviation they went by was precious, they'd refused all communication. The Cataphiles, though, were cheerful urban explorers, ever eager to share their illicit experiences with outsiders. Some were more than a little publicity-hungry. As lamentable as Candace found that as OpSec—if the cops *really* wanted to shut them down, it'd take an afternoon—it served her well.

They'd responded readily, first to her also-disposable Gmail account, then by texts. The Cataphiles and the UX had come to terms with the mysterious joker-ace queen *Maman Nuit-Perpetuelle* and her shadow domain. She preferred to use the English word *Evernight* for her domain as well as herself, they said.

Candace's day job—the one she was trying to get out of, and had now stuck herself back deeper in—mostly involved negotiation. Deals were made.

Luckily, Mama Evernight wasn't eager to kill or disappear anybody. She had ways of warning trespassers—and not just when they were actively in her domain. Many of her "children," as they called themselves, spent some or even most of their time aboveground, engaged in panhandling and petty thievery—as well as in spying and serving as emissaries for their secret queen. But if you pushed her—you went down into the Dark, and were seen no more.

"I just hope Mama doesn't think I'm defying her," Candace said out loud. Though she'd long thought herself a loner, she was starting to feel too much alone, here, with only dead-people parts for company.

Something stung her again, this time in her right ankle.

She let out an involuntary yip of surprise and fear. Looking down, she saw to her horror that something sinuous and thin had snaked out of the ripple of leakage water and up inside the leg of her slacks.

Wishing desperately for a knife, she tried to tug free. More tendrils came dripping from the water. She felt them slither up her leg, around it, their touch slimy on bare skin that tried futilely to shrink away, gripping with remarkable strength. The stinging sensation hit again, stronger than before, a fire in her nerves.

I have your attention now, little one. Calm yourself. If I wished you harm, I'd have caused it already. Now state your business aloud.

The words formed in her head as mysteriously as the stray thought had before. This time there was no question it wasn't hers. *Is it coming through the tendrils?* "I've come to see my brother," she said. Her voice was steady, or mostly so.

She knew the voice in her head was right: she was *had*, here and now, and no mistake. And while she was a long way from trusting its intention—*Well, if this isn't the creature I've come to see, it's the creature I need to get past to do so.*

Good. I taste your honesty in your blood, your nerves.

The stinging stopped. The horrid grip relaxed. The tendrils, now a skein, thrilled their way back down her bare leg, across her socks and boots to vanish beneath the water.

Ahead of her a yellow glow shone around a curve in the walls of bones. Three figures appeared, at least approximately human. Each held a torch overhead. One held two, and still had a hand free.

"Come with us," said the three-armed, meter-and-a-half-high being covered in living, writhing slugs in a mellow baritone voice. "Mama Evernight wants to see you."

♣

What first drew Candace's eyes, in the high, echoing dome-shaped chamber of skulls, deep within the twist of the secret Catacombs where outsiders never came, were the three figures who sat on plain wooden stools by the far wall, staring at her with wide eyes. Their silent, motionless regard and the skeins they held put her in mind of the Fates from Greek mythology she learned at primary school.

The middle Fate, a gaunt waif of a woman with lank dark blond hair, silhouetted by what seemed quite ordinary utility lights on stands by the hollow-eyed walls, spoke to her. "Mama Evernight bids you welcome to her domain."

"Thanks," Candace said, right before it hit her.

They're not holding those skeins, she thought. *The skeins are holding* them. Formed of intertwined threads of black and purple and blue and the deep red of blood, they connected each of the three unmoving figures to what Candace had thought was a mere mound of bones jutting from the middle of the wall, at the farthest point from the entrance through which her joker guides M. Sluggo, the Archive, and dog-faced Toby had previously led her.

♠

"You may call me the Archive," the minute, wizened, evidently ancient man said, as they marched between ossements by dancing flame-light. Candace suspected that, while the other three likely needed the illumination, the paraffin-smelling torches they carried were meant to make an impression on her. They did.

Of her three guides into the underworld, he was the most normal-looking, aside from the fact he stood a good head shorter than Candace, which made him small indeed.

"Not the Archivist?" she asked.

He tapped the short white hair that covered his head. "No. I keep our history here. I am older even than Mama herself. Though I was among the first, who followed her here, when we escaped the sweeps."

"The sweeps?"

"When the wild card hit, France was still badly broken, recovering from the War. It was a time of profound paranoia, in which French men and women were still brutally purging one another for collaborating with the Nazis—whether they had done so or not. And above all, the survivors feared plague. Paris had been spared the worst of the war's ravages, but elsewhere in Europe, the First Horseman of the Apocalypse rode his white horse, and reaped lives."

"I think I see where this is going," Candace said, with a tightening in her gut. Along with the one that came from the surroundings—and the knowledge that, while the floor here was dry, the faint striations visible twining among the bones were some kind of presence that not only lived, but somehow *watched*.

"Yes. Parisians reacted to the wild card outbreak in unreasoning horror. Especially when most of those infected died horribly. The fact that most of those who lived were somehow twisted and transformed—and a very few given inhuman powers—made it all the more terrible. So the unafflicted folk, the nats, began rounding up all the sufferers they could catch, and conveying them to the outskirts, where the *banlieues* rise today.

"When Mama Evernight realized what was happening she gathered as many of the infected as she could, even the ones who drew the Black Queen, but could still be moved, and led them to the only sanctuary that remained. A place where the normal and fearful were unlikely to follow."

"Here," said Candace. It seemed the response he wanted by his pause, though it made her feel like Captain Obvious.

"Here," the Archive agreed. "Down here with the dead, we made first a camp, and then our home. For the dying we provided what comfort we could, from medical supplies we stole from the upper world, as we did our food and other necessities. Or were given to us by sympathetic souls above."

"And the others?" Candace asked, though she knew the answer. "The ones taken to the camps."

"A few escaped," the Archive said. "The rest were never seen again. Not the jokers nor even the aces. We—Mama's children who are able to bear to walk beneath the light—searched for survivors for decades after. We found none."

"We didn't learn this at school."

"No. It was suppressed—officially forgotten."

"But France is a haven for wild cards! No place more than Paris. I mean—isn't it? I saw jokers living freely on the surface." *Even gang bosses, like the Corsican who steered me down here. And I thought "Tony the Nose" was a mere Mob nickname. . . .*

He shrugged. "When the fear and frightened anger passed, came shame. Also, the American persecution of the Four Aces influenced opinion. You know us French, since you come from the Congo: we love to use the Americans as counterexamples."

"Yes." She didn't bother asking how he knew she was Congolese. *My accent.*

"Soon after she led us down here," the Archive said, "Mama Evernight, who had drawn the Black Queen, lay down and died. So we built her a bier of bones and mournfully left her, with a grand chamber all to herself."

◆

"I am Cécile Shongo," Candace said to the woman who had spoken, using the pseudonym under which she'd entered the UN refugee-protection program, after she fled the Nshombos' fall.

The speaker's pallid skin was covered with weeping sores. *I hope that's her joker,* she thought. She knew quite well that Xenovirus Takis-A was not infectious, and anyway, she already *had* it. But she had no idea what kind of terrible creeping cruds lived down here that *were.*

"I've come to help my brother. May I see Mama Evernight?"

"You do," said another woman, middle-aged, normal-looking but for the eyes she now turned on Candace, black without sign of whites. "She lies—"

"—before you," said the third Fate, a stout man whose apparently nude body looked like a mass of calluses jumbled together. He nodded his lumpy head at the projecting skull-mound.

It wasn't a random heap, Candace realized. It was a catafalque of long-dried bones. On it lay the body of a woman, which appeared to have melted partially into the loaf-shaped structure, then . . . hardened again, like candle wax. The skeins from the three seated speakers ran to that body, which was manifestly incapable of motion. What looked like hair surrounding the flattened features was more tendrils. Candace now saw in the shadows—for while darkness was no barrier to her vision, the transition from light made it rather more difficult for her eyes to process what lay in shade than when she was a nat—that strands ran from the corpse's sides and limbs to vine down among the bones that held her up, and vanish into holes at the base of the curved bone wall.

She looked back at the blond, sore-covered woman, then in confusion from her to her companions. "You mean—"

They nodded and spoke in a unison somehow more eerie than one completing another's sentences: "That is our mother, the Queen of the Underworld."

♥

"But she wasn't dead," said M. Sluggo, his lips' . . . appendages . . . writhing to a bubble of what Candace guessed was laughter. "But none of the old beards suspected she had risen, or awakened, or whatever it was, until something stung 'Tit Beni's ankle here, and a voice spoke in his mind."

"Li'l Benny?" Candace said. It seemed a shockingly disrespectful name for the diminutive Archive. Especially from a joker altered as extremely as Sluggo.

"My nickname before I completed my own transition," said the Archive equably. "You know why one might be saddled with such, no?"

"You were exceedingly large?"

"I was enormous. Over two hundred and eight centimeters tall, and strong as a corpse-wagon horse." He chuckled ruefully. "With possibly some yet to grow. They say that the wild card has a mischievous streak, that grants those whom it touches what they most desire. Though I hate to think so many people long to die in horrible fashion. So say, rather, it's influenced by what dominates one's subconscious at the time of changing.

"I was bookish, uninterested in sports and less in the lifetime of manual labor my father planned I should follow him in. I became obsessed with the thought that my size was a cross, and wished profoundly to be smaller. I was lucky, I suppose, in the joker I drew. Though I never envisioned becoming as you see me."

I prayed to the Virgin to draw the Black Queen, Candace thought, *because that was the only way I saw to escape the Hell I was trapped in. I didn't get that wish. But, indeed, Darkness permeated my mind, my soul, and so . . .*

"Apparently the wild card agrees with you," Candace said. "You seem to have aged quite well." He must be at least in his eighties now, in February of 2014.

"In a way," he said. "But that's one of the gifts Mama Evernight grants to those who agree to help her in special ways."

She didn't really want to explore that subject much further at the moment. "So she can do more than just sting?"

"Oh, so very much more," said M. Sluggo. Slugs writhed all over him in merriment. He seemed a cheerful sort. Toby nodded his black and white head and let his big pink tongue loll extra-far over his pink gums and black underlip. "She can make you feel *goo-ood*. She spoke in your mind as she did Benoît's that first day back, didn't she?"

That alarmed Candace more. "Did she read my thoughts?"

"No," the Archive said. "She cannot do that. But she can read the chemicals in your blood, and the electrical impulses which sing along your nerves—sense your mood, your feelings. And she can manipulate them in order to communicate her thoughts directly into your mind. Although she finds that strenuous, and prefers to talk through her Speakers."

"But she seemed to respond to what I was thinking."

"Out loud, right?" Sluggo asked.

"I guess. How did she know what I said?"

"Her fibrils can do a lot more than sting or sample your biochemistry. They hear, and smell, and taste, as well as touch. Though they cannot see; Mama is blind, which scarcely inconveniences her."

"*Taste?*"

Candace thought about the whiff of sewage in the water by her boots after she left the tourist parts of the Catacombs, and her stomach turned over. *Wow, I'm learning so much about myself down here. Such as that apparently I'm still capable of getting grossed out.*

The three laughed, in their various ways. "Our Mother cannot afford to be squeamish, you see," the Archive said. "Her body needs sustenance, and lots of it. In time, everything that dies below Paris, she consumes. And a great many things come here to die."

"And her—fibrils—extend into the sewer system?"

"A rich source of nutrients," the Archive agreed.

"How far *do* they go?"

"Throughout much of the ancient subterranean network that underlies Paris," the Archive said. "Somewhere upwards of a hundred and sixty kilometers of tunnels, currently. The rest she either is still gradually infiltrating, or does not care to, for her own reasons."

They passed an opening to a large side passage, or possibly chamber, dimly lit by electric lights hung from the limestone ceiling. Parts of it were obscured by sheets of plastic hung from lines, or other makeshift sight barriers. In the area she glimpsed, Candace saw living people among the bones.

They were working, or talking, or just hanging out. Some faces were additionally illuminated by screen-glow from laptop computers or smartphones. Another sawed with a hacksaw at a piece of metal on a stout bench. Some sewed, some did things she couldn't make out. Most chatted; many laughed. Children played.

Some were obviously jokers, some were not. At least one was an ace of sorts: a little girl of maybe ten squatting in a red dress with daisies printed on it, her face all solemn with concentration as she entertained half a dozen younger kids by passing a lively orange flame across her palm and over her knuckles, like a magician walking a coin over her hand.

What shocked Candace was how *normal* they looked, after all the dark glamour people on the surface had built around Evernight. They were clearly poor people. But they were nothing more or less. Just people, leading their lives as best they could.

"Huh," she said. The Archive glanced up, saw the direction of her eyes, and smiled.

"Yes," he said. "This is the real underworld. This is what Mama Evernight devoted her life—and whatever's come after—to building and maintaining for us."

"Not very Infernal, is it?" M. Sluggo asked.

"I'm reserving judgment on that one," Candace said.

♣

"What's going on," Candace asked what she had mentally dubbed the Three Fates in confusion.

"We speak—"

"—For Mama Evernight."

"She connects to us with her fibrils—"

Candace forced her reeling mind to quit focusing on the fact that the words came out of the mouths of three presumably different people in sequence, yet as smoothly as if spoken by a single person, and concentrate on what Mama Evernight was saying through them.

"—and stimulates the words inside our minds, in a way familiar to you by now. We also supply whatever trace nutrients are currently needed to keep her and her fibrils aware and functioning. In return she stimulates in us a profound sense of well-being."

Great, Candace thought. *Mama's Milk is morphine. Well, whatever works.*

"I'm no physiologist," she said, understating mightily as curiosity got the better of judgment, again, "but it seems like she—you'd—need a lot of processing capacity to handle all the information your, uh, neural network provides you. And even in your current condition"—*whatever you'd call it*—"don't you need more than just, uh, food to function?"

"Mama's cerebrum has absorbed and supplanted most of the bier beneath her," said the Archive. Though her three escorts had extinguished their torches when they entered electrically lit tunnels long before they reached Mama's resting place, they'd all accompanied her here.

"I have other assistants," Mama's serial voice said, "who share their bodily organ functions with me. They lie in separate chambers; I call them my Sharers. Those who converse for me I call, unoriginally enough, my Speakers."

Madly, Candace wondered what Mama called those who handled excretory duties. *Never mind,* she thought. *I don't need any asshole jokes just now.*

But she felt compelled to gesture at the walls and say, "Are they—?"

"Compensated, among other ways with a deeper sense of bliss than my Speakers are. And yes, most of them are voluntary."

And yes, you've reminded me how absolute your law is down here, Candace thought. "I'm told my brother is here," she said. "I need to see him, please. I—I haven't seen him in years. I thought he was dead."

"The fugitive from the Leopard Men," Mama said.

Candace nodded.

"He is here, and safe. He brings danger with him. But I shelter him."

"Why?"

The three Fates shrugged as one, which Candace had to step hard on herself to keep from dissolving into hysterical laughter at. Not because she was afraid of offending Mama Evernight. Because she was afraid she wouldn't stop.

"In a way, he belongs. He is one of my children: he's broken. Too broken to function on the surface. Evernight isn't just for jokers, you know. You, an ace, are broken, too, or you would not be here."

Seeing Candace's expression through her Speakers' eyes, Mama said, "How could I not know? I tasted your blood, child. How well I know the bittersweet tang of the alien virus."

"What about the Cataphiles? Are they all broken, too?"

"Not in the profound way you and my other children are. They are but hobbyists, and never penetrate to this side of the secret entrance they showed you from the Gate of Hell area. Not if they do not wish to receive a brisk warning—at best."

Candace moistened her lips. Despite the humidity down here, they had grown rather quickly dry. "May I see him?"

"Yes."

Candace felt her whole body slump as tension gushed out of her. She actually swayed, once, as she stood. "Thank God. And thank you, Mama."

"Wait and see. Now, as for your ace: you need not divulge your powers at this time, since you clearly do not wish to do so. I try to allow my children the greatest possible freedom. However, though you have comported yourself well so far, I must urge you to continue to act in strict accordance with the laws of hospitality. Specifically, the duties of a good guest, which you are in our house—my house."

So I'm a good girl, am I? I'll show you, you sanctimonious cadaver. She held her head higher and stared Mama Evernight in the hollowed, ossified eyelids where her eyes used to be. "So long as I don't feel threatened, I'll behave."

"Oh, I do not threaten. Rather, I warn. Briskly, as I warned you. If the situation merits it, I shall issue a second, sterner warning."

Candace was already repenting her brief episode of oppositional defiant disorder. But not enough to let go of it completely. "And then?"

The Fates smiled. "If you keep misbehaving," they said as one, "Mama *spank.*"

♠

When her burly joker escort opened the door with a pangolin-scaled arm, Candace's heart jumped into her throat.

It's him! It's really him!

He looked at her and his brown eyes got wide. But he said in low voice, "Call me Hébert."

He spoke Lingala, a major lingua franca in both Brazzaville and its twin Kinshasa, as well as in much of the Congo River basin. They had grown up speaking it as a second language, after French. Emotion almost choked off her reply. "Cécile."

Then tears flooded her vision, and they hurled themselves into one another's arms so hard they almost clashed foreheads, and for a time there was nothing but hugging and sobbing incoherent endearments, the simple joy and grief of two lost children who had found each other again.

Almost nothing. The survivor part of Candace's brain didn't fail to notice the door was promptly shut behind her. And locked. A *stout* door.

Finally they broke apart in unison—in Candace's case, at least, largely for air. With deep inhalations came a return of control. And attentiveness. Her brother's room, she saw in a quick glance around, was tiny and spare, with bare limestone walls enclosing a bed, a chair, a writing desk, and even a flush toilet. *Not bad,* she thought. *For a cell.*

"Sis," Marcel said in French, with the tears still streaming down his dark face. "You've got to get me out of here." He spoke French now. His earlier use of Lingala meant he thought Mama didn't know that language—and was probably listening.

"First," she said, forcing her mind and soul to steady, "you need to tell me how you came here. How the Hell did you wind up with the Leopard Men?"

"The same as you did," he said, with an alkaline rasp. Lingala again. "They kidnapped me. It was when they rounded up Mama and Papa for liquidation for asking too many questions about what happened to you."

Candace clamped her mouth down on the puke that tried to gush up from her knotting belly. Knowing intellectually what had happened to her parents was one thing. Having it confirmed . . . *But you "knew" Marcel was dead, too. Hold onto that.*

"It was your success in their child-ace force-growing program, you see. They wanted to see if you and I shared a predisposition to draw an ace from the wild card."

That rocked her back in horror. "They dosed you with the virus?"

He shook his head. "I didn't pass their preliminary tests. They were only looking for candidates who might become not just aces, but a highly specialized kind."

"Were-leopard."

He nodded and continued in French. "They kept me on anyway. They needed somebody to clean their latrines and wait on them—that was beneath the dignity of one of Alicia Nshombo's *crème de la crème*, you know? When it all came crashing down and they had to flee, they took me with them. Because they still needed a lackey.

"By the time the group that had me made its way here, they'd found a new use for me. They were already building a new organization to carry on the Revolution. But they discovered I liked to learn and do book things, and that turned out to be more useful to them than shining their shoes and cleaning their weapons. By the time I turned thirteen, I was accountant for Léon. He's chief of the Leopard Men cadre here. He's a true Leopard."

"A shape-shifter?" Candace sucked in a sharp breath. Supposedly the were-leopard ace was Alicia's own: the power to grant the gift of shape-shifting to a few, fanatically loyal, especially gifted followers. And supposedly it died with her. But it hadn't.

There were never more than a handful of true Leopards. Fewer survived the PPA's fall. *Any are too many,* she thought. "I've heard of him," she said. She forced a shaky smile. "I can believe that's what they wound up having you do. You always were the studious one."

The Leopard Men who ran the child-ace horror camp were the kind of swaggering bullies, not necessarily stupid but aggressively anti-intellectual, who'd taken to calling themselves "Alpha" in the USA. They'd find clerk-work womanish and weak.

He grinned. "And you were always frivolous, *hein?*"

She shrugged. *For an accountant, he's turned out pretty sturdy,* she noted. Apparently even being a clerk for the Leopard Men's shiny new criminal operation was strenuous. Once a runt even shorter than she was, at seventeen he'd shot up to 172 centimeters, seven taller than her, and filled out considerably. More wiry than bulked-out, but well-packed with muscle.

"So why did you blow up a bus kiosk? That's the kind of no-question terrorist attack my contacts tell me the Leopard Men have been staying away from since they got here. Also, it was lame."

His smile got wider. "It stirred up the French, though, didn't it?"

"The Western powers are all paranoid about terrorism. The idea someone might do to them what they've spent centuries doing to us terrifies them. Which I guess makes sense. But all the more reason to ask why they had you do such a thing, when the Leopards've worked so hard to make themselves look like nothing more than a criminal gang elbowing for power in the big city."

"They wanted to test my resolve. Also send a message to the Corsicans, the Maghrebi out in the *banlieues,* and the Traveler mob what could happen to them if they kept trying to push the Leopard Men off the top of the heap."

That's stupid, Candace thought. *And utterly characteristic of Leopard Men.* She was lucky, in a perverse way, that her training had been mostly masterminded by the American ace Tom Weathers. Who even if he did turn out to be just another brand of evil imperialist, and crazy to boot, was a thoroughly *professional* revolutionary terrorist. And an experienced one. He'd taught her well. "So how did you wind up here, of all places?" she asked. "You've always been afraid of the dark."

"I freaked out. The blast scared me so much I shit my pants and just *ran.* That's why I'm wearing these castoffs the Evernighters gave me. The hole I ducked down brought me straight to Mama's people."

I was wondering why you were dressed like a street beggar. The Leopard Men had always been sharp dressers, affecting dark suits and neckties even in the hot, humid Congolese bush.

"I guess they were right to test me, no? Because I failed. When I calmed down, I realized they'd figure I was going to sell them out. And I'd heard of this place. You can't be on Paris's underside and not. We—the Leopards and I—even knew where some of the entrances to Mama's little kingdom were. Why not? It wasn't as if even they dared to try to come to Evernight without permission."

"Which Mama wasn't about to grant them."

"Oh, no. She hates terrorists. She doesn't like plain violent criminals much better."

"So why *did* they take you in?"

"They said it was because I *belonged* here. I was broken, as they put it: a young, exploited kid, forced to do things I didn't want to, scared shitless—literally—and looking for a way out. A refuge. Evernight's all about refuge. So, they're sheltering me. Even though it's bringing the exact kind of heat on them that Mama's tried for years to avoid, they tell me."

"Are you worried they'll turn you over to the authorities?"

"They'd never turn anybody over to *les flics.* Mama's even more absolute than the Corsicans about that. If they decide I'm really a terrorist, they'll just send the National Police my head, along with a note handwritten by Sortilège. She's one of Mama's Speakers, even though she's mute. She only communicates by Tarot readings and writing on an Android tablet. She has really beautiful penmanship, I guess."

"Is that why you're so eager to get out? It looks to me as if this place is just what you've been hoping for: a safe haven."

"Sis, it's the closeness. And the dark. You remember. I always slept with a night light, and you always used to tease me."

She grinned. "It was my job as your older sister."

"You didn't have to enjoy it so much. But—I guess I have a touch of claustrophobia, too. They kept us locked in cargo containers when the Leopard Men first smuggled me into France, as many kids as they could cram in each. A lot of us freaked out. I did. But I never fell to the bottom of the heap and suffocated, anyway."

She shook her head. *The Nshombos and their goons had so much to answer for,* she thought. *But, on the bright side, most of them did.*

He grabbed her hands. The tear-flood had started down his cheeks again. He was still full-faced, as he'd been as a child, although clearly not from boyhood pudge anymore. "Please—Cécile. I beg you. I'm going mad here. You've got to get me out!"

She squeezed tightly back. "Leave it to me."

"Mama's children say they don't dare let me go! What can you do?"

She smiled. "In my current life," she said, "you might say I have become a professional negotiator, of sorts."

◆

Yes, the words written on a Samsung Galaxy Tab 2's 254 mm screen read. *I will release your brother. If you will do something for me.*

She really does have exquisite handwriting, Candace thought. *Even with a stylus on a screen.*

A new trio of Speakers now surrounded Mama on her catafalque. One was the fortuneteller with the long, lank blond hair who called herself Sortilège. *By no coincidence whatever, I'm pretty sure.*

"Tell me," Candace said.

"You know about the *Groupe d'intervention de la Gendarmerie nationale?*" asked another Speaker, a pallid kid with black emo hair hanging in his almost-as-black eyes, and a Pinocchio nose she was pretty sure he hadn't been born with.

"Of course. Who doesn't?" *What kind of properly trained terrorist would I be if I hadn't heard of GIGN?* "They're the special-operations branch of the national military police."

"Yes," said a green-skinned older woman, the third of Mama's current interpreters to the outside world. "Their Paris squad is especially brutal. And they have nearly talked the civil authorities into launching something they've wanted to do for years."

An operation to wipe out Evernight, Sortilège wrote. She even wrote the underworld domain's name in English. Candace suspected Mama called it that partly to piss off the surface city's stick-up-the-butt *Académie française* language-fascist types.

"You don't mean kill everybody?" she asked. "How would they get away with such a thing? This isn't off the scope in the Third World—some corner of Africa nobody in the West knows or cares about."

"Isn't it?" asked Scene Kid. "What comes down here is buried. It's been that way since the Catacombs were formed."

At the very least, they mean to murder Mama, Sortilège wrote.

"And that would mean death for all of us, as sure as by shooting," the green woman said.

Candace frowned. She was no bleeding-heart, as the Americans would say. She was certainly no revolutionary—her adventures in the Nshombos' Holiday Camp for Wayward Child Aces had burned any inclination in that direction right out of her. But now, she suddenly discovered, there was still some shit she would not eat.

And not incidentally, the practical side of her brain reminded her, *it would mean Marcel's death as well.* "But what can I do? I'm just a tourist!"

We need you to negotiate on our behalf, Sortilège wrote.

"—With the Mayor's Special Aide for Wild Card Affairs."

"We understand you are a skilled negotiator, in your day job back in Canada," added Scene Kid with more than a bit of a smirk.

She glared at all of them in turn, resenting the bald admission of the eavesdropping she'd taken for granted would happen. And then for good measure at Mama Evernight, although she could no more see with her fibrils than her long-dead and withered eyes. "How do you expect me to do that? Just march into City Hall and say, 'I'm Cécile Shongo and I want to see the Mayor's Special Aide for Whatever the Fuck'?"

"Yes," the green woman said blandly. "You have an appointment."

Sortilège held up a smartphone. Candace's phone. The sender's name on the SMS message display read *Boumedienne.*

"We have her number," the Speakers explained. "We deal with her frequently. But this matter is delicate and requires negotiation face-to-face."

Candace sighed. This place looked and felt so much like something out of a nineties horror flick that she had difficulty remembering it was the twenty-first century, even down here. "What's in it for me'?"

"Freedom for your brother. And you, of course. On condition that he perform no more violent acts. And you must get him out of the country within twenty-four hours."

"Deal. It's been real, but there won't be a lot keeping me here after he's free."

"One more thing," Green Woman said.

You must answer for your brother's compliance with your own life as well as his, the Galaxy said. *If he violates these conditions—*

Her other hand held up a card depicting a skeleton in plate armor, riding a white horse. Candace didn't know much about the Tarot, but she did recognize a Death card. Even without *"Le Mort"* helpfully printed at the bottom.

"I'll do it," she said.

♥

With its colonnaded walls and high, round-arched ceiling the Hôtel de Ville looked to Candace more like a big train station decorated in *Fin de Siècle* Whorehouse–style than City Hall for a metropolis.

The two white dudes in the dark suits tailored close enough to display their brick-like physiques, if not the handguns in their shoulder holsters, with dark sunglasses and earphones stuck to their bald-shaven, brick-like heads, who immediately detached themselves from the columns to march purposefully toward Candace, couldn't have looked more like Official Thugs if they were on a poster for next summer's big action blockbuster.

Dark them! screamed in Candace's brain as fear electrocuted her. *Dark the whole room and run! Cut their fucking throats, to be safe!* She'd scored a sweet lockback-folder knife from Toby for a not-too-extortionate price, and apparently the Paris City Council thought metal detectors on the entranceways wouldn't fit in with the Giant Fantasy Renaissance Castle look of the building's exterior or the gaudy insides.

She forced the voice of terror to shut the fuck up and sighed in resignation.

"Madame Shongo," said the slightly taller goon, "we need you to come with us."

"What are you doing?" she yelled at the top of her lungs. "I'm a Canadian citizen! I have my rights!"

The other goon suddenly materialized—metaphorically, not literally, a distinction you always had to make in a world where any random could be an ace—at her left elbow and pinched her above it with what might as well have been an ace's steel claws.

"Not with us, little girl," he said softly in her ear. "So, do you do this the easy way, or the fun way?"

She let her shoulders slump. She *knew* she didn't have any rights—not with guys who looked and dressed like that. But she did have a cover to maintain. "All right," she said back quietly. "I'll come with you. You can't blame a girl for trying, though."

"Of course we can," said Thing One.

♣

"What are you doing here?" the tall white man in the light gray silk demanded. He was the only one among the seven white men in the room whose suit wasn't black, and the only one without a clean-shaven scalp. His buzz cut had the look and color of steel shavings. "Why do you come to see Madame Boumedienne?"

"I *told* you," she said. "I came here to help a friend who got in trouble with the law and wound up in the Catacombs."

They had forcibly sat her down in the middle of a small but fancy room, overheated by a musty-smelling radiator painted white. It was somewhere down a rat-maze path, into a wing of the sprawling structure that pretty clearly saw little use these days. They hadn't tied her to the antique, Louis the Something-Ass–looking chair, but they had thoughtfully spread a blue tarp on the floor beneath it.

Buzz-Cut bent down, grabbed the chair arms from her right, and spun her to face him. "Do you know who I am?" he hissed in her face. His breath had a strange smell, strong, astringent, and not at all pleasant.

"You are Colonel Emmanuel DuQuesne of the GIGN," she said. "Head of Section such-and-such I didn't bother to remember. You introduced yourself when your brutes brought me in."

"Section 23," he said, straightening. There was something odd about his voice, something she couldn't quite pin down. As if he had something in his mouth, was the closest she could get. "It is a name synonymous with terror. Terror prevention to the media. And to everybody else . . ." He smiled unpleasantly. He was not a man who struck Candace as one who did a lot of things pleasantly.

She knew the type.

"You're not here to help the black terrorist rat who dove down into the sewers the other night? He's a Congolese, we know. As are you."

"I'm Canadian now," she said levelly. "I'm looking to help a friend. He's French, white, and a joker. Jacques Gendron. I met him at college in Montréal."

By great good chance, just such a person had entered Evernight a month ago. She'd met him for the first time moments before departing Evernight by one of the countless secret ways, which happened to lie near a Métro station. *Of course,* she thought, *if GIGN has actually tapped the Special Aide's phone, I'm fucked.*

"And on behalf of such a one, you agreed to serve as emissary for the Queen of the Underworld to the Special Aide?"

"We were close."

He curled his lip in disgust. "So what exactly is your business here?"

"Confidential. You'll need to ask the Mayor's Special Aide that question. I bet she has the proper forms available online."

He glared at her. His eyes were very dark. She expected him to strike her then. Instead he gestured to his Goon Squad. "Her leg," he commanded curtly. "The left one."

She was seized from behind and professionally pinned to the chair. Another goon knelt to clamp an iron grip on her right leg. Two more straightened out the left and pulled the dark-gray wool leg of her business-suit pants up to bare her calf.

"So," DuQuesne said, eyeing her as he might the fruit at a stall in the open-air market in the Goutte d'Or, "you still display the leanness characteristic of the true African, little cunt. The softness of the North American black has not infected you."

"I try to keep in shape," she said. *I could try and sound more terrified,* she thought, *but I don't think at this point it's going to matter.*

He bent down, bringing his pale, scarred face near her bare skin. A thrill of horror ran through her. *He's not going to try to kiss me? Eww!*

Instead he opened his jaws wide. Two long, curved fangs swept down and forward from the roof of his mouth, and locked into place in the gaps where his canines would be. Before she could react, he bit down hard, right into her calf muscle.

It was as if her lower leg had been electrocuted and firebombed at the same time. She convulsed and shrieked so loud it tore her throat.

He stood up, looked her in eyes now brimming with tears. His fangs clicked back into place as he closed his near-lipless mouth on a look of obscene satisfaction.

"They call me *La Vipère*," he said. She knew now why he talked funny. "For, like a viper's, my bite carries venom. Do you feel it burning in your veins?"

"Yes!" She managed not to shriek it.

Agony was not a new sensation for Candace Sessou. The child-ace factory had used "therapeutic" torture to stress its subjects, to encourage the retrovirus to express in them as an ace. But not pain like *this*. It felt like lava blooming beneath her skin.

"My ace," he said, "allows me to inject a blend of such a strength and composition as I choose, within certain limits. In your case: a mild dose of proteases with a neurotoxin kicker. I could inject enough nerve-killer to stop your heart—or enough protease venom to explode the blood cells throughout your body in a rolling tide of unendurable agony. You think you screamed just now? It's nothing."

"Why are you doing this? I told you all I know!" *Please believe me,* she thought.

She knew she could Dark them—or she could, provided the pain died back enough to let her concentrate her will. But that wouldn't get her out of here. They didn't need to see to hang onto her. Or for this sadistic madman to bite her again.

"Have you? Really?"

"*Yes!*"

He nodded. "So be it. You must be telling the truth. Such a slip of a girl could never hold out against even so minor a pain. Let her go."

Let her go? She couldn't believe she'd heard him right. But the GIGN men released her legs and arms and stepped back. She slumped forward in her chair. She stopped herself from grabbing her poisoned leg. She wasn't sure if that would increase the damage the venom did. Or cause it to spread.

It did burn less now. A little. *I can . . . manage.*

"Are you still here? Up. You're free. Get your black ass out of my sight before I nip you there to encourage you to move it."

"Why did you *do* that to me?"

"There will be no lasting damage, I assure you. Well, very little. You should be able to walk now. As for why—well, yes, to assure myself that your story was true, far-fetched as it seems. Also I wanted to make sure you weren't hiding any ace powers—such people are dangerous. Of course, if you had any such, you'd have used them in an attempt to escape the agony. Futile, of course. But you couldn't have known that."

Want to bet? she thought.

"Also, to impress you—and your monstrous mistress below the ground. Her powers and mine are not so very different, you see. We both possess a potent sting; we have likewise senses the average human does not. We share the gift of manipulating human biochemistry. Even if I lack her power of using neurochemical interfacing to control the human mind."

Which Mama can't do. Well, told me she can't. I may have no more reason to believe her than I do this . . . reptile. But guess which one I'd rather trust?

"And finally—" he smiled and let the fangs snap down again briefly, "—for the fun of it. This is a stressful job I have, keeping Western

civilization safe from savage animals. You can't begrudge me a little
sport, can you?"

♠

"This program is far advanced, I regret to say," the Mayor's Special Aide
for Wild Card Affairs said. "Much against our wishes, as I trust you understand. Our mission is to help people, not—anyway. Tell me what Mama
Evernight has to offer, to induce me to do more to stop this tragedy than
I have already."

Maryam Boumedienne was a handsome, gracefully dignified woman
of North African descent. She stood a head taller than Candace and was
willowy despite clearly being well into middle age, with hips broadened
from child-bearing. The hair wound into a mathematically precise bun
at the back of her narrow head was black showing only threads of silver.

She frowned slightly. "But first—tell me, please, what she's offering you,
to get you to agree to negotiate for her?"

"My brother's freedom," she said.

"Your brother the wanted terrorist?"

She shrugged. "Nobody's perfect. But we'll address that later. Yes. That
brother."

Madame Boumedienne's office was positively restrained in its décor, al-
beit still large enough to hold a good-sized elephant or modest Brontosau-
rus. The walls' bare, gleaming oak veneer, the modern-looking desk and . . .
relatively modern . . . chairs, the black and white parquetry floors and
simple ceiling all contrasted hugely to the frou-frou explosions of the corridors Candace had made her way through, after *La Vipère*'s henchmen
cut her loose. Those were all ornate chandeliers and fat white women with
their boobs hanging out *everywhere*: topless in heroic bas-relief on the
walls; cavorting nude with Pegasuses on the ceiling paintings. Whoever
had decorated the place had had *serious* issues.

The Special Aide was still looking at her expectantly. "She offers you
continued peace and well-being in the city."

"A threat?"

"No. An observation. Consider: A modern city needs its refuse dump."
She felt no shame at cribbing from one of the Archive's lectures. "Plus an
extensive sewer system."

"Much of which has been co-opted into Evernight," Boumedienne said.

"Well, they don't actually live in the sewers. Or not many. In any event,
consider the service Evernight provides: a catchment for those, jokers, nats,

even minor aces, who find themselves unable to function in the surface world."

"But we offer services for those poor people," Boumedienne said. "That's among the duties of my department, not to put too fine a point on it."

"And I'm sure you do your best, Madame. But, with all respect, please consider what a wonderful job those social services must have done for these people, these Evernighters, that they'd choose to live in a place with bones for walls instead."

Boumedienne winced. "Point taken. And—it's true. We cannot provide for the particular needs of everyone. We must provide for the common welfare."

"Mama Evernight and her children define 'uncommon.'"

"True. But even leaving aside your brother's recent terrorist act, as you request, there are people of highly dubious moral character living down there."

"There is also a large, thriving, tightly knit community of people peaceably living their lives. It's not too much to call it a family. I have seen it with my own eyes. And—Mama does enforce what few rules she has laid down quite strictly."

"She was one of the 'dubious characters' I was referring to."

"Is it worth wiping out an entire community to get at her?"

"The operation would not necessarily kill everybody down there. Despite the expressed desires of some."

I wonder who? Candace thought. "How many do you think it would be necessary to kill, then? Whom would you kill?"

"Why, none—if it could be helped. But, but—it would be a humanitarian intervention. Some collateral damage is sadly inevitable. But in the service of the greater good."

"Madame Boumedienne, those killed by humanitarian intervention stay just as dead, the arms and legs and faces stay blown just as far off the wounded, as in war by any other name you want to give it. I've seen it up close. And I tell you: anybody who thinks such a thing as 'humanitarian warfare' is even possible does not understand what at least one of those words mean!"

The Special Aide looked uncomfortably away.

"Let me put it another way," Candace said. "Would you shut down the sewers of Paris because they had some alligators in them?"

"Well—they're really Nile crocodiles. And there are not so many of them. And they *do* keep down the rats . . ."

"You begin to see my point."

"All right. This is all very well and good. But I need more. Give me something that I can take to the Mayor—to the national authorities—which will persuade them to stay the Gendarmerie's hand." A beat. "Please."

Candace leaned forward across the neat desk. "Mama abhors all crimes of violence, including terrorism. You must know that, from your years of dealing with Evernight. So she makes no threats. She merely asks you to imagine the effects on the peace and well-being of your city's straight citizens and tourists in the event of even a successful decapitation strike: the horde of angry, embittered jokers and fugitives that would fill the Métropolitain stations and pour up from every manhole and access tunnel in Paris."

The pale-brown eyes got wide. "Shit," the Mayor's Special Aide said.

Candace sat back, nodding. "Precisely."

Boumedienne frowned at nothing for a few moments. Long enough for Candace to start getting itchy about her brother's fate. And her own. *There are too many games going on at once here,* she thought, *and I don't trust any of the players. Except DuQuesne, to be awful.*

"Very well," the Special Aide said at last. "I think I can persuade them with that . . . graphic image. Even the upper ranks of the Gendarmerie National—even the commanders of GIGN themselves—realize that such a measure as they propose is extreme, and likely to produce blowback. When I share your description of the nature of such blowback, I think they'll reconsider."

"So you agree to Mama's terms?"

"Yes. Now, let's talk about yours."

"I've guaranteed my brother's continued good behavior to Mama, which guarantee I likewise extend to you." *Even though you don't seem the sort to kill me if he breaks my promise.* "He will honor that guarantee. He's desperate. Desperate enough even to behave."

"Even so, he's still wanted for an act of terrorism."

"I've also promised Mama Evernight to have him out of the country within twenty-four hours. That would get him out of your hair."

"'Terrorist,'" Boumedienne repeated. "That's a magic word these days. It makes rights and justice go away. Along with a good deal of sense."

"That's true. But in exchange for his freedom, he's willing to provide all the details he knows about the Leopard Man leadership cadre in Paris—which means all of France. Names, dates, plans, the works. *And* he was Léon's own accountant."

"You mean—"

"He'll give you their financial records, down to the PIN numbers on their pseudonymous bank accounts."

"That—that would excuse a very great deal."

"And after all," Candace said, "it's not as if anybody was hurt. It was only a bus kiosk."

"It's not as if anybody else was *there*. The only reason we identified your brother was that several surveillance cameras captured him in the act. We were able to match his face with an individual Gendarmerie agents have photographed in the company of known Leopard Men, and near known Leopard Men locations. Still—the kiosk will cost 63,000 euros to repair."

Candace whistled. "So much?"

"You know government contracts." Madame Boumedienne stood up and offered her hand across the desk. "All right. You have made yourself a bargain. I know the Mayor will see the wisdom of your proposals, and the President as well. As for the National Police and the Gendarmes—well, they'll either see the light of wisdom, or do as they are told, depending. I cannot yet guarantee acceptance. But I think the chances are good."

Candace almost deflated into a limp rubber sack like an empty balloon. "Thank you," she said, pulling herself together enough to rise and clasp the proffered hand.

"You are a brave woman, Madame Shongo," the Special Aide said. "Your brother cannot know what a remarkable sister he's fortunate enough to have."

"Probably not," Candace said. "He's my younger brother."

Boumedienne laughed, but quickly went serious again.

"I only hope your courage turns out not to have been rashness in the end. Good day to you. And good luck."

◆

Where is he? Candace asked herself, checking her smartphone again. It was 2258. Two minutes later than last time.

It was chilly. Her breath puffed out visibly to join the mists creeping out of the Seine to fill the Place Vendôme with the smell of diesel exhaust and grease-trap rankness. The lights glowed dim and yellow, and few people walked abroad. A pair of lovers gazed arm in arm up at the statue of the flying ace Captain Donatien Racine, known as Tricolor, atop the famous column commemorating his defense of Paris from the 2009 attack by the Radical—her old crush and mentor, Tom Weathers. A shabby man—one of

Mama's children?—marched past the gate to the Tuileries, swigging wine from a bottle and mumble-singing indistinctly to himself.

Her own warm buzz of success and champagne was starting to curdle in her stomach. *Should I have let him go off by himself?*

Like everybody packed anxiously into Mama Evernight's crypt, her brother had gone manically happy when Madame Boumedienne called to announce that the President himself had ordered the Gendarmerie to stand down from its planned attack. Candace's bargain had been accepted.

I at least had sense to worry when Marcel said he was going out without me. Briefly. She'd been in a happy place she'd almost forgotten existed, swilling Moët & Chandon from the bottle like the mumbling hobo minstrel, dancing and chanting along to "La Marseillaise" echoing off the bone walls from big speakers playing off somebody's iPod. She had the hairy arm of the two-and-a-half-meter-tall joker called Bigfoot across her shoulders from one side, and the hard, dense arm of the Mauritanian joker-ace who called herself *La Brique* from the other. *He's so happy and excited,* she remembered thinking. *Why not let him go?*

She had pulled together enough to suggest that she come along and watch his back. But no, Marcel said. He had to go alone. He'd stashed thumb drives containing key financial records with a Christian refugee from the Albanian civil war, a shopkeeper who'd suffered mightily from Leopard Man extortion. He'd been planning his escape for a long time, he said.

His contact had the paranoid hypervigilance of an alley cat. If Marcel brought anyone along, he'd shut down and hunker behind steel shutters. So Candace nodded; her brother kissed her fervently on the cheek, thanked her for the hundredth time, promised to meet her in the Place Vendôme at 2100, and left Evernight.

Their flight from Orly left at 0130. Darkness was beginning to muster in Candace's stomach, and tension knotted around the black sensation. To distract herself from her thoughts, and the growling of the terrible thing that lurked in her under-brain, she glanced up the column's bronze, already green four years after its construction. Despite the French government's official reversal of its initial genocidal approach toward those touched by the wild card into operatic concern for their welfare—powered both by guilt and a desire to twit the Yankees for their Four Aces witch hunt—it kept tight rein on everyone who drew the ace. Everyone detected they conscripted into government service. As a consequence, France had few publicly known ace heroes to adore. Because Captain Racine's heroics had been broadcast live worldwide on video news feeds, the government opted to make him the public face of its shadowy ace corps—and a tourist attraction.

Candace recalled her encounter with another official French shadow-ace that afternoon, shuddered, and felt unclean. Tricolor's bravery was real. But it was being used to hide a lie.

Her iPhone started playing the signature tune from Van McCoy's "The Hustle," a current favorite song twenty years older than she was. She almost dropped it yanking it from her purse. "Hello?"

"It's Sluggo," her caller said. "Your brother's been spotted heading for the Leopard Man HQ in the Goutte d'Or. You must come at once."

She barely remembered to end the call with a stab of her thumb before turning and sprinting for the nearest Métro stairs.

Marcel, Marcel—what have you done?

Already, she feared she knew.

♥

When the stench struck her like a fist through the open front door, Candace flicked her knife blade into place. She stepped cautiously out of the feather-light sleet falling on the lower slope of the Mount of Martyrs into the normal-looking two-story gray stone house, cramped on a block of near-identical houses with steep slate roofs, to which Samuel L. Jackson's voice on her GPS had led her from the Château Rouge Métro stop at a dead run.

She opened her mouth, and Darkness rolled out to precede her. Nothing could see through it but her, and those she temporarily allowed to. A were-leopard might hear and smell her well enough to strike, but a far more likely nat gunman would see nothing to shoot at.

Not that anyone she saw was in any shape for shooting. Two bodies, male, and what she thought were parts of a third were sprawled in attitudes of violent death. Their guts and all their blood were on the sodden throw rug—an oddly domestic touch for Leopard Men—the doorway that opened to her right, and the stairs themselves.

She let it lie as she passed by. She didn't need it. Also the recoil from 7.62 cartridges and steel buttplate hurt her shoulder.

The smell was familiar. Fear and fresh blood and shit. She hadn't smelled it for years. *Except in my dreams.* At the house's rear an oblong of relative lightness showed a back door also ajar. Another body lay on its front past the stairs, with its head turned to the side. Half its head. The rear half.

"You have strong jaws, you treacherous bastard," she muttered.

From ahead, she heard a snarling and a spitting, and she ran.

She crossed a short, bare yard that stank of pee and weed, just missed stepping on one of a litter of discarded wine bottles and falling, and clambered up onto a stone wall just higher than her head.

A narrow alley confronted her. In the next yard, two leopards fought, a larger and a smaller.

They squatted on spotted haunches, yowling and swiping for each other's faces. Though both were covered in blood, the larger one's left shoulder lay open to bone, blood running in the rain. As Candace drew herself upright, balanced on the rounded wall-top with the help of a couple years' ballet classes in Cape Town, she saw the bigger gather itself and leap on the smaller.

Rather than spring to meet it, the lesser leopard rolled backward across its twitching tail onto its butt, accepting the attack with its forepaws. The larger cat's momentum flung it all the way onto its back. The bigger landed on top, its hind claws raking at the lesser's belly.

The smaller leopard's jaws clamped on its throat.

A natural leopard killed larger prey by holding its throat closed in its teeth until it suffocated. But Leopard Men—the few, the proud, the weres—they loved the taste of blood. Their shared ace had given them mighty jaws and razor teeth. And what was power, if not to be used to the utmost? To be enjoyed?

With a heave of its round head, the smaller leopard ripped the throat clean out of the one atop it. The bigger one fell onto its side on the flagstones, kicking and gushing.

Candace's heart seemed to pause its beating.

The smaller cat jumped up—and continued rising, to stand bipedal, hunched over as if in pain. To her relief and fury mingled she saw it was Marcel, naked. A taller, older African man, likewise naked, lay bleeding to death at his feet.

Her brother swayed. He was awash in blood. But Candace saw no sign of deep wounds beneath the gore.

"Marcel!" she shrieked. He turned his blood-masked face to her. Their eyes locked.

He turned and staggered around the hip of the darkened house with surprising speed. Too late, it came to her to try to Dark him. *Not that I know how I'd capture him without one or both of us getting hurt, if he turns again.*

She jumped down from her wall, scrambled over the next, vaulted the dying Léon, and ran after her brother. He was weakened by exertion, and mostly by the stress of transforming from a seventy-kilogram boy into a seventy-kilogram cat, with its drastically different skeleton and muscles, and back again to human.

She ran out past the house and stopped. Two figures stood on the street, looking at her. "M. Sluggo," she said, panting more than she should have. "Toby."

Toby uttered a greeting bark. He sounded cheerful. Then again, having a dog's head atop an otherwise-human body, he probably always sounded cheerful, unless he was growling. "Our people have your brother, and are taking him below," Sluggo said mournfully. Or so she took it from the flaccid dangle of his slugs. "You must come with us. You won't make us compel you, too, will you? Please?"

She sighed. "No," she said. "Lead me to the Underworld, psychopomp. Do I need to give you a Euro?"

Sadly Sluggo shook his head. "Alas," he said, "I have no boat. Come on."

♣

"You betrayed me."

On the march down and down into the everlasting dark, and round and round through corridors of bone and stone, Candace had wondered what exactly she would say when—if—she confronted her brother.

Now the two were locked in the same cell he'd been held in before. She was as much a captive in Evernight as Marcel was. She just wasn't restricted to this room.

She knew, now, what she'd say, having said it. But she was still surprised at how levelly she spoke.

He sneered. His handsome, earnest-schoolboy features twisted in a look of hate so pure it rocked her on her heels. "Don't talk to me about betrayal!" he screamed. Then more quietly: "You betrayed us, Darkness."

"Don't call me that."

"You and the others—the Hunger, Mummy, Wrecker—you were heroes of the Revolution, the fighting vanguard of our glorious PPA! Yet you deserted Alicia and the People's Paradise in their greatest need. You deserted the Revolution."

She glared at him through narrow eyes. *He's still my brother. Even after what he's done.*

"Fuck your Revolution," she said, in a low, intense voice. "It was all a bunch of lies Alicia and her brother told us to serve their greed and power-lust. We killed more black people than the imperialists did. By far. We even murdered more of our own—people inside the PPA—than any outside enemy ever did."

Marcel scoffed. "What about Captain Flint and the Highwayman and their living atom bomb that killed so many of our soldiers?"

"Who do you think did most of the Nshombos' murder for them? Not us; we were few, though we murdered our share, many times over. Your precious soldiers. I don't waste tears on them. Any more than I do the British aces, scapegoated by their own to assuage their tender colonialist consciences. I'm not saying the imperialists were good. I'm saying we were worse. Sometimes I wish we'd all died in the blast, too—us child aces. It would have been better for the world. And probably us as well."

But saying that, she felt a pang of loss, for the other stolen ones, her comrades in living through a Hell no one should have to endure, much less children. It lent an acid splash to her next words. "The Nshombos made us monsters, Marcel. You and me both. But they were the greater monsters by far. That's what I turned against. And I'm glad!"

"You only say that because you were the whore of the white devil! The one who misled us, and murdered the Doctor!"

"Oh, come the fuck off it, Marcel. Tom Weathers wasn't a good man, but one thing he was not was into literally fucking children. Even though he helped your precious Nshombos fuck us all!"

And just like that, he *shifted*—partway. Her own reflexes were naturally fast. But she was only able to skip back and turn her head far enough fast enough that the claws at the end of his left arm, now spotted-furred and inhumanly jointed, only gashed her right cheek, instead of tearing her whole face off her skull.

That's some great control you have there, bro, she thought as she opened her mouth and Darked him.

He screamed in leopard fury and lashed out. She backed up to the locked door and pounded on it with her palm, hoping *Gros-pieds* and Brick outside would realize what was happening and let her out.

He turned toward her. His head was still human. The look on his face was not. Though his arm was still transformed—he probably hadn't recovered the energy for a full change—he didn't have a leopard's senses. But he didn't need them. He could hear just fine. And it wasn't hard to make out where she was. He gathered himself to leap. Candace made ready to dodge, hoping she was faster than his mostly human body.

The door opened behind her. Her brother shrieked as fibrils lashed from tiny holes hidden in the stone walls and tangled his arms, his face.

"Don't kill him!" she screamed, as rock-hard hands yanked her backward into the corridor. "Please!"

"I will not," an eerie voice said from her right.

She turned. Between bone walls stood the Archive, small and neat, bearing the distinctive multi-colored tendril leash of one of Mama's Speakers around his neck.

"Not now, at least," he said, the voice his own but echoing the cadence and timbre of a woman long dead—and eternally alive. "Now you must come and learn your fate."

♠

"Please don't kill Marcel, Mama," Candace said the moment she entered the Queen's burial chamber. "I beg you. Take me instead."

A middle-aged Vietnamese woman called Pétunia had cleaned the wounds her brother's claws had opened on her face, closing them with a healing ace. "There might still be scarring, dear," she'd told Candace.

Candace only shrugged. For a moment she'd thought the fact the Evernighters tended her wounds meant Mama didn't mean to kill her. Then it occurred to her Mama might just not want Candace passing out from blood loss before hearing her death sentence.

"Your life is forfeit anyway," said Ariane, the blond woman covered in weeping sores. Apparently the first shift of Speakers she'd encountered was back on duty. "Along with his."

"And yet you'd try to bargain your life for your brother's, even after what he did to you?" That was Evadne, the middle-aged woman with the all-black eyes.

"He's my brother. It's not as if my life is such a fucking carnival, anyway. Just—just keep him. I know you can't let him go. But alive. Kill me."

Aristide, the naked, callused man, said, "You may redeem your life and his. And your freedom."

"Though as you say, your brother must remain in Evernight always."

Evadne gestured toward a big LED TV, which had been set up by the curving wall to one side. Sortilège turned the volume up with her lower left hand.

"—Valentine's Day Massacre," an angry white guy with tie askew was ranting in French. "We cannot allow our streets to become the Wild West as the Americans do. And even when one terrorist kills others, worthy of death though these victims were, they were still victims of a monstrous crime. And it was still an act of terrorism, by a fugitive sheltered in the hellish underworld beneath our sacred city!"

"You want me to kill the loudmouth?" Candace asked. "I mean, I can see why, but all respect to you, Mama, that's not the sort of job I—"

"You misunderstand." As before, Candace had started ignoring the Speaker, and heeding the one who Spoke. "As you might gather from his overheated rhetoric, your brother's actions have made a marked impression. Especially on the authorities."

"Oh, shit," Candace said.

"Yes. Though details of the agreement with us have been covered up as a matter of routine, it's been leaked that the Mayor and the President agreed to give Evernight a reprieve on the grounds they prevent a wanted terrorist from striking again. They have been deeply humiliated. And they react as powerful men who have been humiliated have the power to do."

"The deal's off."

"More than that. Much more. Our watchers have seen an armored van leave the building in the 1st arrondissement that Section 23 of GIGN uses as its headquarters. It is rolling for the Pont Neuf that crosses the Seine to the Left Bank."

"That evil bastard DuQuesne got his green light," Candace said, sick and angry. *Marcel, Marcel, what did you even* think *you were doing?*

◆

The slim fibril whipping out of nowhere to wrap Candace's left wrist was so unexpected she almost tripped and fell face-first in the nasty-smelling water that ran ankle-deep in this stretch of the old Paris mining tunnels that made up most of Evernight.

They've found my commune beneath the Moulin Rouge. The words sang in her blood with the urgency of adrenaline. *You must hurry. They're wearing masks, and spraying gas from canisters.*

"Shit." Alarm thrilled through her, even more jangling than Mama's neural intrusion. "Mama, you've got to pull your fibrils back down the tunnel away from there. *Now.*"

I can't! My people need me. They're falling down already. The poor innocents! I hope it's only knockout gas.

"It's not. It's nerve gas, Mama. Pull back!" Talking out loud at a dead run was taxing her wind, but fear and anger helped keep her moving.

Surely they'd never do—

"You never met DuQuesne. This is *exactly* what he'd do. I'm surprised he didn't just plug up the known entrances and flood the whole tunnel network with the shit." *Except they'd never plug all the cracks and holes, if they had a decade to try,* she thought. Apparently even *La Vipère* had some scruples when it came to killing straight Parisian citizens and tourists in droves. Or his superiors did.

My senses there are growing fuzzy, her blood keened.

"Fuck. This isn't an attack on your colony. It's an attack on *you*. Pull your fibrils back now, a quarter kilometer at least or more if you can! It should take a while for the neurotoxins to travel up them." *I hope.*

I can't abandon my children!

"They're already dead. Think of the rest of Evernight!"

But Candace knew as she spoke that breath was wasted. She was already whipping out her knife to slash through the tendril that had stayed stubbornly twined about her wrist for the last thirty meters. It gave a bit, like rubber tubing, but parted.

She stopped, knelt. The main skein of Mama's fibrils ran along the base of the wall, just above the water. She grabbed it with her left hand. It was surprisingly heavy. Candace wondered just how many rats and ODing drifters Mama had had to metabolize to *make* so many kilometers of the stuff.

Mama read her intent. The cords of slimy tissue suddenly blazed her hand, like a live wire, like fire. Worse than the agony of *La Vipère*'s bite. She screamed—then hacked through the bundle with a single stroke.

"I hope you like my way better than being dead," she said aloud, panting from exertion and the throbbing torment in her left hand. *I also hope my way works.*

She'd already begun to sprint, out of reach of Mama's intact and wrathful tendrils. She opened her mouth, and Darkness poured out, to fill the tunnel network before her.

♥

The rake-gaunt nat woman's hysterical shrieks of terror went silent when Candace touched her eyes. "I can see," she said wonderingly. Candace could barely hear her over the strangled squalling of the infant who had apparently been nursing when the Dark came upon them and stole away their sight.

She looked at Candace with wide pale eyes—Candace saw no colors in her Dark. "I can see!"

"Yeah. Now lighten up your grip on the baby. The baby can't breathe." The woman recoiled from her. "Now. Or I'll have to break your arm."

That snapped the woman out of it. She switched her constrictor clutch on her child to a gently fervent hugging and rocking.

Candace seized the hand of a wizened old man nearby, who looked as if all that was keeping him upright was the dark beetle carapace that covered his torso and legs, and pressed it against the woman's arm. Stunned by his sudden, unexplained blindness, he didn't resist.

Candace had hit a nest of maybe twenty Evernighters, all of them as sightless as if their eyes had been gouged out, none of them handling it much better than the nursing mother had been. Candace knew she'd never have time to touch everybody's eyes and let them see through her Darkness. She felt bad about literally poking the first woman's eyeballs, but she was the first at hand and there was no getting through her panic to get her to close her eyes.

"Take his hand. Good. Now lead the way back down the tunnel toward Mama Evernight, quickly as you can. The rest of you, come to my voice. Join hands, and form a chain."

"Why should we?" somebody asked.

"Hard men are coming to kill you. Hurry up. We got no time."

At ten, including a couple of little kids, the chain got unwieldy. By this time most of the others had calmed down enough that she could get the young man closest to her to shut his three eyes so she could touch the lids. "You link up with the rest and follow the first group. Quickly!"

"Who are you?" Twenty meters along the first woman, who now could see, had turned her face back over her shoulder to Candace as she staggered.

"Life," she said.

She looked the other way. The way she was bound.

I'll never save them all, she knew with sickness in her soul.

"And death."

♣

Screams flew to meet her as she ran. Some ended in choking. Candace's steps didn't falter, though it felt as if she'd been stabbed in the belly.

An elderly woman staggered toward her around a curve, wheezing and staggering, keeping contact with the rough limestone tunnel wall on her right with an outstretched hand. Her labored breathing seemed to result from terror and exertion, not nerve agents, and she was moving toward what she clearly hoped was safety with all the speed her body still had.

A few meters behind her, leisurely strolling, came a GIGN Section 23 operator. He had his own gloved right hand to the wall and was holding a nozzle in the other. "We told you, you old bitch," he called out. "If you run, you'll just die tired."

He sprayed her. The gas the operators carried obviously had some sort of dye in it so they could see where it went. Ironically, Candace was the only one to see it now; their night-vision goggles, whether low-light or equipped with active infrared which lit the wearer's way with an IR flashlight, couldn't penetrate her Dark.

The Evernighter woman started a shriek as she felt the loss of neuromuscular control grip her chest and begin to strangle her like a python. She fell to her knees, beating futilely against the wall and floor as she gagged and dry-heaved.

Fast-acting shit, Candace thought. Her feelings had gone dead numb. But her mind raced ahead. *I can't enter that cloud. I can't help, only join the dying. And then nothing will stop these monsters.*

She made herself hang back, despite the urgency thrilling in her nerves that made it a kind of agony *not* to run forward.

The operator walked forward, still feeling his way along the wall. He didn't spray more gas. Of course, their supply was limited to what they could carry.

All Candace had to do was flatten herself against the opposite wall, and wait.

"Hello, Gaspard," she said into his ear from behind. She knew his voice, muffled or not; DuQuesne had named him when he hustled her in for interrogation. Candace had keen senses and a keener memory. "Hope you got enough jollies with that pain-compliance grip on my arm to last you a lifetime." Candace grabbed his mask, yanked it up his face, thrust her knife into his throat, and *slashed.* The blade cut easily through muscle and cartilage and rubbery jugular veins. He couldn't even gurgle a warning through his own blood on their communications net.

She put the mask on her head but left it up. Gaspard rolled side to side on his belly, hands struggling to slow the blood that was gushing onto the use-smoothed stone floor. She knew there was a chance, however small, he could survive the severed veins. She stabbed his neck again beneath his left ear and cut his carotid artery. His body bucked up off the floor and went limp as his brain, deprived at once of half its blood, shut down.

Candace wiped her blade on his ass, folded it, and slipped it in her jacket pocket. She pulled the mask down over her face, ignoring the stink of Gaspard's breath and the garlic he'd had for his last meal, and tightened it as best she could. She was far smaller than he was, but the respirator and goggle set were clearly not custom-fit.

If there's a leak, she thought, *at least that'll spare me from having to live with what I'm going to do next.*

She stood straight and walked on around the bend. The old mining tunnel widened into a gallery, and she confronted a gray-scale image of agony and despair, like an animated Doré etching of *The Inferno*. The dying writhed and choked with tears and snot running from eyes and mouths, clutching each other, stretching hands that pled toward the masked men. Who could hear and feel their suffering, even though they couldn't see it. They kicked their victims in their faces and laughed at the torments they inflicted like Dante's demons.

Twenty doomed souls? Thirty? Candace couldn't tell. She took a deep breath and released the grip of iron self-control she'd maintained for five hard years.

She stalked forward, as feral and merciless as her brother in his leopard form, walked up to the closest GIGN operator, and stripped the mask right off his face. Then skipped away twirling it by the strap as he dropped to his knees, clutching at his throat.

The next two operators sensed something amiss, put themselves back-to-back with the gas-nozzles raised defensively. "Bruno?" one said in an Eastern European accent.

Candace tossed Bruno's mask away and pulled his off. His partner helpfully turned his head for her to strip his too. They actually dropped their sprayers to cling to each other as their mouths filled with saliva and then their lungs ceased to work, kissed by the fast-acting "next level" poison gas. "Touching," she said, and moved on.

She knew the next one, too, who stood above a large woman lying dead on her back with eyes and mouth agape. He'd been the one who seized her left leg and bared it to *La Vipère*'s tongue. He'd seemed to get into fondling her bare skin a little more than professional cruelty required.

Candace planted herself right in front of him. "This is for groping me," she said, and shin-kicked him in the balls. He had some kind of cup on under his trousers. It didn't help him much. She whipped his gas mask back off his head as he doubled toward her.

A hand brushed her left shoulder, then clamped like trap-jaws on her biceps. "Got you, you bitch!" He had his gas-nozzle thrust almost against the weird bifurcated snout of her respirator mask and was spraying it with mad optimism—as if the nerve agent wouldn't have killed her long since if it could. She whipped her knife out and open.

A single vicious slash across the back of the hand that held her laid open glove, skin, and tendon to bone. His fingers went slack. She slashed his throat, then pulled off his mask for good measure as he dropped to his knees grabbing at his gullet as if to slow the bleeding.

She looked around. And then there were none. *Where's that snake DuQuesne?* she wondered. "He got past you when you were focused on the others," she said aloud into her mask. It was as if some third party offered commentary.

She turned and ran back the way she'd come—toward Mama's chamber, the heart of Evernight. No less a monster than she was now, her enemy was likewise no less focused. He was still bent on poisoning and killing Mama, and destroying Evernight.

The mask made breathing hard. Candace ran. Around the bend she saw *La Vipère's* back. Still blinded by her Darkness, he forged determinedly on, left hand outstretched to touch the limestone wall. She slowed her pace to a brisk walk. No point winding herself. She still moved faster.

Ten meters beyond the bodies of the woman and Gaspard he stopped, turned, and stripped off his mask. "I hear you," he said. "Which terrorist are you? Your steps don't sound too heavy." He stood smiling, seeming calm. But his mouth was open far enough that she could see his fangs twitching partway down from the roof of his mouth and then back, as if to nerves.

She took her own mask off. "I'm the little black bitch you tortured," she said, stalking forward. She watched him closely for a move to draw the Manurhin .357 Magnum revolver holstered beneath his left arm.

"Shongo?" He looked and sounded surprised.

"My name is Candace Sessou. I was one of the PPA's terrorist child aces. I'm one of the most wanted terrorists in the world. I am The Darkness. I'm going to kill you."

"Impressive. And you're telling me this why?"

"One of us at most leaves here alive," she said softly, "so why not?"

Three meters from him now, she slipped to the tunnel's far side so he couldn't target her by sound. She meant to slip behind him and use her knife.

DuQuesne laughed and stuck his tongue out at her. The childish gesture made her stare harder at him. "I thought you'd be dead, having failed your infernal mistress. Well, you will be soon." Again his tongue flicked out. It made Candace's skin crawl. *What's* wrong *with this—*

He lunged straight at her and punched her in the face.

Sparks burst behind Candace's eyes and she sat down hard on a dry patch of floor. *Fuck,* she thought. *Lucky shot.* She rolled right, started to get up.

A boot in the side lifted her in the air and dumped her on her right hip. He kicked her again in the pit of the stomach. The air blasted out of her lungs.

He kicked her in the face. She fell onto her back, stunned.

His weight landed hard astride her hips. She slashed at him with her knife, but her eyes wouldn't focus and she missed. She struck him in the chest with her left fist but had no strength.

For a moment they banged forearms off each other. Then the *Vipère* caught her right wrist and pinned it to the yellow stone floor. He trapped her left a moment later.

He leaned toward her, opening his mouth. The fangs swung down from their slots in his hard palate with cruel deliberation. The venom-stink washed over her. "Poison's not the only gift my ace gives me, little terrorist," he said. "I can taste you from several meters away." The fangs retracted enough to let him waggle his tongue at her.

Her wits were starting to coalesce again inside her battered skull. *That's why he had to run away from the fight and leave his men to die. He couldn't take his mask off to find me without dying from his own gas.*

The irony failed to cheer her. He was leaning his face slowly closer to hers. "And now I'm going to bite you," he said, "right in the face. Just a touch to paralyze you. Now that you've so conveniently come to me, I have a little time to play before I kill the Queen of the Underworld. . . ."

Sheer outrage drowned initial terror at her utter helplessness, that he was playing with her now because he was by far the stronger.

. . . And because he doesn't know I have a knife.

She rolled her right wrist and cut the back of his left one with the folder's locked-back blade. He uttered a strangled cry and reared up. Both grips on her wrists slacked slightly. *But enough.* She couldn't match her muscles to his, but she was wiry strong. She eeled her hands free, gashing his left palm on the way out.

Inhumanly wide-spread jaws darted for her face, the long fangs fully extended. She stabbed between them, into the roof of his mouth.

He screamed shrilly. She writhed out from under him and jumped up. He was clutching the knife-hilt with both hands, trying to yank it free. *Guess I jammed it in there pretty well.*

He let go with his right hand and yanked out his heavy revolver. She was still almost muzzle-contact close. She threw herself backward, hoping his tongue couldn't taste her with her knife in the way.

The noises he made had turned to furious gobbling. Now as she landed on her back and rolled, they rose in pitch and urgency. And then were muffled.

She rolled against the wall, expecting the smash of a bullet every instant, and looked at him through the dark. DuQuesne had what looked like a bandanna wrapped around the lower half of his face.

Where'd he get that? Is he trying to bandage himself—

She noticed his eyes were so wide she could see whites all around his irises. A dark mottling shot through with black veins crept up the visible half of his face as his choked cries rose an octave.

"Oh," she said, as thick bundles of fibrils lashed from the floor and walls to entangle DuQuesne's neck and arms. "Looks like Mama can do that blood-exploding thing, too. I bet that hurts."

She stood up and watched Mama Evernight's hemolytic stings have their way with *La Vipère*. The instant he fell still and silent, she turned and started the long limp back to Mama's burial chamber.

She knew what happened next, and that she didn't want to watch.

Everything that dies below Paris, She consumes.

♠

"You have done well," Mama said in her borrowed voice. She had three Speakers Candace hadn't seen before and was too tired to pay much attention to. But the others were all there in the crowd in Mama's outsized crypt, along with most of the other people she'd met before, like Toby and Sluggo and, of course, the Archive, as well as a bunch she hadn't met. "I understand why you severed my fibrils. There was nothing else you could do, and nothing either of us could have done to save more of our people."

"Yeah," said Candace.

The current Speaker, an elderly man, gestured toward the television set. Though its volume was low, Candace could hear the blond news-reader woman talking about the tragic cave-in which had killed seven members of GIGN's Section 23, inside the old mines for a nocturnal training exercise.

"The President knows that Colonel DuQuesne made unauthorized use of nerve gas against French citizens," the Speaker said. "Or if he authorized it, he has conveniently forgotten it, chosen to cover the whole thing up, and has had Madame Boumedienne on the phone to extend us the olive branch. We've won."

"We have purchased tickets for you on a flight leaving Orly in three and a half hours," a young man with what looked like small fish-fins sticking out of his face and head at odd angles said. "The authorities will be more than happy to see you go. Do you need to collect any baggage?"

"I never travel with anything I can't walk away from." *Is there anything I can't walk away from?*

"Then my children will convey you there. You may leave as soon as you wish. And—thank you."

"Yeah." Candace shook her head. She felt tears start. Fears of loss and anger and a thousand more things than she could name. "They won't stop, you know. They won't leave you alone. Whether it's run by compassionate imperialists, or the brutish kind, the system's still *imperial*. It can't put up with competition or defiance. And it will not stop until it overwhelms you, one way or another."

"We will survive," Mama answered with serene conviction. "Whether it means digging deeper, or something else—we will survive. It's what we do."

"Me too," Candace said. "Now, about my brother—"

In a moment she heard him shouting behind her. "Candace, please, you have to help me! *Please.*"

Brick and Bigfoot had dragged Marcel in. He had on another set of castoff clothes. He also had a fibril skein around his neck, ready to sting him if he tried to shape-shift.

"I did help you, Marcel. And you were helping *La Vipère* all along. How did he turn you? Was it the torture? That was bad, I know. He bit me too. So I killed him."

I probably didn't need to add that last, she thought foggily. *Oh, well.*

"He offered me the Leopard Men," Marcel said. "He said he'd back my play to take over the Paris cell, then allow me to run the whole organization. As his tool, of course. They thought he would control me. But young people are hearing the message of the True PPA. The old ones had gotten soft, even Léon. He had no idea what I would build once I controlled the Leopard organization!"

"So you were playing him the way you played me?"

"It was for the Revolution," he said, as pious as Mass.

"No," she said. "You *thought* you were. In fact—"

In her reduced state she reeled physically from revelation's impact. Toby steadied her arm with a black and white dappled hand.

"—DuQuesne was playing you to take down the Leopard Men. The way he played me, to force the President's hand to stop equivocating and let him kill Mama and wipe out Evernight without any more debate or delay."

"No! He couldn't have been!"

"Because he was so trustworthy?"

His eyes went wide, and his mouth shut.

"As you see," Mama said gently through a Speaker, "we can never let him go."

Candace sighed. "Yes. I do see that. You changed, Marcel. And not for the better."

She looked at Mama's form, embossed atop her bier of bones. "But remember your promise. You can't kill him, either!"

"I keep my bargains. You won his life as well as your own. But your brother must stay here forever in Evernight. He will Share his organ functions with me, and do his part to sustain me. And through me my people, to whom his foolish actions have brought so much harm."

"See, Candace? See? They're going to tear me apart, and rape my body for my organs!"

"That's not how it works, young man," the Archive said. "Mama Evernight will connect her body to yours as she does to ours when she needs to: with her fibrils. You will not suffer. She will stimulate your brain chemistry so that you lie in perfect endorphin bliss. It's like sleep, but better; I know."

"I wish that horrified me as much as it should," Candace said.

"No, no!" Marcel shrieked, struggling wildly and uselessly. "They're going to drug me! They'll kill my soul while this undead monster sucks me dry. You can't let them do this to me, Candace! *I'm your brother!*"

"I might try," Candace said, "if only you had chosen to *be* my beloved little brother. Instead of letting them turn you into a swaggering macho revolutionary asshole like—like the Radical. But then, if you'd chosen to be my brother, we'd already be gone. Free. And a lot of innocent people would still be alive.

"You've earned this, Marcel. You've earned far worse. I still love you. I'll always love you. But I am done with you."

"No! No, please. You're my sister! You can't abandon me. You can't!"

"Marcel," she said. "I can't trust you, and they won't. There's nothing else to do. I love you. Good-bye." She turned for the exit to the surface world and walked away.

"You betrayed me!" he screamed behind her. *"You betray everything!"*

She stopped. Not looking back, she said, "Only what betrays me first." And walked on.

Lies My Mother Told Me

ZOMBIE BRAINS FLEW THROUGH the air, leaving a trail of blood and ichor on the throne riser of Michelle's parade float. She smiled as another bubble formed in her hand. This one was larger and heavier—the size of a baseball. She let it fly, and it caught the zombie full in the chest and exploded. The zombie fell backwards off the float and was trampled by the panicking crowd.

Michelle saw more zombies moving toward her. They clambered over the floats in front of hers, pushing people aside as they flowed up the street. Another zombie crawled up onto her float, using the papier-mâché arbor for purchase. The arbor came loose, and Michelle watched in dismay as the sign reading "The Amazing Bubbles, Savior of New Orleans" broke off and fell into the street. Her daughter, Adesina, who'd been hiding under Michelle's throne, let out a frightened shriek. Michelle released the bubble, knowing it would fly unerringly where she wished. When it hit, it would explode and leave a big, gooey zombie smear all over the decorations. Her beautiful float was getting ruined, and it really pissed her off.

There were three things Michelle hated about Mardi Gras: the smell, the noise, and the people. Add in a zombie attack, and it was going to put her off appearing in parades altogether.

◆

To make sure she could bubble as much as needed during the parade, she spent the morning throwing herself off the balcony of her hotel room . . . until the hotel manager came up and made her stop.

"But I'm doing the Bacchus parade," she explained. "I won't be able to bubble through the whole parade if I don't get fat on me. And the only way to do that is to take damage. A lot of damage. A fall from a fourth story is good, but not great."

At this point, the manager turned an interesting shade of green.

"Look, Miss Pond," he said. "We're all grateful that you saved us from that nuclear explosion three years ago, but you're starting to scare the other guests. It just isn't normal."

Michelle stared at him, nonplussed. *Of course it isn't normal,* she thought. *If I were normal, New Orleans would be a radioactive hole in the ground and you'd be a black shadow against some wall. I didn't ask for this. None of us wild carders did.*

"Well," she said, thinking if she just explained it to him, he'd be less freaked out. "It isn't as if when I get hit, or slam into the ground, or even when I absorbed that explosion that it hurts me. I just turn that energy into fat. Actually, it feels pretty good." *Too good sometimes,* she thought. "So you don't have to worry that I'm in pain or anything like that."

But his expression said he really didn't want to hear about her wild card power. He just wanted her to knock it off. So she stopped trying to explain and said, "I'm sorry I frightened the other guests. It won't happen again." It meant she didn't have as much fat on her as she wanted, but she'd make it work.

Adesina was still watching TV when Michelle closed the door after talking to the manager. She was perched on the foot of the bed, her iridescent wings folded against her back and her chin propped on her front feet. Just seeing Adesina made Michelle smile. Michelle had loved the child from the moment she'd pulled her from a charnel pit in the People's Paradise of Africa a year and a half ago.

Michelle still couldn't believe that Adesina had survived being injected with the wild card virus, much less being thrown into a pit of dead and dying children when her wild card had turned her into a joker instead of an ace. She shook her head to clear it. The memory of rescuing the children who were being experimented on in that camp in the African jungle was too fresh and raw. And her own failure to save all of them haunted her.

And Michelle wasn't certain how Adesina might develop. Right now she was small- to medium-dog sized. Her beautiful little girl's face was perched atop an insect body. But there was no telling if she would stay in this shape forever. She'd gone into chrysalis form after her card had turned and come out of that in her current state. It was possible she might change again—it all depended on how the virus had affected her.

"What on earth are you watching?" Michelle asked.

"Sexiest and Ugliest Wild Cards," Adesina replied. "You're on both lists. One for when you're fat and one for when you're thin."

Christ, Michelle thought. *I saved an entire city, and they're really judging me on how "hot" I am? Seriously?*

"You know, these lists are really stupid," Michelle began. "Everybody likes something different."

Adesina shrugged. "I guess," she replied. "But you *are* prettier when you're thin. They always want you to do pictures when you're thin."

Shit, Michelle thought. *That didn't take long. We've been in the States a year, and already she's thinking about who's prettier. And who's fat and thin.*

"Do you think a boy will ever like me?" Adesina asked. She turned her head and looked at Michelle. Her expression was serious. *Oh God,* Michelle thought. *It's too soon for this conversation. I'm not ready for this conversation.*

"Well," she began as she sat down next to Adesina. The bedsprings gave an unhappy groan under her weight. "I . . . I . . . I don't know." *Oh, great.* This was going well. "I don't see why not. You're beautiful."

"You have to say that," Adesina said. "You're my mother." She rubbed her back pair of legs together and made a chirping noise.

"Well, no one falls in love with you just because of how you look," Michelle said.

Adesina turned back to the TV. "Don't be dumb, Momma," she said. "Everyone loves the pretty girls."

A lump formed in Michelle's throat. She swallowed hard, refusing to cry. There was no way to ignore it. Every TV show, magazine, billboard, and website had some pretty, young, skinny, half-naked girl selling something. And up until a couple of years ago, a lot of the time that girl had been Michelle—but that was before her card had turned. And now Adesina was worrying about this crap. Michelle was at a loss.

She stared at the TV. The bumper coming in from the commercial break flashed a rapid succession of images. There was footage from the various seasons of *American Hero.* There were some still black-and-white photos from the '40s when the wild card virus had first hit. And then there were pictures of Golden Boy testifying before the House Un-American Activities Committee. Shots of Peregrine at the height of her modeling days looking like the ultimate disco chick—with wings. *Of course, they have pictures of her,* Michelle thought. *She's gorgeous.*

"Since 1946 when the alien bomb carrying the wild card virus exploded over Manhattan, they've walked among us," the voiceover began. "The lucky few aces and the hideously maimed jokers. But who cares about that? We're here to determine the hottest of the hot and grossest of the gross—wild card style."

Michelle grabbed the remote. "Okay, that's it," she said, snapping off the TV. "Look, honey, America is a stupid place sometimes. We get all caught up in unimportant junk like that show, and we forget the stuff that really means something. And I am really sucking at this Mom thing right now. The truth is that the world is going to be unkind sometimes because you're different. But that doesn't have anything to do with you, honey. It's just that the world is full of idiots."

Adesina crawled into Michelle's lap—such as it was when she was in bubbling mode—and put her front two feet on either side of Michelle's face, pushing away Michelle's long, silvery hair. "Oh Momma," she said. "I already *knew* that. I just get scared sometimes."

Michelle kissed Adesina on the top of her head. "I know, sweetie. I do, too."

♥

It wasn't so bad up on the float. *Lots of sightlines,* Michelle thought. *That's good and bad.* Good because she could see anything coming, bad because it put Adesina at risk. But being Michelle's daughter was going to put Adesina at risk no matter what.

The crowd was especially boisterous in this section of the parade route. Maybe it was because they'd had longer to drink. The parade had been going on for a couple of hours, and now it was heading into the French Quarter.

Michelle's float was decorated in silver and green. A riser with a throne was at the rear, and a beautiful arbor of papier-mâché flowers arched over the throne. Adesina had commandeered the throne for herself while Michelle stayed out on the lower platform to toss beads, wave, and bubble. Michelle thought Adesina looked adorable in her pale lavender dress—even if it did have six cutouts for her legs and another pair for her wings. Michelle's dress was the same color, but made of a Spandex blend. As she bubbled off fat, the dress would shrink along with her.

A couple of drunken blondes yelled at her, "Bubbles! Hey Bubbles! Throw me some beads!" They pulled up their tops, revealing perky breasts. Michelle was unimpressed, but she threw them beads anyway.

"Momma," Adesina said. "Why do they keep doing that?"

"Got me," Michelle replied. "I guess they think they'll get more beads."

"That's dumb."

Michelle tossed more beads, then started bubbling soft, squishy bubbles that she let drift into the crowd. "You said it. Sadly, I think it works. I just tossed them some myself."

There was a commotion up ahead on the parade route. Michelle stopped bubbling and tried to see what was happening. The crowd was panicking—people were shoving, and others were caught in between, unable to move.

The frenzy moved toward Michelle's float like a tidal wave. Some of the crowd spilled off the sidewalks into the street, knocking down the containment barricades, and then they began clambering onto the floats in front of hers. Cops tried to calm the crowd and started pulling people off the floats, but they were soon overwhelmed.

And that's when she saw them: Zombies coming up the street.

Joey, she thought. *What the hell are you doing?*

Then she saw a zombie grab a guy in an LSU T-shirt and snap his neck. Michelle was horrified. But she immediately slammed that feeling down. She couldn't help him—she had a job to do.

As she scanned the crowd, she saw the zombies brutalizing anyone in their way. A couple of cops tried to stop one of the zombies, and they each got a broken arm for their trouble before Michelle blasted the thing. And then she realized the zombies were heading for her float.

"Momma!" Adesina's frightened voice came from behind Michelle. She spun around and saw a red-faced, pudgy man and a skinnier man in a striped polo shirt climbing onto the float.

"Hey!" Michelle shouted at them. "It isn't safe here. They're coming for me."

"Behind you is the safest place to be right now," the pudgy one said. "We're not going."

Michelle sighed. "You're leaving me no choice here, guys." The bubbles were already forming in her hands, and she let them fly. The bubbles—big as a medicine ball and just as heavy—bowled the men off the float. Michelle heard them cursing. "Hey," she yelled. "Language! There's a child here!" She picked up Adesina, tucking her under her left arm.

"Momma," Adesina complained. "You're embarrassing me."

"Sorry sweetie," Michelle replied. "Now behave while I take Aunt Joey's zombies out."

Michelle let a tiny, bullet-size bubble fly at the closest zombie. Its head exploded, sending bits of brain, skull, and decaying flesh into the air. It was immensely satisfying. Unfortunately, this only made some of the people in the crowd even more panicked. And now Michelle could feel her dress getting looser. *Dammit,* she thought. *I knew I needed more fat.*

Michelle spotted another zombie and let a bubble go. There were more shrieks as its brains and pieces of its skull splattered everywhere. The float rocked as the crowd pressed against it, and she struggled to keep her balance.

"Momma, please, put me down."

"Not on your life," Michelle replied, yelling to be heard over the commotion. "Zombies and panicking nats are not a good combination. It would be too dangerous, so, yeah, that is not going to happen."

Adesina let out an exasperated sigh. "You're mean," she said.

Michelle destroyed another zombie. She felt her dress get a little looser. The zombies were coming faster, and one-handed bubbling wasn't getting the job done fast enough. "Oh darnit," she said, putting Adesina down. "Go stay under the throne. And let me know if anyone—anything—tries to get up here."

♣

If there was anything Dan Turnbull liked better than blowing shit up in a first-person shooter, it was making a mess that someone else would have to clean up. His mother had left his father six months ago, and since she'd been gone, neither of them had cleaned up much of anything. Stacks of dirty laundry were piled like Indian burial mounds in different parts of the house. A variety of molds were growing on plates in the kitchen—and in the fridge, heads of lettuce were now the size of limes. Rancid, greasy water filled the sink, and Dan wasn't sure if the sink had stopped draining or if the stopper at the bottom needed to be pulled. What he knew was that he wasn't putting his hand down there to find out.

But lying up here on the roof of the St. Louis Hotel looking down on the mess he'd made just now, well, *that* made him seriously happy. Zombies were breaking up the Bacchus parade, and that Bubbles chick was trying to stop it.

He watched her pick up the freak she called her daughter while at the same time she methodically blasted the shit out of the zombies. And he had a grudging admiration for how cool she was, given the situation. She didn't get hysterical or spaz out the way most women would. No, she just mowed those zombies right down without ever hitting a single civilian. And he wondered what it would be like when he grabbed her power.

It had been a rush when he'd grabbed Hoodoo Mama's power. Of course, he'd only taken one other ace's power before, and that had been an accident.

He'd been walking down the street and had bumped into a teenage girl. Reflexively, he grabbed her bare arm to steady himself. The expression on her face when Dan's touch had taken her power was high-larious. He'd been so surprised that she had a power, he'd used it without thinking, and teleported himself across the street, slamming into a wall as he materialized.

When Dan realized he'd almost teleported into the wall, he started shaking. In a few moments, after the adrenaline rush of fear had passed, he looked around to find the girl. But she'd vanished. *Of course, she had,* he thought. *What else would she do?*

Unlike the teleporting girl, Hoodoo Mama's power about blew his skull off. But he was only going to get one chance at using it before it reverted back to Hoodoo Mama, and he had orders to make a mess. What was happening out on the street was megaplus cool. He'd done his job well.

There were all kinds of local news video filming the parade, but this was the view he wanted. A nice long shot of the whole scene. He'd brought a video camera to get it, but he knew there would be plenty of civilians making recordings, too. Those would be on YouTube before the end of the day. What mattered was having a lot of videos of all hell breaking loose. And the one that showed it all in perfect detail would be the icing on the cake.

It didn't matter to Dan why his employers wanted a mess. For 5k and an hour's work, it was a no-brainer. He didn't even care how they knew about his power. His father had started demanding rent, and Dan had no job. And he had no intention of giving up his status as top shooter on his server. It had taken way too long for him to get there, and his team needed him. A job would just get in the way of that.

With his video camera tucked into the pocket of his baggy jeans, he climbed down the fire escape and slipped down the back alley. A couple of stragglers from the parade came toward him. As they got closer, he saw that they were girls. They were trying to run, but drunk as they were, it was more like fast staggering.

"Oh my God," one of them said to him. She was wearing what looked like a pound of beads. Long dark hair framed her face, and he wondered if she was drunk enough to fuck him. "Did you see what happened back there?"

He shrugged. "Looked like a bunch of drunk assholes. Like every Mardi Gras."

They gave him a baffled look. "No," the other one said. She wasn't as pretty as her companion. *There's always a dog and a pretty one,* he thought. "I mean Bubbles. She was so incredible, like, she just demolished those zombies. Oh shit, I think I have some zombie on me." She wiped at her shirt.

"Looked like she just made a mess of things to me," Dan replied. Neither girl had looked at him with anything like interest, and it annoyed him. He'd been the one who'd made everything go crazy, not Bubbles. He'd made her look bad too. It was his job to make her look bad. These chicks were drunk and stupid. He started past them, then impulsively grabbed the one with dark hair by the arm.

"Asshole!" she yelped, yanking away from him. But he hadn't wanted to grab a feel—he was checking whether she had a power. But there was nothing. She was an empty battery. It made him sad—and he hated that feeling more than anything.

"Jerk!" The uglier one snarled at him and looked like she might actually do something.

But then he put his hand up, using the universal gesture for a gun. He sighted down his finger at the girls.

"Bang," he said.

♠

The zombies were nothing more than piles of dead flesh now. Zombie goo was splattered everywhere, but that couldn't be helped. *You kill zombies, it's gonna make a mess,* Michelle thought.

The parade had stopped, and some of the crowd who had climbed up onto the floats to get away from the zombies were making no effort to get down now. The rest of the crowd had poured into the street and surrounded the floats as well. It was a compete logjam. People were sitting on the ground crying. Some of them were wounded.

Adesina crawled out from under the throne, and Michelle picked her up. "You okay?" Michelle asked, kissing her on the top of her head. Adesina nodded. "Will you be okay sitting on the throne?"

"Yes," Adesina replied. "But there are some men trying to get up here." Michelle put Adesina on the throne, then spun around. A couple of different men were pulling themselves up.

"Guys, other people are going to be needing this space," she said, growing a bubble her hand. She'd lost most of her fat during the parade and zombie fight, but there was still enough on her to deal with a couple of drunken douches.

"Hey, it's really crowded down here," complained one of them.

Michelle shrugged. "I don't care," she said. "Right now, this isn't a democracy. I'm queen of this float, and I refuse."

"Bitch."

"That's Queen Bitch, and there's a child here. Watch your language. Besides, the people who are injured need to be up here more than you do." The men grumbled, but dropped back down and began pushing their way back through the crowd.

The cops were trying to restore order. Michelle called out to them, and they began bringing the wounded to her float. One of them stayed and started triage. Then Michelle heard sirens and a surge of relief went through her. Blowing things up and taking damage was the sort of thing she excelled at. But the aftermath was always more complicated and messy than she liked.

Now that things were starting to calm down, one of the krewe running the parade got on the loudspeaker for the float in front of hers and encouraged people to get out of the street and back up on the sidewalks. A couple of teenage boys helped the police reset the barricades.

Michelle pulled her phone out of her dress pocket as she moved away from the wounded. Michelle hated purses and because her clothes were specially made, she always had pockets added. Though why women's clothes never had pockets was a mystery to her. She scrolled through her favorites and then hit dial when she found Joey's number.

"What the hell is wrong with you," Michelle hissed as Joey answered. "Do you have any idea what a fu—freaking mess you made here today?"

There was a long pause on the other end of the line. "What are you talking about?"

A fine red curtain of rage descended on Michelle. "I'm talking about zombies attacking a parade," she whispered. "Killing people in the crowd—and they were coming for me and Adesina."

"You fucking think I'd do something like that, Bubbles?" Joey's voice was tremulous. It sounded worse than when they'd been in the People's Paradise of Africa and Joey had been running a hundred-and-four-degree fever. The hairs on Michelle's arms rose.

"Are you saying there's another wild carder who can raise the dead? Am I going to have to deal with two of you?" The red veil lifted, just long enough that another horrible thought slipped in. What if this had been just the first wave? *Honestly,* she thought. *Enough with the goddamn zombies already.*

The laugh that came over the line was hollow and mirthless. "For a smart bitch, you're awful fucking stupid. Obviously, we need to fucking talk. When can you get to my house?"

"I'm stuck here," Michelle replied. She looked around at the wounded on the float and the cops trying to get the crowd cleared out. There was zombie ick all over the sidewalks, and Michelle really wanted to smack Joey hard. "I'm kinda busy."

"Just get here quick as you can."

The connection went dead. Michelle stared at the blank screen.

"Are we going to Aunt Joey's now?" Adesina asked, tugging on Michelle's dress.

"Soon," Michelle replied, surveying the ruins of the parade. "Soon."

◆

If there was one thing Joey hated, it was nosey cocksuckers sniffing about her business. Not that Bubbles was usually a nosey cocksucker. Given what she said had happened at the parade, Joey could even understand her being fucking pissed. But now she had to explain what was going on with her children.

The problem was that she had no idea.

One minute she'd been making her way back from the bakery up the street—early because it was Mardi Gras, and there would be tons of tourist dickweeds otherwise—and the next thing she knew, it was as if a light had just shut off inside her head. Usually, she knew where every dead body lay for miles around, and she often had zombie bugs and birds moving about keeping an eye on things. And today had been no different, until the lights went out.

She'd been "blind" for a few hours, and then, just as abruptly, her power was back. Truth be told, she'd been out of her mind while her power was gone. And she'd been scared. Really scared. She couldn't remember the last time she'd been this frightened. *Yes, you can remember that time,* a whispered a voice in the back of her mind. But Joey shut that thought down hard and fast—or tried to. *What did your mother say about lying?* the voice persisted. *Well, she'd lied, too,* Joey reminded herself. Her mother had lied, and left Joey alone, and what had happened after that . . .

Then Bubbles had shown up on her caller ID, and Joey had been relieved. Bubbles was the most powerful person she knew. Bubbles would keep her safe.

But when Joey picked up the phone, Bubbles started giving her shit. But

Joey didn't know what had happened. And if she was being honest with herself, she was scared. What if she was losing her power?

Without her children, she wasn't safe. Without them, she was just Joey Hebert, not Hoodoo Mama. Without Hoodoo Mama, no one, not even Bubbles, could protect her.

And when she thought about not being Hoodoo Mama anymore would mean, she began to shake.

♥

There wasn't much that Adesina didn't like. She liked American ice cream, American TV, and American beds. Ever since Momma had brought her to America, Adesina had been making a list of all the things she liked.

She liked Hello Kitty, The Cartoon Network, and taking classes from a tutor (even though sometimes she missed being in school with other kids). She even liked the way the cities looked. They were so big and shiny, and everyone talked so fast and moved around like they were all in a big rush to get somewhere important. Even if it was just to go to the grocery store.

And she liked Momma's friends. Aunt Joey (even though when they'd lived together in the PPA Momma had kept yelling at Aunt Joey about her language), Aunt Juliette, Drake (even though he was a god now and they never saw him anymore), and Niobe. Sometimes they were invited to *American Hero* events, and she got to meet even more wild carders. But she liked Joker Town the best of all because no one there ever turned around and stared at her.

And she had liked being in the Joker Town Halloween parade with Momma, but she didn't like this parade now at all. Aunt Joey's zombies had attacked, and people were hurt. So they were going to Aunt Joey's and Adesina knew Momma was mad. She didn't need to go into Momma's mind to know that. It was pretty obvious.

Once, she and Momma had had a conversation about her ability to enter Momma's mind. Momma had made her promise she wouldn't do it anymore, but it was difficult to control. Once she'd gone into someone's mind, it became easier. She couldn't go into nats' minds—only people whose card had turned. She'd discovered that while they were still in the PPA.

And she wasn't going to tell Momma that she had already been in more people's minds than Momma knew. Sometimes it just happened when she was dreaming, but mostly it happened if she liked someone. The next thing she knew, she was sliding into their thoughts.

The police and ambulances came. The ambulance took the wounded away, and the police cleared out the crowd so the parade could head back to the storage facility. There was no more music, no more beads thrown, and no more bubbles.

Adesina didn't mean to, but she found herself in Momma's mind. Momma was worried. Worried about Aunt Joey and what she might have to do to her if Aunt Joey really had made her zombies attack. She was worried about Adesina and how much violence she was around. And she was worried about the people who'd been hurt at the parade.

Adesina wanted to tell her that zombies weren't as bad as being in the charnel pit. And that that wasn't as bad as what had happened to her after she'd been injected with the virus and her card had turned. Even though Adesina's mind wanted to skitter away from that memory, it rose up. She couldn't—wouldn't—forget what had happened.

The doctors had grabbed her and strapped her down to the table with brown leather straps that were stained almost black in places. Then they slid a needle full of the wild card virus into her arm. She'd looked away and stared up at the sweet, fairytale pictures they'd put on the stark white walls. But the girls in the pictures were all pale, not at all like Adesina.

The virus burned as it rocketed through her veins. She looked away from the smiling children in the pictures and stared at the ceiling. There were reddish-brown splatter marks there. Then blinding pain swallowed her and she was wracked with convulsions. Her body bowed up from the table. She tried not to, but she screamed and screamed and screamed. And then there was darkness and relief when she'd gone into chrysalis form.

The doctors didn't want jokers, they wanted only aces, and so they threw her body into the pit with the other dead and dying children. But she wasn't dying. She was changing. And while she was cradled in her cocoon, she found that she could slip into the minds of other people infected with the virus.

That was how she'd found Momma. Both of them were floating in a sea of darkness. But Adesina wasn't lonely anymore, not now that she had Momma.

But if she said anything about that time, Momma would know she'd been in her mind. So she grabbed Momma and made her sit on the throne and cuddled in her lap until the parade came to its final stop.

♣

Bullets flew across the smoking landscape, past the charred and burned wreckage of tanks and jeeps. A grenade exploded next to Dan, and he took a massive amount of damage. His health bar was blinking red, and he was out of bandages.

"Jesus, RocketPac, you were supposed to take that bitch with the grenade launcher out," Dan snarled into his mic. He'd logged on as soon as he'd gotten home from the parade. "You fucking faggot."

"Suck my dick, CF," Rocket replied. Feedback screamed into Dan's headset. "If you'd given me the suppressing fire, I could have gotten close enough to get a shot off. Go blow a goat, you asshole."

"Turn down your fucking outbound mic, bitch," Teninchrecord said to Rocket. "And your goddamn speakers, you big homo. CF, tell me again why the fuck we let this useless scrub onto the team."

Dan fell back. He's been using a bombed-out building for cover, but it was clear it wasn't doing any good. And he needed to find some bandages. If they made it out of this without losing, he was going to kick that useless POS RocketPac off the team. He couldn't figure out how this team he'd never heard of was pwning them. Especially since they had the utterly fag team name "We Know What Boys Like."

A shadow passed in front of the TV. Dan jumped and dropped his controller. "What the fuck!"

"Mr. Turnbull, we need to talk," Mr. Jones said as he picked up the controller and handed it to Dan. He wore a sleek dark gray suit, a white shirt, and a black tie. No one Dan knew ever wore anything like that. Dan was certain Jones wasn't his real name, but he could identify with not wanting everyone to know who you were. And Dan didn't want any more information than necessary about Mr. Jones.

He was afraid of Mr. Jones because Mr. Jones looked like he could snap Dan's neck without blinking an eye. Mr. Jones reminded Dan of a coiled rattlesnake.

Dan ripped off his headphones and yanked the headphone jack out of his computer. "That's a voice-activated mic," he snapped, but his hands were trembling. "I don't want those dipshits knowing who I am in real life. And I told my dad no one was supposed to come down here when the sign was up."

Mr. Jones shrugged. "Your father isn't home and I don't care about your little game," he said.

"I did what you asked," Dan said more defensively than he wanted. "I've got the video here on this USB drive." He stood up and dug around in his pocket until he came up with the lint-speckled drive.

Mr. Jones plucked it from Dan's fingers, then delicately blew off the lint. "I doubt we'll need it," Mr. Jones said, slipping the drive into the breast pocket of his suit. "There are already more than fifty YouTube videos up. More going up by the minute. And the local news interrupted programming to report on it. CNN and Fox are running breaking-news tickers, and we know they're working up their own spin on things. You did well."

Dan didn't know what to say. He was both flattered and scared. "Uh, thanks," he replied, and jammed his hands into his pockets. Out of the corner of his eye, he saw that his CntrlFreak avatar was down. *Shit.*

"We may need you to do another small task for us," Mr. Jones said. He held out a thick manila envelope. "The payment. And a little extra."

A tingle slid up Dan's spine as he took the envelope. He thought about touching Mr. Jones's fingers to see if he was an ace but, for the first time, it occurred to him that he might be out of his depth. "Sure, dude, whatever," he said. "But coming to my house, uh, maybe we could meet somewhere else?"

Mr. Jones's smile was shockingly white against his dark skin. "Looks like your team lost," he said, nodding at the monitor. "Combat Over" flashed on the screen. "I'll see myself out."

Dan took a long, shuddering breath when he heard the front door close. Then he opened the envelope and started counting.

♠

The cab pulled to a stop in front of Joey's house. Michelle paid the driver, and she and Adesina got out. The house was a dilapidated Victorian with peeling paint and an overgrown garden surrounded by a wrought-iron fence. Dead birds nested in the trees and perched on the utility lines. In unison, they all cocked their heads to the left.

"Knock it off, Joey," Michelle said as she opened the gate. It gave a screeching complaint. *Has she never heard of WD-40? Even I know about that.* "Save it for the tourists."

"Caw," said one of the birds.

"Jerk," Michelle muttered.

A relatively fresh female zombie answered the door. She wore a cheerful floral print dress and was less filthy than most of Joey's corpses. *The dead don't groom,* Michelle thought. *They are so nasty.*

"Follow me," the zombie said. But it was Joey's voice Michelle heard. All the zombies had Joey's voice, and that was okay when the zombie was a woman. But it was weird as hell coming from a six-foot-tall former line-backer as it sometimes happened.

"For crying out loud, Joey," Michelle said. "I know every inch of this house. You in the living room?"

The zombie nodded and Michelle pushed past it. Adesina flew up to Michelle's shoulder. "Momma, don't be too mad," she whispered.

"I'm just the right amount of mad," Michelle replied. Then she sighed, paused, and tried to get her mood under control. Adesina was right. Joey never responded well to an angry confrontation. Angry was Joey's stock-in-trade.

The living room was mostly bare. There were tatty curtains on the windows and a sagging couch against one wall. The new addition to the room was a large flatscreen TV. Across from the TV was Joey's Hoodoo Mama throne with Joey perched on it. She was slightly built and was wearing a shapeless Joker Plague T-shirt and skinny jeans. There was a shock of red in her dark brown hair and her skin was a beautiful caramel-color. A zombie dog lay at her feet, and two huge male zombies flanked her chair.

Michelle and Adesina flopped on the couch. Joey frowned, but Michelle ignored it. "So, you want to explain what happened?"

The zombies growled, and then Joey said, "I had fuck all to do with it." Her hands were gripping the arms of her throne, and her knuckles had turned white. "I can't believe you think I'd do something like that."

"Are you saying there's another person whose card has turned, who lives in New Orleans, and who can raise the dead just like you?" Michelle gave Joey her very best "Seriously, what the hell?" look. "That's a lot of coincidences, Joey."

"No, there's not a new fucking wild card who can control zombies," Joey said, leaning forward in her throne. "There's one who can fucking-well snatch powers."

"Jesus, Joey, language." Michelle glanced at Adesina, but she was already engrossed in a game on her iPad.

"Oh fuck you, Bubbles," Joey said. "Adesina has heard it all and more. Haven't you, Pumpkin?"

Adesina glanced up and shrugged. "Yep. You cuss. A lot. But I'm not going to."

For a moment, Joey looked hurt. "Michelle, are you planting weird fucking ideas in my girl there?"

"No, just normal ones."

"That's a goddamn fool's errand for a joker."

Michelle glared at Joey. "Back to your mystery wild card," she said. "What makes you think your powers were snatched? Maybe you just lost control."

The two big male zombies started across the room towards Michelle. Calmly, she dispatched them with a couple of tiny, explosive bubbles to the head. It took her last reserves of fat, but she wasn't putting up with any more of Joey's aggressive zombie shit.

"Motherfucker! Goddamnit, Bubbles, look at this dick-licking mess! Christ!" The female zombie came in and began cleaning up the remains. "I'm fucking fine," Joey continued. "What happened wasn't my cocksucking fault. I went out to get some pastries at the bakery. On my way home, I bumped into someone, then bang, my power just went away and I couldn't see any of my children anymore."

Her voice trailed off, and she looked so sad and scared that Michelle believed her. Michelle knew that Joey's card had turned because she'd been raped. But she didn't know any details and really didn't want to know them. She imagined that Joey must have felt as helpless now as she had then.

"Do you remember anything specific about how your powers were stolen?" Michelle asked. A wild card who could grab powers was frightening to contemplate. They needed to figure out who it was. But even more, she needed to protect Joey from having her powers stolen again. Joey had never been especially emotionally stable—Michelle reminded herself that a lot of the wild carders she knew were just shy of permanent residence in Crazytown—but seeing Joey's reaction now worried Michelle. Whatever having her power grabbed was triggering in Joey was bad. And Michelle was beginning to think it might be more important to help Joey deal than to get the person yanking her power.

Joey shook her head. "Fuck me, I've tried. I just remember being jostled, then . . . nothing."

Adesina tugged on Michelle's arm. "Momma, look," she said, pointing at the TV.

There was a long shot of the Bacchus parade as the zombies were attacking. The image zoomed in on Michelle as she began killing zombies. Joey turned up the volume on the TV.

". . . ack on today's Bacchus parade. Michelle Pond, the Amazing Bubbles, was on one float and was the apparent target of the zombie attack. More horrifying is that Miss Pond had her seven-year-old daughter with her. Though Miss Pond managed to stop the attack, it is troubling that she had her daughter at an event where she would be exposed to such adult sights as women showing their naked breasts for beads. This isn't the first time that a public event featuring Miss Pond has turned violent. It does make one wonder about her choices."

Michelle jumped up from the couch. "What the fuck!" she yelled.

"Language," Joey said.

♦

Adesina was worried. Momma was looking at videos of the parade on her laptop. Aunt Joey had switched off the TV after the news report, but Momma had pulled her laptop out of her bag and started looking for more reports online.

She'd found a lot of them. And even though Adesina tried not to, she couldn't help slipping into Momma's mind. And what she saw there was fear and anger and worry.

So she slipped out and started playing "Ocelot Nine" on her iPad again. Getting Organza Sweetie Ocelot out of the clutches of the Cherry Witch was easier than understanding the workings of the adult world.

♥

Michelle's cell was buzzing. It had been buzzing since the attack on the parade. But she'd been ignoring the calls—she already knew things were screwed. The old adage, "There's no such thing as bad publicity" was complete crap in her experience.

But she hadn't realized just how bad it was until she saw the news reports at Joey's house. And then she'd gone on YouTube and saw all the amateur videos.

It made her sick. *Of course, there was going to be video everywhere, you idiot. It was Mardi Gras. Hell, it's just the way things are now. Not a moment unobserved.*

And there was still the issue of how Joey had lost her powers. More to the point, Joey's reaction to losing her powers was preying on Michelle's mind. She couldn't leave Joey alone in that state. Michelle decided she and Adesina would stay with Joey tonight and try to figure out what had happened. Much as she hated even considering it, Michelle thought she might have to ask Adesina for help. But God, she didn't want to do that. She didn't want to send her baby into Joey's mind. There were things Adesina did *not* need to see at her age—or any other age as far as Michelle was concerned.

Since Michelle had decided that Joey shouldn't be alone for even an hour, the three of them cabbed it back to Michelle's hotel. Both Joey and Adesina were hungry, so Michelle left them in the hotel coffee shop while she went up to the room to pack a bag.

She slipped out of her dress and tossed it onto the bed. Then she pulled on a pair of baggy drawstring pants and a T-shirt. She needed to get fatter—throwing herself off Joey's roof hadn't done much—and her clothes needed to cooperate with a variety of sizes.

As she was packing an overnight bag, her cell began to ring again. She grabbed it off the bed and glanced at the number. It looked familiar, so she answered it saying, "Michelle here." She threw underwear, baggy pants, and T-shirts for herself into the bag, and then tossed in Adesina's favorite dress and nightgown.

There was a pause on the other end of the line. "Hey, Michelle. It's me." For a moment, Michelle's stomach lurched. It was Juliette. They hadn't spoken much since Juliette had left the PPA. And when they had, it was awkward. Sleeping with Joey had ruined Michelle's relationship with Juliette. And no matter how she tried, Michelle knew that there were some mistakes that couldn't be forgiven. "I saw some of the footage from the parade online," Juliette said.

Michelle's hands started shaking. *Crap, crap, crap.* She thought. *This is not the time to get emotional.*

"Yeah, it, uh, was intense."

"Was it really Joey?"

Michelle went into the bathroom and started grabbing toiletries. "She says, 'No' and I believe her," Michelle said. "This just isn't her style. She says someone stole her power, and right after the attack, her power came back."

There was another long pause. "So, you've been seeing her while you're there?"

Crap, Michelle thought again as she dumped the toiletries into a travel case. Then she released a stream of rubbery bubbles into the bathtub. A couple bounced out and rolled around the bathroom floor. Michelle kicked them, and they ricocheted off the wall. One hit her hard in the thigh.

"Yes, I went to see her," Michelle replied, reflexively rubbing her leg. *Stupid bubbles.* "Hello? Zombie attack. Who else am I going to see?" She went to the mirror and looked into it. *Stupid girl.* "We're not screwing if that's what you're asking. And we haven't since that one time. And you

broke up with me and I'm pretty sure that means I'm allowed to see anyone I like. And I'm really sorry."

Shit.

"You done?" Juliette asked.

"Yes," Michelle said meekly.

"I'm glad you went to see her. This thing is a PR disaster for both of
you."

This flummoxed Michelle. "I thought, well, I mean . . ."

"Look, Michelle, this isn't about you and Joey and me. This is about
Adesina. You suck as a girlfriend, but you've been a good mother to her.
And I really hate the idea that someone's playing a political game that'll
impact on Adesina's life."

Michelle slid down the bathroom wall and sat on the floor. The tiles
were cold against her butt.

"I'm not sure what you mean. Why would this affect Adesina?"

An exasperated sigh, not unlike the one Adesina often gave, escaped
Juliette. "How can you still be this naive? You're too damn powerful and
too damn popular. They can't do much about the powerful, but they will
happily destroy peoples' fondness for you. They need to marginalize you."

Michelle opened her left palm and let a light bubble form in it. She let
it go and it floated around the bathroom. "Well, who would do that? And
why use Joey?"

"Oh, it could be a lot of people: the NSA, CIA, and the PPA, for starters.
Also, the Committee might be involved, though that's less likely. It could
even be an entirely new group with their own agenda. And it's tough to
come at you directly, but going through people you love . . ."

"I don't love Joey," Michelle said emphatically. What she wanted to say
was, "I love you. Please come back." Instead she said, "I've been off the
radar for almost a year. It doesn't make any sense." Michelle rubbed her
middle finger between her eyebrows.

"But you're back and already you're doing parades that remind people
how you saved New Orleans. Not to mention that you adopted Adesina
who is just about the most adorable joker in the world."

Michelle smiled. "Yeah, she is filled with adorableness, isn't she? I
think she has a creamy chocolate center, too."

Juliette laughed, and Michelle thought her heart might break. "I'm
gonna email you a link to something," Juliette said. "This is what's at
stake and how far they're willing to go to marginalize you."

Will this bullshit never stop? Michelle thought. *I'm just trying to have a life.* "Thanks for the help, Juliette. And . . . I'm sorry. I know it's not enough, but I'm really sorry."

There was another long pause. "Yeah, I know," Juliette said. Then the line went dead. *Great,* Michelle thought, rubbing away tears. *Just great. You're never going to make the Joey thing up to her, so stop trying. You're lucky she even called.*

But Michelle knew Juliette hadn't called for her sake. She got up and ran cold water over a washcloth and held it against her face for a few minutes. The last thing she needed was Adesina seeing that she'd been crying. Her daughter saw too much anyway.

♣

Even though her power was back, Joey was still grateful that Michelle was spending the night. She had her children, of course. But now there was the nagging fear that at any moment, someone could grab her power.

Adesina was sitting on the coach playing that goofy game. *What the fuck are ocelots anyway?* Joey thought as she sat down next to her. "So, you really like this game?" Joey asked. She wasn't a fan of video games, but she'd played a few here and there.

Adesina nodded. "The ocelots are really cute, and Organza Sweetie Ocelot is amazing. She has these cool powers and she just goes right after the Cherry Witch who wants to take all the ocelots' food and land . . ."

Joey tuned Adesina out. It was something she did on occasion. She just stopped listening and let herself slide into her children. There were dead dogs and cats. Dead people. Dead insects. She moved into them all, seeing through their dead eyes. Her children were the reason she was safe. No one could escape the dead. They were all around. So no one could get the drop on her.

But losing her powers for a few hours had been horrible. She tried to push away the memory of losing control—but that made another, darker, memory come to the surface. Bile rose in her throat, and sweat broke out across her back. No, she wouldn't let it come back. She was Hoodoo Mama. She'd already killed that motherfucker. That was over and done—he couldn't touch her anymore.

"Aunt Joey! Aunt Joey!"

Joey opened her eyes. It took a moment for her to snap out of the memory. Adesina was sitting on her lap, and her front feet were on Joey's face.

Tears were streaming down Adesina's cheeks. "Aunt Joey, please stop!" she cried.

"What the fuck?" Joey said. "What are you doing, Pumpkin?"

"You were stuck," Adesina replied. She slid off Joey's lap and wiped at her tears and runny nose with her feet the way a praying mantis might groom itself.

Joey got up. "I'll get you a Kleenex," she said, running for the bathroom. She grabbed the box off the back of the commode and headed to the living room. She saw Michelle running into the room from the other side.

"What the heck is going on here?" Michelle asked. "I could hear Adesina crying from upstairs." *What the ever-fucking hell?* Joey thought. *Am I really losing it? Fuck me!*

Michelle went to console Adesina. Awkwardly, Joey held out the box of tissues. A withering glance was all Joey got from Michelle as she pulled tissues out and started dabbing Adesina's face.

"You want to tell me what happened?" Michelle asked Adesina. But Adesina wouldn't answer. She just curled up in Michelle's lap and closed her eyes.

When Michelle looked up, Joey wished she weren't on the receiving end of that look—and despite herself, Joey took a step back. *What happened?* Michelle mouthed silently. Joey shrugged and shook her head. And then Joey was pissed. Michelle *knew* she'd never do anything to hurt Adesina.

"Adesina," Michelle said softly. "Look at me."

For a moment, Adesina just lay there, but then she slowly opened her eyes. There was a stern expression on Michelle's face and it struck Joey as mean. "Adesina," Michelle continued. "Did you go into Aunt Joey's mind without permission?"

"What the fuck are you talking about, Bubbles?" Joey asked. There were too many things she didn't want anyone to know about, much less have the Pumpkin see.

"Adesina can go into the minds of people who have the virus," Michelle said. "And I know she's been in yours before. Adesina, I told you about doing that, didn't I?"

Adesina nodded, and a tear slipped down her cheek. "I'm sorry, Momma," she said in a quavering voice.

"There are grown-up things you shouldn't be seeing, and it's an invasion of the other person's privacy. Like when you don't want me going into your room without asking."

That made Adesina burst into tears. Michelle hugged her. "It's okay, you just have to be more careful, honey." She looked up at Joey. "I think I'm putting Adesina to bed. It's been a long day."

"Yeah," Joey said. "Yeah, it really has."

♠

After Michelle got Adesina settled for the evening, she went back downstairs to talk to Joey. She found her in the kitchen, pulling bottles of beer out of the fridge.

"You wanna tell me why the ever-lovin' fuck you never mentioned that Adesina can get into my cocksucking mind?" Joey demanded handing Michelle a beer.

Michelle twisted off the bottle cap, flipped the cap in the trash, and then took a long swig. "She's knows she's not supposed to. And the one time before when she ended up in your head, it upset her so much she swore to me it would never happen again." What Michelle wanted to tell Joey was that being in her mind had made Adesina violently ill. That the garbage Joey was dragging around was toxic to Adesina and most likely to Joey, too. But Michelle knew that telling Joey anything was a losing proposition.

Another hard pull of the beer made Michelle's head swim a little. Aside from jumping off Joey's roof before they went back to the hotel, she hadn't done anything to bulk up again even though she'd meant to. She was thinner now, even more so than when she'd been a model. It meant she got buzzed much more quickly. And that wasn't feeling like a bad thing at all at the moment.

"Did she tell you what she saw?" Joey asked.

Michelle shook her head. "I didn't really ask her much about it. She's only seven. But really, how much of what's in your head does she need to see?" It was a cruel thing to say, but Michelle didn't much care. No, that wasn't true. She was just worn out.

"I don't want the Pumpkin seeing . . . things." Joey chugged her beer, plunked the empty bottle on the counter, then went to one of the cabinets and pulled out a bottle of Jack Daniel's. "Best fucking way I can think of to forget. You want a shot?"

Michelle shook her head, then killed the rest of her beer. Golden warmth encased her. Her lips went a little numb. "That's not going to help us figure out what happened to you. And I actually thought about having Adesina go into your mind to try to find out what happened. But that's obviously a terrible idea." Michelle took another beer out of the fridge. *Screw it,* she thought. *So I get hammered. My life is rapidly going into the toilet.* "Oh, and I talked to Juliette when we were at the hotel. And then she sent me some links. The new meme out there is that I'm a terrible mother who routinely endangers the life of her child."

"What the fuck is a meme?" Joey asked after she took a swig of the JD.

◆

Dan jammed dirty laundry into the washer, then dumped laundry soap on top. Laundry pissed him off. If his mother hadn't left, the house would be clean, there would food in the fridge, dinner on the table, and he would have clean clothes when he needed them. Instead, he was going commando in some ratty jeans (and he hated that commando shit), and his T-shirt was so smelly it grossed him out.

But the day wouldn't be a complete loss. He and Teninchrecord had booted RocketPac from the team, and they were interviewing replacements in an hour. He knew that they needed someone good, but weeding out the noobs and scrubs was going to be hilarious. After starting the washer, he headed back down to the basement. He'd replaced his old sofa with a tricked-out gaming chair using some of the money he'd gotten for grabbing Hoodoo Mama's power. The chair had built-in speakers and an ergonomic design in black leather that perfectly cradled his ass. His dad was at work, and Dan was looking forward to settling in for a nice long gaming session.

Except when he got to the bottom of the stairs, he saw that Mr. Jones was ensconced in his chair. *Son of a bitch,* Don thought. "Most people might start by knocking on the front door."

Mr. Jones smiled, and Dan didn't like it at all. "Dan, you might remember I told you the other day we might have need of you again. It appears we need you sooner than we expected."

For a moment, Dan thought about trying to get more money this time. But Mr. Jones's persistent smile made him leery. "What are you looking for? More of the same? There's all kinds of Mardi Gras stuff happening."

Mr. Jones had Dan's controller in his hands. He hit the start button, and Dan wished he could just kill him. The password page came up, and Mr. Jones punched in Dan's password.

"What the fuck?" Dan said.

"Do you seriously think we don't know everything there is to know about you, Dan? Your password is nothing. The location of your mother?

That was simple, too. In fact, Dan, with the exception of your power, you're just not that complicated."

Mr. Jones was putting Dan's CntrlFreak avatar through his paces. And he was kicking major amounts of ass. It made Dan feel sick.

"Then why not just have me take Bubbles's power and then kill her?" Dan asked.

"Because we may have need of her in the future," Mr. Jones replied. "In your scenario, you could use her power once—and then, if she were dead, it would be gone and you couldn't take it again. A matchless resource would be lost."

Mr. Jones executed a perfect jump and roll with CntrlFreak, then single head-shotted two combatants. "Perfect!" flashed on the screen.

"Not everyone is as uncomplicated as you are, Dan," Mr. Jones continued. "Take the lovely Miss Pond, for instance. She's ridiculously powerful, and yet, she cares little for that. But her friends, well, they're what matter to her.

"I could have had you steal her power, but that wouldn't have mattered to her. And we're not in the business of destroying people. We're in the business of managing them."

Watching Mr. Jones play the game made Dan want to jump straight out of his skin. And he didn't really give a shit about why Mr. Jones was doing anything he was doing—or why he was asking Dan to do anything. Just so long as they paid him. But he itched for Mr. Jones to put down the controller, get out of Dan's new chair, and tell him what the hell he wanted this time. The rest was just jacking off as far as Dan was concerned.

"But tormenting her friend," Mr. Jones said, smiling beatifically, "well, that's another matter. That will teach her the lesson I mean for her to learn. That no one she loves is safe. That she can't protect them. There are a lot of people in the world now who are extremely powerful, Dan. Controlling them isn't always about their personal peril. It's about explaining to them the limits of their power. The world may be changed because of the virus, but people, well, they're still the same."

Mr. Jones made CntrlFreak do a diving jump over several dead bodies, then he rolled up into a perfect kneeling position, gun extended, and squeezed off a single-bullet killing shot.

"We'll need you tomorrow morning," Mr. Jones said as he put another bullet into the head of another player's avatar. "I'll send a van to get you at 6 A.M."

"Winner!" flashed on the screen. Mr. Jones got out of Dan's chair and tossed him the controller. "Have fun playing," he said.

♥

Michelle woke up feeling muzzy-headed. She'd only had two beers, but at her current weight, it had hit her like a Mack truck. Actually, it wasn't that bad. She'd been hit by a couple of Mack trucks. And even a bus once. It was frustrating that there wasn't a large vehicle handy at the moment. She'd have to make do with having Joey's zombies pound on her for a while to get fat.

She rolled over and saw Adesina curled up in the center of the extra pillow. Michelle smiled. She reached out and touched Adesina's new braids. They'd been experimenting with different hairstyles, trying to find one Adesina liked. But Michelle suspected Adesina just enjoyed having her hair done.

"Stop playing with my braids, Momma," Adesina said.

Michelle pulled her close, saying, "But they're so awesome! I'm jealous!"

Adesina giggled, opening her eyes. "We could braid your hair. It's long enough."

"Yes, but it would look like crap the next day, and yours looks amazing. Let's go downstairs and see if Aunt Joey has anything for breakfast in the fridge besides beer."

♣

But when they got downstairs, Joey was gone. There were no zombies in the parlor and none in the kitchen. And when Michelle went outside, there wasn't a single dead pigeon in sight.

Dammit, Michelle thought as she pushed open the gate, left the yard, and began looking up and down the street. *I told her not to go off alone. And now I've got to do something I really don't want to do. I am so going to kick her ass when we find her.*

"Adesina," Michelle said. "I know I told you not to go into Aunt Joey's mind, but we need to find her fast."

"It's okay, Momma," Adesina replied, flying into Michelle's arms. As Michelle cradled her, Adesina closed her eyes.

A minute later, her eyes snapped open. She squirmed out of Michelle's arms and floated down to the ground. Then she began running. Adesina could only fly short distances, but she ran fast. Michelle followed, wishing again that she'd piled on some fat.

Adesina ran down the street, turned right, then left. Then she ducked into an alleyway. The stink of puke and rotting garbage hit Michelle in a wave. A large dumpster squatted at the end of the alley. Adesina slowed as she reached it, and Michelle heard sobbing. She stopped running and hesitantly approached the far side of the dumpster.

Joey was sitting on ground with her back against the building's brick wall. Her arms were clasped around her legs, hugging them tight against her body.

"Joey," Michelle said softly as she crept forward. *Oh God,* she thought. *I should have been there for her.* "Joey, honey, it's me. It's Michelle."

Joey's shoulders shuddered, and then she looked up at Michelle. "Jesus, Bubbles," she said, her voice jerky from crying. "I shouldn't have come out here alone. They took my power again. I can't see any of my children."

Adesina flew to Joey's shoulder and gave her a quick kiss on the cheek, then hopped to the ground. "It's okay, Aunt Joey, we're here now," she said.

"I just wanted to get some pastries for breakfast," Joey said, wiping her nose on her sleeve. "Croissants, maybe a few turnovers. I know the Pumpkin likes turnovers. I just wanted to get something for breakfast. And then everything went dark."

Michelle reached out and took Joey's hands. They were shaking and cold. "C'mon," she said, pulling Joey to her feet. "Let's go home."

"But I didn't get the goddamn pastries," Joey said, stubbornly. "There's nothing for breakfast. The Pumpkin needs breakfast."

"We can get breakfast later, Joey," Michelle said as she slowly pulled Joey down the alley. "Adesina will be fine without breakfast for a little while longer, won't you, sweetie?"

Adesina flew back up and into Joey's arms. Joey reflexively caught her. "I'm not hungry at all, Aunt Joey."

"But you need something to eat," Joey said stubbornly. "I was going to get pastries." Joey toyed with Adesina's braids. "My mother used to braid my hair."

Holy hell, Michelle thought. *She's unspooling. We've got to find whoever is stealing her powers. And barring that, figure out a way for her to cope with losing them. And why steal Joey's power? Why not mine?* She'd rarely felt this helpless. She couldn't figure out a way to help Joey and she couldn't stop the person stealing Joey's power. It was infuriating. *When I find the person who's doing this to Joey, I will end them.* But she knew that was a lie. She'd give up ever finding them if she could only keep Joey safe.

"We could stop and get some turnovers on the way home," Joey said. She hugged Adesina tight. "You want something for breakfast, Pumpkin?" Adesina glanced at Michelle.

"We should get you home," Michelle said. "I'll go out after and get something."

Joey shifted Adesina into one arm, then grabbed Michelle's wrist. "No," she said. "You can't fucking leave me alone. Please. Not while my children are gone."

"It's okay," Michelle said, gently pulling Joey's hand away. "I won't go anywhere if you don't want me to. We'll figure it out." Michelle put her arm around Joey and led her home.

♠

"So, where do you want me to use the zombies?" Dan asked. He was sitting in the paneled van with Mr. Jones and some other dude who was driving. It felt like his head was about to come off. Hoodoo Mama's power was kicking around in his skull and rattling his bones. It sang in his blood. It wanted to *move*.

"Dan," Mr. Jones said in a bored voice. "Don't be impatient."

Dan scratched at his arms. The power felt different this time. Angrier. This was the first time he'd grabbed a big ace power more than once. He'd assumed it would be the same, but it wasn't. It felt like its own entity. As if he'd swallowed a bowl of bees.

"Mr. Jones," he said. "I'm not feeling so good."

Jones turned and looked at Dan. "Would you care to be more specific?" he asked in a flat voice.

"I . . . I . . . I'm not sure," Dan stuttered out. "Hoodoo Mama's power feels different this time. I'm having a hard time keeping it in. I've never grabbed a power like hers more than once." He didn't want Mr. Jones to know how strange the power felt this time.

Mr. Jones's cold, dark eyes appraised Dan. Normally, this would have scared Dan, but the power he felt was bad and getting worse by the second.

"How annoying," Mr. Jones said. "We didn't anticipate your power would be so . . . inconsistent." He turned back around, and then said to the driver, "It's early, but let's do the drop."

The van jerked forward. Dan's head hit the side window. "Ow," he said, but neither Mr. Jones nor the driver said anything.

A few minutes later, the van stopped. Dan looked around. Victorian houses lined the street. Most were shabby-looking and rundown.

"Bring me a zombie," Mr. Jones said as he pulled an envelope out of his breast pocket. Gratefully, Dan reached out and found a wealth of dead all around. "What do you want?" he asked. "Rats, dogs, cats?"

Mr. Jones glanced over his shoulder with an expression of contempt on his face. "Bring me a dead person, Dan."

Dan got the closest one he could find. It was a relief to be using the power. He could feel it starting to drain away from him. The buzzing died down to a dull hum. "Where do you want it?" Dan asked.

"Bring it here, have it take this note, and send it to that house two doors down across the street. Have it ring the bell and give the note to whomever answers the door."

"The one with the wrought-iron fence?" Dan asked to be sure. He didn't want to make Mr. Jones mad.

"Yes."

Dan did as he had been instructed.

◆

The doorbell rang. Joey jumped, and Michelle reached out and patted her on the arm. It didn't help. She felt Joey trembling.

There was a zombie standing on the porch when Michelle answered the door. It held out an envelope. Michelle took the envelope, and then the zombie fell over into a heap.

The envelope was addressed to Michelle. *Okay,* she thought warily. *This isn't weird at all.*

There was a single sheet of paper inside the envelope.

Miss Pond,

We haven't been introduced, but my employers are big fans of yours. They've admired your many good works for years now. That said, they think you've had quite a nice run, but it might be time for you to retire and take a long vacation from the public eye.

The incidents with Joey Hebert are just a small sample of what we can do to people you care about. Persist in having such a public profile, and we will take more drastic measures. Perhaps something having to do with your child.

I look forward to meeting you soon.

Sincerely Yours,
Mr. Jones

Michelle stared at the letter, trying to figure out who sent it. "Mr. Jones" was a transparent pseudonym.

Was Juliette right? Was this whole thing designed to marginalize her? And why target Joey? Joey helped the people who needed it who lived on the fringes of New Orleans society—why would anyone want to shut that down? Sure, some of them were grifters and other shady types, but some were homeless people who just needed looking after.

And me, Michelle thought. *What the hell? I'm not affiliated with any agency anymore. I don't try any of that vigilante bullshit. Why would anyone even care?*

"Michelle!" Joey said as she came running down the hall. "My children! I can fucking see them again!" She danced gleefully around Michelle then glanced outside. "Why is that body on the porch?" The body sat up as Joey possessed it.

Michelle held the letter out to Joey, who took it and read it quickly.

"Is this Mr. Jones the motherfucker who's been taking my power?" Joey was jumping from one leg to another as if she'd been hitting the Red Bull hard all day.

"I'm not sure," Michelle said. "He could just be an errand boy. There's no way of knowing. My guess is that they're going to do something again—I just don't know why they're going after you." She looked at Joey and didn't like what she saw.

Joey's eyes were wide, and she was jittery as hell. Losing her power wasn't just making her nervous—it was making her angry, too.

"Joey," Michelle said. "I know losing your power is horrible, but you told me when we were in the PPA that knowing where all the nearby dead bodies were all the time made you kinda crazy. Wasn't it a little bit of a relief when it went away?"

Hands shaking, Joey gave the letter back to Michelle. "No, yes, no," she said. "In the PPA there were so many bodies. And so many of them were dead children. You remember, Bubbles. And at first, when my powers vanished, I was just me. And that was nice. But then I started remembering how it was before I turned into Hoodoo Mama . . ." Her voice trailed off.

Michelle frowned as she closed the door. "I don't know what to do. It's clear they want me to stay the hell out of the public eye, and they're willing to fu . . . mess with you to get me to do it. Maybe I should reach out to someone from The Committee."

"No!" Joey exclaimed. "No! I don't want anyone to know this is happening. What if they take my powers away forever? Jesus, Bubbles, what the fuck would I do then?" Her face began to crumple as if she was about to cry, and then a furious expression replaced it. "And, Bubbles, I want the fucker who's been yanking my power. This Mr. Jones mother-fucking turd prick-ass bastard is going to pay."

"I'd like nothing more than to see him pay, too," Michelle said. She needed Joey to remember what had happened when her powers were taken. That was the most important thing right now. "This time was like the last time, right?"

Joey nodded, but she was still shaking.

"So," Michelle said. "They grab your power, use it, and then you get it back?"

"Yeah."

"Then my guess is they *can't* keep it. Otherwise, they'd just grab both our powers and be done with it. That's what I'd do. And you were out both times they took your powers, so maybe there needs to be line of sight, or proximity?"

Joey nodded and looked relieved. "I'm glad you're here, Bubbles," she said, with just a hint of a smile. "I mean, you know I still think you're a cocksucking bitch, right?"

"Well," Michelle replied. "You got that half right."

"Let's see what the Pumpkin wants for breakfast," Joey said as they went into the living room.

"Unless it's beer and bourbon," Michelle replied, "we've got to make a grocery run."

"You go make the run," Joey said. "I'll be okay here for that long. But I'm pretty sure I heard her saying she loooves bourbon for breakfast. Girl after my own heart."

♥

Momma and Aunt Joey were laughing. Adesina felt the knot in her stomach loosen a little—until they came into the room. Then it was clear to her that they were putting a nice face on things. She didn't need to slip into their minds to know that.

There was a smile on Momma's face, but it wasn't one of her real smiles. And Aunt Joey was smiling too, but Adesina could see the ghosts in her eyes.

"You up for some breakfast?" Momma asked as she sat on the couch next to Adesina.

"Your mom says you're not down with bourbon for breakfast," Aunt Joey put in. "I keep telling her you're my homegirl, but she doesn't believe me."

Adesina made her sincere face. "I'd love bourbon for breakfast, Momma."

"Okay," Momma replied. "But I'm going to pour it over your cereal. Yum."

"Gah," Adesina said. Once she'd been very bad and snuck a taste of Aunt Joey's bourbon. It was disgusting. "I want French toast."

"I'll go to the market," Michelle said as she leaned over and kissed the top of Adesina's head.

"Be careful, Bubbles. They could grab your power," Joey said. She bent down to tie the laces of her ratty Converse sneakers. Her hands shook as she did so. "It was bad when they took my power. It'd be much fucking worse if they got yours."

Momma shrugged. "I've been out in public, and they could've already gotten my powers. So I don't think they're interested in it, Joey." She leaned over and kissed Adesina. "Don't let Aunt Joey do anything stupid like go out of the house, sweetie."

"I won't, Momma," Adesina replied.

♣

Dan rubbed his face. He'd been about to explode when he'd had Hoodoo Momma's power. Even after using it, he was still jittery as hell. But maybe that was because he was stuck in a van with Mr. Jones and the creepily silent driver.

"Uhm, can you drop me back at my house?" he asked as he fidgeted in his seat.

"Yes, Dan, we will drop you off at your house," Mr. Jones said with barely concealed distaste. "I'm very disappointed in you, Dan. These things need to be timed properly and you didn't do your part."

A cold slippery feeling slid into Dan's gut. "Uh, I know," he replied. "It's like I told you. I've never grabbed a big ace power twice. And I didn't know it would be so weird the second time. I just don't know what happened. I'm sure it was nothing."

Mr. Jones didn't reply. Dan rubbed his palms on his pants. A silent Mr. Jones was worse than a talking one.

He decided that the next time Mr. Jones wanted him for anything, he'd just say no. It'd never occurred to him that there might be limitations on what he could do, or that yanking a big power more than once might have blowback. He needed to figure out what the real parameters of his ability were. And there was no way Mr. Jones was interested in helping him with that. Mr. Jones was interested in whatever weird-ass, mind-fuck shit he was up to. And nothing else.

The van slowed in front of Dan's house. Dan was reaching for the door handle before it came to a stop. But before he could open the door, Mr. Jones's hand was clasped hard around his wrist.

"Just a moment, Dan," he said. "I forgot to give you your pay." He held out a fat manila envelope.

For a fleeting moment, Dan thought about turning it down. But then he took it.

"I'll be in touch," Mr. Jones said.

Dan nodded. What he wanted to say was, "Fuck no, you crazy prick. I'd rather eat ground glass than deal with you again."

And it wasn't until he got to the front door that he realized Mr. Jones had no wild card abilities in him at all.

♠

I'm not afraid, Michelle thought. *Well, not much anyway.* The streets were still pretty empty despite the fact that it was Mardi Gras. She went into the local corner store and began grabbing what she needed to make French toast.

"Hey, you're the Amazing Bubbles, aren't you?"

Michelle looked up and saw a young girl. She was maybe sixteen with hair dyed black, black clothes, black Doc Martens, and a wealth of silver-studded and spiked jewelry. A pale face with heavy black eyeliner and crimson lips completed the look. Michelle wondered how she hadn't sweated through everything, including the heavy pancake make-up.

"Yeah," she replied. "I am." She dropped a loaf of bread into her basket and started to the dairy section. The girl followed.

"I thought what you did at the parade was awesome," the girl said. "I mean, you were really great."

Eggs, half-and-half, and butter went into Michelle's basket. "Thanks," she said as she walked to the produce section. "Just doing what I can."

What if this is the wild card who can grab powers? Michelle thought. *What kind of sick asshole would send a girl after me?* But then she realized that if this was the wild card who'd grabbed Joey's power, she would be just as helpless as Joey had been.

"Well," the girl said, "I just wanted you to know I really admire you. You've been my favorite wild card since *American Hero.*"

Michelle smiled at the girl. If they were going to grab her power, they would be doing it soon. "Would you like an autograph?" she asked.

"Oh, I couldn't ask for that," the girl said. "But would you mind a picture of us together?" She held up her phone.

"Sure," Michelle replied. Michelle put her arm around the girl and smiled as the picture was snapped. "And what's your name?"

"Dorothy," the girl said as she looked at the image. "Hey, this came out amazing."

Michelle laughed. "Well, I am a professional. Or I was."

"Hey thanks," Dorothy said. "Uhm, I just want you to know I don't think you're a lousy mother. I don't care what anyone is saying."

Michelle tried to keep her expression neutral, but she was irritated. And then she reminded herself that this was the way it was. You become famous, and you give up part of yourself. And Michelle knew she was lucky. Even with all the weird crap in her life, she could pay the bills, and give herself and Adesina a decent life. So she made herself smile brightly and say, "I really appreciate that, Dorothy. It was nice to meet you."

"Mr. Jones would like to see you and Joey Hebert in two days, nine in the morning, at Jackson Square," Dorothy said. "He thinks it's time for you to meet in person." She gave Michelle a bright smile, then vanished.

For a moment, Michelle just stared at the spot where Dorothy had been. *Yeah, I was not expecting that,* she thought. Then she went and grabbed a bottle of vanilla extract. It was going to be one of those lives.

◆

Joey was washing the breakfast dishes while Michelle dried. It was nice. Nice and normal, and that made Joey mad. She didn't know why. But she knew it wasn't the way she should be feeling.

After they'd finished eating, Michelle had asked for a couple of Joey's zombies to knock her around and fatten her up. It took a while, but eventually, Michelle stopped looking like a horrific thinspiration photo and was pleasantly plump. Joey thought Michelle looked especially pretty when she was plump. Joey liked her girls curvy.

Then they'd come back inside and started cleaning up the kitchen. Adesina was flopped on the couch playing her game, so Joey didn't bother to have her help. Sure, her mother might have said they were spoiling the child, but Joey didn't see it that way.

"I had another message from Mr. Jones," Michelle said softly while wiping a dish.

Joey looked over her shoulder to see if Adesina had heard. But she was still engrossed in her game. "What the fuck did he want?"

"He wants us to meet him in Jackson Square day after tomorrow morning at nine," Michelle replied. "Oh, and the messenger was a sixteen-year-old girl who can teleport."

"We're not going to go, right?" Joey asked. "That would be fucking insane." Joey wanted to hit something. Hard.

"I'm going," Michelle whispered. She kept drying dishes as if it were the most normal thing in the world to do while talking about some thug who wanted to steal your powers. "It's the only real choice we have. Unless you want to go underground, leave your home, and assume a new identity. Avoiding these people—whoever they are—just gives them power over you."

"But they've already got power over us, Michelle," Joey hissed. Soapy water splashed on the floor as she angrily dumped the frying pan into the sink. "In case you've forgotten, they've yanked my power twice. Maybe they'll yank yours next."

Michelle nodded, then opened the silverware drawer and began putting utensils away. "They might," she said. "But if that happened, it wouldn't be the end of my life. I'd go back to what I was before. It wouldn't change what I've done and it wouldn't change who I am." Michelle slid the drawer shut.

"Well, it's fucking easy for you to say, Bubbles," Joey replied. "You had a life before your card turned. I had jack shit. Except for my mother." The thought of her mother made a hideous lump form in the back of Joey's throat. She swallowed and tried not to cry. "I was just a kid when my card turned."

And even though Joey had banished almost every moment of that day, flashes of what had happened would still swim to the surface. And she knew if she hadn't turned into Hoodoo Mama, she would have died then.

"I know it's easy for me," Michelle replied gently. She dropped the towel on the counter and turned to face Joey. "And that's why I need to do something to help you. If you'll let me."

Joey threw her sponge into the sink. "And what the fuck do you think you can do?"

Michelle grabbed Joey's hands. "I can have Adesina go into your mind—into your memories—and she can . . . help you."

Joey grew very still. "What do you mean?" she asked.

"You know that Adesina can go into your mind? Well, when we were in the PPA, after all the fighting had stopped and we stayed to help the children we'd found there, Adesina went into some of their minds and she . . . she took their pain away. She made them forget what had happened to them." Michelle paused, and then she dropped Joey's hands. She picked up the dishtowel, folded it, and then hung it on the rack. "I stopped her from doing it because I didn't like how depressed she got afterward."

"Well, why would you fucking let her into my mind knowing that she's already been in there once before and it wasn't a fucking fun time?" Joey's hands were shaking and she jammed them into the pockets of her jeans. "I don't want her in my head. And I don't want to remember. I *won't* remember. Why should I?"

"I've been giving this a lot of thought," Michelle said. "And I talked to Adesina about it—to see if my plan would even work. She'll be in your mind, but not in the way she usually goes into someone's mind. I'm going in for her. Well, more like with her." Michelle rubbed her forehead and sighed. "I'm not describing this well. Adesina has linked two separate minds together before—by accident. So it'll be difficult. But she wants to help. And given our time frame, I don't see that there are any other solutions. So, yeah, I'm not going to be winning Mother of the Year any time soon."

"Fuck," Joey said, rocking back on her heels. She shook her head. "I don't think I can let Adesina do that. What if she sees . . . something a kid shouldn't see? What if *you* see?"

"Joey," Michelle said, exasperation hard in her voice. "We can't go on the run from these people. Christ, I can't even figure out who they work for. You freak when your power is lifted. I think have a way to fix that—or at least a way to make the memory this is triggering go away. You have to be okay with not having your power. Otherwise, they can get to you. And I can't be here all the time. You need to deal with this. Yeah, it's a suck solution, but it's the only one we have. Do you really think I'd do this to my daughter if I could think of any other option? And may I remind you that Adesina is in danger from these assholes, too?"

"Honestly, Bubbles," Joey replied as she rocked back and forth on the balls of her feet. "I've seen you do some pretty bad shit."

"Yeah?" Michelle replied as she turned away from Joey and began putting dishes in the cupboard. "Welcome to the working world."

♥

It took another two hours of arguing before Joey finally agreed to let Michelle and Adesina into her mind—and then only with the understanding that if Joey gave the word, the experiment ended.

"Where do you want to do this?" Joey asked. They were in the living room, and Joey had cleared out the usual zombie guard because Adesina mentioned that they were stinky.

"It's easiest when the other person is asleep," Adesina said. "That's how I found Momma. When she was in the coma."

"Well, I'm not tired," Joey said.

"We could go upstairs and use the guest bedroom," Michelle suggested. "You could lie down and just try to relax."

"Fuck," Joey muttered as she turned and stomped out of the room. Michelle and Adesina followed her. And Joey couldn't help noticing that Michelle didn't say anything about her bad language in front of the child.

♣

Adesina had a fluttery feeling in her tummy. She was pretty sure she could bring Momma into Aunt Joey's mind. But once they were there, could Momma really protect her? Adesina loved Aunt Joey, but there were things lurking in the dark corridors and rooms there that scared her.

Aunt Joey lay down on the bed, and Momma lay down beside her. Adesina hopped up and snuggled between them. Aunt Joey's body was rigid, her arms stiff and tight against her side. Momma rolled onto her side, reached out, and took Aunt Joey's left hand. Aunt Joey sighed, then relaxed a little. And then Adesina slid into Momma's mind.

It was a comfortable place for Adesina. Momma's mind was like a big, open house. There were pretty views out the windows and lots of bright, airy rooms. There were a couple of rooms Momma wouldn't let her go into, but Adesina didn't mind. Momma had explained that some of it was grown-up stuff, and some of it was private.

And there were bunnies in Momma's mind, too. Adesina liked the bunnies, but never could figure out why Momma had so many of them.

"Hey there, kiddo," Momma said. She was standing next to the windows looking out at the view holding a fat rabbit. "You ready to do this?" She turned toward Adesina, put the bunny down, and Adesina ran and jumped into her arms.

"I'm ready, Momma," Adesina said. And then she reached out for Aunt Joey.

♠

One moment Michelle was in her own mind, or at least Adesina's interpretation of her mind—and the next, she and Adesina were in the front entryway of a version of Joey's house. But it was bigger than Joey's actual house. There were corridors that spawned from the main hallway. Michelle saw that they were lined with closed doors.

"Joey?" Michelle yelled. She tried not to shout in Adesina's ear, even though she knew she wasn't really carrying the child in the crook of her arm. "Where are you, Joey?"

"Here," Joey replied from behind her. Startled, Michelle spun around. There, in the multi-colored light from the stained-glass windows in the front door, was Joey. She looked frailer and younger than she did in real life.

"You scared the crap out of me," Michelle said. She reached out and touched the intricately carved chair-rail that ran the length of the hall. "Your house looks different in here."

"Yeah, I don't know if that's me doing it or the Pumpkin," Joey replied as she slowly turned around and took in the front entrance and hallway. "I guess if I ever got around to sprucing the place up, it might look like this. And that front door is really fucking cool."

Michelle kissed Adesina on the head and then put her down. "End of the line for you, kiddo," she said. "I want you to stay here, okay? Aunt Joey and I need to go the rest of the way alone."

"Wait," Joey said. She brushed by Michelle and opened the first door on the left. "I did something for the Pumpkin."

Adesina and Michelle turned and peered through the doorway. Inside the room were overstuffed couches upholstered in a faded chrysanthemum print. The couches were positioned in front of a large flatscreen TV. A couple of burly zombies played checkers on a table under the bay window. Several otters sat on the couches eating popcorn and watching cartoons on the TV. Adesina gave a squeal of delight, then ran into the room and hopped up on the couch next to the smallest otter.

Michelle looked at Joey and then cocked her head. "Really? Do otters even eat popcorn?"

"My head, my rules," Joey replied with a grin that surprised Michelle. "Besides, Adesina really loves those otters."

"I know," Michelle said. "Weird, huh? I guess we should get going."

Joey's smile faded. "Yeah, I guess we should."

"You're going to have to lead," Michelle said. "I have no idea where to start."

"I do," Joey replied. Her voice was sad. "It's this way." Then, much to Michelle's surprise, Joey took her hand.

They went to the second to the last corridor leading off the main hallway and turned into it. There were sconces lining the walls here, but several of the bulbs had burned out. The walls were painted a dull gray, and the hall runners sported an undulating pattern in chartreuse, smoke, and brown. There were three doors along each wall in this hallway, and there was a door at the far end as well. Joey slowed, and Michelle had to tug her hand to get her to move forward again.

"I know you don't want to do this," Michelle said. "But it's the only choice."

Joey stopped in front of the first door on the right. "I know," she said as she reached out and threw open the door.

Sunlight spilled into the hallway. They stepped through the doorway. The light was so bright that, for a moment, Michelle was blinded. She blinked, and blurry images turned into people.

Michelle and Joey stood at the top of a hill. Below them, a tall, willowy woman in a blue sundress was laughing at something a bandy-legged man standing beside her had said. She took a long drink from the tallboy in her hand. Around them ran a short, skinny, young girl.

"Mommy," Joey whispered. Then she pointed at the little girl. "And that's me down there, too."

"How old were you?" Michelle asked. She couldn't take her eyes away from the scene. Everything about it was golden and warm.

"Eleven," Joey replied, her voice wavering. Michelle glanced at her.

"Why are you crying?" Michelle asked, perplexed. "You look so happy here."

"It's the last fucking happy memory I have."

Michelle looked back to the scene. Joey's hair was done up in braids, and she wore a pink T-shirt and overalls. She threw her head back and laughed and laughed, the perfect image of her mother.

"Screw this," Joey said. She yanked them out of the room, then slammed the door shut. The golden light was gone, and they were back in the gloomy hallway.

Joey dropped Michelle's hand, then ran to another door and yanked it open. Michelle sprinted to catch up with her. Inside, Joey's mother was sitting on a bed with Joey. Joey's mother wore a tatty floral housedress and her hair hadn't been combed. Joey was wearing a blue T-shirt with faded, but clean, jeans.

"I'm never gonna leave you, baby girl," Joey's mother said, her words slurring. She patted Joey's head and toyed with her braids. "I don't know where you get these crazy ideas."

There was a sick look on Joey's face. "You've been spending a lot of time in bed, Mommy," Joey said, touching her mother's cheek. "And you forget stuff. And you never want to eat anymore . . ." Joey's voice trailed off.

"Oh, baby girl, you know your mother has a bad memory," her mother said as she lay back against the pillows. Michelle saw now that Joey's mother's belly was distended and her skin was ashy. Even the whites of her eyes were yellow. Joey's mother was ill—very ill. "Always have had a poor memory," Joey's mother continued. "There's nothing to that. Your Uncle Earl John is here to help me remember things."

"Mommy," Joey said, inching closer to her mother. "I don't like Uncle Earl John. I don't understand why you're with him."

"Baby girl," her mother said as she pushed herself up again. It looked like it took an effort. "When you get older, you'll understand that it's hard to make a living. Your Uncle Earl John takes care of us. He buys us what we need."

"I don't fucking want what he buys," Joey said in a surly voice.

Her mother slapped her across the face.

"Don't you take that tone with me," Joey's mother said. Her tone was angry, but her eyes were scared. "And don't you use that nasty language."

Young Joey rubbed her cheek, and adult Joey mimicked her. Michelle wanted to say something to help, but she was at a loss. Her parents had been horrible, but at least they had never hit her.

Then Joey's mother began to cry.

"Oh God," she said, pulling young Joey into her arms. "I'm so sorry, baby girl. I love you and I just want you to be safe after . . . I just want you to be safe. Uncle Earl John will keep you safe. He promised."

"It was the only time she ever hit me," adult Joey said, her voice hitching with tears. "She never let *anyone* touch me. Not ever. None of those cocksuckers she married. None of the ones she just fucked. They could beat the hell out of her, but never once did she let them hit me." She pulled Michelle out into the hall again and slammed the door shut.

"Where to now?" Michelle asked. At the dead end of the hall was a door flanked by flickering sconces. She pointed at it. "What about that one?"

"No," Joey said, taking a step backward while wiping the tears from her cheeks.

"Maybe it's what we're looking for," Michelle said, grabbing Joey's hand and pulling her toward the door.

"Michelle, don't!" Joey cried.

But it was too late. Michelle was already opening the door. She stepped through the doorway, dragging Joey along, and found herself on a rise overlooking a cemetery. A small knot of mourners was gathered around one of the small crypts.

Michelle saw young Joey. She was wearing a dark blue dress and was sobbing. Next to her was the man from the first room. He was rubbing Joey's back, and the sight of that action made the hairs on Michelle's neck stand up.

Abruptly, Michelle found herself in the living room of a shotgun house. There were casserole dishes laid out on card tables, and a group of women were fussing over the dishes and Joey. Michelle could see into the kitchen where a group of men were talking and drinking. The women in the living room clucked over the men's boozing between attempts to get Joey to eat. But Joey just sat curled up on the ratty sofa and cried.

The scene shifted again. It was dark outside, and in the back of the house, Michelle heard someone banging around. Joey was still on the sofa, her legs pulled up under her chin. Her face was vacant. The guests had left, and someone had cleaned up the living room.

"Hey, baby girl," came a loud, slurred voice. Joey didn't respond, but Michelle turned. The short man with bandy legs leaned against the doorjamb. There were sweat stains on his shirt, and he'd pulled his tie loose. It was the man from the funeral. Joey's Uncle Earl John.

"Baby girl!" he said louder. Michelle could smell the liquor on his breath. "You hear me?"

For a moment, Joey didn't answer, but then she turned toward him. "Don't call me that," she said in a flat voice. "No one but my mother calls me that."

"Well, your drunk-ass, junkie momma is dead as a doornail," he said, pushing himself from the doorjamb. He staggered into the living room. "All the money I spent on that lush, down the drain. But you, well, you're going to fix it. Goin' to clean my house; goin' to fix my dinner, and goin' to get in my bed."

He grabbed her. Joey shrieked and tried to yank her arm away. But he held on tight and jerked her off the sofa.

Michelle instinctively tried to bubble—but nothing happened.

Of course not. This was Joey's memory, and Michelle was just a spectator. And then Michelle realized that her Joey—grown-up Joey—was gone.

"Let me go!" Joey screamed, but her voice and face switched back and forth from child to adult Joey. "Let me go!" She kicked, but it didn't do any good. Joey was just a skinny slip of a thing.

No. No. No. No. I don't want to see this, Michelle thought. *God, I don't want to.*

The memory began to fragment. Michelle found herself in a bedroom. A slice of light fell across the bed from the open bathroom door. The heavy smell of bourbon was everywhere.

♦

The ceiling had a stain on it, a brown water stain from a roof leak. Joey remembered exactly how it looked. The edges were darker than the center. And then he was grabbing her legs and forcing them open. Joey screamed, and he released one of her legs and fumbled with his pants. The stain looked like Illinois.

There was a heavy weight on Joey's chest. She couldn't move. The world spun, and she thought she was going to be sick. She rolled over and started gagging. Earl John pushed her off the bed.

"You puke in the bathroom," he said.

Joey crawled to the bathroom. The floor tiles were blue and until today, Joey had always loved the color of them. She lifted the seat on the toilet and dry heaved. Nothing came up because she hadn't eaten in two days.

Something ran down her leg. She wiped at it. Her hand came away sticky and smelled like the river.

♥

The memory jumped again. Earl John was holding Joey facedown on the bed. Joey pushed her face into the pillow and breathed in her mother's smell that still lingered there. It was Mommy's favorite rose perfume. Joey heard her own pathetic cries and Earl John's grunting, but it sounded as if it were coming from somewhere else. Somewhere far away.

Then he was done and he rolled off Joey and went into the kitchen. There was the sound of the refrigerator opening, and a glass being filled with ice cubes.

Joey wanted to die. She could die here with Mommy's smell in her nose. They'd be together, and she wouldn't have to feel the disgusting stickiness between her legs anymore.

"You just stay like you are, baby girl," Earl John said. "I'm going to break all your cherries tonight."

Joey didn't know what he meant. But she knew Mommy wouldn't want him to touch her. Mommy never let any of them touch her. Ever!

Earl John threw back his drink and set the glass on the dresser. He started toward Joey and there was another jump in time.

Someone was banging on the front door. Then there was the sound of wood smashing. Earl John jumped up, went to the side table, and pulled a gun out of the drawer.

"What the hell?" he said as he turned around. Then he gave a high-pitched shriek. Joey rolled over and saw Mommy in the doorway.

"You hurt my baby," Mommy said. But it was Joey's voice that came out of her mouth. "I told you to take care of her."

Earl John shot Mommy twice in the chest.

But Mommy just smiled.

"Can't hurt us no more, Earl John," she said. Joey mouthed the words, too. "Can't hurt us no more, you fucker."

And then, Mommy ripped Earl John's head off.

♣

Joey sat in the middle of the bed, her knees pulled up under her chin. She hurt all over. Mommy came and sat on the bed, too.

"I'm sorry, baby girl, I shouldn't have left you alone," she said. Her voice was still Joey's.

"It's okay, Mommy," Joey said. She crawled to Mommy and put her arms around her. Then she laid her head on Mommy's shoulder. "You're here now." Then Joey looked around the room. Earl John was scattered everywhere. The sheets were gross and streaked with blood. Then she looked at herself. There were bruises on her legs and arms and blood on her thighs. She started to shake. "What do I do?" she asked. "I gotta do something."

Mommy laughed. "Well, baby girl, you need to get dressed. But before you do that, you should wash up. Use my shower."

Joey slid off the bed, but her legs were weak and barely held her. Mommy grabbed her and helped her get to the bathroom. Mommy ran the water in the shower until it was warm—almost hot. She helped Joey into the shower, and then Joey lathered herself over and over until all she could smell was Mommy's soap.

Then Mommy helped her get dressed and braided her hair again. And together they went into Joey's room and packed a suitcase. Then Mommy went back into her own bedroom and rifled through all of Earl John's things until she came up with all the cash he had. Joey waited for Mommy to finish.

"Where are we going, Mommy?" Joey asked when Mommy returned.

"Wherever you want, baby girl," Mommy said in Joey's voice. "Wherever you want."

♠

After Joey's mother saved her, the memories fragmented.

But the one constant from that terrible night onward were the zombies. After reanimating her mother, Joey began to raise more and more of the dead. They were often in different stages of decomposition, but the smell didn't bother Joey at all. And the more zombies Joey raised, the stronger she felt. And Mommy was proud of her.

But, like all zombies, Mommy began to fall apart. It was then that Joey realized her mother was really gone.

Joey put her mother back into her crypt and left her there. Then she plunged into the underworld of New Orleans and turned herself into Hoodoo Mama. As Hoodoo Mama she ruled the grifters, the street hustlers, and the people who were lost and stuck on the fringes. Joey was a queen in this world, and her justice against men who hurt women was swift and terrible.

And Hoodoo Mama never let anyone hurt Joey again.

♦

And as she watched all of this, Michelle realized she'd been wrong. Even though Michelle wanted nothing more than to erase the horror of what had happened that night from Joey's mind, it wouldn't be right to do it. What had happened was part of Joey now. It had made her who and what she was. There were ways for Joey to deal with her pain, but having Adesina just cut that part out was wrong. To do so would banish Hoodoo Mama forever.

They'd have to deal with Mr. Jones and his power-stealing ace some other way.

As soon as she realized that, Michelle found herself back in the hall with Joey and Adesina. Joey was sitting on the floor.

"Sweetie, how did you get here?" Michelle asked Adesina. "I thought we said you were going to stay back in the otter room."

"I know, Momma," Adesina replied. She was sitting on her back legs with her front legs in Joey's hands. Tears were running down Joey's cheeks. "But Aunt Joey needed me, and you were stuck."

"Did you see anything?" Michelle asked nervously.

Adesina shook her head. "No, just some zombies. But they're every-where in here."

Michelle plopped down on the floor next to Joey. "You okay?" she asked.

Joey shook her head. "I don't know," she said. She looked at Michelle. Tears stained her cheeks, and her eyes were red and puffy. "My mother came back for me and she made him pay. She told me she'd keep me safe." Tears ran down her cheeks. "Fuck, I hate crying," she said. "And I never, ever, wanted to think about that again. Hoodoo Mama shut it away."

"Look," Michelle began as she reached out and wiped the tears from Joey's face. "What happened to you was unspeakable. And you were just a child. You did what you needed to in order to survive."

"Fucker asked for it," Joey said with a hiss.

"Oh, I think that barely begins to cover it," Michelle said. She sat down in front of Joey and took her hands. "But you were just a little girl then. Even if they steal your power, you're a grown woman now. They can't control you."

"But if I'm not Hoodoo Mama, who am I?" Joey asked with a plaintive cry. "You saw what happened to me. If I'm not Hoodoo Mama, how can I stop those fuckers?"

"You're Joey fucking Hebert," Michelle replied. "And Joey fucking He-bert *is* Hoodoo Mama whether she has a wild card power or not. That's who the hell you are. And day after tomorrow we're going to tell this Mr. Jones he's gonna stop fucking with *both* of us."

"Momma," Adesina said. "Language."

♥

It was muggy and hot the morning they were to meet Mr. Jones. Joey's eyes were gritty from lack of sleep, and she rubbed them. She'd heard Michelle get up in the middle of the night and go downstairs. Then she'd come back up to bed around four. Joey had assumed she couldn't sleep, either.

At 8 A.M., there was a knock on the front door. Joey went to the door flanked by two linebacker-sized zombies. She found a blond woman wear-ing a neat navy blue suit on the porch. Then she saw a black SUV with tinted windows parked in front of the house.

"Good morning. I'm Clarice Cummings, and I'm here to pick up Miss Pond's daughter," the blond woman said politely. "Will you tell her I'm here?"

Another one of Mr. Jones's scams, Joey immediately thought. Her zombies stepped toward the Cummings woman. "Yeah, I call bullshit, lady. You can tell Mr. Jones to fuck all the hell off. Or I could just send you back to him in pieces."

"Joey, it's okay," Michelle said as she ran to the front door. "I called in a favor. Thank you for the help, Ms. Cummings. Adesina will be right here."

Ms. Cummings smiled, and Joey decided she liked her just a little. "I'm happy to help. Adesina is one of my favorite pupils."

"Miss Cummings!" Adesina exclaimed, pushing herself between Joey and Michelle's legs. "Momma, you didn't tell me Miss Cummings was going to be here!"

Michelle grinned. "I wanted it to be a surprise. Besides, you've missed too much school this week. Now you're going to go with her, and I'll come to get you later this afternoon."

"I don't have my school bag," Adesina fretted.

"That won't be a problem," Miss Cummings said. "Everything today is on the computer."

Adesina jumped up and down excitedly. Miss Cummings laughed, then turned and started down the steps. Adesina followed her.

"Don't I get a kiss?" Michelle asked, her voice mock sad.

Adesina spun around, and then flew up into Michelle's arms. "Sorry Momma," she said planting a big kiss on Michelle's cheek.

Michelle kissed Adesina's forehead. "I'll see you soon," she said, and then she put Adesina down.

Adesina ran back to Miss Cummings and began chattering excitedly about lessons.

Joey shook her head. "I don't fucking get it," she said. "I hated school."

"Well, Adesina loves it," Michelle said. "And I needed someplace safe for her today. Before we came back to the States, I talked to Juliette about how to approach Adesina's education. I didn't want to send her to regular school, and it would have been dumb for me to home-school her. I even thought about moving to Joker Town and having her go to school there, but I was worried everything there would be about being a joker. And I wanted her to have as normal an education as possible."

Joey laughed. "You mean as normal as possible for a joker who can go into other wild cards' minds? With a mother who's one of the most powerful aces on earth?" She turned and went inside. "You coming?"

"I guess," Michelle replied. She followed Joey inside, and then shut the front door. "Anyway, Juliette found out about this program for kids with wild cards. They monitor their development, they get classes, and they give them a place where they're not the only wild card. And it's a mix of deuces, aces, and jokers. They also allow a really flexible schedule. Adesina started there when we got back from Africa."

Michelle and Joey went down the hall into the kitchen. Joey pulled out her coffee pot and Michelle got the coffee from the cupboard. She toyed with the edge of the bag.

"There's one more thing," Michelle began. "Miss Cummings knows that Juliette gets Adesina if anything happens to me."

"But nothing is going to happen to you," Joey said. "I mean, what can they do to you?"

Michelle shrugged. "Who knows?"

But they both knew. If Michelle's power could be stolen, she could be killed.

♣

Michelle hadn't been back to Jackson Square since she'd absorbed Little Fat Boy's nuclear blast. There was a shrine to her in one corner of the park. Flowers and handmade signs decorated a small official placard.

She knew Mr. Jones had chosen Jackson Square to screw with her. Absorbing that blast had done something terrible to Michelle. It had driven her half mad and had caused her to fall into a coma where she'd wandered alone for over a year. That is, until Adesina had found her and pulled her out of that dark, insane place.

The Square and surrounding area was oddly vacant and Michelle didn't like that at all. She and Joey were the only people there. Even Café Du Monde was bizarrely vacant. And there were usually at least a couple of homeless people camped out on the benches. But not this morning. No doubt part of Mr. Jones's preparations.

She scanned the area. Mr. Jones hadn't arrived yet, but she and Joey were a little early. Joey was keeping watch on the whole square using zombie birds and insects. They'd agreed that Joey wouldn't make a big display of zombie power. Not only because they wanted Mr. Jones to see they were cooperating, but in case Joey's power got taken again, there would be fewer dead things for the other wild card to use.

"How the hell did they clear everyone out of here?" Joey asked. She jammed her hands into her jeans pockets and rocked back on her heels.

Michelle shrugged. "I have no idea," she replied. "But they must have clout to clear it during Mardi Gras."

"You're early," Mr. Jones said.

Michelle jumped, and then turned. Dorothy and a young man in a hooded sweatshirt were standing next to him. A bubble formed in her hand. She made it heavy. When it released, it would be fast as hell. When it hit, there would be carnage. They might nab her power, but she was going to get one last bubble off. And make it count.

"Hello, Michelle," Dorothy called out brightly. Today she was wearing a pale blue dress with a striped apron, and her hair was done up in pigtails.

"You're running with a bad crowd," Michelle replied. The bubble quavered in her hand. "But cute outfit."

Dorothy grinned and smoothed her skirt. "Thanks! My mother always said I'd end up in trouble."

It was an odd group: The girl, the boy in the hoodie, and the man who was so obviously a kill-first-ask-questions-later type. Michelle knew Dorothy's power was teleportation, so she wasn't the power thief. That just left Mr. Jones and the kid with the unfortunate complexion.

"I'm just here for a little conversation," Mr. Jones said with a toothy smile. Despite the mugginess and rapidly rising heat, he looked cool. Michelle wondered how that was possible. Even his suit was crisp and impeccable.

"Dorothy you already know. This is Dan. He's the one who's been lifting Miss Hebert's power."

"Fucker!" Joey yelled.

"Oh, most likely not," Mr. Jones said. "If you were downwind of him, you'd know why."

"Hey!" Hoodie Dude said.

"Why are you telling us this?" Michelle asked. "I mean, can you not see this bubble? Can your boy yank both our powers before I get this bubble off?"

Mr. Jones smiled, and Michelle really wished she hadn't seen it. She'd battled crazy people before. She'd even fought people she was convinced were evil. But Mr. Jones was worse. His eyes were cold and dead. And the suit and all of his smiles couldn't disguise that he was devoid of humanity.

"I thought I was clear, Miss Pond," he said. "Killing me—or even all three of us—won't stop my organization. Consider me an errand boy. I make deliveries, send messages, take out the trash. In the great scheme of things, I am unimportant."

He smiled again. It didn't improve upon repetition.

"For instance," he said. "I could kill young Dan here." Then, in one swift motion, he reached into his jacket, pulled out a Glock, and held it to Hoodie Boy's head.

"Fuck!" Joey said.

"Shit!" Hoodie Boy said.

Michelle let her bubble fly—but Dorothy touched Mr. Jones and Hoodie Boy, and they teleported ten feet to the left. The bubble hit the wrought-iron fence surrounding the park and blew an enormous hole in it.

"Settle down, Miss Pond," Mr. Jones said. "I'm just trying to explain that even useful people reach an end to their usefulness. Dan's been handy, but his power, unlike yours, now appears to be unpredictable. But we adapt."

"Jesus, dude," Hoodie Boy said, his voice quavering. "I'll do whatever you want, just don't shoot me."

"Miss Hebert has a very nice power, but her psychological profile is . . . subpar," Mr. Jones continued with a slight smile, ignoring Dan. "She's too unstable to be of any real use to us other than to manipulate you."

Michelle wanted to blow a hole in him, but knew that Dorothy would just teleport them again.

That's when Michelle heard it. A faint rustling noise above her.

She looked up and there—spiraling down towards them—were hundreds of zombie birds. Dan, Mr. Jones, and Dorothy followed her gaze.

"How irritating," Mr. Jones said. "Dorothy . . ."

The girl grabbed the back of Dan's hoodie, and they ported. They reappeared next to Joey, and Dan grabbed her hand. Joey shrieked.

The zombie birds suddenly started flying erratically, crashing into one another.

Then Dan screamed, and his face turned red. Veins bulged out from his neck.

"Dan," Mr. Jones said calmly. "You're such a disappointment." He grimaced and leveled his Glock at Dan again. One moldy pigeon flew into Mr. Jones's face, and then Dan and Joey gasped at the same time.

The flock of zombie birds coalesced again and began to lower onto Mr. Jones and Dan.

"You played with my pain, fucker," Joey said. "That wasn't nice."

Dan scrambled to his knees and lunged at Michelle. He touched her bare arm, and there was a terrible wrenching inside her. The world tilted and went gray for a moment. Then the contact was broken, and Michelle staggered backward. She was empty inside as if someone had scooped out part of her. It was awful.

Dan made a whimpering noise and fell to his knees as bubbles filled his hands and rose into the zombie birds coming for him. But instead of exploding, the bubbles just kept floating upward as if made from soapy water.

Then Michelle's power flowed back into her like a tidal wave. It filled her up and made her whole. Relief surged into her. She was Bubbles again.

Dan was still on the ground. It was clear to Michelle that his power-snatching ability was spent. So that just left Dorothy and her teleportation, and Mr. Jones and his Glock.

"Little girl," Joey said, her voice cold. "Dorothy's your name? I suggest you bounce back to the fuckers who sent you, and you tell them that we're off limits. Or there will be more of *this*."

And then, in an eyeblink, the zombie flock descended on Mr. Jones and Dan.

Dan just lay there, twitching and crying, as the birds blanketed him. Michelle had a momentary twinge of guilt at seeing him buried under the birds, but then she remembered how she felt when he lifted her power and a cold anger filled her.

Mr. Jones pulled his Glock and began firing, but his bullets were useless against the zombie flock. Then he lowered his gun and aimed at Joey, but it was too late.

The birds engulfed him, and he shrieked as they ripped his flesh. He dropped his gun and began yanking the birds away from his face, tearing them to pieces as he did. But there were too many. And still they rained down on him.

"I'm Hoodoo Mama, fuckers," Joey said. Her tone was icy and imperious. "And this is *my* parish."

Dorothy squeaked, then vanished.

It grew dark, and Michelle looked up again. The sky was filled now with thousands of dead birds blotting out the sun. Crows, pigeons, waterfowl, sparrows, and more that she didn't recognize. She'd never seen Joey resurrect so many dead things at once before.

And when Michelle looked back at Joey, she was filled with awe. The scared and nervous girl Michelle had been trying to protect was gone. Joey's eyes had turned solid black, and her face was filled with rage. It seemed as if she were growing larger and larger. As if she had become a force of nature.

No. She had become a force *beyond* nature.

A force stronger than death.

She had become Hoodoo Mama.

And God help anyone who messed with her.

In the next instant, Mr. Jones vanished, enveloped by the zombie flock. He screamed and screamed and screamed. Blood pooled under the mass of birds.

"Oh Jesus!" he shrieked. "Help me! Jesus, help me!"

"Jesus can't save you, fucker," Joey said in a cold voice. "No one can."

Then the mass of birds collapsed as Mr. Jones crumpled to the ground. Even then, he kept kicking and screaming.

"Mommy," he cried. "Mommy!" His voice rose up into a high-pitched keen.

Then he fell silent. For almost a minute, one of his feet would pop out of the mass of birds as he kicked and flailed.

But after a while, Mr. Jones stopped doing even that.

And Dan was already still and silent.

Joey turned then and looked at Michelle with a beatific smile on her face.

"I think you were right, Bubbles," she said. "I think I *am* going to be okay."

With that, Joey threw her arms wide open and spun around. Ten thousand zombie birds swirled around her and rose back up to the sky.

Nuestra Señora de la Esperanza

by Carrie Vaughn

THE THING ANA CORTEZ remembered most about being shot was not realizing she'd been shot. It was more than adrenaline or the chaos of the situation. It was thinking, *this can't possibly be happening.* No way was this really happening. When you have ace powers, you're supposed to be able to save the world. But then you get shot.

She'd been part of the group that ditched *American Hero* to try to do some good intervening in Egypt's civil war. And maybe they had done some good—they'd done *something,* at any rate. Maybe they'd stopped a conflict that would have raged out of control; maybe they'd saved some lives. But they'd killed, too. *She'd* killed. She avoided news coverage and replays of the event, but she still saw it playing over in her mind: a crack in the earth opening under her touch, part of an army falling in, hundreds of soldiers buried alive . . . Self-defense, she told herself. Those soldiers had been about to attack her and the people she was helping to defend. It had been mostly instinct. She hadn't believed she was capable of such massive power, of so much destruction.

And then she got shot. She didn't think she'd been in serious danger of dying—help had been close by. Michael—Drummer Boy—carried her to a first aid tent, his six arms feeling like a cage around her while she was still trying to figure out exactly what had happened, her blood spilling over them both. Others had died; friends had died. She was lucky. That was what she kept telling herself.

A month had passed. She was home now, on the dried-out fringes of Las Vegas, New Mexico. She'd been told to go home, visit her family, rest. She didn't really want to be here. If she slowed down, if she rested—if she came home—she might never get out again. Her getting out of here the first time was almost a miracle.

But she was here. She couldn't sleep. Her heart ached.

The family home was a double-wide in a trailer park in an okay neighborhood. She'd grown up here and had never really noticed how tired the place looked—especially compared to the Hollywood madness. Still, it looked a ton better than some of the places in Egypt she'd seen. Everyone here got enough to eat, had running water, cars, and jobs. It was all a matter of perspective.

Kate, aka Curveball, her teammate from *American Hero* turned best friend, had wanted to come with her and look after her, but Ana had said no, that she needed the time alone to think. But really, if she were honest, she didn't want Kate to see where she came from.

Just her father and younger brother Roberto lived there now. Her mother had died when Roberto was born; Ana didn't remember her well.

Her third afternoon home, when she couldn't stand lying on the sofa and staring at the TV anymore, she walked to church. She had something she needed to do.

She used a cane. The muscles in her gut still hadn't fully mended from the gunshot wound, and she needed the help. She moved slowly, like an old woman, leaning on her cane and rocking with every step. A truck drove by with a couple of guys in the cab. One of them shouted out the open window, "Earth Witch! Hey! We love you, Earth Witch!"

She managed a smile, waving with her free hand. They drove on.

Yeah, and she was famous. Local girl makes good. She'd never get used to it.

♠

She arrived at Our Lady of Sorrows, the church where she and her brother had been baptized and confirmed, where her parents had been married, where her mother's funeral had been held, where every Sunday of her life until a few months ago she came for Mass. The old sandstone building with its two square towers loomed like an elegant grandmother, straight and tall. Ana hobbled into the vestibule and made her way to the carved-wood confessional.

Inside, she closed the curtain, set the cane against the wall, and slowly, very slowly, lowered herself to her knees. She needed a moment to catch her breath. Her injured body ached. Almost, though, the ache comforted. It was dull, like being worn out. Not sharp, like the initial injury had been.

The shadow on the other side of the screen moved. It was Father Gonzales, who had presided here for ten years, who had counseled Ana's father

Manuel, who had tutored and advised Roberto, and who every Sunday had asked Ana, "Is everything all right? Do you need help?" She'd always proudly said that her family was well and didn't need help. They were coping. Sure, Papá drank too much and things were harder without Mama to help. But they were fine.

She was glad he was here. He might understand. Might have words of comfort, because things weren't so well for her at the moment.

"Bless me, Father, for I have sinned." They continued with the ritual, speaking familiar words without really hearing them.

Then Father Gonzales asked, "What's wrong, child?"

Her eyes stung, and she bowed her head. She wouldn't be able to speak all this without crying, but she tried to keep her voice steady. "I've done something terrible."

"Don't be afraid. You're safe here; you know that."

He watched the news. He read the newspapers like anyone. He knew what she was going to say. This shouldn't be hard.

"I killed people," she said, and took a deep breath. And it wasn't so bad, now that she said it. The tears fell, and her voice was tight. "I don't even know how many, really. I don't . . . I can't even say if I meant to or not. It happened so fast." She saw it again in her mind's eye, how the earth split open, swallowed all those soldiers, and closed back over them again with a crack like distant thunder.

She swallowed, because she had more to say. "I did it to protect my friends, to protect so many people. But I know that doesn't justify it. Doesn't erase what I did. I want to ask for forgiveness."

Father Gonzalez was quiet for a long time. Each passing moment made Ana's heart clench a little more. This was what she'd been afraid of: God will not forgive you for this. God doesn't forgive mass murderers, even when those murderers have the very best of intentions, even when the people you killed were going to kill you with guns and tanks.

Finally, he said, "You're sorry for what you did?"

"Yes. I am." She nodded emphatically. "I'm so sorry."

"Then here is your penance. If you are truly sorry for what happened, and you seek true forgiveness from God, then you will never use your ace again. You must abandon your power."

She held her breath, forgetting to inhale. Whatever she had expected to hear, that wasn't it. Not use her ace? Might as well tell her heart to stop beating, it was that much a part of her.

"Can you do that, Ana?" Father Gonzales continued. "Scripture tells us that if our eye offends us, we must pluck it out. Your power has wrought harm. Therefore, you must renounce it. Do you understand?"

Without thinking, she shook her head. Her power was all she had in this world. She had nothing else, nothing to do, nothing to live for. But that was pride speaking. Vanity. Selfishness. Another sin.

"Father—I'm sorry, no. My power—it's a tool. I used it badly. That doesn't mean I should abandon it. Does it?"

"You said it was instinct. That you don't even know if you meant it. What if something like this happens again? Will you be able to stop it? Or will you be back here in a year, confessing more deaths?"

What if he was right? It made sense—if she was really sorry, it should be an easy thing to walk away. Still, she shook her head. "I can use it to save people. If I have a chance, I should save people, shouldn't I? God wants us to do good in the world—"

"Are you willing to risk it?"

Now she was crying quietly, tears falling as she tried to catch her breath. The wound in her gut throbbed, as if it too was saying, *Walk away*. She clutched the St. Barbara medallion hanging around her neck, which her mother had given her and she always wore. St. Barbara was the patron saint of miners, geologists, and ditchdiggers.

What would Kate and the others say to that? Kate, Michael, John Fortune, Bugsy, they were all in New York right now, forming the Committee on Extraordinary Interventions, a project they all believed in: using their ace powers for good. She was going to be a part of that—and here she was, full of doubt.

When she found her voice again, she said, knowing that she was probably lying, the worst time to lie, here in the confessional talking through Gonzales to God, "I can try. I'll try. I'm so sorry."

"I know you are. You're a good girl. I know you'll do the right thing."

On the way out, she stopped in the bathroom to wash her face, then set off on the long walk home. Only a couple of blocks away, a pickup stopped next to her. She ignored it until her brother Roberto leaned out the window. Eighteen, in his last year of high school, he'd already been accepted to UNM. She was supposed to help pay for it—with her ace power, with all the opportunities that opened up for her after her stint on *American Hero*. What now?

"Ana, hey, are you even supposed to be walking?"

She stopped her hobbling trek and hid a smile. "Not really."

"Thought so. Get in, I'll take you home."

She did, grateful in the end that she didn't have to walk back. "I guess you knew I'd be out here, at church."

"Kind of. Yeah."

A long pause, tires rumbling on asphalt. Then he said, "Did it help?"

She started crying again, quiet tears. She quickly wiped them away, but even if he hadn't seen the tears themselves, that movement betrayed them.

"You talked to Father Gonzales? What did he say?" Roberto said, glancing at her. She just shook her head.

Back home, their father Manuel was standing on the steps outside the trailer door.

"Papá's up," she said.

"Yeah. He's the one who sent me after you. It's like he just woke up. You know, to everything. It's kind of weird."

Old worries awoke in her: was he well, or was he drunk? Would he be mad at something she'd done? Would he want to eat and be angry that she hadn't fixed anything? She had to calm herself; he'd gotten by this long without her. She didn't have to take care of him anymore.

Still, as she approached the door, limping on her cane, she braced for whatever he might unleash at her.

Roberto slipped around him, smiling brief encouragement at her. Papá didn't look at him but stared square at Ana and didn't say a word.

"*Hija,* you shouldn't be walking around hurt like that," he said, in Spanish. He knew English well enough but spoke it rarely, especially when he drank.

She answered in Spanish. "I know. I did it anyway."

"Gone to church, right? How did it go?"

Surely he could tell by the look on her face. She felt heavy. She felt like God had turned his face from her, ashamed.

"Ana, sit here with me a moment." He lowered himself to the top step and patted the space next to him.

She did, easing down with her cane, leaving her leg straight to keep the injured side of her body from cramping.

"What happened?" Manuel asked.

"Father told me not to use my power anymore. He said it's wrong, the power is evil, and if I was really sorry—"

Manuel's look darkened, his jaw tightening, like a rage was taking him. But nothing like the drunken angers where he screamed until he sobbed. Consciousness lit his eyes. This anger had a target.

"He had no right to tell you that. *No* right, do you understand?"

"But what if he's right? What if he's right about me, and I can't do anything but hurt people?" She was crying again.

"Ana, I have to tell you a story I should have told you long, long ago. I've been a bad father, Ana. Terrible." *Un mal padre,* terrible words.

"Papá, no—" she said reflexively, because she should, because it was the right thing to say.

He took her hand in both of his. "No, it's true. Let me speak. You should have had a family around you, aunts and cousins to teach you. Grandmothers. You've had no women in your life to teach you, and so you go out to earn a living like a man, and it isn't right. I made you do that—I made you go out when I should have kept you home, kept you safe. I was too greedy. I made you do all the work. And now what kind of wife will you make? You should be married now. You should have babies. I should have been glad to take you to the church myself, to marry you off. Your mother would be so ashamed of me."

"Papá—" Once again, she wanted to argue reflexively. Part of Manuel had died with her mother. That didn't mean she'd be ashamed.

Ana was born with the wild card virus in her—born an ace. She'd had her power her whole life. She was eight when her father started hiring her out to the neighbors for ditchdigging and gardening projects. She'd always earned her way with her power. She'd been proud of that. It wouldn't do any good to tell him she didn't particularly want to be married off and matronly, at least not at this point in her life. That was what he focused on; she wasn't going to be able to steer him off it.

"But she would be very proud of you, Ana. Very proud. I have to tell you—you might not come back home again, so I have to tell you now."

"Papá, I'll come back, I'll always come back." And they both knew the bullet hole in her gut gave the lie to that.

"I have to tell you about your grandmother. Your mother's mother, in Mexico. She was one of the cursed ones. A joker. You know that, yes?"

Ana had known that her grandmother passed the wild card virus to her mother, who passed it in turn to her. Her mother had been latent until she turned the Black Queen when giving birth to Roberto. But she hadn't known any more than that.

"They say she is like a vine, that her skin is green, and instead of limbs, branches grow from her. But Ana, what I haven't told you is that she is also holy. A great *curandera. La Curandera de las Flores.* Because flowers bloom from her, and she plucks these flowers from her own body, dries them, and makes medicines from them. She cures thousands of people. When your mother was born—she was like a seed, growing larger and larger, and when they opened it up, there she was, a little baby. Everyone said that she was cursed, too. Though your grandmother helped so many, people shunned her. Called her *bruja*. She sent her daughter away, to live with cousins in America where she wouldn't be called the daughter of the witch.

"Ana, the power you have, it comes from your mother and her mother. The priest is wrong. Your power comes from God, and from the mother of God. I know they call you *brujita*, and we all laugh. Everyone laughs because they're really frightened. But your power is holy—I believe that with every drop of my blood. I always knew that God would call you away from me because of it. God has called you, Ana."

Ana had never heard Manuel Cortez speak so many words together. His face flushed from the passion of it, and his look was filled with all the tales he'd never told of their family, his beliefs, and his fears. The shadow of her mother watched over them, and the even dimmer shadow of a grandmother. Ana imagined a picture of her: a woman who rose from the earth like a tree, her face turned toward the sun.

I come from a family of witches, she thought. *I'm not surprised. Perhaps it isn't so bad*, though she didn't feel particularly like God had called her. More like she had walked into the desert without a path to follow.

Her father wasn't finished: "But the thing you must know about your Grandmother Inez, the most important thing—she's still alive, Ana. If you don't believe me that God has called you, go to her and ask her. Make a pilgrimage. Talk to your grandmother."

◆

Ana should have laughed, but this was the most real thing she'd heard since she'd come home. Of course she should go talk to her grandmother. Roberto loaned her the truck and gave her a list of instructions that made her rethink the whole trip.

"Keep the extra gas cans full, because you never know—you know how it gets out here, a hundred miles between gas stations. And there's an extra container of radiator fluid. You'll definitely need that. I'm not sure what's wrong with it, but you see smoke coming out of the hood, it's probably the radiator. Just stop and top it off and you'll be fine. There's a clanking comes out of the engine sometimes, but don't worry about that—"

"Roberto, I don't know anything about keeping a car running like that! How do you expect me to remember all this?"

Her little brother—three inches taller than her—took a patient breath and explained it all again, opening the hood to show her the parts and pieces, the difference between the radiator and the washer fluid reservoir, and everything else.

Again she expressed despair, and he looked at her in exasperation. "Ana, you battled the Righteous Djinn in Egypt, I think you can drive a beater truck to Mexico and get back in one piece."

Well. When he put it like that.

She brought along a case of bottled water and a cooler filled with ice and sandwiches, made sure she had her passport and birth certificate in hand, gave Roberto a hug, looked for her father to do the same, but he wasn't home. He'd probably vanished on purpose to avoid an emotional scene.

"Call if you need anything," Roberto said, helping her climb into the driver's seat. The soreness seemed to be fading. Having a distraction probably helped with that. She brought her cane along, propping it on the passenger seat. "And have a good time!"

She wasn't sure that was the point, but she gave him a salute anyway. "Love you, Roberto. Take care of Papá."

And before dawn, she was off.

♥

Until she got onto *American Hero,* she'd been alone, the only wild carder in an inconsequential New Mexico town. But now, she had friends.

She called Kate on the road. Curveball, the blond and beautiful softball player turned human rocket launcher who would have won the whole show if she hadn't ditched it to go to Egypt. Ana liked her a lot.

"Ana! When are you coming back?"

Kate was apartment hunting. They were supposed to share a place in New York. Assuming Ana went back. She didn't want to say that part.

"I don't know. Something's come up. I'm driving to Mexico."

"What?"

"I know, kind of crazy."

"Is this a family thing?"

"Grandmother. I didn't even know she was alive until my dad got all emotional and told me to go find her."

"Can't say no to that, I guess."

"Not really. And . . . well, I need to talk to someone, and she's supposed to be a good person to talk to."

She could hear the hurt in Kate's voice. "You can't talk to me?"

"I've already told you everything. This is . . ." A Catholic thing, a church thing, a family thing . . . "I'm still kind of messed up about what happened, you know?"

"Yeah," she said. Kate had killed too, her thrown missiles blowing up tanks and helicopters and the people inside them. But not at the scale Ana had.

"How're things going there?" Ana said, feigning brightness. She wanted to hear about Kate, not talk about herself.

"Good, good. I think I found us a place. It's tiny but near a subway stop. People here tell me that's important."

"I'll have to take their word for it."

"John's taking me out to dinner."

Kate and John Fortune were a thing, now. They'd been a thing before, but Egypt had cemented it. "That's good. Isn't that good?"

She hesitated a beat. "It's great. It's just weird, being in New York instead of L.A., and being part of the U.N. instead of in Hollywood. And John not being totally himself. He's still John, and I still like him a lot, and . . . Well."

John, who was now playing host to a powerful parasitic joker, Sekhmet, who gave him superpowers. The ace he always wanted. And Kate stuck by him, because that was Kate.

"Have fun, okay?"

"When do you think you'll be back, Ana?"

She had to say, "I don't know. I gotta go—there's traffic ahead."

"Okay. Call me later. Be safe."

Ana put her phone away. There was no traffic, not in rural freaking New Mexico. She clutched the St. Barbara medallion and tried not to think too hard.

♣

The border crossing in Ciudad Juárez went smoothly. No reason it shouldn't have; she had all the right paperwork. But there was always that worry in the back of your mind that they'd decide to search, that they'd make up some excuse to stop you, that they'd hold you for hours, or worse. Crossing back into the U.S. might be a different story—but it wasn't like she'd be smuggling anyone in the open back of the truck. There wasn't even a tarp back there. She kept telling herself everything would be fine.

The officer asked the reason for her visit, and she answered, "To see my grandmother. She lives in the country southwest of Juárez." Her father hadn't known exactly where. He'd given her vague directions. She was hoping to find a name in a phone book somewhere.

Then the unexpected happened. The border officer looked at her passport, looked at her through the open window, back at the passport, and again like five times before furrowing his brow and saying, "I'm sorry . . . but are you Earth Witch?"

That was when she remembered: she was famous now. For a split second, she thought about denying it, saying she was just an anonymous traveler. But her name was right there on the passport, and for all she knew, this guy was a fan. "Yes," she said, her smile thin.

The guy broke into a huge smile. He called over the other officers. There was some chaos. Cell phones came out and pictures were snapped.

"Can you do something right here? Dig a hole or make an earthquake or something?" one of the officers asked. It was a ridiculous question, on the road inside the glass-and-concrete bunker of the border crossing. He'd gestured vaguely off to a patch of dirt on the other side of a chain link fence.

But mostly Ana heard Father Gonzales: *renounce your power.* Pluck out your eye.

"I'm sorry," Ana said. "I really probably should get going."

A line of cars had queued up behind Ana's truck, so they settled for autographs, and Ana obliged them. Maybe getting back into the U.S. wouldn't be a problem at all.

Mostly, she smiled and said thank you a lot as her new friends told her how much they loved *American Hero* and thought she definitely should have won. Kate, with her athletic build and bright smile, was so much better at this sort of thing than she was. Ana was glad for the barrier of the car door.

And then she was in Mexico.

♠

She had never been to Mexico, which seemed ridiculous now that she thought of it. It had always been there, just a day's drive away. Her mother came from Mexico. Her father didn't, or didn't recently. His family had started out Mexican, but the borders moved around them. There'd never been a reason to go to Mexico until now.

Juárez didn't exactly inspire her to want to spend *more* time in Mexico. It was a city, urban, crowded with buildings for miles in all directions. It had a claustrophobic, washed-out feel to it that made her homesick. Never mind its reputation as murder capital of the world. She wasn't going to stop, right? Just drive straight through, following her father's not-exactly-detailed directions. *Take the main road west out of town and then keep going, maybe thirty miles. You might have to stop and ask someone.*

Yeah, this was all seeming like less of a great idea than it had when she started out.

Much of the town seemed normal—houses, shops, streets with cars parked, people walking. She could tell when she passed through a less-normal part of town—probably even a dangerous one. People vanished; the streets were empty, except for one or two cars that were dusty, abandoned. Graffiti covered the walls, slogans and gang signs in black spray paint, crossed out by more spray paint and replaced by different slogans. Ana kept her eyes open and didn't see much of anything, suspicious or otherwise.

She was almost out of town when the clanking coming from the truck's engine got louder. Roberto didn't tell her what to do if that happened. The whole cab started shaking.

"Come on, come on, keep going," she muttered, as if she could coax the vehicle into turning healthy.

Then smoke started pouring out from under the hood. The temperature gauge on the dash spiked into the red. Perfect. She pulled over to the curb before something blew up. Groaning, she rested her head on the steering wheel. Broken down on the outskirts of Juarez, in one of the obviously not-great neighborhoods. That was exactly what she should have expected on this trip.

Fine. Like Roberto said, she'd battled the Righteous Djinn; she could handle this.

First thing she did was pop the hood and step back from a billow of white pouring out. She had enough common sense to figure she ought to let the engine cool some before she started pouring things into it. She really hoped adding radiator fluid did the trick, because Roberto didn't give her fixes for anything else.

Sighing, she sat on the front bumper and looked out at the road. It seemed to run to the end of the world. No gas stations, of course; no mechanics visible in the immediate vicinity. The truck had broken down at the edge of a neighborhood—short stucco houses, TV dishes attached to some, old-fashioned antennae to others. A dog barking somewhere. The place didn't look abandoned, but its emptiness seemed strange.

She really wanted to get moving.

Sure enough, the radiator reservoir was low, just like Roberto told her it would be. Her little brother, looking out for her, which made her smile.

At the sound of the gunshot, she dropped to the ground, hunching by the protection of the driver's-side wheel well. The movement had been reflexive, a hard-won instinct honed those weeks ago in Egypt. Her heart was racing, and the wound in her gut throbbed, remembering.

She had no way to tell where the shot had come from or if others would follow. Best thing she could do was get the hell out, so she got to work. Funnel in the opening of the reservoir, bottle of radiator fluid open, she poured. Hoped the little that splashed out wouldn't cause problems.

Another shot rang out and was answered by automatic gunfire. A full-on gun battle was happening, way too close.

She'd just about gotten the cap screwed back on the radiator when a sedan squealed around a corner a few blocks away and came barreling toward her. Someone leaned out of the back window, firing a handgun at some unseen pursuer. In a few more seconds, Ana and her truck were going to be in the crossfire.

She expected to see another car chasing the first, some gang or drug cartel dispute gone mobile. And it did, this one a small pickup truck with yet another guy leaning out the window with a gun.

A third car roared into the intersection, just in time to cut off the first. All three cars squealed to crooked stops not thirty yards away from her. Shouting followed, and things were about to get really ugly. She didn't know why these guys were in a three-way shootout. She didn't much care; she just wanted to get out of here without getting creamed by a stray bullet. But of course, they were blocking the road. She could backtrack, find another way. Hope she didn't draw their attention. Hope they didn't feel a need to get rid of witnesses.

Or she could use her power. Her hands burned from wanting to use her power.

"Screw this," she muttered, and put her hand on the ground.

If you're really sorry, you won't use your powers. You'll stop getting in trouble. You'll stop *causing* trouble. She could never promise to not use her power, because she couldn't put it on a shelf or lock it up. It was always with her, a part of her. And she couldn't just huddle under her truck, hoping it would all go away.

In Egypt, she opened the ground beneath her attackers, buried them. Here, she did the opposite: raised pillars of earth, platforms of clay. She pictured it, sent the power through her hands and into the ground, which rumbled with the strength of an earthquake. Ten feet, twenty feet, she pulled in the soil from underneath, from all around, from the crust of the earth. Asphalt ripped, the street broke, and the three cars shot upward, each on its own platform. There was lots of shouting, and the guns stopped firing.

The towers of earth, twenty feet tall, eased away from each other, separating the cars. Men opened doors, trying to climb out, three out of the first car, two from the others. Near as Ana could tell, they all had guns, they just didn't know who to shoot at anymore. She tried something—a little more complex, but it should work if she could manage it. Gathering more dirt from beneath the street, she raised the sides of the pillars, building up walls around the cars. Just thick enough to keep them from thinking of shooting.

Before the wall went up, one of the guys tried to climb down from the third car, scrambling over the edge and sliding off his dirt platform as it lifted him higher. Shouting, he slid down the side of the pillar, clawing uselessly as the slope went vertical and space opened up—he was going to fall a dozen feet and end up broken. Setting her jaw, clenching her hand in dry earth, she altered the path of the dirt under him. The vertical pillar expanded, sloped back out, and caught him in a bowl-shaped hillock. Instead of falling, he rolled up one side of the bowl, back up the other, then came to a stop, panting for breath. He'd lost his gun somewhere on his fall. Good.

When she stopped, she imagined she could still feel the ground shaking under her. Her muscles ached as if she'd been running.

Finally, she stood and regarded her work. It was like giant termites had appeared in the middle of town and built uneven, clay-colored mounds in the street. Bits of dirt and gravel still rained down from the sides. The surrounding street had sunk in, about twenty feet in all directions, from the dirt she'd pulled up.

She sighed. Once again, she'd done a lot of damage. Still, she never would have been able to do anything like this before *American Hero*, before Egypt. She never would have gotten this angry. It was a good anger. Focusing. And she just stopped three cars full of guys from shooting each other. What did that do to her tally of damage from Egypt? What would Father Gonzales say?

She hadn't even been able to keep from using her power for a whole day.

"Hey! Hey, chica! Who the hell are you?" The guy, shouting Spanish, was leaning over the edge of his bowl and looking down at her. He was in his early twenties, about her age, dressed in jeans and a faded Dallas Cowboys T-shirt.

"Someone who's trying to fix her car without getting shot!" she called back.

"What are you, some kind of fucking ace?"

That was fairly obvious. Was it weird that it was kind of encouraging that he didn't recognize her from TV? "What's it look like to you?" She realized suddenly: her Spanish had an American accent. She'd never noticed that before.

She finished with the radiator fluid and closed the hood.

"Hey—you gonna get me down from here? You gonna get my friends down?"

"Your friends? They were shooting at you. Or you were shooting at them. Or something."

"None of your business. Get me down from here."

Glaring, she ignored him. She'd pretty much made a wreck of the street and wondered how much of a detour she'd have to take to get out of town. She probably at least ought to make an effort to put things back the way they were.

"You going to behave? Tell your friends to behave?"

"Yes, Christ, yes! You could fucking bury us all if you wanted!"

Yes, she could.

She'd churned the ground enough; she'd never be able to get it back to perfect, but she'd get close. First, she lowered the platforms, returning tons of dirt to the sinkhole she'd created, raising the surface back to level. She pictured it all as one giant blob, a chunk of clay she could stretch and mold however she needed to. Working slowly, steadily, she returned the earth to some kind of street-like configuration. The asphalt maybe had a lot more cracks than it had before. She left the walls up around the three cars, just so she wouldn't have to deal with the gangbangers and guns. The guy on his own slope returned to street level and ran a dozen steps away, as if the ground was haunted.

It was a cliché move, but she brushed her hands off when she was done. "You guys can dig out of that on your own, after I'm gone."

The guy was staring at her handiwork, hand on his temple like he had a headache. He was rough, a scar on his chin, his skin baked to sandstone brown. Tattoos decorated his arms and neck; a bandana was tied on his head in a way that was no doubt coded.

From within the dirt cages she'd constructed came angry shouting and curses. But nobody was shooting, which was the whole point.

"You're *La Bruja de la Tierra*, yeah? From *American Hero*?"

She just looked at him, because who else would she be?

"So, what the hell are you doing here? Why aren't you in Hollywood or New York, being a big star or whatever?"

A snapped non-answer was on the tip of her tongue, but she hesitated. Who knew—maybe he could help. "I'm looking for someone," she said. "My grandmother."

"Yeah? She live around here? Maybe I know her—"

"She lives out in the country. I figured I could ask when I get out there."

"Try me. I know everyone."

"Why would you want to help me?"

He put his hands up. "Hey, peace."

Well, maybe he did know everyone. "Her name's Inez Salerno. She's a joker. I guess people call her *La Curandera de las Flores*. The joker *bruja*."

She expected him to shake his head and send her on her way, but he showed a flash of recognition. Her grandmother had a reputation—he knew her, or at least of her.

Suspicion shut down his expression. "Why do you want to find Inez? What can you get from her that you can't get up north? You've been on TV—you must be rich, you can get anything you want."

He was testing her. He had the stance of a gatekeeper. *This thing is ours,* he said, *and you are a stranger here.* That he seemed to be protecting Inez made Ana feel better.

"I just found out she's still alive. I need to see her. I need . . . advice, help. Something." She sounded helpless, like a child. The sound of her own pain startled her.

"Your ace. You got it from her?"

"I got the wild card gene from her, yeah. The ace was dumb luck." She hadn't been infected with the virus like so many others. She was one of those of the second, third, and fourth generations who'd inherited. Enough generations had passed since the first Wild Card Day, the recessive wild card gene was recombining, popping up where it wasn't expected. It was part of the genome now; Ana was proof of it.

"If you find her—you think she'd really want to see you?"

The question had never occurred to Ana, and it made the whole trip even crazier. She didn't have any pictures; she didn't know anything about Inez.

"*No sé,*" she said. "I don't know. All I can do is find her and ask."

He nodded. "There's a side road. Not the main highway. Last right turn before you leave town, then a left. That's the road you want. Take it for a couple of hours, at least until dusk. You won't find her before dusk. When you see the evening star, that's when you stop. Understand?"

She could ask for more exact directions—how many miles, what kind of landmarks—but her instincts told her she was lucky to get this much. The surreal directions seemed exactly right for a quest that had started out vague.

"*Sí. Gracias.*"

The guys in the dirt cages were *still* shouting. Some dirt crumbled down the outside—one of them probably hitting at the wall from the inside. They'd figure out they could escape soon enough, and she needed to be gone by then. She got back into the truck, said a prayer, hoped the problem really was just the radiator fluid, and turned the key.

The engine coughed a couple of times, but it started. Clanking, just like before, but working.

"*Bruja,*" the man called over the sound of the engine rattling, into Ana's open window. "Her friends call her *La Señora de la Esperanza.*"

The lady of hope. Maybe this was really going to work.

He waved to her as she drove on.

◆

She hadn't had nightmares after Egypt, not that she could remember. But she hadn't slept well. If she couldn't find her grandmother by nightfall, she didn't know what she was going to do about finding somewhere to sleep. Pulling over to the side of the road was an option, but then she really wouldn't sleep. She might as well just keep driving. Wisely, she'd filled up with gas before leaving Juárez. And filled up the cans in the truck's bed.

Ana had probably been nuts to trust that gangbanger and his crazy directions. Now here she was, on a flat waste of desert scrub, nothing visible for miles, not even a cactus. The road was an actual paved road, which was good. But it was a narrow two lanes, the lane markings were cracked and faded, and she hadn't passed any kind of sign in half an hour. She hadn't passed another car in an hour. It had been two since she left the outskirts of Juárez. The sun was setting, the sky's blue deepening to twilight, and her gut was aching. She pulled over, set her hazard lights, and dug in her backpack for her bottle of aspirin. Look for the evening star, he'd said, like she was Peter Pan or something.

Except there it was, a diamond-bright light low on the western horizon, above the crooked silhouette of mountains. Up ahead was a light, an ancient dim streetlight standing watch over a small building. It had been just far enough away that she hadn't seen it. Not until that streetlight came on.

She started the truck again and pulled over in front of the building. It was a gas station but abandoned, the windows boarded up, the two pumps out front so old-fashioned, they had numbers that flipped over mechanically on plastic tiles.

The place seemed like another mirage. A threat, even. She ought to just drive on past it. It would be a trap that would open under her, swallow her up. Except in the fading light, her eye caught something else.

A footpath led away through the dust and desert. A paler stripe of yellow earth worn into the beige by many feet. It went on maybe a mile or two, though distance was hard to judge in this arid landscape, then sloped down to a nearby arroyo. While the building and skeletal pumps of the gas station were foreboding, the footpath seemed like an invitation. Another mirage, this one leading to an oasis.

It would be a long hike in her injured state. She would probably definitely regret leaving the truck alone out here. But why else had she come all this way? What other reason would there be a path at an abandoned gas station, unless to point the way to somewhere?

Yeah, to a drug stash or cartel hideout. And if that was the case, she could handle it.

She grabbed her backpack with its water bottle and headed out.

♥

She shouldn't be walking, not this far. Her doctor wouldn't like to see her walking. Roberto and Kate would both give her a hard time for this. What happened to resting?

Because if she'd sat down, if she'd lain on the sofa to do nothing but watch TV and think, she might never have gotten up again. This hurt, but this was better.

It was full dark now. She hadn't thought about setting off at dusk, hadn't thought about how long such a walk would take, or that she maybe should have waited until morning. Setting off immediately had seemed the most natural thing in the world. The moon was high overhead, close to full. She could see the dirt path cutting across the desert, like it had been painted. It glowed, almost. Her cane bit into the dirt. The rhythm was solid, stable, if lurching.

The path began sloping up, and at the top of the rise, she stopped because of the scene spread out before her.

A beautiful hacienda nestled in an oasis, a lush depression tucked in between the hills. One story, sprawling, made of clean white stucco, it was surrounded by a waist-high wall, and a tall archway decorated with tiles opened into a paved courtyard with a well. Golden lights shone from all the windows, a glowing halo. Outside the wall, a pond spread out from the front, surrounded by willow trees and rose bushes.

For no particular reason, the path worn into the dirt became paved with pale cobblestones just a few steps from where she'd stopped. The path led right to that archway.

She took a breath and smelled perfume, sweet and heady. There were flowers, everywhere flowers, climbing roses arcing over pergolas, clematis climbing fences, a dozen different kind of lilies lining the walkway, and never mind what season it was, they were all blooming together. She could imagine getting drunk on the smell of all the flowers. Finding a grassy spot to lie down and sleeping for a month, safe in paradise.

She felt like she had been walking for a very long time, and seeing this place made it worthwhile.

As soon as she crossed under the archway into the courtyard, a small man in a pale shirt and loose trousers appeared. He had a mustache and his hair was carefully combed. He'd probably come from the front door, though she wasn't sure. Ana stopped, a little confused—her steps had been carrying her, almost unconsciously, toward the front door. This was the right place; it had to be the right place. But the man, frowning, intercepted her.

Before he could say anything she asked, in her clearest Spanish, "I'm looking for Inez, does she live here? *¿Está aquí?*"

"*¿Quién es?*"

She hoped this was the right place. She swallowed the lump out of her throat. "Ana Cortez. Her granddaughter."

There was no reason the name would mean anything to him, but recognition lit his eyes and he nodded. "Yes, of course! We've been expecting you."

Ana stopped herself from asking how. From asking anything at all. She merely followed him when he guided her inside the house.

Just as many plants, vines, and flowers grew inside as out. Instead of painted walls or art, vegetation decorated the place. There must have been hundreds of pots and planter boxes, and all of them had something growing from them.

The short man chatted as he led her through room after room to the back of the house. "My name is Antonio, I'm the caretaker here and run errands for Inez. Been working for her for, oh, twenty years, I think. Ever since I shut down the gas station, you know? Can I just say—it's so good of you to come. I was really hoping you would come. You see, you're just in time."

"Just in time for what?"

His smile turned sad. "She's very sick." He turned away and passed through another doorway into a darkened room.

His tone gave the statement a dark weight. The phrase was a euphemism. She was sick, and she would not get better. Ana's steps slowed as she tried to imagine what she would see when she walked into the room. She had no idea.

"Inez? *Señora*, you have a visitor."

The room smelled pleasantly like a greenhouse, of damp earth and new growth and the perfume of flowers. Around the walls were shelves, tables, cabinets, and all of them were piled with pots, jars, boxes, and growing things. Grow lamps clipped to stands and hanging from the ceiling focused on the vegetation and gave the room a glow like it was lit by a pale sun.

The bed in the corner seemed like nothing so much as a hillock of grass, and the woman lying propped up on a mound of mossy-velvety pillows seemed like she must be growing from the earth.

"Inez?" Antonio said again, gently prompting the woman awake.

Abuela Inez was a joker; Ana had known this. But she'd never seen any pictures, so the image before her was new. The old woman's skin was brown, wrinkled; she might have been any *Mexicana* who'd spent her life working in the sun, except the furrows and whorls across her body were so regular, the shape and color of bark. Vines and sprouts grew from her the way hair would have on another person. Her face, eyes, and smile were human, and she woke up and reached a twig-like hand to Ana.

"*¡Por supuesto, maravilloso!* Ana, I knew you would come."

And suddenly, everything was fine. They'd known each other forever. This was her mother's mother.

Ana knelt by the bed and took her grandmother's hand. It was warm, like bark that had been in the sun. "*Abuela*. How did you know? How do you even know my name?"

Her smile grew wide, her green eyes laughed. "Oh, I knew. I was keeping an eye on you even if it didn't seem like it. And Tony—he brought over his son's laptop so I could watch your TV show. You were so beautiful on the TV, so powerful. *I* think you should have won." She patted Ana's hand.

Ana wanted to laugh, because that was exactly the kind of thing a grandmother was supposed to say. "I think I did win. I made friends. I have so much to look forward to. I got out of New Mexico, and I can get Roberto into college. *We* won."

"I'm so glad to hear you say that! It's so hard to tell on the TV—but I'm glad you and the others are truly friends. Friends are so important. But Ana, right now, you don't look like someone who's won."

Ana started crying, which she should have expected. Just quiet tears falling. Now that she was here, she couldn't get the words out as to why she'd come. It seemed ridiculous to kneel before a woman who was so obviously ill, probably dying, and say, *I need to be healed.*

Inez's gaze fell to Ana's shirt, to the St. Barbara medallion shining on its chain. The old woman lifted it, studied it.

"This is from your mother?" Abuela asked.

Ana nodded. "I've had my power since I was little. Mama said I needed someone to watch over me."

"Saint Barbara is a good patron. Your mother chose well. I knew when I sent Susana away that I would never see her again."

"Was it really so bad, that you had to send her away at all?"

"Aren't you glad I did? If I hadn't, there'd be no you, no Roberto." She chuckled, patted Ana's hand, settled a bit more deeply, more comfortably, against her pillow. "Maybe it wasn't so bad, but if she'd stayed here she would have been *La Hija de la Bruja* her whole life, never her own person. She was such a bright light, she deserved more than that."

"I miss her."

"Oh my dear, of course you do. Now, you came here because you're hurting. *Dígame todo.*"

Ana didn't say anything. What was there to say? She lifted her shirt, exposing the puckered pink scar of the gunshot wound. Inez urged her close and ran a gentle hand over the wound. It felt like the brush of a flower petal.

"It's healing well, but I imagine you're still in a lot of pain? Deep in the muscles? I have something for that—on the shelf behind you, look for the blue glass with the lid . . . the small one . . . there it is."

Ana followed her directions and fetched the jar, which was filled with some kind of yellowish, pungent ointment. When she rubbed it into the wound, it soothed. The earthy scent of it relaxed, and it left a warmth against her skin.

"Papá said you make your medicines from the flowers that grow from your own skin," Ana said. "Is that true?"

Inez gave her a wry look. "Of course not. That's just a story. A folktale. Did he also tell you that your mother was born out of a pea pod?" Ana chuckled, nodded. "I was in labor for two days with her, there was no pea pod! People say all kinds of things about me—don't mind them. I use the plants from my garden. But I do have something of a green thumb, yes?" She held up her thumbs, which were indeed green, bristling with hairs that looked like grass. "Now, here you go. Twice a day, it'll be better in no time. And you probably shouldn't be walking around so much."

"That's what the doctor said."

Inez lifted a greenish brow as if to say, *Of course he did.* "Now, what else is bothering you?"

Because she knew it wasn't just the pain. Ana leaned against the bed; Inez rested her bony, woody hand on her hair.

"The priest back home told me not to use my power anymore. That if I'm really sorry for killing all those people, I won't use my ace again. I came because . . . because I don't know what to do. I can't not use it. If I don't use it, what good is having it at all? But I don't want to hurt anyone. If it's too dangerous for me to use it . . ."

"This is an old complaint, my Ana. When the priest tells you one thing and your heart tells you another, who do you listen to? When the priest says *this,* but you hear God saying another. Do these powers come from God or the Devil?"

Ana looked up. "They came from *aliens.*"

"Exactly. So what does your heart tell you?"

"If I can help people, I should. Avoid the bad. Don't fight in any more wars."

"Sometimes we can't avoid the wars. But that shouldn't stop you from doing what you can, you think?"

"I knew that. Maybe I needed to hear someone else say it."

They sat together in silence for a time, Ana lulled by her grandmother's touch, by the beautiful smells of the plants and flowers. No wonder everything grew so lush here—it all felt so safe.

"Are you hungry?" Inez asked after a time. "Have you eaten at all today?"

She couldn't remember. "Not really."

"Go into the kitchen. There's fruit and lemonade in the fridge. Go bring us some."

Ana went, and noticed that her gut hardly hurt at all.

They had a picnic by the bed, but Inez didn't eat anything, Ana noticed. Sipped a little of the lemonade and seemed pleased to watch Ana eat. Something else hung in the air. The conversation wasn't over, and so Ana wasn't surprised when Inez spoke again.

"Ana, will you do something for me?"

"Of course, if I can."

"I will need to you dig my grave."

Ana answered reflexively, "*Abuela,* I don't think—"

"I want to be buried here, where I've lived my whole life and where everything good I've ever done is. Your mother was born here and your grandfather is buried here. But Tony is too old to dig, and I don't want heavy equipment barging through my garden. But you, Ana—you could do it in a moment. I think it's why you're here, why you came to me now. Will you stay with me and make my grave when the time comes?"

"Yes, I will." It was the only possible answer.

♣

It happened quickly, just two days later. Ana was at her side; Tony stayed by the doorway, stifling tears. She fell into a deep sleep and never woke up. It was so very peaceful. Nothing like an earthquake. Ana held her hand and was sure that Inez had stopped breathing for a long time before Ana even noticed. Tony said that Inez had been waiting for the right time to let go; she'd been waiting for Ana.

Tony made a simple wooden casket for her. He called his teenage son to help him carry it out to the spot that he'd marked out, where Inez had wanted to be buried.

"Don't you have to dig the hole first?" Tony Junior asked.

Ana said, "No. Just set it down. I'll take care of it."

Because Inez had known, and this was exactly how her *abuela* wanted it.

Ana knelt, pressed her medallion to her chest with one hand, touched the other to the earth, digging her fingers in. She could feel its depth, its life, cut through with a billion roots of all the growing things around her. Gently, she opened a hole, the particles of soil serving as a million hands supporting the casket, lowering it as the ground parted to make space for it. There was a noise like ants walking, or rain falling on a desert. The earth simply swallowed her. The surface continued churning until her grandmother had traveled deep enough to her last resting place. Ana dug the hole and buried her grandmother in the same moment.

The shifting earth fell silent, and the three of them stayed still, watching.

"Do we need to call a priest?" Ana asked finally. "To say a blessing?"

"We'll do it," Tony said, and they all bowed their heads as he recited an Our Father and a Hail Mary. Then it was over.

♠

Tony walked her back to her car, a hike of several miles that seemed much more ordinary than the walk to the hacienda had been. "You can't be too careful out here," he said. "All the gangs and thieves and monsters. It's very dangerous."

She just smiled.

The truck was fine, right where she left it. She checked the gas, checked the oil, topped off the radiator again just to be sure. Gave Tony a hug—he and his family would keep looking after the hacienda.

At last, she set off on the empty road and made a call.

"Ana!" Kate greeted her. "I've been texting and calling, but nothing was getting through—where have you been?"

"I don't think there was any reception where I was. Anyway, I'll tell you all about it. The important thing is, I'm coming home. To New York."

♠ ♥ ♦ ♣

Discards

by David D. Levine

IN A DARK, STINKING room on the outskirts of Rio de Janeiro, its discolored cinder-block walls scarred with generations of graffiti, Tiago Gonçalves lay sweating and thrashing, delirious with fever.

For a bed, Tiago had the box spring from a child's crib, stained and torn, over which was thrown a threadbare sheet that had perhaps once been pink. A battered plastic milk crate nearby held one pair of jelly shoes, three shirts too big for his skinny frame, two pair of shorts, some underwear, a plastic mug and spoon, a toothbrush, and half a cake of soap. That was all. But his most treasured possessions sat proudly atop the crate: an oil lamp assembled from discarded cans and bottles, using braided electrical insulation as a wick; a Swiss Army knife, its long-vanished plastic side panels replaced with scraps of teak painstakingly shaped to fit the hand and polished to silky smoothness; and a bouquet of flowers he had made by twisting together bits of colorful plastic bags.

All of these things Tiago had rescued from the landfill. But there was no one to rescue Tiago. He had lain here for . . . he didn't know how long, days maybe, without anyone to care for him. The other three *catadores*—"collectors" of recycled materials—who shared this twenty-reais-a-week room had lives and problems of their own. At least João had shared some of his water and fried manioc cakes.

Tiago shivered in his sweat-soaked sheet, which clung to him like it was his own skin. He ached all over; he could barely raise his head. He wondered if he might be dying.

He knew death. He had seen death far too often in his fifteen years. Every time there was a war between the gangs of drug *traficantes* that ruled the *favelas*, bodies turned up in the dump. Sometimes they were headless and handless, oozing black blood from the severed stumps. Once Tiago had unearthed a tiny newborn baby, the umbilical cord still attached, from a bag of rotten food scraps. Rats had eaten its ears. At seven he had seen his father gunned down by the police while stepping from his own shower, during a drug raid based on mistaken information.

His mother, too, was dead, or at least that was what he assumed. Two years ago she had gone off to look for work and never come back. Most likely she had been unlucky enough to catch a stray bullet from some *traficantes'* battle, never identified, and buried anonymously in a public cemetery. But deep inside he harbored the fear that she had tired of him, of the strain of caring for a hungry, curious boy as an unemployed single mother, and had run away, back to the countryside from which she had come before he'd been born.

He should never have been born. Just by existing, Tiago made things worse.

João poked his head around the tattered bath curtain that separated Tiago's space from the rest of the room. It must be the end of his work shift; time passed strangely in this delirious room without windows. "Oi, Tiago! Just checking to . . . *Nossa Senhora!*" Even in the near darkness, Tiago could see the shock in João's eyes, sudden wide white circles in his dark face.

"Wha . . . ?" Tiago struggled to sit up. "What's wrong?"

"Have you seen your *face?*"

"No . . ."

João vanished, the curtain falling back, leaving Tiago blinking in dazed concern, heart pounding with fever and dread. João returned a moment later with the mirror from the men's washroom, a shining triangular scrap with a deadly point. Without a word he held it up so Tiago could see himself.

At first he thought that what he was seeing was just an effect of the fractured mirror. Then, as he continued to stare and the mirror shifted slightly in João's hands, he realized it was reality.

His face, formerly an ordinary but unlovely dark brown, had changed. It was now a dramatic hard-edged jigsaw of black, brown, and pink. One eye was still brown; the other, the one whose surrounding skin was lighter, was now hazel. His nose was divided down the middle—the left side had dark skin and a broad African nostril, the right was tawny, a slim Tupi Indian beak. Neither side matched the nose he remembered.

With wonder he touched his cheek. It was his own skin, not a mask—he could feel his fingertips lightly brushing his face—and its texture varied slightly, the pale skin smoother and the darker skin having a more waxy feel. The line between the two was distinct, but didn't feel like a seam or a scar. He rubbed at it, first in concern and then in panic, but though both sides reddened and warmed, the color did not come off.

His hands were the same patchwork of colors.

Suddenly alarmed, he sat up and pulled his shirt open. Triangles and rectangles of a half dozen different shades ran all the way down his chest and stomach and into his pants. Legs and arms too. His own hands on the parti-colored skin felt like ice.

He realized he was making noises—*ah, ah, ah*—frightened, animal sounds. He clamped his mouth and eyes shut, hugged himself with his arms, and rocked, trying to calm himself.

"You got the virus, man," came João's voice through the keening in Tiago's head. "The wild card." He sounded half-terrified and half-awed.

"No!" Tiago moaned into his knees. But he knew it was true. What else could cause such a change to happen overnight?

The curtain rattled and Tiago opened his eyes. It was Eduardo, the oldest of the four and the one who collected the rent. *"Que diabo!"*

"He got the wild card," João said, helpfully.

Eduardo clapped one hand over his nose and mouth and backed slowly away. "You can't stay here," he said, muffled. "You take your things and go, right now."

"But it's almost dark!" João protested.

Eduardo glared at João. "You wanna end up like him? Or worse, like some kind of fungus glob?" He shook his head, turned back to Tiago. "No. You go, now. Take your germy stuff, too. We'll have to burn your mattress."

João looked back and forth from Eduardo to Tiago. Tiago—still trembling, chilled, disoriented—just sat and stared back at him. Then Flavio, the fourth boy sharing the room, came in.

Flavio took one look at Tiago, shrieked, and fled.

"That's it!" said Eduardo. He yanked down the curtain and threw it out the door. *"Cai fora!"* Beat it!

Tiago looked to João, but the younger boy just shook his head slightly, blinking in stunned incomprehension. He would find no support there.

Shuddering, barely able to stand, Tiago dragged himself out of bed. The Swiss Army knife he put in his zippered shorts pocket, along with his few bills and coins; the lamp and flowers would have to remain. The remaining contents of the milk crate he dumped onto the sheet, gathered up into a bundle, and slung over his shoulder.

He couldn't even manage a good-bye. He just glared at the two other boys as he dragged himself out the door.

◆

As he trudged down the street—really just a dirt track between houses assembled from cinder block, scrap lumber, and discarded doors, illuminated only by the flickering light of methane fires from the dump—he considered that he didn't have enough money for even a shared room, and no one he knew had any extra space, even for one skinny little boy. Too late, he realized that he should have asked Eduardo for his share of the weekly rent back. But then again, Eduardo had probably already paid it to the landlord, or would claim to have done so.

The *catadores* worked around the clock. If he hurried, he might make the late shift, where he could pick up a few reais—if anyone would work with him. He turned his feet toward the Catadores' Association yard, where the pickers received the fluorescent vests that showed their authorization to work and caught a truck to the landfill.

But when he arrived, he found the yard empty, with stacks of sorted plastics, papers, and metals sitting silently beneath the buzzing floodlights. The last truck had already departed. Only old Vitor, guardian of the cash box, remained, sitting on an upturned plastic bucket and smoking.

As he approached, Vitor looked up lazily, then jerked to his feet. *"Porra!"* he swore, the bucket rattling away behind him.

"It's just me, Vitor. Tiago. The one who always brings the nice clean PET bottles." But his hopes were already fading.

"Curinga!" the old man replied, crossing himself and backing away.

Tiago's lip curled and he prepared to spit back a matching insult at the weak, shabby old man. But then he realized that Vitor's slur, *curinga*, was just the literal truth.

Tiago had become a *curinga*—a joker. A twisted, pathetic victim of the wild card virus.

He didn't belong here, not anymore. Not even the *catadores*, the lowest of the low, would associate with him. He was diseased, abased, offensive. There was only one place for him to go.

"I just need some money, man," he said. He realized that tears were leaking slowly down his cheeks. He ignored them. "I need to get to Bairro dos Curingas." Everyone knew Rio's Jokertown—the neighborhood where the virus's most unsightly sufferers gathered. There, at least, he would fit in. But Rio was a long way from the landfill, and he would need bus fare. "Can you give me an advance on tomorrow?"

Advances were strictly against the rules, and they both knew that Tiago would not be working tomorrow. Nonetheless, Vitor went into his little shack and returned with a small wad of money, which he flung at Tiago. The bills landed on the ground halfway between them.

Tiago sighed and took a step forward, reaching for the money. But before he could touch the bills, they fluttered up, seemingly of their own accord, to his outstretched fingers . . . and stuck there.

He blinked, shooting Vitor a glance that said *Did you see that?* But the old man just stood there trembling, clearly just wishing the scary *curinga* would go away.

"Thanks, man," Tiago said. He pulled the bills off his fingers—they came away easily—and stuffed them into his pocket without looking.

As he trudged away toward the bus, Tiago wondered what the hell had just happened. Probably it was just a breeze that had moved the bills, and as for the sticking to his fingers . . . Well, what was there here at the dump that *wasn't* sticky? Anyway, he was still feverish. Maybe he'd imagined the whole thing.

♥

The few other people at the bus stop kept their distance, muttering and casting glances, and the driver eyed him warily. But he accepted Tiago's fare—it was almost all of what he'd gotten from Vitor—and Tiago found a seat way at the back of the nearly empty bus.

Hours passed in diesel-scented, lurching motion. People got on, people got off; no one sat near Tiago. From the occasional muttered *"Curinga!"* he knew that it wasn't just the stink of the landfill on him.

The last time he had traveled this route had been a couple of months after his mother had disappeared. He'd spent the first month in a series of wretched little homes, handed from one to the next; there was no government assistance for abandoned children, he had no relatives that he knew of, and none of his mother's friends had the space or the money to house a hungry teenaged boy for more than a few days. But then the boyfriend of a woman who'd taken him in had tried to take Tiago's clothes off. He'd kicked the man in the nuts and fled with only the clothes on his back.

After that he had lived on the street, becoming increasingly hungry and filthy, until one of the other street kids had let him in on a scheme:

she had heard that the landfill at Jardim Gramacho was a place where you could make money by picking through the garbage for recyclable metals and plastics. It was smelly, difficult work, she said, but an honest living, and she knew someone who would give them a ride . . .

Weak, skinny, and ignorant, he'd barely survived his first few weeks as a *catador*. But eventually he had learned the ropes: where to go for a vest and a ride, how to be the first to a fresh load without getting run over, how to identify the plastics that paid the most per kilo, which of the buyers would cheat you. Eventually he had gotten good at it, even begun to take pride in his work—taking people's discards and helping to recycle them into something useful. He'd stayed alive, if not prosperous, for two years; he'd even made a few friends.

Now all that was gone—taken by the virus.

He leaned his head against the chill darkness of the bus window and wept.

♣

"Bairro dos Curingas!" called the driver. Tiago roused himself, shook his head to clear it, collected his bundle of belongings, and stumbled out the back door just before the bus roared off.

He stood, blinking and shivering, on the black-and-white pavement. He was sick and weak and hungry, and with three changes of bus he had barely slept; it must be past midnight. But now he stood at the gate of Rio's Jokertown.

It was not what he had expected.

Curingas there were, to be sure. A man with writhing snakes for hair stood on a corner handing out leaflets. A grossly fat woman, wider than she was tall and with warty red skin, sat at the entrance of a club, calling out to passersby in multiple languages. Two scantily clad women, both with attractive bodies but hideous faces, danced on a balcony illuminated by spotlights.

But it was not what Tiago would consider a *bairro*—a neighborhood—at all. It was a commercial district, bright with neon and brash with music and chatter even at this late hour. People thronged the sidewalks, most of them normal looking and almost all of them white or light skinned. Tiago supposed that many of them were *turistas* rather than *cariocas*—Rio natives.

A man bumped into Tiago from behind, making him drop his bundle. As

Tiago bent to pick it up, the man slurred a drunken apology and stooped to assist him.

The man stank of alcohol, with shabby clothes and gray hair. His eyes were red and bleary . . . and extended on stalks from his face.

Tiago swallowed, but he would need to learn to accept *curingas* if he was to be accepted himself. "Hey," he said. "I'm new here. I'm looking for something to eat, and a place to stay."

"Plenty to eat here," said the eye-stalk man, waving down the street. Doorway after doorway gleamed brightly, and enticing smells mingled in the air.

But every one of those brightly illuminated doorways had a sentinel. Some of them were guarded by large, no-nonsense men in tuxedoes; others had only a friendly-looking attractive woman in evening dress, but Tiago suspected that those women had burly men backing them up. And although a few of them had mild deformities, none were frightening or disgusting.

The whole place stank of money. And Tiago . . . simply stank. "I don't have a lot of cash," he told the eye-stalk man. The few remaining reais in his pocket probably wouldn't buy a packet of peanuts at a fancy restaurant like these.

The man's eyes wavered and literally crossed, making Tiago slightly queasy. "Santa Teresa's gone to hell anyway," he muttered. "Just a tourist trap, anymore. The real *curingas* have gotten pushed out to the *favelas*." To some people, *favela* meant neighborhood or community; others sneered it to mean slum. The difference depended on where you stood: on the *morros*, or hills, with the poor, or on the *asfalto*, or pavement, with the rich.

The black-and-white pavement of this place was hard beneath Tiago's jelly shoes.

One of the burly tuxedo-clad men—his skin was black as night and white ram's horns curled from his forehead—was keeping a wary eye on Tiago. Tiago knew that look; he'd seen it plenty of times while he was living on the street, before he'd gone to the landfill. It was a look that said *I know you're just waiting for an opportunity to zip in here and take some of those hot* empanadas *off the bar, but I've got my eye on you.*

Above the neighborhood gateway, a huge neon sign of a burly man in priest's garb, with tentacles where his mouth should be, waved a welcome to the crowd below. The shadows shifted in the moving light from his waving arm, but the neon *curinga*'s welcome was not for Tiago.

"Where do the real *curingas* live?" he asked the eye-stalk man.

"Up there," he replied, gesturing vaguely toward the hills.

Tiago shouldered his bundle and began to walk.

♠

He walked for hours, asking directions of passersby as he went. Most gave him a cold glance, or even less acknowledgment than that, and breezed past without stopping. Some spat at or threatened him. One or two threw coins, and though he had not asked for money he was not too proud to scramble after them. And a few, a very few, tried to help. The consensus was that the *curingas* were mostly to be found in Complexo do Alemão, a large complex of *favelas* in the hills of the city's North Zone—three hours' walk or more away. Even if he had had enough money for the bus, none were running at that hour. Finally, too tired to go any farther, he hid himself beneath a heap of trash bags, arms and legs wrapped around his small bundle of possessions, and slept.

He woke at dawn to the sniffing noses of rats, and breakfasted on stale *pão de queijo* rolls rescued from the garbage behind a café just setting up for the day.

He knew he was approaching the *complexo* as the graffiti got denser and more elaborate. The ones that were executed entirely in black paint, he knew, were gang tags—they indicated which group of drug *bandidos* controlled this territory, though he did not understand their code. A further, more definitive sign was the rising terrain, as the wide, straight, paved streets of the *asfalto* gave way to the steep, curving, narrow streets of the *morro*. Eventually he found himself at a high concrete wall, plastered with graffiti and topped with an iron fence: the boundary of Nova Brasília. Of all the *complexo*'s *favelas*, this was—or so he'd been told—the largest, poorest, most dangerous, and densest with *curingas*.

He followed the wall until he came to a gateway, where two muscular young men lounged on folding chairs. One had bat-like wings, too small to be functional; the other had a shaven head crowned by a circle of white lumps—molar teeth—and was drinking a Coke.

Both men carried machine guns.

The man with the teeth wiped his mouth and tossed the can, rattling, into the gutter. That made Tiago wince—back at the landfill, aluminum cans fetched almost two reais per kilo. "Welcome to Nova Brasília," he said. "What's your business?"

"I'm a *curinga*," Tiago replied, gesturing to his face. "I need a place to stay."

"He's a *curinga*," the man replied, smiling at his partner, who smiled back. The man with the teeth dropped the smile and glared at Tiago. "We don't care what you look like, you don't come into this *favela* unless you're on approved business."

"Approved by who?" Tiago replied. These men wore civilian clothes and carried no identification.

"Comando Curinga," the man with the teeth replied—Joker Command. It was a name Tiago hadn't heard before, but it echoed the names of the drug gangs Comando Vermelho and Terceiro Comando—Red Command and Third Command—which were all over the radio. "We took over this *favela* from the Amigos dos Amigos back in March. And no one goes in or out without our say-so."

The bat-winged man shrugged. "Nothing personal, kid."

By reflex, Tiago snagged the Coke can from the gutter as he walked away. But half a block later he stopped.

He had walked all night. His belly rumbled. He had no money and nowhere else to go.

The man with the wings was, at least, not actively hostile.

He looked at the can in his hand.

Then he sat on the curb and took out his Swiss Army knife. Using the can opener, small blade, and corkscrew, he cut and carved and shaped the can's soft aluminum until it was a bird—a stupid-looking cartoon bird with big round eyes and a spray of shredded aluminum feathers on its head. It was ugly, fragile, and covered with dangerous edges, but kind of adorable.

He went back to the gateway and presented the thing to the bat-winged man. "Here," he said, "I made this for you."

"Did you now?" said the bat-winged man, with no visible emotion, but he put out his hand and took it. The one with the teeth frowned at him, but said nothing.

The man turned the stupid little bird over, poked at its beak, and considered it at arm's length while Tiago's heart stood still. He expected the man to crush it in his fist and toss it away.

But instead he just grunted, "It's cute. My girlfriend will like it."

"So . . . can I come in?"

"All right," the bat-winged man said, ignoring his partner's glare. "And did you say you needed a place to stay?"

Tiago swallowed. "I did."

The man eyed Tiago for a moment, considering, then scribbled on a scrap of paper. "This is my cousin Luiza's address. Tell her Felipe sent you."

Tiago tucked the paper in his pocket. "I don't know my way around. Can you tell me how to find it?"

◆

Luiza lived at the top of a "street" so steep, narrow, and twisty that not even a bicycle could traverse it. Tiago's heart pounded from the climb as much as his nervousness as he rapped on the rusted metal door.

The door was pocked with bullet holes.

"Yeah?" came a voice from within, over the thumping funk music.

"I'm looking for Luiza."

The door creaked open a finger's width. One eye peered through the gap. "I'm Luiza."

"My name's Tiago. Your cousin Felipe sent me." He briefly described the circumstances.

The eye regarded him for a moment, then the door closed. There was an extended rattling sound, then it reopened more fully, letting out a blast of music and a sweet whiff of *maconha*.

Luiza was a girl not much older than Tiago. Thin, with the black hair, medium-dark skin, and prominent cheekbones of one with a lot of indigenous heritage, she looked nearly normal except that her eyebrows were made of feathers—long, black, and shiny like a raven's. They made her dark eyes look fierce and predatory. She wore a white sleeveless top and camouflage pants, and her belt and pockets were heavy with cell phones, pagers, beepers, and media players.

"That's a lot of gadgets," Tiago said.

"Cool, huh?" Luiza uncrossed her arms and looked admiringly down at her array of devices.

"Why do you need three cell phones?"

Luiza smirked. "This one works." She pointed to the oldest and most scarred of them. "The rest are for show. But pretty soon I'll be able to afford all this for real. So will you. Everybody wins in this business . . . except for the losers." She pointed a finger at the side of her head and mimed a gun going off. "Bang, you lose."

She ushered Tiago inside, closing and locking the door behind him. The room was dark, the window covered with old newspaper. Boxes and bags of Tiago didn't know what, but could guess, were piled in corners. Most of the rest of the floor was covered with mattresses; a giant sound system pounded the air. "You know the drill?" Luiza said, raising her voice above the music.

"Drill?"

Luiza rolled her eyes. "What we *do* here?"

"Uh . . . no."

Theatrically she cradled her forehead in her hand and shook her head. "Nossa . . ." She looked up. "Okay. You'll be an *avião*, right?"

Tiago was completely baffled. "I'll be a jet plane?"

"A *courier*! Look, do you know *anything*?"

"I guess not." But he was beginning to understand.

"You pick up the packages, at the dock, and bring them here," Luiza said, making each word clear and distinct as though Tiago were a complete idiot, and deaf to boot. Which he likely would be if he stayed in this noise too much longer. "Then you take deliveries to the *bocas* and the bigger customers. If you get arrested, they just let you off because you're underage. *Entende?*"

Tiago understood all right, but didn't like what he was hearing. He'd seen too many people messed up by drugs and killed by *traficantes* to want any part of the process. But this was the only lead he had on a place to stay. He thought quickly. "No, no, you misunderstand. Felipe didn't send me here to be an *avião* . . . he liked the little bird I made. I thought I could maybe make things like this and sell them." It wasn't exactly a lie. The bat-winged man *hadn't* said anything about Tiago being a drug courier, he *had* liked the bird, and Tiago *did* think—or at least hope—that he could sell them.

Luiza looked extremely skeptical, but the invocation of her cousin's name seemed to pacify her somewhat. "Well . . . okay, you can sleep in the corner. But you have to pay your share of the rent."

Tiago was skeptical too . . . that he wanted anything to do with this crowd, that Luiza wouldn't kick him right out once she talked with Felipe, that he would be able to afford whatever his share of the rent was, that he would be able to sleep at all with this noise. But it would be a roof over his head, for as long as it lasted. "It's a deal."

♥

Tiago spent the rest of the morning prowling the streets for raw materials. His years as a *catador* stood him in good stead . . . He could spot reusable materials from a long way off against any background, no matter how messy, and could tell from the outside of a garbage bag what it was likely to contain. He picked up bottles, cans, plastic bags, broken electronics, and even a pair of metal shears that could be repaired. Those would be useful for cutting things his Swiss Army knife couldn't. The best find was a tube of glue, mostly dead and hard but with a little usable glue left at the bottom.

In the afternoon he stuffed bits of packing foam in his ears against the music and reassembled the things he'd found into things he thought he could sell. He made a bunch of aluminum can birds—all goofy, all different—some plastic bag bouquets, a sort of teddy bear from brown medicine bottles, and an airplane made of old greeting cards that was colorful and actually flew. He probably spent too much time on that last one.

As he worked, *aviões* came and went, picking up or dropping off packages and money. Most of them were boys, mostly dark, and mostly *curingas*, but there were also some girls and some normal-looking people—which he learned were called by the *curingas "limpos"* or "*nats.*" Some looked curiously at Tiago, but mostly they seemed focused on their jobs; also, a lot of them were somewhat or more than somewhat stoned. Tiago decided he was happier not getting to know them any better than that.

When hunger and fatigue made him stop, he packed up the things he had made in an old suitcase he'd found and headed down the hill in search of someone to buy them.

It was a long walk from Luiza's place at the top of the *morro* to the nearest busy tourist street. He had to endure questioning from the armed Comando Curinga guards at the *favela*'s entrance, and handed over the brown-bottle teddy bear as a good faith offering. On the way he scrounged some pizza crusts for his dinner. Eventually, following his ears, he found a well-trafficked corner with a spot by the wall where he could spread out his wares.

Mostly people just passed by, and that was okay. In general the city people, *cariocas* and *turistas* alike, didn't seem afraid or disgusted of him because he was a *curinga*, but on the other hand they weren't interested in him either. But some of the playboys—well-dressed young men—sneered or spat or kicked at him. One group of playboys kicked his little display across the sidewalk, laughing the whole time; he never did find all of the items. He did sell some birds and a couple of bouquets, though, earning a handful of reais for his day's labor.

He hadn't been there all that long when a couple of self-important men came and stood over his little sidewalk shop. They were big and beefy and pale and wore uniforms and carried big guns, but they weren't police.

Luiza had warned him about these militias. "Mostly ex-cops, or off-duty cops," she'd said. "The real cops won't charge you if you're underage, but these guys don't care—they'll just kill you unless you pay up."

Tiago hadn't realized that he had set up shop in a militia-controlled area.

"We can't have street trash like you bothering the tourists," one said, his eyes hidden behind reflective sunglasses.

"I'm not—" Tiago's mouth had gone dry. "I'm not bothering anyone."

"You're blocking traffic with your garbage," the other one said. He nudged one of Tiago's birds with his shiny boot tip.

Tiago pulled the bird back out of the way. "Sorry."

"Sorry won't cut it," said the first. He leaned down and took the glasses off; his eyes were just as hard and cold without them. "There's a fine."

Tiago looked from one to the other. Neither of them looked the type to forgive a fine in exchange for a handcrafted bird or a bunch of plastic flowers. "How much?"

The man smiled, but there was no humor in it. "How much you got?"

Without a word, Tiago held out the money he'd made.

Without a word, the man took it.

"*Cai fora!*" said the other.

Tiago scrammed, as ordered.

♣

The day wasn't a total loss. He hadn't given the man everything; the proceeds of his first few sales were safe in his zippered pocket. And he'd retained his unsold stock, some of which he managed to sell by walking beside *turistas* and offering it to them on the move. But the effort was great, and the strain of keeping a wary eye out for militia was significant, for the paltry few reais this brought in.

It was very late when Tiago returned to Luiza's apartment. He was so tired he had no trouble falling asleep despite the pounding bass, and he slept right through until the next morning when Felipe slapped him awake.

"What is this shit?" the bat-winged man said, shaking a plastic bouquet in Tiago's face.

"Plastic flowers?" Tiago blinked quickly, panic and sleep mingling in a confused mess in his head. "I sell them to pay the rent. I'll do better today."

Felipe threw the flowers on the floor. "You were meant to be an *avião*!"

Luiza stood behind him, arms crossed on her chest, feathered eyebrows making her look like one of the vultures that always circled above the landfill.

They were all vultures—the *traficantes*, the militias, the playboys, the cops who'd killed his father. They perched at the top of the heap and took their pick of whatever got stirred up by the people below, people trying to recycle trash into something beautiful or useful.

"I can't do that," Tiago said, knowing that it might get him hurt or worse.

But Felipe just made a disgusted noise. *"Cai fora!"*

♠

He'd lived on the street before, and he could do it again. He was older and smarter and tougher now.

He stayed within Nova Brasília, mostly—*curingas* were not as welcome in the other *favelas*, even less so on the *asfalto*. He learned where and when the militias patrolled and how to avoid the *traficantes* and the cops. He found the warm dry places to sleep, the dumpsters where the food wasn't too spoiled, the places to drink and wash, the hidey-holes and routes for escape.

When he could, he remade trash into something he could use or sell. But he couldn't carry a lot with him, and no matter how much money he made it was never enough. Though many of the necessities of life could be scavenged, there were always things that required cash, like paying the militia for protection.

He begged when he had to.

Eventually he began to steal. First food from sidewalk markets, then goods from shops, then unattended cell phones and purses from café tables. He was small and lithe and fast and he knew the *favelas* better than his pursuers. But even that didn't bring in enough cash. Sometimes the militia beat him when he couldn't pay their "fines."

He could feel himself wearing away.

♦

One of the things Tiago learned was the locations of the *bocas* where the playboys from the *asfalto* came to buy drugs. He liked to hang around nearby—but not too close—because the rich young men, stupid and stoned, tended to lose track of their expensive phones, watches, and even, sometimes, sneakers. He could get in, grab the goods, get out, and turn the items into cash before the playboy had even left the *favela*.

Late one night he was lurking near a *boca*—hiding in a trash pile, looking just like the other discards—when he saw a whole gang of sharp-dressed playboys laughing and lurching their way along the street. They were clearly stoned out of their minds.

Then the lead playboy in the pack stopped to light a cigarette, and as he took the lighter from his pocket, a huge roll of bills came halfway out with it. The playboy didn't even notice as he paused, puffing his smoke alight.

Tiago just about salivated at the sight. That was enough money to get him a good hot dinner and a room for the night. A couple of nights. Maybe even a week. But the man was too far away and surrounded by his friends.

Gritting his teeth in frustration, Tiago reached out for the money—a greedy, useless, symbolic gesture.

And the wad of cash whipped from the playboy's pocket and flew across the street into Tiago's extended hand, where it stuck.

With wonder Tiago tugged at the roll with his other hand, but it seemed firmly attached. It was as though it had somehow become part of him. He could *feel* every bill, all wrapped and nestled around one another like a warm pile of puppies.

How could this be?

The playboy noticed the motion, slapped his pocket, looked around, and saw Tiago sitting astonished and staring at the roll of banknotes wedded to his hand. "Hey!" the playboy shouted, breaking the spell, and gave chase. His companions followed.

But Tiago's reactions were faster than the drug-soaked playboys', and with his head start and his knowledge of the *favela*'s twisted streets he soon gave them the slip.

♥

Later that night, warm and dry and wrapped in a towel after a long hot hotel bath, Tiago sat on the bed and watched in incredulous awe as some of his remaining bills flew up from the coverlet to his outstretched hand, wrapping around it like a glove of multicolored paper. All he had to do was *want* it to happen, and it happened.

He made a fist, opened it, turned the hand over. The paper crinkled but remained firmly attached. Then he relaxed, and the bills simply fell away, leaving both money and skin unharmed.

The power, whatever it was, could pull bills all the way across the room, at least, though the farther it got the more he had to concentrate to make it happen.

It worked on bills, but not coins. It worked on note pads and towels and pillows, but not the television or the glass ashtray or the iron bedstead. It worked on the lampshade, but not the rest of the lamp, and he had to scramble to catch it before the whole thing toppled to the floor and broke. Paper, wood, fabric, and plastic, yes; glass, metal, stone, and water, no. He wasn't sure, but thought that maybe the power worked only on things made from plants and animals.

It could pull, but not push. The only direction he could move anything was toward himself.

He tried the carpet and the mattress and the wooden desk. He could feel the tug—when he really tried to pull the desk, his feet slid along the carpet—but he wasn't strong enough to move any of them.

Maybe if he practiced he would get stronger. There was no telling; the wild card virus was unpredictable. Sometimes it created hideous *curingas*, sometimes it created aces—people with supernatural powers, like the lady with wings on the Peregrine Toothpaste billboards or the contestants on the TV show *Heróis Brazil*. Apparently this time it had done both at once.

His dreams were all of pulling and snatching and flying. Happy dreams.

♣

Soon he was doing tolerably well, lifting bills, checkbooks, passports, and other small paper objects in a way no other thief could and most people didn't think to protect themselves against. Operating from a distance, patient, and stealthy, he almost always got away clean; his victims rarely even saw him, and often didn't immediately notice that they'd lost anything. He earned the respect of the fences and always got the best price for his goods. In a way, he told himself, he was still recycling—turning paper into cash.

Tiago slept in a warm bed with a full stomach nearly every night. He was making so much money that he could afford to let other street kids crash with him. Some *curinga* girls, and a few of the boys, were *very* grateful.

He made friends. He learned the limitations of his powers.

He started to get cocky.

♠

One day he found himself in a situation that, just a few weeks earlier, would have seemed completely insane. He was in an enclosed space—a former nightclub, long abandoned, now used as a drug warehouse at the wholesale level—watching from just across the room as a major drug deal went down.

Fernandinho Oliveira dos Santos, head of the Comando Curinga, had just entered the room. One of Tiago's fences had let him know that dos Santos would be meeting with the head of a Colombian syndicate to discuss distribution of a new and very potent variety of cocaine. The Colombian would be bringing a sample.

If Tiago could steal that sample, the fence had assured him, he could write his own ticket. Not only was the sample itself worth thousands, its unexplained disappearance during the meeting would set the Curinga gang and the Colombians at each other's throats—a situation some others would pay handsomely to precipitate.

The fence had let Tiago practice on a bag of his cocaine. Tiago had found no difficulty drawing the stuff to himself at distances of up to half a block.

He was well situated, hidden behind a pile of broken furniture with a door just behind himself. He had scoped out his escape route. He was ready.

Tiago watched dos Santos carefully as he paced, puffing a cigar and talking on his cell phone. The *grande chefe* of the Comando Curinga resembled a warthog, very broad of shoulder and belly, with gray skin and enormous tusks protruding from the corners of his mouth. His tailored suit was white and shiny and immaculate, his shoes polished, his open-collared shirt a delicate shade of orchid.

His hands were big and thick as bowling balls and looked like they could crush stones.

Tiago swallowed nervously and hoped the pounding of his heart was not as audible outside his head as inside.

Dos Santos grunted, nodded, and clicked the cell phone shut, then spoke low to his lieutenants. They quickly positioned themselves around the room, covering all the entrances and exits—except for the door behind Tiago, which was half-collapsed and seemingly led nowhere. Only Tiago knew that a fast and skinny kid could slip out of the back via that route, leaving larger and slower pursuers floundering in heaps of broken wood, fallen plaster, and torn-up carpet.

The Colombian, a slight and elderly *nat*, entered with two of his own lieutenants, one of whom carried a briefcase which was attached to his left wrist by a chain. After cordial greetings in Spanish and a toast of *cachaça*, the briefcase was unfastened and opened.

Tiago tensed. He might not have much time to make the snatch. And the two drug chieftains were both leaning very close over the briefcase.

The Colombian lifted the sample from the case. It was a brick the size of a Bible, wrapped in aluminum foil and sealed in a plastic bag. But the wrapping wouldn't stop Tiago—it was the plant-based stuff within that his power affected.

Dos Santos unwrapped the brick and peered at the white stuff inside, sniffed it, then called in one of his lieutenants, who did things with test tubes and colored papers. Tiago noted that no one was even tasting, never mind snorting or injecting, the stuff. None of them were that stupid.

There was a nerve-wracking amount of discussion, comparison, and inspection . . . all in Spanish, of which Tiago understood only a tiny fraction. He kept waiting for an opportunity to snatch the sample, but dos Santos or one of his lieutenants kept a tight grip on it at all times. Sweat ran down Tiago's sides; he fully expected to be spotted at any moment.

Then Dos Santos set the package down on the table and reached to shake the Colombian's hand. This might be his only opportunity.

He tensed to spring, then reached out and pulled the package to himself.

The shining foil-clad brick flew through the air in plain sight of everyone in the room. They all followed it with their eyes as it flew to Tiago and landed right in his hands.

Tiago jumped up to flee . . . and the pile of broken chairs and tables behind which he'd been hiding suddenly collapsed, knocking him down and trapping his foot.

As if in slow motion, he saw dos Santos and all the other *traficantes* pull guns from their jackets, belts, and briefcases.

And Tiago reached out with his power—blindly, unthinkingly, instantaneously, more powerfully than ever before in his life—to pull every bit of stray trash in the room to himself. Papers, plaster, broken furniture, big swaths of rotting carpet, even the Colombian's jacket . . . all flew onto Tiago's body, covering him completely.

But it did him no good. A moment later he heard the overwhelming sound of multiple automatic weapons firing in an enclosed space, and felt the pain of the bullets striking home. Back, side, legs exploded in agony.

Shrieking in pain, he jerked to his feet. He stood up . . .

. . . and up, and up, and up.

He found himself standing with his shoulders pressed against the ceiling, looking down at the stunned, upturned faces of the *traficantes*.

Was this death? Was he floating up to Heaven?

It didn't *feel* like death, or like Heaven. Every motion felt ponderous, labored. Even moving his hand through the air felt like swimming.

He raised the hand to his face . . . and it was a hand made of trash. A junky, moving sculpture of broken chair legs, bits of plaster, and torn papers in a vaguely handlike shape. He made a fist, and the trash hand moved as though it were his own.

His whole body was made of junk. And it was enormous.

With wonder he put his hands to his face. Fingers of plaster and shattered wood touched eyes that felt like two empty coffee cups, their lids blinking at the contact. His tongue felt like carpet, but it tasted his fingers' filthy plywood.

How was this even *possible?*

Again came the rattle of gunfire, not so loud this time, but again accompanied by the pain of bullets impacting his body. He screamed and backpedaled . . . and crashed through the wall behind him.

He fell heavily onto the floor of the room beyond, feeling wood and plaster cascading down on him from the shattered ceiling. When he struggled to his feet, somehow he had become even bigger. As he straightened he found himself looking down at the ceiling joists of the room he'd just left.

Pops and flashes of gunfire came from behind the mangled wall and ceiling, along with shouts and screams. Points of pain peppered his lower body.

He turned and ran, smashing through walls, gouging holes in the floor with his enormous feet. And then he was out in the alley behind the former nightclub, the night air cool on his face, his hands, his back. Behind him the building folded in on itself, the ancient, rotting wood cracking and slumping into a haphazard, unrecognizable pile.

Shuddering with fear and released tension, he collapsed in a heap. Literally. He fell down in the alley and his body—his gigantic trash body—simply collapsed, sloughing off of him, until it was only a heap of garbage all around him, leaving his own, original body unharmed in the middle of it.

Unharmed. Despite all the bullets he had felt striking him, somehow he was uninjured.

He was still clutching the foil-wrapped brick of cocaine.

He threw it into the wreckage and ran.

Tiago went to ground in his deepest, safest hidey-hole, way in the back of the old abandoned Coca-Cola factory in Nova Brasília. The place was a warren of squats, but he'd found a way to creep along a narrow alley and squeeze through a crack in the wall to a dry, protected space under the floor. He stayed there, shivering with reaction, all night, mind racing and unable to either sleep or concentrate.

When hunger finally drove him out of there, he kept his head down and his ears open. The word on the street was that the old nightclub had collapsed, killing eight people, including the *grande chefe* of the Comando Curinga and a major Colombian drug lord. Officially, it had been an accident, though some suspected a bomb. The lack of fire made that theory less plausible, but it was rumored that gunshots had been heard just before the collapse. Whatever the cause, the loss was a major blow to the Curinga gang, and both Terceiro Comando and the Amigos dos Amigos were beginning to muscle in on Curinga territory . . . including Nova Brasília.

There were no rumors of a giant man made of trash having been seen at the scene.

But even if no one but him knew it, he had killed eight people. True, they had been drug lords—terrible people, people the world was better off without—and they had tried to kill him first. But still, it was a terrible burden to bear. And who knew how many more would yet die, because Tiago had interfered?

With dos Santos dead, the *traficantes* would have to find a new balance of power. There would be assassinations, bombings, and gun battles all over the *favelas* as the various gangs struggled for dominance, complicated by the Colombians' quest for revenge. Dozens or hundreds of gang members would be killed, and unknown numbers of innocent bystanders. People like Tiago's mother.

Again, just by existing, Tiago had made things worse.

♥

He slept on and off for nearly an entire day, awakening in the late afternoon to the sound of banging and shouting above him. Curious, he crept up a disused escape stair to the factory's rafters, from which he could peer through an open inspection hatch into the cavernous main floor.

A huge swarm of militia in riot gear were evicting the people who lived in the factory, pushing and shoving them along with shouts of *"Cai fora!"* Behind them, workmen were tearing down the wooden and fabric partitions those people had put up to divide the giant space, tossing the wreckage and the squatters' furniture into dumpsters. Other workmen were putting up lights, mounting speakers, and erecting a stage.

A man in a purple suit—his skin was purple too, his ears like fish fins—stood on the half-built stage, directing it all. *"Rápido, rápido!"* he called, clapping his webbed hands. "Get those squatters out of here! Clear out that garbage! Tonight Comando Curinga is gonna present the biggest *baile funk* Rio has ever seen!"

A *baile funk*—funk dance—was something Tiago had heard of but never experienced. They sprang up suddenly, raved for a night, and then vanished, like poisonous mushrooms. Loud, energetic, and sexy, they were places where playboys and girls from the *asfalto* mixed and mingled with the denizens of the *morros*, getting a thrilling taste of authentic *"favela* chic." And drugs . . . lots and lots of drugs. The *bailes funk* were *the* place for playboys to enjoy *maconha*, cocaine, and crack in quantity, and the bands, funded by drug gangs, performed *funk proibidão—* "prohibited" music—whose lyrics glorified the gangs and their *grandes chefes* as heroes.

He had to get away from this, and quickly. But when he went to leave, he found his alleyway and alternate exits blocked by equipment or by gangs of workmen.

He retired to his hidey-hole under the floor, where he held his ears against the thump and bang of the *baile funk* setting up above him. It would certainly be worse when the music and dancing started, but unless an opportunity appeared to slip out before the dance began, he would just have to wait it out.

♣

The music started at eleven, a vast pounding beat that made Tiago's belly feel like it was being squeezed and sent gouts of dirt down from between the floorboards. Brightly colored light swept through the cracks, and the smells of *maconha* and alcohol were strong.

And then the dancing started, right over his head, and instead of feeling squeezed he felt as though he were being stomped on by elephants.

He couldn't stay here. The noise alone would kill him.

He climbed up the rickety stairs to the rafters. The music here was nearly as loud, but the dancers' thumping feet were not so punishing, the air was fresher, and he could see what was going on.

Below Tiago a sea of bodies surged rhythmically—hair tossing, arms waving, heads pumping—thousands of people, driven to a frenzy by the music, the colored spotlights, the band's shouted lyrics, and the vast quantities of chemicals they'd ingested.

With the darkness, the smoke, and the strobing, intermittent light there was no telling whether the thrashing figures were dark or pale, *curinga* or *nat*, even male or female. There were no individuals, there was only the dance.

Even though he hated the *traficantes* who had funded and were profiting from this dance, hated the way they'd evicted so many innocent poor people to have it, hated the damage they did to the community . . . even so, as Tiago looked down on the throbbing dance floor, he realized that in this melee even a *curinga* like him could fit in. His parti-colored skin would just look like a trick of the light.

He didn't have to partake of the drugs; he could just dance and enjoy himself. He might even meet a girl. A nice girl, a kind girl, an adventurous and openhearted girl who could love a *curinga* . . .

And then the screaming started.

A wave was spreading through the crowd from somewhere below Tiago's point of view—people trying to run away from something, crashing into other people, pushing them onto the dance floor. There were enough of them, screaming loud enough, that the noise could be heard even over the pounding funk.

Then the source of the wave and the screaming came into view. It was a large group of men—*nats*, from what Tiago could see, big and brawny, wearing bulletproof vests and carrying long machine guns. They were walking in phalanx, yelling at the crowd and pushing toward the stage.

A group of burly leather-clad *curingas*—Comando Curinga soldiers—came rushing from the stage area to meet them. But the invaders had the Curingas outmaneuvered and outgunned, and they were cut down by automatic weapons fire from both sides as well as from the main, visible group. Many audience members fell as well. The music stuttered to a halt.

Panic ensued, the crowd surging back and forth, but the invaders had men at all the exits. Then one of them raised his weapon and fired a long burst into the ceiling; Tiago heard the bullets ricocheting around the rafter space. The screaming intensified.

The man who had fired his weapon pushed his way to the stage, jumped up onto it, and grabbed the microphone from the lead singer. "Shut up!" he said, his words booming across the hall along with a squeal of feedback. "Shut up shut up shut up shut *up!*" he continued, until the crowd finally did just that. "Okay, listen up!" he shouted over the remaining moans and whimpers. "We are the Amigos dos Amigos and we are taking control of this dance, this *favela*, and this *complexo*. You will all line up over here"—he gestured to his left—"and give these nice men your money and your drugs. You can keep your phones and watches; we can't be bothered."

"Fuck you!" came a voice from the back of the hall, followed by a hail of bullets. It must be the Curingas, counterattacking; apparently the Amigos hadn't gotten them all. The Amigos returned fire. The packed crowd heaved and flowed in every direction, running and climbing and crawling over one another as they tried to get away.

Tiago shook off the horrified paralysis that had overtaken him with the first gunfire. He should get to the stairs, get down to ground level, and get *out* of the building, right away.

That was what he should do.

But what he did instead was far stupider.

He jumped through the inspection hatch.

As he fell, he *pulled* with his power, harder than he'd ever pulled before. From the dumpsters in the corners of the hall, where they'd been shoved by the workmen who had cleared the squatters out, came huge quantities of trash—broken partitions, torn curtains, shattered tables and chairs— flying through the air and melding on to Tiago's plummeting body.

He hit the floor with an enormous crash, which stunned him and knocked the wind out of him. But then he shook his head and hauled himself up.

And up.

He was already twice as tall as even the biggest of the *bandido* soldiers, but he needed more. Again he pulled, and more trash sailed through the air from the dumpsters and the heaps in the corners and the piles behind the bar.

Tiago became enormous—a gigantic statue of a man made of wood and cardboard and empty drink bottles and torn posters. He stood in a bare patch of dance floor, the colored lights still swirling all around, as the crowd and both gangs scrambled to get away from him. But one of the Amigos took a shot at him as he backpedaled.

Instinctively Tiago raised a hand to protect himself. With a splintering *crack* the bullet smashed one chair-leg finger.

Tiago cried out—it hurt like a sonofabitch. But it was only wood; no matter how much their bullets had hurt his huge body of junk, the drug lords at the abandoned nightclub had not managed to injure the real body inside it. He shook the hand hard and it re-formed, pieces shifting and grinding, until it had five fingers again.

Then he reached down with the renewed hand and smacked the Amigo into the bar, where he lay still.

More Amigos opened fire on him. Or maybe they were Curingas. It didn't matter. He charged into the group, ignoring the tearing pain of the bullets striking his trash body, and picked up one *bandido* after another, flinging them into the dumpsters with the other garbage. Maybe some *catador* at the landfill would find them and make something useful of them.

Screaming from behind Tiago drew his attention. A huge wave of people was trying to leave through the front door, but they had crashed into a countercurrent: police in riot gear coming in. They were firing indiscriminately, hitting innocent audience members as well as *bandidos*.

At that Tiago's blood really boiled.

He waded through the crowd, bellowing "Out of my way!" The voice of his garbage body was tremendous, hollow, echoing. The people tried to comply, scurrying away in all directions.

Tiago met the cops and stood staring down at them. Looking stunned, they stared back at him. The crowd pulled back in a big circle around the confrontation.

"Leave these people alone!" he told them.

One cop stepped forward, leveling his rifle at Tiago. "This is police business! *Cai fora!*"

He picked the man up and shook him until the gun flew from his hands, then set him gently down. He wavered momentarily, then collapsed to the floor.

Tiago looked around, but no one else stepped forward to challenge him.

"The ones without guns haven't done anything but look for a good time," he said. "Just let them go home! The *bandidos* . . . you can do what you want with them."

A few audience members edged toward the door, reached it, sprinted into the darkness. More followed them, then more and more.

Tiago stood, hands on hips, staring down at the cops, while the crowd flowed past them. No one tried to stop them.

Soon the dance floor was mostly empty, and some of the cops were handcuffing the gang members Tiago had thrown into the dumpsters. But other cops were conferring, looking over their shoulders at him, maybe planning a concerted assault. Plainly it was time to go.

But for some reason he suddenly felt very tired.

As a matter of fact, he had to sit down right now.

He sat down harder than he'd planned, bits and fragments clattering off him as he slumped to the floor. Gently, quietly, he relaxed, his giant trash body slowly sagging into a pile of random garbage with a skinny *curinga* teenager lying in the middle of it.

Somewhere, something was dripping. Somewhere close.

That's a lot of blood, he thought, and passed out.

♠

He awoke to find himself handcuffed to the side rail of his bed.

The metal rail of the bed, in a white, sterile room that stank of antiseptics. The hand that wasn't cuffed had tubes taped to it. It itched. There were beeping noises.

The thing that had woken him up was the sound of shouting from the hall outside. He couldn't make out the words, but through the frosted glass of the door he could see several figures and much gesticulation.

Then the door opened, and a woman in an expensive suit came in. A pale woman, with lipstick and high heels. She had a briefcase. In the hall behind her, a uniformed cop and a doctor were both yelling at her.

"Take it up with my lawyers!" she told them, and slammed the door.

She closed her eyes, took in a breath, and released it. "So," she said brightly, turning to him, "I'm Cristina Moraes from the Rede Globo television network. I gather you are Tiago Gonçalves?"

"Where am I?"

"You're in the hospital. I'm told you will recover nicely, but you lost a lot of blood. The bullet nicked one of the big veins in your leg." She gestured to his leg, which he saw was elevated and bandaged. It itched too, now that she mentioned it. "You'll be here for a while yet."

So apparently one of the bullets he'd shrugged off had made it all the way through his armor of trash to the real body within. He would need to be more careful next time.

If there *was* a next time. The presence of cops and lawyers outside his hospital room implied that he was in a *lot* of trouble. "So what's going to happen to me?"

"Well, that depends on you." She set her briefcase on the bedside table, sprang open the catches, and brought out a sheaf of papers. "If you sign this contract, we will make all those pesky criminal charges go away, and you will be a contestant in season six of *Heróis Brazil*. You'll appear on television, earn a nice little weekly stipend plus expenses, and maybe win a cash prize. But the real money is in endorsements and speaking fees. Depending on how well you do in the competition, of course."

Tiago flipped through the contract . . . pages and pages of fine print. "And if I don't sign?"

She shrugged. "Then I walk out of here, and, well, whatever happens to homeless orphan *curinga* boys with big legal troubles and big medical bills . . . happens to you."

"I see." He closed the contract. "I guess I don't have much of a choice."

"I'm glad you understand." She looked at him, tapping her lower lip with one finger. "I think we'll call you . . . Garbageman."

"No," he said, and she blinked. "I don't just pick up garbage and take it away. I turn garbage into something useful. Call me O Reciclador." The Recycler.

She paused, considering. "I think we can work with that," she said. "So do we have a deal?"

"There's just one problem." He looked at the contract, and his eyes stung with tears. "I . . . I can't read. I can't even write my name."

Again the pale woman blinked. "Well. We'll have to do something about that." She held out her hand. "In the meantime, do we have a handshake agreement?"

His right hand was the one cuffed to the bed, so he shook with his left.

♠   ♥   ♦   ♣

The Elephant
in the Room

by Paul Cornell

"MY DEAR," SAID MY mother, "when your father told me you'd joined the circus and would be turning into an elephant, I had to come over immediately."

And I suppose that was true.

Mum, you see, on hearing about my biggest, though perhaps not my most prestigious, theatrical gig thus far, had decided, to my horror, to come to New York. Dad had stayed home, thank goodness. He was probably looking forward to enjoying his shed. But Mum, on being told that the New York School for the Performing Arts had placed me with the prestigious Big Apple Circus, had darted across the Atlantic like a salmon. Sorry, I should be more specific. I'm still, I suppose, not quite used to living amongst . . . I mean living *as part of* . . . a community who have special, you know, *powers*. So I should emphasize that that was a simile. My mother cannot turn into a salmon. (That is, I suppose, one of the little-talked-of features of living in a neighborhood like New York's Jokertown, where someone of one's acquaintance might actually go green with envy or fall to pieces: One has to indicate where the line of metaphor is drawn.)

I'm making this all sound so very lighthearted, aren't I?

I met Mum at JFK in the company of Maxine, a Jokertown Yellow Cab driver of my acquaintance who really *drives* her vehicle. That is to say, she runs it off her own calorie intake. This, if one can do it, is, apparently, a good deal, economically. It means that Maxine is happy to be paid in junk food, which also makes economic sense for her passengers, and makes hers the hack that jokers and poor drama students head for after the show, with a bag of White Palace and fries for change. This ability came to her suddenly, when she was a child, when she was involved in a frightening car accident, and, in that extraordinary way which makes it very clear that our brains know our bodies better than we do, managed to turn the birthday meal she'd just eaten with her loving parents into a sudden burst of automotive power that saved their lives. Long term, however, it meant she lost her family. Within the year, actually. Because that moment she used her, you know, *power* for the first time was also the moment she . . . changed. They couldn't deal. They put her up for adoption. Nobody took her. You get a lot of stories out of those children's homes that got packed with ace and joker kids back then. These days, they're the stuff of Young Adult novels, but I bet the truth of it was even more grim. People *understand*, to some degree, the original release of the wild card virus in September 1946. They *feel* for the first generation of those infected, be they powerful ace or differently bodied joker. They feel the loss of those who "drew the Black Queen" and died on the spot. They feel for the deformed and stillborn children of those infected. They're not quite as able to categorize their emotions for those of us unlucky enough to get infected in subsequent decades. The virus is still out there in the jet stream. It's been found on every continent. (At some point in my childhood it must have been drifting through rural Dorset.) Maxine, at the moment she expressed it, changed into, and now looks like . . . well, a pile of rubber tires with a pair of googly eyes on top. Okay, yes, you know, like that advertising character. I've never said it out loud within earshot of her. That would be cruel. She makes reference to it every now and then, a nod out of the window when we pass a hoarding: "That's my dad." She says tourists who've come to gawk at the jokers sometimes go, "No, really?!"

My mother, however, rolled her luggage on wheels to the edge of the sidewalk in the airport pick-up area, and when Maxine got out of the cab to help her with it, went way beyond any awkwardness and into the land of outright social horror. She saw Maxine and screamed.

I had to basically wrestle her into the cab, while looking desperately around to make sure there weren't any jokers about who might be offended. Maxine was silent all through the journey back, while Mum was a stream of "Honestly, darling, you can't blame me, we don't *have* jokers in Dorset. I thought I was *dreaming*. I was prepared for your joker friends to be horrifyingly ugly monsters, not, I'm sure *charming*, if rather disconcerting, giant, blobby, vastly *flexible*, to fit in that seat up front, I mean you *must* be . . ." And this was all without the slightest forensic trace of guilt, as if we all yelled about this stuff all the time at the top of our voices in Jokertown.

"Maxine doesn't self-identify as a joker," I told her, my voice already a hiss. "She thinks of herself as an *ace*: someone with *useful* powers."

"Ah, of course, because jokers are your actual *monsters*," said Mum, "who can't do anything useful."

I stared at her, once again horrified by the prospect of taking this woman into my ghetto. "Except . . . sometimes they can, and very few of them self-identify as *monsters*—"

"So it's all a bit of a mess, classification-wise? How very American, not to have proper names for what things are. And what *is* this 'self-identify' business you keep on about?"

"It's about how they want to see themselves!"

"Darling," she said, "I'd like to see myself as Keira Knightley, but it's what the world sees that matters, isn't it? Hey, with your own, you know—"

"My *powers*."

"Yes, yes, well, you'll be picking up a bit of Maxine's *power*, won't you, how did you put it? 'Like hi-fi'?"

"*Wi-Fi*."

"Yes, that! I mean you'll be sort of automatically catching on to what she's doing—"

"Unless I stop myself," I emphasized. "I can do that now."

"Well, well done darling, but don't stop yourself right now, because surely, if you're doing it too, you're contributing to keeping this car moving." She saw the look of befuddlement on my face and sighed, speaking as if to a toddler. "So you'll be contributing to the petrol money! I think we should negotiate a discount." She turned to start doing just that, but before she could I decided I had to put the possibility of being thrown out of the cab before my own comforts and make the ultimate sacrifice.

"Mum," I asked quickly, "how are my aunts?"

Which immediately distracted her onto her favorite subject, a conversation which was only dangerous to my nerves rather than to my health. My, you know, *power*, if you haven't read the reports of what happened, is that I pick up other peoples' powers (yes, like Wi-Fi) and start expressing them myself, utterly randomly. Well, until the last few weeks, when, as I said, I've managed to gain a level of control. But still, if I'm caught unaware, if, let's say, an ace passes me in the street, and their power is that they can turn into a pile of goo, well, there I suddenly am, a pile of goo with a sign saying GOLF SALE stuck in it. As happened that one time when I was, erm, between acting engagements. It took all my willpower then to literally pull myself together as the ace, unaware that it was all about proximity for me, and not *noticing* goo when it was *other* people, dawdled nearby, getting himself a coffee, passing the time of day. I ran the risk of being lapped up by a small dog, until I managed to rear up at it. And of course, once reintegrated, I was atop my clothes rather than in them. As happens to me rather too often for my taste. My taste in those matters would actually tend toward the not at all.

I'm distracting myself. Like I won't have to finish this if I do that. Like it won't have happened, then. Sorry. Anyway. I was able to just about ignore mother's usual drone about what the aunts were doing back in Dorset, all of which was, as usual, formidably dull. But she segued out of that into her equally doleful round up of cousins and distant relatives the provenance of which remained a mystery, while New York, bloody incredible New York, which she'd never seen before, sailed past the windows like an in-flight movie. I had to lower my own window to get some early autumn air in my face to stay awake. Just as Mum started talking about the sleeping pills which had got her through that terrible flight. She was intending to use them to manage her awful jet lag. I was already feeling that, of Mum and I, only one of us was going to survive the next few days, and that it was going to be me, frankly, because I already wanted to murder her with a crowbar, just bash it across the back of her latest stupid hat, time after time after—

Sorry. I really need to calm down. Just thinking about the start of all this makes me so . . . well, there I am now. I'm angry. Which is better than sad, I suppose. But it's such an impotent anger. At how things worked out. At how things are. When I don't think they have to be. They really don't. No, let's not go there. Not yet, anyway. Not until I have to.

Sorry. As I think I already said. Many times, probably.

Hello. My name is Abigail Baker.

I am a serious actor.

Until just before the landing of my mother, I'd been having the summer of my life (apart from being arrested and accidentally publicly naked quite a few times during it), working at the Bowery Repertory in Jokertown, the lovely Old Rep, on loan from the School, and making my debut as a stand-in. . . . But actually, you may well have read about that, as I said.* It was all over the media, for all the wrong reasons. In the end Mr. Dutton, the theater owner, got a team of lawyers involved, and I didn't even have to spend a single night behind bars, though I do now, technically, have a criminal record. And, erm, a suspended sentence. Well, several. Anyhow, now the Old Rep's autumn season was approaching, and with it the end of my placement there, and, having shown me off to the audience in a range of parts that frankly hadn't stretched my talent to its rawest extremes, Mr. Dutton had, rather too quickly to my mind, agreed

*Possibly in *Fort Freak*, in which Abigail makes her first appearance.

to the Circus asking to benefit from my newfound notoriety when it came to my last role before the new school year began.

They actually asked for me. I don't know if my mum ever got that, or if it just added to it for her.

Anyway, that was another reason why I wasn't entirely comfortable with her being in New York. I'd covered up all that unpleasantness, to her, with euphemism, made easier by the positive spin the joker-friendly elements of the media had given it. I'd sent her all the right press cuttings and crossed my fingers about whether or not the sort of newspapers my mother reads would take an interest. That was all I had to worry about. Mum doesn't do online media. She once, prompted by her favorite columnist, called me up to warn me that Facebook could literally kill me where I stood. As it turned out, she hadn't ever quite been aware of the me-being-arrested part. She does tend to mention these things if she hears about them. So that was fine. It joined the encyclopedia of details concerning my life of which my mother was unaware. On the day of which I speak, for instance, I had concealed any of my tattoos that might be visible with several layers of foundation.

But there was one big thing I hadn't told her about. One big thing who, when Maxine angrily thumped Mum's luggage onto the sidewalk in front of my humble apartment building, was waiting inside. Because he'd insisted. Because he was strung out to the point of distraction and kept grabbing my hands and urging me that since we were together, he wanted my parents to know we were together, wanted them to see he was a good guy. I hadn't said to him that that wasn't exactly true. I'd have meant it as a good thing, but right now I didn't know how he'd take it. I didn't know how he'd take anything. I looked up at the building, wondering how this was going to go.

"So," said Mum, completely ignoring Maxine standing there staring at the packet of mints she'd offered her as a fare, "remind me, darling, when's your first public appearance as an elephant?"

"Tomorrow afternoon," I said, trying to indicate to Maxine with mere expression that, next time, I'd bring her at least a hamper. "At the matinee. And that's great, I thought you were going to say something about where I lived."

"Oh my dear, I wouldn't dream of hurting you like that. That's why I said something irrelevant to the moment, you see, to distract us both. But now you've spoiled that little act of grace on my part. You never were one for the social niceties." She glanced back to Maxine. "You know, your friend should come to the circus with you, she'd get straight on the bill.

She'd do so well. Bouncy bouncy!" And with an engaging grin, like this was the best idea ever, she actually made a motion like a trampoline.

My mother had told me that she liked circuses. And, she'd said on the phone, also elephants. I didn't wonder at the time that she'd never mentioned that before. She told me then that she and Dad had met at a circus. That they were there with their parents. I imagined at the time that, with the austerity of Britain in decades past, said Big Top probably consisted of three mice, a spoonful of jam, and a man in an interesting hat. And that my mum, even at such a young age, would have spent the evening telling my putative dad at horrifying length about what her mother's sisters were up to. But now I wonder if that story was even true.

Anyway. Sorry. My expression to Maxine gained several extra dimensions, to the point where I hoped it intimated that next time I saw her I would provide her with nothing short of a feast. Finally, she just shrugged, her arms bouncing off her sides, and got sulkily back into her cab. Mother looked to me with an expression that said her words had once again fallen, inexplicably, on stony ground, and rolled her noisy luggage toward the front door of my block. Where, to my increasing worry, a greater class of horror awaited us.

◆

His name, and I'm pretty sure it's his real one, is Croyd Crenson. He was infected by the wild card virus in 1946, and since the events I mentioned that you might have already read about, with the being arrested and the nudity and everything, he'd been, erm, my boyfriend. He doesn't look his age. He just looks as if he has ten years or so on me. Okay, maybe twenty. All right, listen, if it was a thing on my part, it was not that much of a thing, compared to being made of rubber or having the ability to reduce oneself to goo. That's something else I've realized about the people who live in Jokertown: Their notion of what's socially acceptable for nats (sorry, I mean, noninfected people) extends quite a way beyond what's okay for those living elsewhere. It's all about what one is surrounded with, what one has as a background to compare oneself to. That, and the low rents, is what makes Jokertown such a vibrant, diverse, Bohemian environment. (That is to say, as Mum would translate it, there are a lot of gay and transsexual people here too. Actually, that's probably not how she'd translate it.)

But, sorry, I was talking about Croyd Crenson. As I probably will be for the rest of my life, now. Croyd has not always been on the right side of the law. And that was very much the situation that summer. The trouble we'd been in, as you may have read, had a lot to do with his then-current ability to multiply objects (and, luckily for me concerning one particular escape from the police, people) with a touch of his hand. He had been using that for nefarious purposes involving DVDs.

I should have realized that something terrible was approaching (other than my mother) when, three weeks before her anticipated arrival, Croyd had appeared on my doorstep with flowers. They were beautiful, and he looked especially charming with his awkward, sad smile beside the blooms. Though his teeth were chattering even then. Croyd isn't one for grand romantic gestures. He's been alive long enough to know that it's the small things that matter: the way he understands a person, and wants to know about that person, and gives that person, if they're me, space to talk. And talk. He is, actually, rather the silent type, now I think of it, although maybe that was just because he was with me—

Oh dear. Oh, I'm crying now. Sorry. Sorry. So stupid.

Anyway. Where was I? Right. Right.

That night, he took me out to this backstreet Italian joker place. Its decor was a combination of Sicily and the kind of twisted outsider tattoo-parlor chic that young jokers in New York had developed, that showed up in mainstream design in ways which made you wonder if said jokers were impressed or pissed off. Lady Gaga having the former effect, of course. Her concerts in Jokertown itself, with free admission for jokers, meant she could plaster her videos with orange and purple swirls if she liked. Croyd knew the owner, like he seemed to know everyone dodgy in New York City, so we got a table on our own, and had the food shown to us by the waiters as they sloped or skittered or flapped out to their customers.

Croyd put his hands on the tablecloth and visibly controlled their twitching. He didn't quite manage to make them stop. The speed of his breathing, in the last few days, had started to worry me. It was all the amphetamines he was taking. Looking back, I'd started to feel nervous around him, not to anticipate his visits with unbridled delight. I could feel him, whenever he put his arm in mine or his hand on my waist, treating me deliberately carefully, like one day he might treat me otherwise. It had started to be like he took a deep breath before I opened my door. But on the flip side of that, the release of that, when I gave him license, in intimate situations, to let all that energy loose . . . yes, well, I think you get the idea.

I suppose he made me feel a lot better about myself. Being with him kind of made one a lady, without anyone ever having to use the word. I hate to say this is true, but I suppose he really was something from the past that I'd tried to escape, that had reached out to me and said I was okay. And at the same time he was something from my new world of jokers and aces, who had helped me to accept being one of that community, to stop standing quite so nervously apart from it. He listened to all my emo bollocks, because, unlike every other man I'd ever met, he seemed to soak up how people felt about one another, seemed to enjoy hearing about it, particularly when it was about me and him. Even when he started to get jittery and raging and paranoid, he still stopped and listened. He made himself do that for me. And he made his own rules, but was nonetheless honorable, outside the law rather than against it, you know, the bad boy thing. But that so minimizes what he was to me.

After dark, we would go for walks in Central Park. People say it's dangerous at night, but we never felt threatened there. We could always make more trees to hide behind or more stones to throw. Or I could reach out into the brilliant shining city above us and call over someone else's useful power. We never had to do any of that.

I often think New York feels like it does, natural and full of energy and about and for people, because it reminds us all of something from our evolution: We scurry about at the foot of what seem like enormous trees, and we've got this clearing in the middle to rush out into and play and fight and change. You see so many jokers there, day and especially night, like that forest clearing is even there for this latest direction of evolution. And we were jokers too. We were part of the night, and so not threatened by it. We sat on benches, and we talked, or I suppose I did while he looked at me.

I see that look in my memory now. It's still a good thing.

And then we would go back to my apartment and shag like bunnies. And nobody ever says that at this point in stories, but they really should. They really should.

Oh dear. There I go again. Sorry.

He looked up from his hands, at that table in that restaurant that night. "The thing is, kid," he said (and I would hate it with a passion if anyone else called me that), "in this next couple of weeks, you don't know how extreme I'm going to get."

I watched his hands as I always did, as his fingertips went to absentmindedly stroke the stem of his wine glass, well, not that absentmindedly, or he'd have found himself with several wine glasses. And so would I have, except that I was managing to hold a place in my head back from his now very familiar, very intimate power. "You've told me," I said. "You need the speed to keep you awake—"

"—And I become a different person because of it. Irritable. Cranky. Sometimes . . . terrifying. That's a word people have used. You haven't seen that. I haven't let you see that. Not yet." I realized with a little jolt that he'd interrupted me. He never did that. "But that's not what I wanted to talk to you about. You know that next time I go to sleep—"

"You'll wake with a new . . . you know . . ."

"Power, yeah." He hadn't been to sleep since I'd met him. I'd wake up in the night, and he'd be sitting up in bed beside me, reading these terrible 1950s crime novels. He once told me he was trying to catch up with all the books from his youth. "That's actually what my own power is. Sleeping. Every time I sleep, my DNA gets rewritten by the virus, and I wake up with a new power. But—" He held up a hand to stop me saying I knew all this. "What I haven't told you is, two other things might happen."

"You might wake up as a joker?" I guessed.

"Yeah. I might wake up with claws or no face or oozing sores, and you'd have to stop yourself getting those too. How you'd feel about that?"

I actually felt annoyed. I think I got that he was testing me. Although I don't know how conscious that ever was for him. But at the time I thought I knew everything that was on that table. "I'd still—" And then I quickly changed what I was going to say. Because neither of us had used that word. Yet. "I'd still feel the same way about you. How could you think I wouldn't? If I'm okay with our joker friends—!"

"Yeah, yeah, but—"

"And if it was that terrible for you, you could just go back to sleep and draw another card, right?"

He paused. He took a deep breath. "Okay, here's the thing. You might have wondered why I've stayed awake so long—"

"I thought you were just finding the duplication thing, you know, useful."

He laughed. And there was an edge to it. "I don't want to lose you, Abi. I don't want to lose you by turning into some horrible monster—"

"But I've said you won't! Don't say that word!"

"And I don't want to lose you by dying."

I stared at him.

"Every time I go to sleep, Abi, I risk drawing the black queen. It's like playing Russian roulette. One day I won't wake up. That's why I stay awake as long as I can before I start hating the way the speed makes me. That's why this time I've stayed awake . . . longer than ever."

"Because of me."

"Yeah." His eyes searched my face.

I hoped I was looking back at him like he needed me to look. I took his hands in mine, and held one of them to my face. If I felt I could have gotten away with it in public, I'd have held it to my breast. "Listen," I said, "you could get hit by a bus. Or, this being New York, probably a cab. Thank you for telling me the risks. But this changes nothing."

He smiled. And yet there was something not quite satisfied about that smile. "You're young," he said. And then he looked up and realized we hadn't been served and let go my hand and started yelling for the waiter. We walked in the park that night, but, looking back, it was more like a march.

♥

We didn't talk about it after that. We both knew where we stood. I found myself accepting the thought that I was a military girlfriend. That my love might vanish forever when he closed his eyes. Or I wonder if I did accept it. I wonder if I got there?

He would arrive at my doorstep with bruises and wave away what happened. "Just some stupid guy, you should see him."

He would get angry at some memory of the past, pacing and raging, "and then he said, this was in 1962, then he said—!" And then he'd realize I was standing there listening to him in silence, and he would make himself stop, panting.

The worst time was when he went to the window and said he thought he could hear police out there on the ledge. And then he looked at me as if he was using me to check on whether or not what he was saying was sane. And then he broke into a terrible false laugh, and clapped his hands at his own "joke" and headed off, saying he needed a drink, and I didn't see him for two days and I thought he'd died.

♣

I should have canceled Mum's visit. If I could. She might have just shown up anyway. It was only because Croyd insisted so hard, insisted like it was a dying man's last request, that I didn't. He was trying so desperately to hang on to something. He so needed to be that decent, upright guy for me. I see that now.

♠

Mother walked into the apartment and was confronted by the sight of Croyd, obviously at home there (though he actually wasn't, we were still in our separate messy apartments), finishing up washing the dishes. Thanks to Maxine's rage-fueled, literally, driving, we were, I realized, a few minutes early. "Mrs. Baker," he said, drying his hands and then holding one out to her, keeping it steady through what I could see was sheer willpower. "Croyd Crenson. It's a pleasure to meet you."

Mother looked at him as if he were a burglar. At that time, Croyd didn't look anything other than nat, though maybe there was something a little too intense about those eyes. Even without the drugs. He was wearing a vest and braces, like something glamorous from a 1940s movie, with his hair slicked back. Mum looked to me without taking his hand. "Who's he?"

I took a deep breath.

"Oh no," she said.

That sound of genuine anguish and despair in her voice may have been the most terrible thing I ever . . . No, actually, it wasn't. But at that moment, it was. I looked to Croyd, afraid that he'd be furious. But he'd kept that pleasant, fixed smile on his face.

"Croyd is my . . ." I had been going to say "boyfriend." But that suddenly seemed such a small, childish word. And the last thing I wanted to feel then was childish. But what? "Lover"? "Partner"?

Croyd didn't step in to help me. It wasn't that he was waiting to hear me describe him for the first time. It was, I think, that he realized that if he butted in, it would look like he'd provided the definition, that he had maybe coerced me into that way of seeing things. Holding on to his kindness, on that ledge above such a drop.

"We're . . . together," I finished.

Mother turned back to him and looked him up and down. "What are you?" she said, as if she were being shown round the zoo.

"Parched," said Croyd, "do you want a G&T as much as I do?"

"I mean—"

"I know what you mean." And that was still so jolly. "What are *you*?"

"Normal."

"Well, hey, me too."

"Oh." She visibly relaxed, as if she'd been told anything meaningful. "Well, *that's* a relief." And she actually took his hand.

I was about to bellow with righteous anger, but eye contact from Croyd stopped me.

"You'll have to forgive me," she said. "I'm just surprised that my daughter never mentioned you."

"She was worried that you might not approve."

She smiled *so* broadly. "I think, actually, I will have that G&T. Now, darling, where are your facilities?"

While she went to the bathroom, I followed Croyd into the alcove I laughingly called a kitchen. "You let her believe—!"

"I will explain the misunderstanding and tell her my true nature. Once she's got used to me. Okay?" And the tone in his voice, for the first time ever to me, sounded like he didn't want to hear any arguments.

◆

The Big Apple Circus stands on Eighth and Thirty-Fifth. It's not that huge a building, but that's kind of what makes the BAC authentic: It's a classic, one-ring circus. As I'd discovered, from rehearsing with them for the last few weeks, the joy of actors at their comradeship and tradition, and especially about those situations where they find themselves in a rep company, is to be felt also in the troupe of a serious circus. Clowns aren't scary when they've devoted their life to their craft, and can project helplessness and pathos past their makeup to make kids squeal with laughter that's about a shared impotence. That fear of them that's arisen in the last few years: That's the product of a world that started accepting second-rate clowns. The Big Apple's joker clowns are especially something to see, not concealing their differences, but using them as props. This isn't a freak show. It's about traditional joker skills, used as they've been used in circuses since the 1950s. On the morning of my debut, I got to the circus at seven, as usual, for my last rehearsal. Mum had departed for her hotel thankfully early the night before, popping a pill and succumbing to the jet lag I'd so desperately hoped for. Croyd had come to the end of his charming ability to listen to stories the protagonists of which he'd neither met nor heard of. But he'd remained resolutely charming, though I was proud he never nodded at her more ridiculous political assertions.

"Meet me for lunch tomorrow," she said to him on the way out to her taxi, "and then we can attend Abigail's debut performance together. I feel we should get to know each other." He'd agreed and feigned enthusiasm.

But after the door closed, and we'd heard the taxi drive off, he ran at the wall and kicked it, so hard I feared for his toes. "People like that—!" he yelled. "How is *she* your mother?!"

I told him about how distant I felt from the ancient and immobile forces that Mother represented. How she always tried to control what I did. I reassured him that we'd fooled her, that he'd done fine. And finally, his heart beating through his chest against my palm, he calmed.

I tried to sleep as he tried not to. He was listening on headphones to jazz that I couldn't help but hear seeping out, as if from some great distance. The man who never slept in the city that did likewise. The saxophone and the little lights way out there finally got into my head and I was unconscious. Which was just as well, because this hadn't been the greatest preparation for my first performance. But we'd both known it would be like this.

Next morning that taut look on his face was one notch more haunted. "Break a leg," he said when I was dressed and ready to go. I kissed him. I held him hard. "You too," I said.

Radha O'Reilly was waiting for me at the performers' entrance. She looks like a petite, incredibly fit fiftysomething (though I hear she's a lot older), with the sort of golden biceps that, to my eyes, demand a bit of ink. But that's not something I ever could say to her, because I'm a bit in awe of her. You'll appreciate the reasons why: She's been a famous ace for decades now, Elephant Girl, someone who walked out into the spotlight and declared who she was before there were the ace and joker communities and celebrities of today. She was the first person who turned into an elephant onstage and expected people to see it as entertainment rather than horror. Today I was to be the second.

"Okay this morning?" she said.

What she meant was, was I receiving her power, and was I able to control it? That was why she always met me outside, so we wouldn't be in a confined space for that moment. I'd been feeling her power from halfway down the street, in that way that I'd used to find so horribly intimate that the first few times I'd come to rehearse I'd been all kind of blushy when I got there. It was true that what we were going to do that afternoon, then that night, then eight times a week was, if anything went wrong, vastly dangerous. But I'd never felt able to ask her if she felt I was the newbie, still likely to mess up, or an actor only trying to be a circus pro, or someone that had been foisted on her, because of my new-found bums-on-seats value, or even if I was any good. She had an utter calm about her that made one both desperately not want to flap around in front of her, and yet more likely to do so at any moment. There goes that language again: Flapping around in front of her was exactly what I was there to do.

I told her I was fine, she finished her none-blacker coffee, and we went inside.

♥

"My mother's going to be in the audience," I said, as we stood in the empty ring, me aching all over after the rehearsal.

Radha looked sidelong at me, taking this new factor onboard. Realizing, I think, that I was letting something out by saying it. "Does that add to the pressure?"

"I suppose."

"Only, I was wondering why you seemed distracted—"

What, distracted enough to dump me at the last moment and send the clown car out a second time? "No! No, there's . . . you know, stuff going on in my life. But when I'm up there, I'm completely focused."

She rolled athletically onto her back, and lay there on the sawdust, looking up through the safety net that we knew would be totally inadequate for our own protection this afternoon, but was entirely to make the audience feel that they were watching something only reasonably death defying. "I do this for my mother, you know."

Feeling a little awkward, I sat stiffly down beside her. "In my case, it's kind of in spite of."

"My mother was on the *Queen Mary* in 1946. The death ship. She was transformed by the virus. She grew thick gray skin. People are still shocked by the pictures of her, but to me that's just Mum. I never heard her voice. I always wanted to. She'd never recorded herself when she was a nat. Dad stayed with her, while the rest of the world threw up their hands and backed away. They were taken in by this cult, back home in India. You'd see this awkward relationship between Dad and the priests. He loved Chandra, but they *worshipped* her. She took it, being seen as a kind of holy object, because, well, we needed a home, this was the only place we could live in peace. She had me seven months after the virus. She had a choice in that. Nobody was sure if she would survive the pregnancy. But they wanted me so much, they always told me that. My mother sacrificed so much, without being able to say a word."

It took me a moment to be able to speak. "That sounds like . . . the opposite of my mother. I think she'd find some . . . horrible words to describe yours."

"What, you're setting me up for meeting her today, all the while thinking of her like that?"

"Would you prefer it if I lied?"

"Well, she is your mother. Perhaps she deserves some falsehoods being told on her behalf. None of us can really judge our parents. I don't believe in karma, but . . ." She shook her head quickly and changed the subject. "I have to introduce you tonight. Have you chosen your ace name?"

"I sometimes think . . . The Understudy."

She considered it, flatteringly seriously. "I like the humility of that. But you'll need to know when to become the lead. You'll need to be strong enough to make that change and have people accept it."

I felt ridiculously close to tears. I shouldn't have got into such a serious conversation with everything that was hanging over my head. I needed to keep a distance. "I'm not ready yet. Nowhere near."

"Not after today?"

"Of course not."

She nodded, pleased again. "Have you told your mother your real name?"

I couldn't even shake my head.

"Before we go on," she said, "decide your name."

♣

This next part of what happened is something that I can only tell you about secondhand, from what Croyd told me when he called me that afternoon. And yet it's the most important thing. So you'll have to accept my memories of his memories. He went over everything several times. The sound of his voice scared me from the moment I took the call. "I have to tell you," he said, "I have to tell you before you see her again. She swore me to secrecy, and I said yes, I don't know why I said yes—"

I was frightened that I was talking to someone who wasn't the man I knew anymore. I also knew, instantly, that she'd done that to him. That the rocklike tradition of what she was had put a hole in him and he was sinking. I said, "Don't tell me, let me come and see you," but he started yelling at me that my career was the most important thing, that I had to stay there and get ready, and he made me swear to keep that promise. Finally, I managed to get him to tell me what happened, and here it is, for you, through all the distortions.

He'd taken Mum out for lunch at an excellent diner he knew in Greenwich Village, one where the dodginess was a little more under the surface than usual, and which had, to use his words, "A billion kinds of coffee, 'cause that always impresses you Brits."

"I'd just like to say," he said, holding her chair for her, "I'm charmed by how open-minded you've been about your daughter and me. I think she's a peach." He frowned at her reaction. "That's a good thing."

"You talk," she said, "like you're from my father's generation. Why is that?"

He'd shrugged. He didn't want to lie again to her, when he'd been going to tell the truth.

"What do you do for a living?"

"Recently I've been a DVD wholesaler. Before that, I was an importer. And I've been known to dabble in the security business." He coughed as the waiter brought them the coffee.

"The sort of thing a con man would say."

Again, he was forced to silence, cornered.

"Your daughter's got a delightful power—"

"Ah, I was wondering if she'd told you. Please don't use that like it's a key to unlock the mysteries of my own approval. Abigail is *infected*. It's a medical condition, not a political cause. I mean, look at her, look what's become of her! I had to come over and see what she'd sunk to. Because I still care about her, you see."

He hadn't expected this. He'd just stared at her.

"Here she is, an exile from her home, because of what people there would say, living in a ghetto—"

"She came to New York for Broadway—!"

"An excuse for when you've lost a life of comfort and ease, and have been reduced to scraping a living by performing as a *freak* in a *circus*."

"She is *not a freak!*"

"And neither are you."

"No!"

"And that's why you lied to me. When you told me you were normal."

And suddenly Croyd was trying, and failing, to hold a dozen full cups of coffee. Like a clown. It burst all over the table. It stained the cloth, it covered his clothes, it burnt him. It missed Mum completely.

"Tell me everything," she said. "I might be sympathetic to your plight."

That's all he told me of the conversation. It was only later I learned there was more to it. I stood there beside the ring with my phone in my hand, shaking. "I thought . . . she was proud of me," I said. I managed to swallow down the end of that sentence. And then I hated myself almost as much as I hated her. "Where is she now?"

"Shopping. We're still going to come to the show together. I don't know why I said yes. I kept thinking about you—"

I hate being angry. I hate rows. I hate people grandstanding like that. I hate disruption. I hate that my mum drags me into all that. "I don't want her here. I don't want to *see* her—"

"Absolutely. You want it, I can get some of the guys to put her in the back of a cab and make sure she gets on a plane."

"Yes. Yes, that's great, do it!"

"Some of those guys I know. Who make sure of things. And you know she's not going to make it easy, she's going to push them. And then they might . . . reciprocate."

"Fine."

He gave up with that. He was just about yelling at me now. As if he was scared that neither of us could seem to find a way to stop the inevitability of all this. The inevitability. It only seems like that now. "And then, what, you're estranged from her? Cut off? You don't have a family no more?"

"I don't *now!*"

♠

I went backstage for costume and makeup. Alice, the makeup lady, had to ask me to relax my face, because she wasn't going to be able to fill in the frown lines otherwise. I managed not to have her have to cope with tears. It was just basic stage makeup, and my costume was a deliberately ordinary frock and dark glasses. Covering up the tats hadn't just been for my mother's benefit.

Radha, in her colorful, loose-fitting stage costume, was waiting for me outside. She looked at me, understood something, and took my hands in hers. "Breathe," she said.

I breathed.

"We're doing this for the audience. We owe them our best performance."

I managed to nod.

"Whatever this new crisis is, you have to put it behind you. For your own sake."

I managed to share a smile with her. I was already there, actually. Or I thought it was. Performing is my home, and I was deciding it was also going to be my family. It and Croyd.

"But most important of all, remember this: If you don't manage to put it out of your mind, and mess up up there, I will fucking *kill* you."

And that was said with such an enormous grin on her face, and such steely eyes, that I was right back to being overawed again. And that took something serious in my brain and fixed it there for the future. Because that was professionalism. There it was. "Understudy," I said, helplessly.

She shook her head. "No. Oh well. I'll just have to name you."

I couldn't find anything to say.

I hurried out toward the side door to join the queue.

♦

That was the plan, you see, for me to head into the venue with the rest of the audience, anonymously. I'd been provided with a ticket that would place me in just the right seat. I hesitated on the corner, looking at the line, worried that I'd join it at just the point Croyd and Mother did. But no, there they were, Croyd rolling his head to try and ease the tension, Mum looking pointedly at him and then all around, as if she was worried to be seen with him. As if the scales of right and wrong there were the other way round. Neither of them knew what the details of the act were going to be.

I joined the back of the queue and, desperately trying to put everything else out of mind, headed in with everyone else.

♥

I took care to sense, as the four sides of bleachers around the ring filled up, if anyone else with, you know, powers, had entered. There were two, both deuces. That is, they had useless powers. One of them could turn her hands different colors, the other one had complete control over the style of his moustache. I relaxed, let my power harmlessly flirt with theirs. My palms ran through a range of hues, my top lip itched, but I didn't let it sprout. If one of the audience had turned out to have a major power I couldn't deal with the presence of, I had a number ready to call on my mobile, and they'd have been led out, with gifts and a refund, before Radha's act. The circus authorities had obviously heard about my earliest experiences in professional theater.

I sat through the clowns, who were a fast-moving bundle of acrobatic sight gags that made the children and a lot of the adults in the audience squeal with laughter. None from me. My gaze, in the moments when the lights were up, had found Croyd and my mother in the crowd. She was looking prim, her mouth a line, suggesting a smile but not being one. I sat through a joker high wire act, the Flying Crustaceans, who used their pincers to snap from trapeze to trapeze. And I thought about me and, you know, love.

When I was in my teens, I'd been too focused on getting away from Dorset and the weight of history there to have much in the way of romance. By which I mean there was, you know, stuff, of the usual kind, involving cider and boys who drove tractors. But I always had one hand reaching out ready to extricate myself. I'd fallen in with Croyd like it was going to be the obvious, central relationship of my entire life, not, like these things seemed to be with some of my classmates at the School, a test drive, the first of maybe many. Maybe I was a bit old-fashioned like that. Made by my mum. There was a terrible thought. I absolutely did not want to be. Had she been right that I'd run here not *to* something but *from* something? I thought about the times when my family had met other families from my parents' class, what their looks had meant, what the lack of party invitations had meant, why I'd ended up only with boys who drove tractors and never those who bought them.

Well. Maybe the bitch was right about some things.

The lights went up on the ring once more, revealing Radha standing there. "Ladies and gentlemen!" she called out. And the audience was silent. And she didn't need a mike. "You may have heard of me. You may think you know everything about me. You know I can do . . . this!" The lights flickered as the back-up generators kicked in, helping the grid handle the sudden demand for power. This was why the show had that sign outside saying no audience members with pacemakers allowed. The BAC had had to rent some serious megawattage to avoid blacking out whole city blocks. With a dramatic gesture, Radha's body suddenly contorted and the space around her did too, like reality had just done a magic trick with a folded handkerchief. Her garment burst from her in a moment which managed to be (and I'm told you can see it slowed down to individual frames on YouTube) both alluring and modest at the same time. She spun to a halt on the spot, taking up much of the ring, in her new form, that of a full-sized Asiatic elephant.

"And," continued her voice, now a recording being played over the speakers, "you probably know I can do . . . this!" And with an impossibly graceful upward leap, and a single flap of her enormous ears, the elephant that was Radha took to the air. She soared straight up, to the top of the big top, then managed, the band striking up a boisterous tune with shrieking electric guitar as she did so, to turn that into an elegant spiral, flashing over the audience, heading down and down, faster and faster. They started to applaud wildly, because most of them, being tourists, although they had probably heard of Radha's power, wouldn't have seen it live before. I didn't applaud, though. Playing my part, I folded my arms over my chest, looking glum. This was not hard.

"But did you know," the recording continued, "that I can also do . . . this!" And as she swung her third turn down toward me, she tensed her trunk, raised it above her head, and then straightened it suddenly in my direction.

The blast of water hit me right in the face.

At that same moment I let down my guard and let her power take me.

We'd practiced this move for weeks, with dummies in the seats around me. (Which had, actually, each been moved an inch farther away from mine.) I took the flight power a tiny instant before I took the transformation. My human feet sprang upward a moment before my body above them burst into its new elephantine shape. My carefully weakened clothes sprang apart, to reveal nothing much in that nanosecond, I really hoped, because I didn't want that to become, you know, my signature move. To the audience, especially to those screaming in horror and glee nearby, it seemed that one of their number had suddenly exploded into being a flying elephant—

—who spiralled up to join, exactly as we'd rehearsed ten times a day, Radha, the two of us flying around the ring equidistantly. She was waving her trunk playfully, suggesting she could do it to many more of the audience too, and the clowns were running about putting up umbrellas over people. "No," cried out the recording, "you're quite safe. Ladies and gentlemen, may I present Abigail Baker, The Actor!" And there was applause as, perhaps with some relief, the audience remembered that I was that girl they'd heard about and, oh yes, they'd wondered what I was going to be doing in the show.

And she'd named me in that instant. Like something out of *The Jungle Book*. In the recording she'd made just before we went on. But I only really paid attention to that later.

Because as I sped above them, I kept looking at Croyd and Mother. Looking and looking. Round and round. Spiralling gradually downward. He was applauding, yelling, bellowing, loving me. Though he'd never used that word.

She was nodding, sighing, acknowledging that this was the best I could do in these sad circumstances. I was such a disappointment to her.

I couldn't help it. I say that, but I know I could have. What was meant to happen now was that Radha and I were supposed to spiral in toward each other, clasp trunks, spin around until the moment it looked like we were going to fly up and hit the ceiling, then change back and fall, naked in the moment before the lights went out, into the net. Costumes would be thrown to us, and donned in the moment before we somersaulted out of the net and onto the sawdust to take our bows.

That's what should have happened.

I got that expression of my mother's locked into my head, bigger and bigger, on every circuit of the room. All her condescension, and all my guilt and anger, always in my way, time after time. And here I was doing this incredible, beautiful thing, here I was, strong and famous and adult, and it was *never* going to be acknowledged, not from this woman whose acknowledgment would have meant everything. To her, all this was shameful. My love was shameful. And so in the end was I.

And I proved her right.

I swear, I just wanted to knock that stupid hat off her head.

I swung deliberately an inch lower. I extended one of my enormous elephant feet as I saw her turning to look up toward me as I approached, looking perhaps a little bored now. Croyd realized a second before she did. He started to yell no.

Him looking scared in that second . . . him starting to cry out in horror, the sudden expression of the fear that had been hanging over us, the things we weren't talking about . . . I think I must have instinctively reached out to him in that second, mentally. I think I must have connected us. For the last time. Because what his power really is, like he said . . . It's sleeping.

I suddenly found a terrible shuddering fatigue grabbing my body. I realized, as the audience before me became a screaming dreamscape of surreal clowns, that I was somehow—

Falling asleep.

With my last conscious thought, I managed to use the power of flight that was about to leave me to throw myself sideways.

I could feel myself spinning as time slowed down to a crawl. It was half a dream, half adrenaline trying desperately to keep me awake as I spun toward those hard bleachers and the flesh and bone of anyone I might connect with in a high-speed crash.

Something grabbed me from behind. And threw me with the strength of an elephant.

And there was Croyd throwing himself forward out of the seats, heaving clowns out of the way, and diving for the safety net. For so much more safety net. Than there had been. In a different place. And he was right underneath me now! If I was still an elephant when I landed—!

♣

I woke up in a hospital. I scrambled up, shouting, demanding to know if everyone was all right—! And standing there at the end of my bed wasn't Croyd or my mother . . . just Radha.

"Nobody got hurt," she said. "You included."

After a moment I was able to talk again. "That was sheer luck," I said finally. "It was all my fault."

"Yes," she said.

"Understudy," I said, starting to cry. Because it hadn't been Croyd who had nearly hurt someone in a careless rage.

"Yes," she said. And it turned out that had been all she'd been there to say. Because she headed for the door. A moment later, Croyd and Mum entered. Like she'd told them I'd said it was okay. They both looked horribly caring and fearful at me. I felt like I was twelve or something.

"My darling," said Mum, and meant it. "My darling, thank God."

The look on Croyd's face said he hadn't told her what I'd been trying to do. He looked more tired than I'd ever seen him.

♠

They let me go home that same day. I was clearly not in shock, having been asleep at the moment when, thankfully as a human being, I'd been caught in Croyd's arms. Mother stayed beside me, occasionally looking at me as if to ask if it was all right she was there. I wondered if she'd somehow intuited that Croyd had told me what she'd said. She looked so frail, suddenly. She looked lost in a foreign country. She wasn't proud of me, but she was afraid for me. It weirdly seemed now like even that much must be difficult for such a small woman to manage. She and Croyd were careful with each other. We went back to my place in the same taxi. We didn't talk.

♦

I found a message on my answerphone from the owner of the circus, asking me to call as soon as I felt able to, to talk about my "employment options."

I went into the kitchen space with Croyd, wondering what Mum would make of the tea we had over here. Croyd held me. He was quaking. I heard a noise from the other room. It sounded like a sob. And then the door opened.

I ran out into the stairwell, but Mum was already on her way down, as fast as her heels could take her. "I can't, darling," she called, before I could shout, "I'll come and see you tomorrow." And then she was gone.

♥

Croyd sat on the sofa just staring at me. He looked desperately sick. "I thought . . . I thought . . ." He didn't look as if he could think anything. He looked like he was about to have a heart attack. Saving me had taken all the strength he had left. His eyes were half in a dream.

I decided.

I went to the kitchen and made him a cup of very strong coffee. In it, I dropped the sleeping pill I'd taken from my mother's purse.

He took a few sips of it, then as soon as he could, threw back the whole mug. He could hardly talk. He was desperately holding on. I put my arms around him, and rested his head on my shoulder, and hoped that I hadn't just committed murder. To go alongside all my other guilt that day. He tried to fight the feeling, tried to fight me, but finally, with an exhalation, his head slumped against mine and he was asleep.

♣

I put him to bed. I piled food beside it, ready for when and if he woke: boxes of Hostess Twinkies. I lay beside him, trying not to think about the evening performance that was taking place amongst all those lights out there, without me. I wondered if I'd finished off my life here alongside his. I kept checking to see that he was breathing. Sometime in the early hours I fell asleep myself.

♠

I woke and he was in the exact same position, still asleep, still breathing. I put a little water in his mouth. I checked my phone and found a message from Mum. She sounded calm, lost. She'd meet me at the same place she'd met Croyd. She said one o'clock, as if leaving it up to me to arrive or not, or controlling me still. One or the other.

I looked at Croyd and decided that he would either wake or he wouldn't. It might be days. I had to see her. I wasn't exactly sure what for.

♦

We sat in the low angled sunlight of the coffee shop. She looked momentarily pleased to see me. Then she locked that expression away. "How is he?" she asked.

"Asleep."

"Yes. I thought it would be soon."

"He told you about his power?"

"Yes. Did he tell you what I said?"

"Yes."

She closed her eyes. "When I'd heard everything, I told him he reminded me of the wide boys my father used to hang around with. He was of that generation, and of that type. I asked him how he could ever be sure that he wouldn't hurt you in a drug-induced rage. My father, after all, gave my mother a black eye occasionally. And so that is something I would never allow, for myself or for you. I asked him that simple question, and he flung the table aside, bellowed at me, threw cups and plates at me, until I was quivering." She looked suddenly ashen at me. "Oh. He didn't tell you that part."

I was furious with her all over again. But I held it in. "I believe you," I said. "But he would never have hurt you."

"I understood that at the time, I think. And I became convinced of that when I saw him risk his life to save you. The elephant almost crushed him, you know—"

"You mean I did."

"I told him he was too old for you. That you could never keep up with him. That you still needed to grow. That he would get frustrated at that, and there would come a time for the black eye. He stopped yelling. He finally started listening to me."

♥

I knew my apartment was empty before I entered. I found mucous and scales and what might have been feathers on the bed. I fell back against the wall.

He was alive.

But he had not stayed. He had not gone out to find a pizza or anything storybook like that.

He wasn't coming back.

I was sure he had done it for me. But perhaps it was apt punishment also. I had, after all, controlled the most important decision he made. Perhaps, that day, we had saved each other's lives and parted because of it. Or perhaps we were just victims of the way the world is still made. I haven't decided yet.

♣

I tried to stop myself, but I gave in. I tried to find him. But I'd left it too long. And he's good at not being found. I might have seen him, amongst the jokers passing me. I kept looking, for a while. I didn't know what he looked like.

Mum and I spent the next few days together. I told her Croyd had gone. She nodded. We didn't talk about what had happened. Or anything else meaningful. We talked about the weather, which was getting colder. We talked about New York, which she'd started to gaze at, from out of the window.

Finally, it was time for her to go home. She asked me when I had to return to school. I told her I still had two weeks. I thought she was about to offer me money, but she thought better of it. She kissed me on the cheek and I smelt the same perfume that I associated with what I'd fled, and felt the age of her skin on mine. I gave her some of the many boxes of Hostess Twinkies I still had lying around, which I was sure she'd give all of to Maxine. I was sure for many reasons.

♠

The media coverage was minor to nonexistent, an accident to an increasingly minor celebrity. A run of shows cancelled, understandably. I rejoined the School much as I'd left it.

♦

I've talked to Mother on the phone twice since then. She's more like her old self. Which is either normal, or evil, or scared, depending on the background she's seen against. The weather over there is much as it is here, getting colder. The aunts are fine. Thanks for asking.

♥

As the snows came to New York, I realized that I'd stopped looking for Croyd in every crowd of jokers. That I'm sure I will see him again. I call myself The Understudy in ace circles now, and will until I feel justified doing otherwise. I don't know how that could happen. But I know it might.

I've finished crying, anyway. Telling this story cleared something away for me. I don't know if I entirely wanted it cleared. But it has been.

There's no justice to any of this. One day I may end up taking care of my mother. She will never apologize for anything. I'm not sure I could ever be sure enough to insist she should. The battles of our adolescence can never be won.

♠ ♥ ♦ ♣

When the Devil Drives

by Melinda M. Snodgrass

"THERE WAS A GUY in the building we brought down, boss."

It was my demolition foreman Sam Karol bringing me this particular bit of unwelcome news. I sat with it for a moment then asked the obvious next question. "Do we know who it is?"

"Not yet, Mister Matthews. I wanted to let you know right away. Auntie Gravity did her teke thing, lifted a block of concrete and there was all this blood and bones and stuff. I pulled everybody off the site."

"Well done. Have you done anything else?"

"No, sir, I haven't even called the cops yet."

That was a relief. "Good man." I stood, grabbed my black leather jacket off the coatrack and shrugged into it. New York was having an unusually cold autumn.

"Auntie's real upset, sir. I wanted to send her home, but figured you should talk to her first."

"You would be correct. Have you told Rusty?" I was concerned that big, slow, stupid and very kindly ace, the actual agent who brought down buildings, had been informed. Rusty would have immediately told the police. Which was not something I wanted.

"No, sir. Figured it would upset the big doofus."

"And you would be right." I clapped Sam on the shoulder. "Let's go take a look at this body."

"It's bound to be ugly, boss. All that blood. It's all crushed and smashed. *Eeoch*." He gave a shudder, then looked embarrassed.

"I expect I'll survive," I drawled.

Sam gave me an "it's-your-funeral" look. At first and even second glance I'm your typical Englishman. A bit too skinny, rather horse faced, and I've got that prissy BBC accent thanks to the fact my mother is a Cambridge don. Sam also knew that in addition to running Aces in Hand I'm a rather famous stage magician. It was no wonder he'd concluded I was a delicate snowflake.

What none of my employees knew is that the magic show had merely been a cover. My real career was as an ace assassin for MI-7, the British equivalent to the American CIA. To be more exact, I killed for the ace division of MI-7 known as the Order of the Silver Helix. Dead bodies bothered me not in the least. Most of the ones I'd seen I'd ushered into that state.

But those days were in the past. I'd parted company with my former employers, and it hadn't been particularly amicable. They tried to hurt people I cared about so I stole a number of their dirty little secrets. They know I'll release them if they fuck with me or mine. Hence we have each other nicely by the short hairs.

After the birth of my son I curtailed my performance schedule, but worries about money—I wanted Jasper to have the best of everything—and my basic restless nature had begun to set in and I walked out on my wife and child. At times I wished I still had access to the shrink who counseled MI-7 agents. I love Niobe and adore my son, but I had left them, and was filling the void I'd left in their lives with money instead of the husband and father. Why? In my more reflective moments I suspected it was because I didn't want Jasper to learn about the less savory parts of his dad's resume. If he knew my true nature would the adoration in those big eyes turn to disgust?

In an effort to keep the money flowing I'd founded Aces in Hand, a company that is designed to deal with real world problems using the extraordinary ace powers bestowed by the wild card virus.

We specialize in building demolition, toxic waste disposal, and nearly instantaneous travel for busy executives. I also design security systems for banks, corporations, and wealthy individuals. Since I had spent years learning how to defeat such measures it was fun to try to counter my own skills. Of course I always left a small imperfection that I could exploit should the need arise.

We had been steadily building, profits were up—well up—so I bloody well didn't need a dead body in one of my job sites affecting our prospects. All of these considerations made me decide that I didn't want to sit in a cab while it fought Manhattan traffic, or take the numerous trains that would be required to ride the subway out to Queens. "Come along, Sam, Ilya's going to pop us over there."

"Uh . . . I'd really rather not, sir. I'll grab a cab."

"We don't have time for that."

"I hate that Between thing."

"It's only for an instant. Don't be such a pussy."

I wasn't going to admit to Sam that I felt the same way. Teleporting may seem instantaneous, but there is a moment in the transition when you are someplace not of this world, or perhaps even this universe. I call it the Between and my employees have picked up the phrase. It had always been a disturbing place. Even more so since the recent unfortunate events in Talas, when eldritch horrors from an alien dimension had invaded the Earth. Now a raging, brooding, inhuman presence washed against any traveler through the Between. Sometimes I thought it reached for me. I didn't want to contemplate what would happen if it ever caught me.

We left the office. My assistant, Dogsbody, a particularly ill-favored joker, looked up. Dogsbody doesn't actually look like a dog. He looks like a vaguely human-shaped turd. His body is covered with black and brown lumps. His eyes are mere slits peering out from between the knobs of flesh. He manages to type and answer the phone because his fingers narrow down to twig-like appendages. "Trouble, sir?"

"I'm afraid so. Can't say when I'll be back. Sam, wait here."

I went to the next-door office. The name plate read ILYA KUUSIKOSKI. I stepped inside, closed the door, stripped, and changed into the clothes stashed in a filing cabinet. They hung on me, but not for long. I accessed my ace and let the bones and flesh start to shift and change. Within seconds I had become a much taller and broader man with red gold hair and gleaming golden eyes.

This other me has had a lot of names over the years—Bahir, Etienne, Christian. Right now he was Ilya Kuusikoski, the teleporting ace who could travel to any part of the globe. I created this bogus employee because we made a lot of money ferrying very busy and very important business leaders and government officials around the world in the time it takes to inhale. I had another persona to handle trips that took my clients in the dark of night. A lot of people know that I'm an ace, that these avatars are just me. Billions more don't know, nor do they particularly care. Wealthy executives certainly didn't care who ferried them around the world, any more than they care to know the name of the pilot on their private jet.

It was a damn shame I'd never managed to access my teleport power without assuming one of these alternate forms. My old handler at MI-7 had raged, cajoled, mocked, and pleaded, but I was unable to overcome the psychological block. I could only teleport as my male and female avatars. Lilith was the queen of the night. Ilya the sun god. *Fucking wild card.* I sometimes wondered if it was due to the fact I'm a hermaphrodite . . . or to use the more PC term, intersex.

I gathered up my Noel Matthews–sized clothes, stuffed them in a backpack, opened the door, and called to Sam. He joined me. I slipped on the backpack, wrapped my arms around the man, held him close. His stubble scraped against my cheek, and he smelled of sweat and concrete dust. He held himself rigidly within my embrace. I pictured an alley near the demolition site and went there.

On this particular morning the alley was empty apart from a skinny cat exploring the interior of a dumpster. It arched its back and hissed as we appeared with a faint *pop* of displaced air. Sam staggered a bit, but as Ilya I was strong enough to keep him upright.

"Go along. I need to change back to me. I'll be right there."

He nodded and tottered off toward the mouth of the ally. I changed, crammed Ilya's clothes into the backpack. I then walked over to the site where a twelve-story building had stood yesterday. Catherine Powell—better known as Auntie Gravity, to fans of *American Hero*—stood beside a partially loaded flat bed. Her round face with its peaches and cream complexion was screwed into a mask of woe. Tears washed down her cheeks.

"Oh, Mister Matthews." She flung herself into my arms, and the smell of the hairspray that kept her bouffant blond hair fixed in place assailed my nostrils. Her extremely large breasts pressed against my chest.

I patted her on the shoulder. "There, there," I tut-tutted.

"I lifted away some concrete and there were these *feet*. It was *horrible!*"

"I know, Catherine, it's terribly upsetting, but it's not your fault. Why don't you go on home? We'll finish clearing the site tomorrow."

"Okay, Mister Matthews," she sniffed. "Thank you."

At that moment the large and lumbering figure of Wally Gunderson hove into view. The big iron-skinned Minnesota ace and I had worked together on a mission in Africa. From that association Rustbelt had concluded that I'm a hero and a real stand-up-guy. A belief I find to be breathtaking in its naiveté, but one which I'm careful to cultivate. It keeps Rusty loyal and working for me.

I gave Catherine a look. "Sam said Rusty hadn't been informed."

She held out placating hands. "I called Wally," Catherine said. "I thought he deserved to know."

"Oh, well done. Now he gets to feel responsible for killing someone," I snapped. Catherine looked hurt and walked away, boobs bouncing in indignation.

The earth actually trembles when Rusty approaches; his body is sheathed iron, and he weighs over seven hundred pounds. He was wearing another of his absurd hats, this time a British driving cap. For some reason the big ace had decided that hats looked good on his overly large head with its steam shovel jaw.

Despite the metal it was easy to read Wally's distress. "Ah geez, Mister Matthews. I'm just sick about this. Do we know who the fella was? We gotta find out so I can apologize to his family."

"You have nothing to apologize for, Rusty. This was clearly marked as a demolition site. If he was fool enough to go inside, well. . . ." I shrugged.

Rusty's ace power enabled him to serve as a one-man demolition crew, without requiring the use of explosives or wrecking balls. Instead the crew would expose an interior girder or rebar and Rusty would unleash his ace, rusting the metal into powder. Since the rust had to eat its way through the entire interior structure, there was plenty of time for Rusty to retreat before the building quietly slumped and collapsed.

"That's not fair, Mister Matthews. Maybe he was a homeless feller just lookin' for a warm place to sleep. It's sure been cold the past few nights."

I turned to the two men who were tasked with doing the final check of the building. "You did a final sweep of the building, correct?"

"Yes, sir. While some of boys were exposing rebar for Rusty to rust me and Dominic went through every floor."

"Interesting. Well, let's get on with it. Show me this body."

"I'd like to come with," Rusty said.

"Fine."

The building had collapsed into the basement. The leather soles of my loafers slipped a bit on the concrete, drywall, and tile as I climbed down the incline. Red rust puffed up and swirled around me like a devil's whirlwind. The upper half of the body was still hidden beneath a chunk of concrete. Only the legs were visible, thrust out from beneath the slab. Concrete dust and blood caked the badly mangled limbs.

"Ding Dong, the witch is dead," I caroled. Sam tittered, then looked embarrassed, and Rusty's head swung toward me questioningly. "Perhaps not in the best of taste, but certainly apt," I said . . . for indeed the shoes thrust out from beneath the slab were a pair of high heels.

"So I guess she was a homeless gal," Wally said mournfully.

"Not when she's wearing Jimmy Choos. Those retail for around two thousand dollars." Lilith owned a few pairs.

That broke through Rusty's distress. "Two thousand dollars for *shoes?* That seems . . . seems . . . well, kinda wrong."

"Rusty, if you're done contemplating income inequality . . ." I made a lifting gesture at the slab.

The big ace gripped the edge of the slab and flipped if off the body the way one might flip a poker chip. Sam immediately turned away and vomited. When several stories of a building come down on flesh and bone it's crushed into hamburger. In this case, extremely inconvenient hamburger.

Rusty's jaw clenched, but he kept it together. "I saw worse in Africa. Do you know who she is . . . was, Mr. Matthews?"

"A veritable witch indeed," I said. I recognized the Yin/Yang necklace that was embedded in the shattered chest. It was Belinda Yamaguchi, owner of Elite Solutions, a competitor who had been increasingly persistent in her attempts to buy my company. All of which I had refused. She had taken to filing bogus and harassing lawsuits against me, keeping my lawyers busy.

I could foresee an unpleasant session with New York's finest. My experience was that cops were lazy and unimaginative. An obvious motive had been handed to them. Along with a convenient suspect.

Me.

♣

Not long after, I faced an absurdly tall and extraordinarily skinny young white man who lacked the nasal East Coast twang. His partner was a small Asian man with a ferocious frown. They introduced themselves—McTate and Fong. Their relative sizes made them look like a bad comedy duo. The interrogation room was painted a bilious shade of pea green and a miasma of fear, despair, sweat, stale coffee, and old vomit clung to the walls and the concrete floor. The only furniture was a dented metal table and several equally battered chairs.

"Coffee?" Detective McTate asked.

"Yes please. I'll take a Venti Iced Skinny Hazelnut Macchiato, Sugar-Free Syrup, Extra Shot, Light Ice, No Whip. And will you allow me to buy you a sandwich, detective?" That I directed to McTate.

"Oh, great, a comedian," Fong growled.

"Anything will be fine," I said.

"Limey asshole." The muttered remark floated back as Fong stalked out of the interrogation room.

"So, pretty terrible what happened," McTate said.

"Yes. Tragic. I'd like to have my lawyer present."

"Really? Why?" McTate spread his hands in that universal and universally insincere cop "trust me" gesture. "We're just having a friendly conversation."

I leaned back in the battered chair and gave him a thin smile. "I find that conversations with law enforcement are rarely *friendly*."

"Had a few of them, have you?" McTate asked.

I gave him another smile, and he gave a put-upon sigh but didn't interfere. I wasn't under arrest, so there wasn't even any limit on how many calls I could make. The efficient assistant at Dr. Pretorius's office said she would get someone down right away. Once the phone was stowed, I dug my hands into my pockets and slouched even deeper into the hard wooden chair.

"So you knew Ms. Yamaguchi?" I didn't answer. "What kind of services does your company provide?" No response. Fong returned with coffee. I took a sip. It was terrible, but I'd drunk worse.

McTate explained I'd requested a lawyer. Fong's expression became, if possible, even more sour. It was a long forty minutes. Finally there was a tap on the door. What entered was not the venerable, brilliant joker attorney Dr. Pretorius. Instead it was a young man, slight, thin, and nervous, trying to juggle his briefcase and a cup of coffee with awkward looking appliances that were hooked onto the flippers that he had in place of arms.

"Hey, Flipper," McTate called jovially. The frown that was laid on the thin features looked forced.

"Are you charging my client?"

"We're just discussing—" Fong said.

"No? Then we're leaving."

While it was the appropriate response for a lawyer, it didn't suit my interests. I wanted to know what the cops knew—or the more likely and alarming scenario what they *thought* they knew. "No, no, Mister . . ." I paused suggestively.

"Oh, sorry, Charles Santiago Herriman."

Why the young man felt it was necessary to give me his full name I wasn't sure, but I nodded agreeably. "So pleased to meet you. I was going to say, I'm happy to answer questions about this tragedy now that you are present."

"Very prudent," Herriman said. "But I would still advise against it."

"Please, one likes to be helpful to our boys in blue."

Herriman shrugged and struggled to drag a chair over. Fong went to help. The lawyer settled down between the cops and me like a jurisprudential referee.

"So . . ." I raised my eyebrows inquiringly at McTate.

He flipped open his notebook. "How did you know Ms. Yamaguchi?"

"We're in the same line of work."

"Which is?"

"We're . . . cleaners."

"That usually has a pretty unpleasant connotation," Fong growled.

"Only if you have an unpleasant mind, detective."

McTate jumped back in. "Her assistant said she was trying to buy your company."

"She made an offer. It was declined."

"Word is she offered more than once. Why would she do that?"

"Because my business model was proving to be more profitable than hers. She was using traditional methods. I use aces to achieve my goals."

"She had filed a complaint against you with the Better Business Bureau and with OSHA."

I shrugged. "Corporate games. I thought nothing of it."

"So you weren't pissed? Looking for a little payback?" Fong asked.

"It would be a rather stupid way to register my annoyance," I said. I added softly, "Do I seem stupid to you?"

"No, you seem like a dick!"

McTate laid a soothing hand on his partner's arm. "We talked with your foreman and the workers who made the final sweep through the building before Rustbelt came in. They said no one was in there." I didn't answer. The quiet stretched between the three of us. Quiet has a devastating power. Most people can't stand quiet, so they say more than they intend. Which is why I kept my mouth shut.

"You're an ace," McTate finally added.

"A *teleporting* ace," Fong added.

They both peered at me. "You sure there isn't something more you'd like to tell us?" McTate suggested softly.

"No."

"Where were you last night?" Fong asked.

"At my apartment."

"Anybody to verify that?"

"No."

"How about this morning?" Now it was McTate's turn. They were so predictable.

"In my office. You can verify that with my assistant. I presume you've looked at the husband. Murder is so often a family affair."

"Do you think *we're* stupid?" Fong demanded.

I rubbed at my mouth thoughtfully. "I'll decline to answer that on the grounds I might incriminate myself."

"Keep laughing, asshole." McTate pulled Fong back into his chair.

My lawyer made sad dog eyes at me. I gave him a not-so-rueful shrug. Deciding I had learned as much as possible from the interview I gave Herriman a significant glance.

He grasped my meaning and stood up. "If you're not charging my client then we're done here."

I also stood and shot my sleeves and retrieved a small bug from my coat pocket. I reached up and clapped McTate on the shoulder as I walked past, setting the bug beneath his collar. Not for nothing had I spent years as a famous stage magician.

"Don't leave town," Fong huffed as a parting shot.

We passed through the bullpen. Hostile stares followed us. Outside not even the stinks and exhaust of Manhattan in general and Jokertown in particular could trump the noxious smells that clung to my clothes. Not that I wasn't familiar with jails. I had been in more than a few during my career with MI-7. "Where is Pretorius?" I asked. My tone had been merely inquisitive, but the young joker reacted as if I'd slapped him.

"Uh . . . in Chicago. Murder trial. I'm—"

"Charles Santiago Herriman. Yes, you said that. Apparently you are also known as Flipper, but if I were you I wouldn't let the cops call you that. Rather undermines your authority."

"I want to have a good rapport with them," he said defensively.

"No you don't. You want them to hate and fear you. To believe you're a stone cold son-of-a-bitch . . . but never mind, you're what I've got. I'm going to call you Charlie, all right?"

I slipped in an earpiece and picked up the end of McTate saying, "*. . . a warrant.*"

"*Home and office?*" Fong's voice.

"*Yeah. Got a feeling this guy is slippery.*"

"*Hey, I hate being the bad cop. Can we switch it up on the next one?*" Fong asked.

"*Sure.*"

"So I better get your story," Flipper said.

"Let's do it over a drink. I need one."

♠

It took one martini to tell what little I did know to Charlie. After he left I had two more while I contemplated my situation. It was clear the cops were wearing blinders and weren't going to look past me. If I was going to avoid being charged I would have to find the real killer and deliver him or her on a platter to the fuzz. I really wished I could see the autopsy report and determine what actually killed Belinda. But first things first. I needed to scrub my place before the cops arrived.

My apartment is a dismal place. It's a furnished one bedroom in the midtown Manhattan Oakwood. Oakwood is temporary corporate housing, but what it really is is ground zero for men who are divorced or separated from their wives. Whenever an actual businesswoman checks in, she will find herself immediately hit upon by the sad and desperate males. The fact I'm still there shows that I'm . . . ambivalent about my decision to leave.

I gathered up my extra passports and driver's licenses, the guns I kept in New York, various knives, the garrote, and my laptop. Once I'd cleaned the apartment down to utter anonymity, I transformed into Ilya and teleported to an apartment I keep in a poor neighborhood in Vienna. I have several of these scattered around the world maintained under different identities. I dropped off the weaponry and documents, and with the sun just kissing the ripples on the Danube I made the jump back to New York before sunset trapped me and I had to wait for full dark back in Manhattan.

I settled onto the couch and checked back in with the Dynamic Duo. They were talking to the grieving spouse. Well, to be more accurate, they were listening to the grieving spouse blubber. His sobs were so shattering that I could hear them easily through the small microphone on McTate's collar. *"I failed her. I let her down. I can't tell her how sorry I am. She was always stronger than me. How did this happen?"*

It went on and on in that vein. I was saved from the litany of self-pity when my cell phone rang with the ringtone that belonged to Niobe—"I'm falling, baby, through the sky."

"Hi," she said hesitantly.

My heart still gallops a bit when I hear her voice. "Hi yourself. You okay?"

"Yeah. I was wondering if you could pick up Jasper? I've got an opera guild meeting that I'd forgotten about."

"Happy to."

"I probably won't get home before seven—"

"I'll pick up dinner for us."

"Thanks, I really appreciate it."

"Anything for you."

"Really? Then you should come home." She hung up on me before I could respond.

◆

Once back in my own form, I called for my car. Jasper attends an upscale private school on the Upper West Side which apes British boarding schools but without all the bullying and buggery. My son was sitting on the front steps with a friend. His backpack rested on the step next to him and his knees, exposed by his uniform, were red from the cold. He was busy weaving the light from the setting sun into intricate patterns to the evident delight of his companion. Jasper was an ace and the result of very tedious and very expensive medical efforts so that his two wild card parents wouldn't produce a child that would die instantly or be a deformed freak.

It was a technique that relied on Niobe's ace power that flipped the dreadful odds associated with the wild card. The doctors utilized the genetic material in her ovipositor eggs and mixed it with my sperm and her normal, human egg. Niobe had mused about donating some of these wild card eggs to other wild card couples, but I had argued against it. It smacked too much of the way she had been forced by the government to birth tiny, short-lived aces. Those other wild card couples could just take their chances with the virus's shitty odds.

Jasper could make beautiful fractal snowflakes out of starlight and sunlight and even the harsh light from electric bulbs. In time he might learn how to plait those photons into something destructive, but I was glad it hadn't occurred to him yet. I really didn't want him following in his father's footsteps.

The limo glided to the curb. He waved a hand through his creation reducing it to glittering shards that flew off in all directions. A quick word to his friend and he ran down to the car as I pushed open the backdoor. He slid in next to me. "Hi, Daddy." He flung himself into my arms and I hugged him tightly. He smelled of child and Sweet Tarts.

I explained about Niobe's meeting. "So what do you want for dinner?"

"Pizza."

I sighed. Eventually he would grow up and we could share an actual meal. I called for a pie to be delivered from John's, and we made our way through Manhattan traffic to the condo on the other side of Central Park. Jasper chatted artlessly about school and soccer practice, and what he should do for his science project. I leaned against the corner of the car and listened while my heart felt too large for my chest.

Once home he scurried to change out of his school uniform, calling out to me to load up *LEGO Takisian Wars* on the Xbox. I did so. He returned and sat cross legged on the floor in front of me, controller clutched in his hands, tongue peeping out of the corner of his mouth as he fought his way through Swarm monsters and other evil aliens.

I sat on the couch behind him and made a list of all the known teleporters or aces with powers that could put a person in a place they weren't supposed to be. At the top of the list was Mollie Steunenberg, the ace known as Tesseract, who hated me with a passion. A quick phone call established that she was still in the nut house and still wearing the ankle bracelet that prevented her from using her power. Next up was the private eye Popinjay, but I couldn't imagine why he would want to fuck me over. Pop Tart, another former contestant from *American Hero*, was a grifter and conniver—my kind of girl—but her power was very limited in range, and somebody would have noticed her on the demolition site. Especially given the way she dressed. She was catcall bait.

This seemed like a dead end, so I turned back to my two employees who had been tasked with sweeping the building. Using Niobe's laptop, I delved into their online life. Like everyone else in the world (except for us in the intelligence biz who know just how dangerous it is) they had left a massive trail across social media. Brent had signed up for no less than three dating sites. It didn't look like he was having much luck, which considering his looks was not surprising. Dominic frequented the fantasy football sites and played online poker. Once I was on a safer machine I would delve into the owners of the various sites where Dominic played.

The doorbell rang. I carefully deleted all record of my activities on Niobe's computer before answering, and even took the added effort to wipe off any fingerprints.

I accepted the pizza, paid the delivery man, gave him a sizable tip, and we settled down to eat. "Do you think the Takisians were good guys are bad guys, Daddy?" Jasper asked.

I chewed thoughtfully and contemplated the aliens who had brought their hell-born virus to Earth some seventy years ago. I thought of those few of us blessed with meta-human powers, balanced that against the hundreds of thousands dead when they drew a black queen, the tens of thousands twisted and deformed by the virus. The key grated in the lock and Niobe entered, dragging her heavy ovipositor tail behind her. Thick bristly hairs dotted the leathery skin. I considered the generations of jokers reviled by their societies or murdered because of their deformities. Niobe rejected by her family because of her affliction. "Bad guys," I said.

"Mommy!" Jasper ran to her and wrapped his arms around her waist. Niobe's acne-scarred face glowed with joy and love. I crossed to her and gave her a hug. She kissed my cheek. She gave a sniff. "That smells good."

"There's plenty left, Mama." Jasper led her over to the table and she tried to find a comfortable way to accommodate the tail. She grimaced and pressed a hand to her back.

I drained the last of my wine, moved behind her, and began to massage the small of her back. She gave a groan of pleasure. "Thanks, that feels good. What have the two of you been up to?"

"Debating the finer points of alien diplomacy." Both she and Jasper looked confused. "Shooting down Takisian ships and Swarm monsters," I amended.

"Oh." She pulled my head down and whispered in my ear. "I'm not sure I like him playing these violent games."

"Don't worry," I whispered back. "He's not likely to follow in my footsteps. He's a far sweeter and better person then I ever was."

"You were and are good to us."

"I should get going."

Niobe checked her watch. "Oh good heavens, look at the time. Jasper, you go brush your teeth and get in your pj's. It's bedtime."

"Awww, Mommy—"

I held up a preemptory finger, cutting off the whine. "Do as your mother says." He drooped off down the hall. Niobe and I shared a look and a laugh. I kissed her on the lips and she held me tight. Her head rested against my chest. "I wish you weren't . . ."

"Me?" I suggested.

"A better you. A you who hadn't left us."

♥

Back at my flat I checked in briefly with Detective McTate, only to hear a toilet flush and then Fong tell him they had caught a new murder. Since it wasn't about me I didn't particularly care. I turned to Brent and Dominic. I needed to set in motion the moves required to get close to them.

Brent was going to be easy. I went into the bedroom and laid out a pretty silk top and a bra. I then allowed the shift to take place. Soon Lilith was looking out of the mirror at me. Jet black hair tumbled to my waist and covered my unnaturally firm breasts. Silver eyes gleamed and my skin was almost marble white. I lifted a strand of hair and wondered if my avatars would go grey when I did. I dressed, grabbed my cell phone, and snapped a selfie.

I joined one of the dating sites frequented by Brent and gave him a wink. I got back a response in seconds. There was no danger my female avatar would be recognized by a guy who worked construction for me. We chatted, and he tried to be sexy and debonair but only ended up seeming pathetic. We agreed to meet for a drink the next night. I hated to delay but it seemed unlikely that a woman as beautiful as Lilith would be eager enough to meet this sad loser right away.

I returned to Austria, booted up my laptop, and located Dominic playing online poker. I lurked and watched. Dominic was not having a good night . . . probably because he wasn't very good. I am a decent poker player online, but superb when there are actual cards involved. Cards that I can manipulate. Meaning I can cheat. I would have to consider if there was a way to draw Dominic into a real game.

I next sent emails under my own address to both men, requesting they come to my office tomorrow morning at 9:00 and at 10:30 so I could get their statements. Then I teleported back to the Manhattan Oakwood.

At that point I was exhausted, and still felt the stink of the precinct even on my Lilith body. I took a long hot shower and crawled into bed. I contemplated shifting back to my normal form, but it makes my joints ache if I change too many times in a day. I had been Ilya, me, back to Ilya, me, and now Lilith. I decided to sleep as Lilith and let the dawn do the work for me. I might be able to sleep through the discomfort of the change.

The top sheet rubbed against my nipples, stiffening them and sending a flare of heat to my groin. Apparently my imperfect body was horny. I considered masturbating, but I found it harder to get the female body to respond, especially when I was distracted. Bringing Lilith to climax was like playing a violin. When I was Ilya I just needed to grab hold. Being a hermaphrodite, I have a vestigial dick that's nothing to write home about, so I usually use my uber male form to find release and relief. By the time I had considered all these ramifications I found myself drifting off to sleep, and the "romantic" moment had passed.

♣

The next morning, clutching coffee and nursing a headache, I sat in the back of the limo heading to the office. We had just pulled up to the building when my phone rang. It was the manager at the Oakwood informing me the cops had arrived with a search warrant.

I told him to let them in, then instructed the driver to take me back to the apartment building. I arrived just in time to hear Fong grouse, "This guy has about as much personality as a piece of fucking cellophane."

"I'm British, what did you expect?" I said.

McTate was just pulling off his gloves. They gave a sharp snap from the force of the pull, the only indication that he might be irritated. "It is a little unusual for a place to look like a hotel room," he said mildly.

"My wife and I separated a few months ago—"

"Kicked your ass out, did she?" Fong snorted. "Can sure as hell see why." I almost told him that I had left them, but forced back the words, angry that I had allowed the man to get under my skin.

"Do you think she'd be okay with us searching her place?" McTate asked.

"I'm certain she would not object."

"There's no computer here," Fong said.

"No. I spend enough time on a computer during the day. I leave work at work. When I'm home I read." I gestured at a pile of library books on the coffee table. "And I watch football—you know, real football—and cricket."

"You're a magician. Where's your equipment?" McTate asked.

"A full show requires quite large props. They're all in a warehouse in Oxford." I gave Fong a smile. "That's in England."

"Keep it up, asshole. You won't be smirking when we nail you," the cop growled. I gave him another smile.

"May we take a look at your phone?" McTate once again, very humble and very polite.

"No. You need a separate warrant for that, also for my work computer."

The cops left. While I was locking up the manager approached. "We provide corporate housing for upscale clients. We don't need this kind of trouble."

"Am I being evicted?"

"We'd prefer that you make other arrangements."

"Fine. Expect to hear from my lawyer." He didn't like the sound of that, but also didn't suggest I stay on. My headache intensified. The day was just getting better and better, and tonight I had a date with a particularly unprepossessing man who also happened to work for me. For a moment I was shaken with a desire to call Niobe and ask if I could stay with her.

I forcibly rejected the notion. Because of me, they were about to be subjected to a police search. No, I would stay in one of my other *pieds-à-terre*.

♠

It took continent-hopping to get ready for my date. I had spent too much time working and hadn't noticed that while it was still light in New York it was now dark in Vienna. Time zones are a bitch when you have to be in the proper form to teleport. I had to wait until it was fully dark in New York before I could teleport to my flat in Vienna and dress as Lilith. Which meant I had to contact Brent and ask if we could push our date back an hour. Once in Vienna I dressed in a short skirt, silk blouse, and knee-high boots with a very high heel. That's actually the worst part of assuming my Lilith form, the damn high heels. Foot binding and girdles might have gone the way of the dodo, but I was convinced that high heels were designed by frightfully insecure and fearful men to torture women. I also retrieved a small SIG Sauer pistol that could fit in a pocket or a purse.

Brent had suggested the bar of the Tavern on the Green, a dreadful tourist trap, but the perfect choice for a simple man trying to seem sophisticated. I teleported into a secluded area of Central Park, and actually met a mugger. Crime has gone down in New York City as the population aged and the city changed. Disney has replaced the porn shops in Times Square, even Jokertown has Starbucks and an upscale Hyatt hotel, and the mask and cloak shops now sell more to tourists than to residents. I left the mugger groaning and clutching his bruised balls and walked on. Passing a trashcan, I dumped the cheap .38 he had been carrying. A few moments later and I saw the lights through the windows of the restaurant as they flowed across the grass and trees.

I went inside and scanned the bar. Brent spotted me, slid off the bar stool, and waved frantically. He was wearing khaki slacks and a silk turtleneck with a sports jacket tossed casually over one shoulder. The debonair *bon vivant*. I recognized the look. Men who have gone to a discount suit broker and placed themselves in the hands of a salesperson who had decided to find his inner valet. It wasn't a bad look. It just *tried* too hard. I stifled a sigh and walked over to him.

"Lilith?"

"Yes. Brent?"

"Yeah."

I slid onto a stool. His eyes dropped to the flash of the milk white thigh I exposed. He gestured to the bartender, who ignored him. Yes, Brent was one of *those* men. I crooked a finger and the young man jumped to attention. I ordered the most expensive cocktail on the menu and watched Brent from the corner of my eye. He blanched. Then I ordered an appetizer of oysters on the half shell. That was another thirty dollars.

Brent was starting to sweat. "So, uh, you just joined Happy Couples. 'Cause I sure would have noticed you before now."

"Yes, I'd tried Ace Affairs, Wild Card Couples, and few of the other wild card dating sites, but aces can be so full of themselves." There was no way of hiding my wild card, Lilith's silver eyes will always give me away.

"So you're not an ace?"

"No." I gestured at my eyes. "Not sure if these make me a joker or not. They are sort of a physical deformity."

"Oh, no, they're beautiful. You're beautiful," he blurted.

"Why thank you, what a sweet thing to say." The oysters arrived. I squeezed lemon across them, stirred the horse radish into the cocktail sauce, dabbed it onto one, picked up the shell and slurped down the oyster. I gestured at the plate. "Would you like one?"

"Uh, thanks . . . uh maybe later."

I ate two more oysters then asked, "So what do you do?"

"I'm in . . . uh . . . I'm an architect."

Poor baby, I thought. Start out lying and you'll only end up in the suds. "Why, how interesting. Have you designed any buildings I might know?"

"Probably not. I just do ordinary stuff. What do you do?"

"Guess." I teased him with a flutter of my eyelashes.

"Actress? Model?"

Well, at least he hadn't said exotic dancer. I gave him credit for that. I lifted the last oyster and held it out to him. "You sure?" He shook his head. I told him I was a dress buyer for Bloomingdale's. He told me that didn't surprise him. He liked my outfit. The inane conversation continued. I learned he was divorced with an eight-year-old son. The longing in his voice as he talked about how weekend visits with his boy just weren't enough caused a flare of pain in the center of my chest. The fact he pulled that reaction from me turned the pain to anger. How dare he be real? I ordered another overpriced martini.

"Do you like kids?" he asked. "Would you like to have some?"

"Not really and no," I snapped.

"Oh, well okay then." He surprised me by fishing out his wallet. "Look, this has been really nice, but I don't think we're gonna work out."

"Beg pardon?"

"I really want to remarry. Have more kids. Family is important to me. Thank you for coming, but . . ."

It was the last thing I had expected, and it rather charmed me. I held out my hand. "No problem, and thank you for being so forthcoming."

He got the bill, turned an interesting shade of grey and handed over his credit card. The bartender came back with a half-sneering half-regretful expression. "I'm sorry, sir, but your card was declined." I watched as Brent fumbled through his wallet, pulling out and then mentally discarding the three other credit cards.

"Let me," I said. "It's the twenty-first century, after all." I pulled out cash and settled the bill. We walked to the door. I gave him a hug and stole his phone.

Once I was out of sight I downloaded the contents of his phone into mine. Then I returned to the bar and handed the phone to the bartender.

"My companion dropped this. Will you hold it for him?"

"Sure. So I'm guessing not a great meet up. Wanna try again with somebody who hates kids too? And I won't stick you with the bill."

"You won't stick me with anything, bucky," I said, and left.

◆

The next morning I was skimming through the downloaded contents of Brent's phone. Pictures of a grinning pudgy boy, an overweight woman with the pudgy boy. His email was mostly messages from the ex about visiting and alimony. Emails from the boy reminding Brent of his baseball game. It was all rather sad, and nothing raised any flags.

My phone rang with Niobe's song. I shut the door to the outer office then stood, cell phone pressed tight to my ear as if it could bring her closer, and stared out the window. A cold autumn rain was sheeting down the glass and the tops of the skyscrapers were lost in the clouds.

"The police came," she said. "They didn't find anything."

"Of course not. I'd never endanger you."

There was a long silence then she asked, "You didn't kill that woman, did you?"

"No. If I had I would have disposed of the body far more efficiently."

"Stop! Don't act like that with me."

"I'm sorry. I apologize."

"One of the cops indicated you might get kicked out of the Oak-wood."

"Very likely. I'll just stay in one of the flats."

"Why don't you come home, Noel?"

"You know why."

"Actually I don't. I still don't understand why you left us."

A stone seemed to have settled in my chest. "I'm not good for Jasper or for you. Better if I just provide you with a good living."

"A child needs their father. You're not protecting Jasper by abandoning him. You're hurting him. You and your father were so close. Why would you deny that to your son?"

"Because I'm not my father! He was . . ." Grief washed over me, as cold and grey as the rain beyond my window.

"A good man?" she suggested softly.

"Yes."

"You're trying to be, Noel. You have been for a long time."

"And what happens when I'm not?"

"We get through it. Together." The stone in my chest had lodged in my throat and I didn't trust myself to speak. After a long silence she said. "Just think about it. Come home. We love you."

I stood holding the phone long after she had hung up.

♥

After Niobe's call I almost cancelled Brent's appointment, but mentally heard Captain Flint telling me to dot every i and cross every t.

Brent now sat in the chair across the desk from me. He looked nervous. "I guess you wanted to ask about sweeping the building. I already talked to the cops."

"I'm not surprised, but I wanted to hear from you directly. Can you tell me anything that might shed light on how Ms. Yamaguchi ended up inside?" I found myself nervously clicking the top on my ballpoint pen. I set it aside.

"Not really. I checked my floors and Dominic checked his." He gave a slight chuckle.

"What?"

"It's sort of funny. Usually Dominic takes the lower floors. He's always whining about climbing all the stairs, but this time he said he'd take the upper floors."

"I see. Did you hear anyone in the stairwells?"

Brent shook his head. "It was pretty noisy outside with the trucks coming in to haul away the debris."

"No strangers loitering around the site?"

His eyes narrowed and his mouth worked from the effort of recall. He shook his head. "No, not that I remember."

I tried to think if I was missing anything, but nothing occurred. I stood. "Well, thank you for coming."

♣

I was dealing with the insurance issues that had arisen due to a dead body on my site when Dogsbody called me on the intercom to tell me Dominic had arrived. As they entered Dominic was casting uncomfortable looks at the joker. The construction workers never came to my office, so this was a first for him.

After Dogsbody left Dominic ran a hand through his thinning and rather greasy hair. "Wow, a joker . . . and a . . . dude. Didn't expect that. Thought a big important guy like you'd have a gorgeous babe." He gave a nervous laugh.

"The city offers tax incentives to companies that hire jokers," I said with an indifferent shrug, thus indicating I was a fellow bigot. It was also absolutely true that I was happy to get the tax break.

Dominic gave me a knowing grin. "Oh, okay, that makes sense then."

"Please sit down." I put a hand on his back and guided him to a chair. At the same time, I lifted his cell phone from his pocket and slipped it into mine. "Thank you so much for coming in," I said, as I perched on the corner of my desk.

"Uh . . . sure. I mean it was . . . terrible . . . what happened. I have no idea how that . . . happened." His eyes shifted left, right, up and down, but he never actually looked at me.

MI-7 had honed my interrogation skills, though I wouldn't have needed them in this situation. Dominic was a terrible liar. I was also beginning to see why he played poker online. "So why don't you just take me through the morning."

"Sam had Fred and Bob opening up the wall to expose the girders. Rusty was hanging around drinking coffee while he waited. Sam picked me and Brent to search the building. We divvied up the floors. He had one through six. I had seven through twelve."

"The indication is that the woman was on one of the middle floors. So it could have been either you or Brent who missed her." Dominic squirmed. "Can you assure me that you checked every room on every floor?"

"Yes, sir. I sure did. I absolutely did. I can't speak for Brent." He paused and licked his lips. "Look, I don't want to cause the guy any problems . . ." *Meaning that he absolutely did.* ". . . but I know Sam has gotten on Brent's case about how he's doing his job. I mean, I've never seen a guy have such bad luck with the subways."

"Meaning?"

"He's late a lot."

"Thank you for letting me know. I'll speak to Sam about that." I stood, indicating the meeting was over.

Dominic dragged his feet as he walked to the office door. "Uh . . . that lady, did she have a family?"

"I have no idea," I answered. "Should it make a difference? She's dead." He flinched at the word. I find it fascinating the American inability to just say died. All these euphemisms—*passed on, went to a better place.*

"I guess not. Just hard on her kids or husband if she did have a family."

"Your sympathy does you credit," I murmured, and enjoyed watching him flinch again.

He left and I settled at my desk and pulled out his phone. I quickly jacked it into my laptop and downloaded the entire contents onto my computer. Then I hurried out of the office and caught him waiting at the elevator. I held out the phone. "This slipped out of your pocket. I found it in the cushions of the chair."

"Oh, gee, thanks, Mister Matthews."

I told Dogsbody to hold my calls and settled in to dissect Dominic's life. Like many people he was lazy about removing old emails and totally eliminating deleted voice messages. It seemed that Dominic had taken to playing in some less savory corners of internet gambling, and he had racked up a very large debt. Judging by their phone messages, the people holding that debt were of the very large and very unsympathetic variety. The threats had grown ever more threatening and the promised bodily harm more graphic. Then abruptly the calls stopped. The day after Belinda found herself squashed by a collapsing building.

There were some sent emails by Dominic that didn't correspond to any received. Somehow the messages to which he had replied vanished off the server. Which indicated a level of technological sophistication beyond what your average thug could muster. Dominic's responses however were damning.

Why would you want to forget the debt?

What do I have to do?

I'm not real comtable with this.

Okay I geuss I can do that.

What was abundantly clear was that Dominic's online creditors had offered him a solution for his financial problems. A solution that Dominic had accepted. Also that Dominic was a shining example of the American educational system.

I selected the relevant emails and prepared to print them, but suddenly a *hack detected* alert came up on my screen and an alarm started sounding. My program began trying to backtrace the hacker, but it was an aggressive assault designed to take over my machine. Most people's computers would never have detected the hack, but I have extra layers of protection and surveillance on all my tech.

The faceless hacker and I sparred and struggled as my fingers flew across the keyboard. Windows flashed by, text scrolled, but he was very good and I was losing. He would be able to download the contents of my machine before I could trace him, and possibly insert something into my files. There was only one thing to do. I hit the burn command, unplugged the computer, poured a cup of tea across the keyboard. It sparked and died. I opened the case, pulled out the hard drive, and beat it into pieces with a heavy paperweight.

Panting a bit from the exertion, I fell back into my chair and considered. Someone with a high level of computer skills had been on the other end of this hack. They had paid Dominic not to make a sweep of the upper floors. I had to believe the man wouldn't have gone through with it if he'd actually come across an unconscious . . . or dead . . . woman in one of the rooms. Someone was clearly trying to destroy me, and since the person who had been actively engaged in that attempt had ended up squashed at one of my job sites, I had to look for another culprit.

One sprang quickly to mind. My former employer.

I paced the office, pursued by the stink from the destroyed computer, and fought the rage that threatened to overcome me. Could this really be the Silver Helix coming after me? The level of sophistication of the hack suggested that.

I was ready to teleport to a working laptop and immediately release all the damning material I had stolen to WikiLeaks, but I stopped myself. It's never wise to react in haste and anger.

I sat back down at the desk and began to write a list. What I knew. What I didn't know and more importantly what I *thought* I knew. I realized there were a lot of blanks under what I actually knew. It made no sense for the Silver Helix to use this method to destroy me when it would also destroy them.

No, the answer had to rest in the details of Belinda's life and company.

♠

I bought a new laptop, settled in at a coffee shop in Jokertown, fired up my personal hotspot, and began to dig into Belinda Yamaguchi. Born Belinda Fujasaki in Los Angeles, California, attended USC where she earned an MBA. Husband Harvey Yamaguchi, MIT, grad school at Cal Tech specializing in computer science. I had a new candidate for the attack on my computer.

I continued digging. Harvey had met Belinda at a mixer. Love bloomed and they married in 1999. One daughter Megan born in 2004. A few years after Belinda founded Elite Solutions Harvey had founded an IT company, Brilliant Solutions. The similarity in names was nauseatingly cute.

After Belinda began her assault on my company I had begun researching ways to take the fight back to her. Buy any outstanding debt, look at her investors and supplier, and see if any of them could be squeezed. I still had the file so I pulled it down from the cloud and started to review. A name floated past—везучий. My Russian was a bit rusty, but the meaning came back to me. *Lucky.* Something niggled at the back of my mind. I had seen that name before. Then I remembered. It was the name of the company that owned the online poker site where Dominic played and had lost so much money.

I took a sip of my now cold coffee, leaned back in my chair, and considered. So what did an online gaming site and a demolition and aftermath company have in common? I turned my attention to the Russian company and had soon traced it back to a particularly powerful Russian mob family in Brighton Beach run by Ivan Grekov. He had money, foot soldiers, and even a few aces on his payroll, but as yet the hapless cops of the NYPD had nothing on him.

Most of construction in New York City is heavily mobbed up. When I'd first founded Aces in Hand several large men with Italian surnames wearing cheap suits, shiny pointy-toe shoes, and large bulges beneath their arms had come visiting. They told me they could rent me equipment at very reasonable prices. I told them I had no need of their equipment. Our discussion became more heated until I pulled a gun on them. They had left threatening retribution. I had changed to Ilya, caught them on the street, and teleported them into the center of the Nefud Desert. The good thing about predators is they recognize when they've met a bigger one. Since then, I've had no trouble.

But Belinda didn't have my particular skills. It was likely that *Gospodin* Grekov had his tentacles in Elite Solutions and Belinda had probably failed to make a payment or make good on some other promise. It also made complete sense for them to dispose of a body and take out the competition all at the same time. I just needed to figure out who and how.

◆

Rather than exhaust myself and play games with the sun-collecting equipment that was scattered around the world, I just went to a nearby electronics store and used cash to buy what I needed. I then hied myself down to Brighton Beach and boosted a car.

Uncle Ivan had a number of offices for his various endeavors, but he seemed to stick close to home, a garish house on Corbin Place. Judging by the houses to either side, Ivan had purchased one of the grand old places, knocked it down, and put up a monstrosity. There does seem to be something about decadent oil sheiks and mobsters that make them crave the vulgar and tasteless. The house was a perfect example.

It was close enough to the ocean that the smell of brine and soft rumble and hiss of the waves carried through the open car window. I sat with my sandwich and a beer, a pistol on the seat next to me, a camera, a change of clothing for both avatars, and a big ears rig that could pick up conversations inside the house. Men came and went. Strong guy, strong guy, thug, young woman with a little girl about Jasper's age.

One of the strong guys took offense at a car that had been luxurious in parking, so he picked it up by the rear axle and moved it. I marked him down as someone who could easily carry a dead body up a number of stairs. The sun was starting to set when a silhouette etched itself against the glow. A flying ace. I sat up and grabbed my camera. The ace dropped onto the sidewalk in front of the house, straightened his suit jacket, and entered.

I had been so excited by the sight of this ace that I lost situational awareness. It returned in a rush when the top of the stolen car was torn back like a man opening a can of sardines.

I scrambled for the pistol, but found myself grabbed by the back of the collar and hoisted, choking, out of the car. I reached back to try and claw his eyes. He headbutted me and red streaks flashed across my vision from the force of the blow. I went limp so he wouldn't hit me again. I needed to stay conscious.

He flung me over his shoulder. Ilya was not accessible at sunset and Lilith could not be accessed until it was full dark. I desperately measured the distance until the sun set. Minutes yet.

I was carried into the house and thrown onto the silk rug. It didn't do much to cushion the landing since there was cold marble beneath it.

"Found him in a car, boss, watching the house. He had lots of surveillance equipment and a gun," the ace said in Russian.

"Thank you, Vladimir."

I groaned and peered up at the dapper little man standing over me. He had perfectly coiffed milk white hair and an absurdly elaborate waxed mustache. He seemed less cherubic after he kicked me hard in the ribs. I recognized Ivan Grekov from my research.

"Who are you? NYPD? FBI? SCARE?"

"None of the above." I climbed to my feet.

Now that I was erect I could evaluate my surroundings. It was a study. A fire burned in the ornate marble grate. A huge polished-mahogany desk, high-backed leather armchairs, and a sideboard loaded with bottles of liquor—most of them vodka—made up the furnishings. The flying ace was also in the room peering at me curiously.

"Wait, I recognize you," Grekov said. "You're that Brit. You have been costing me, *tovarich*."

"Cutting into Belinda's profits, was I? Is that why you killed her?" The three men exchanged glances and began to laugh uproariously. "Okay, I gather that's an erroneous conclusion. Care to enlighten me?"

Grekov exchanged glances with his thugs. "Why not? But nothing comes for free, Mr. Matthews. Same deal I had with Belinda. Thirty percent of your gross."

"Sure," I said. Now that I had been inside the house I could return and kill him any time I wanted.

He was smart enough to have a momentary worry over my prompt agreement, but greed and a lifetime of feeling untouchable made him continue. "She had fallen behind on her payments. I hope you'll do better."

"I'm sure I can. Now keep your side of the bargain."

"Harvey, Belinda's husband, called me a few nights ago. Blubbering about how he'd done a terrible thing. Could I help him. Once I understood the problem, I saw a way to kill two birds with one stone, so to speak. Take over her company and yours as well."

Grekov gestured at the flying ace. "I sent Boris to deal with the problem."

I couldn't help myself. "Ivan, Vladimir and Boris? Really? Could you be any more of a cliché? Sorry, you were saying?"

The old man looked amused. The two aces glared, but Boris picked up the tale. "I went to the condo. Guy had shot his wife. He was bawling about how he had let her down. I didn't pay much attention . . ."

I wasn't paying any attention either. The sun had set. It's not easy to move during the change, but needs must when the devil drives, so as my bones were shifting I lunged for Boris. I wrapped an arm around his throat, and with my free hand ripped the gun from its shoulder holster and pressed it into his side.

He took to the air and slammed me against the ceiling. It almost knocked the breath out of me, but I tightened my grip on both him and the gun, pictured our destination and teleported—

♥

—To a jail cell in Cairo with which I was intimately acquainted. Since we were ten feet up in the air it was a hard landing. I scrambled away from Boris and jumped to my feet. Fortunately he was disoriented by the transition. By the time he rolled to his feet I was holding the gun on him.

Shock had robbed him of English. He stuttered in Russian, "Wha—what the fuck? What *are* you? Where am I?"

"In a jail cell in Cairo. I pay a monthly bribe to the warden to keep it for my private use. You never know when you might want to sequester someone," I replied in the same language.

"Fuck you, you bastard!"

"Currently the proper term is bitch." I shot him in the leg. He screamed and clutched at his calf. Blood welled between his fingers. He started crying.

"Oh dear God, stop blubbering. It's a flesh wound. You work for a mobster. Didn't you think this was a possibility? Tell me about what the husband said."

He wiped snot onto his sleeve and glared at me. "He said she'd found out some stuff. He was bawling that he was a coward, that he'd let her down. I picked up the body and flew it to the building. Landed on the roof, carried her down to the eighth floor, and left her. That's all I know."

"Excellent. I'll be back for you later. And you can tell the police everything you just told me."

"You're leaving me? But I'm bleeding."

"You won't die of it. I suggest you use your shirt for a bandage, and tie it in place with a shoelace."

I teleported back to my office.

♣

I sat at my desk and gently probed my aching side while I considered. So Belinda had "found out something." The question was what. I decided I probably had a couple of broken ribs, likely from Ivan's kick. I added that to my list of things to settle after I had dealt with Harvey.

Affairs were the usual culprit in a spousal murder. I knew that Harvey was a computer savant, so I didn't try to directly hack him. Instead I dug into his employees; affairs usually start at the office. I found nothing beyond the fact he seemed to be a thoughtful employer, always remembering his employee's birthdays, even their children's birthdays. In short, everything I wasn't. I had no idea when Dogsbody or Sam or any of the rest of them had been born, nor did I give a damn.

I managed to break into his accounting program, though I was pretty sure an alert had been sent. I wasn't going to have much time, but fortunately I got lucky. Harvey had his accounting service pay his personal bills. If he had a mistress, a gambling habit, a coke addiction, I could find it. But before I jumped back out I noticed something far more interesting than his green fees at the Dyker Beach Golf Course, or the large stuffed unicorn he had, presumably, bought for his daughter, or the bouquet of roses.

His company was hemorrhaging money.

He had been pulling money out of Belinda's company, and he was trying to hide it with creative bookkeeping. Which would explain why Grekov hadn't been getting his cut. If Grekov had threatened Belinda, she would have tried to figure out why her profits were dropping. She discovered the embezzlement and confronted Harvey. The rest of the tale told itself.

I hit erase on the laptop, burned the hard drive back to factory settings, leaned back in my chair, and considered. So . . . did I take this to the bumbling cops? No. A direct approach was needed. I went back to work and located the Yamaguchis' home address. Another search revealed that the condo had been purchased in 2010. I went through the archive pictures from the real estate company so I could study the rooms.

The placement of furniture is always a danger for me. Fortunately there was a very nice photo of the master bath. I was still taking a risk by tele-porting in, but my search hadn't revealed any filings for building permits, so I was reasonably sure the large Roman style tub hadn't been moved.

I muttered a prayer to a god I didn't believe in and teleported—

♠

—And landed, mercifully, in a bathtub that was dry and person-free. I stepped out and morphed back into my own form. It hurt like a mother with my broken ribs. I noted the expensive fixtures, the His and Her sinks. The His was filled with soap scum and whiskers congealed onto the side. There were a few pieces of blood-stained toilet paper wadded up and strewn across the countertop, revealing a shaky hand with the razor. The marble tile around the front of the toilet showed pee stains. It didn't look like Har-vey had been doing all that well since he'd become a murderer.

I slipped through into the master bedroom. The bed was unmade and there was a sour smell. I moved on, searching for Harvey. I had to hope the daughter was like most teenage girls and out with friends, doing after-school activities, or in her room with the door closed and texting with someone.

The condo was very quiet which made the ticking of the large grandfa-ther clock seem very loud and very ominous. I passed an open door that showed a pretty canopy bed and a large collection of stuffed animals. The unicorn was there. Thankfully the unicorn's owner was not.

Harvey was in the kitchen slumped at the kitchen table. An open bottle of Bunnahabhain "40," which retailed for around two grand, was at his elbow. Judging by the level in the bottle Harvey was not sipping. I added that to his list of crimes.

He jumped as I walked into the room. The stainless steel surfaces in the very modern kitchen threw back my slightly distorted reflection—a dark haired man, wearing gloves, in a suit and carrying a gun. It was no wonder Harvey jumped and caught the bottle with his elbow. I got there before it completely tipped and spilled the nectar inside.

"You . . . you," he stammered, and shoving back his chair he inched away from me.

"So you know me. Good, saves time."

"Wha . . . what do you want?" It wasn't just fear slurring his words. He was clearly pissed.

"Well, for starters a glass. I'd rather not use yours."

"Uh . . . okay." He tottered to a cabinet and took down another high-ball glass. He picked up the bottle, peered at the glass like an archer focusing on a distant target. I put away my pistol, took the bottle, and poured three fingers of scotch into the glass and refilled his.

I pulled out a chair and sat down opposite him. His bones seemed to have vanished, because he melted more then sat.

"I take it that Belinda found out about your embezzlement. So is it going to be the accident defense *she had a gun and when I tried to take it from her—*"

"No, no it wasn't like that." He started blubbering. "She was scared. She couldn't understand why profits were down so much. It was making it hard to pay Grekov. She was crying."

He gulped down the scotch. I refilled his glass. "I felt so guilty so I . . . I confessed. Told her what I had done. She started screaming at me. That Grekov was going to come and hurt us all, and it was my fault. I was angry. *She* was the one who had put us in danger by getting us involved with that crook."

I took a sip of scotch. "So you work for Grekov too."

"No. I just handle IT for his companies. I'm not involved in any of that . . . other stuff. I'm not a criminal."

"Yes, you are a model of courage and rectitude. Are we getting close to the part where you kill your wife?"

He flinched. "She called Grekov, told him what I'd done, and begged him to forgive us. She then put me on the phone. Grekov told me what I had to do to win back his trust. He wanted me to hack into banks and credit card companies. I wanted to be a hero for my daughter. Instead I was being forced to become a criminal."

I took another drink. Playing therapist was boring the shit out of me, but there was also an uncomfortable resonance to my own life.

"Yes, terrible," I snapped. "So what happened?"

"After we hung up, Belinda went to fix a drink. I got my granddad's Luger. He fought in Europe in World War Two. They didn't trust a Japanese guy to fight in the Pacific. He took a pistol off a dead German, brought it home as a souvenir."

"Boring and irrelevant," I snapped.

He goggled at me then continued. "I was so angry. I followed her in here and shot her. When I realized what I had done I was going to kill myself . . ." He threw back the scotch.

"But you got cold feet. Or maybe that cold barrel in your mouth gave you second thoughts."

"I thought about Megan, my baby. To lose both her parents . . ." He was crying again. "I realized Grekov could help me. Get rid of the body."

"By framing me for murder."

"I didn't know Grekov would do that," he whined.

"But you sure as fuck didn't do anything to clear me!"

"What could I do? I'd go to prison and my daughter would be alone."

"Where's the gun now?"

"Here."

"Good, that simplifies matters."

"What do you mean?"

"Let's get the gun. Then I'll explain." Fortunately he was too drunk to argue or consider where this might be going.

He led me to a home office and took the Luger out of the bottom drawer of the desk. When he straightened, he saw I was holding my pistol. "I've got a gun too," he blustered. "I could shoot you. Say you threatened me."

"I can assure you I have a great deal more practice with firearms than you do, I'm not pissed, and I have no compunction about killing people. As for threatening you, you are quite right. I'm going to."

The man had already proved he was a coward, and my demeanor can be quite menacing. He shuddered and handed me the Luger. I pocketed the ancient pistol.

"Now, you have three options. You can go immediately to the police and confess. You'll stand trial and go to jail, but Megan can come visit you, so she won't be a total orphan. You can write a suicide note and finish what you started. Or I'll kill you and write the note for you. Your choice."

"You . . . you can't match my handwriting . . ."

"Oh please, it's 2017. Who does a handwritten note today? I'll put it on your iPad."

He spread his hands beseechingly. "Please, my daughter . . . she needs me."

"And my son needs me. Your daughter is fucked no matter what you do. The question is which outcome screws her up the least. I would suggest it's daddy in jail, but it's entirely up to you. Now, it's late, I'm bored, and it's decision time. So what's it to be?"

He stood, head bowed, for a long time. He then lifted Detective McTate's card off the desk and pulled out his phone. I laid the Luger down and backed out of the room. He might be a worm, but I wasn't going to risk turning my back on him. As I left I heard him say, "Detective, I . . . I have something to . . . to tell you."

I went into the kitchen, washed my glass, and returned it to the cabinet. Pushed back in the chair, gritted my teeth and turned into Lilith, and left.

Back at the Oakwood, I listened to Harvey's confession as I stood looking out at the lights of midtown. There were still a few loose ends to settle. I returned to Cairo, grabbed Boris, and dumped him on the steps of Fort Freak, the Jokertown police station. I then printed out Dominic's incriminating emails and mailed them to Detective McTate.

It was nearly dawn by the time I returned to my flat. I was tired and hurting and I dreaded the change. With each transformation my ribs' objections had become more acute. I dry swallowed four aspirin, sucked in a deep breath, and let Lilith melt away.

My suit had blood on it from Boris's wounded leg. I undressed and taped my ribs. I eyed the bed and decided sleep was not attainable right now. I returned to the window and watched the sun's rays glint off the roofs of skyscrapers. The music of the city—car horns, sirens, revving engines—was muted beyond the glass. A flying ace was circling the spire of the Empire State Building.

I had told myself I had left my family to protect them. The truth was I had only been protecting myself. I had been afraid to see love turn to disgust if Jasper ever realized who I was and what I had done. I had called Harvey a coward. I deserved the label myself.

◆

They were at the breakfast table when I walked in. They looked up in surprise. Jasper flew across the room. I dropped the suitcase I was carrying as he leaped into my arms.

"Daddy!"

I held him close. Niobe's eyes met mine across the top of his head. She took in the suitcase I was carrying and a look of satisfaction and relief filled her eyes. "Jasper, go get your satchel while I finish packing your lunch."

He pulled back and gave me a desperate look. "Will you be here when I get home?"

"No." And before he could react I added, "But I'll be here when I'm done at work."

"Okay!" he shouted and ran out of the room.

Niobe approached me, tail dragging behind her. "So, are you really back?"

"Yes."

"What changed your mind?"

I thought about the child who was soon going to be without a father and felt a tug of guilt.

"I realized I didn't need to be a hero to my son or to you. I just needed to be here."

The Atonement Tango

by Stephen Leigh

MICHAEL—AKA "DRUMMER BOY," aka DB, as most of the people who knew him called him—saw Bottom peering out through the rear curtains of the stage where their band, Joker Plague, was set up to play to the audience in Roosevelt Park. Through the thick velvet, they could hear people clapping and shouting impatiently. "Well?" Michael asked as Bottom let the curtains close.

Bottom glanced back at him: the head of donkey on a man's body. The thick lips curled over cartoon-character teeth; he held the neck of the Fender Precision already strapped around his neck. Michael twirled the drumsticks held in each of his six hands. "It's a decent crowd," Bottom told him. "Nearly all jokers, of course."

"A 'decent' crowd? You mean a mediocre one. Shit." Michael pulled one of the curtains aside, looking out himself. The front of the stage area was packed, the audience there applauding in unison and pumping fists in the air, but the crowd thinned out well before it reached the end of the park's field. When Joker Plague had played here during their heyday ten years ago, the crowd would have spilled out onto Chrystie and Forsyth Streets, which the Fort Freak cops would have closed off.

But that was years ago. The Joker Plague faithful were here, but . . .

They were rapidly becoming an "old" band. While they could still pack the smaller venues, in the past they had played huge arenas to thousands—not just to jokers, but to crowds of nats as well. They still had fans, still put out the requisite new album every year or two, but their new material never got the airplay, coverage, and good reviews that their old stuff had, and the nats now paid no attention to them at all.

Playing music had been his refuge when everything in his life had turned to shit. Now he was losing that too. Even the jokers' rights events where he'd once been so visible had mostly vanished, just like Joker

Plague's fame and days with the Committee. He was becoming "that old guy, whatshisname" that they dragged out on stage to give a few lines before the "real" talent appeared.

Washed-up and useless in his mid-thirties. Playing a parody of himself now. "Fuck." Michael let the curtain close.

"What's the problem?" Shivers asked. He was the guitarist for the group, who had the appearance of a bloody devil newly released from hell. Everything about him was the color of blood: his skin, his face, his hair, the twin horns jutting from his forehead, his trademark Gibson SG guitar. Shivers, like the other members of the group, didn't seem to notice or care how they'd fallen. If they were no longer making the money they used to, money managed to come in and it was sufficient. "It's showtime."

S'Live—a balloon-like face gashed with mouth and eyes, thin and impossibly long arms protruding from his head like a living Mr. Potato Head—hovered in the air near the back. The Voice, the lead singer for the group, was there as well: invisible but for the wireless mic that floated in the air near Shivers without any apparent hand holding it there. Their head roadie, a joker built like a two-legged, seven-foot-tall pit bull (and with the same breath), gave them a double thumbs-up at Shivers' statement.

"Shiver's right," the Voice said in his mellifluous, rich baritone. "Let's get on with it. There's a couple chicks waiting for me back in the hotel room, getting themselves ready, if you know what I mean." He laughed. The Voice lifted the mic, flipping the switch on the barrel. "Are you ready?" he bellowed, his voice amplified to a roar through the PA system, the echo from the nearest buildings bouncing back to them belatedly. A mass cry from the audience answered him. "C'mon," the Voice responded. "You can do better than that! I said, are you *ready?*"

This time the response could be felt through the risers of the stage, throbbing with the affirmation. The microphone bobbed through the air to the curtains, and the Voice's invisible hand held them open.

Michael clicked on the switch for his wireless throat mics and went through, tapping with his drumsticks on the rings of tympanic membranes that covered his bare, muscular chest, all six arms moving. From the openings on either side of his thick neck, the sound came out from the two throat "mouths" to be caught by the mics there: a throbbing, compelling drumbeat, the lowest bass ring pounding a steady, driving rhythm through the subs of the PA system.

The crowd erupted as a spotlight found Michael and the stage lights began to throb in time with his drumbeat. Then Shivers came through with a single, killer power chord that screamed from the Marshall amps at the back of the stage. S'Live glided through the air to his bank of keyboards, and Bottom strode to the other side of the stage, thumb-slapping his bass in a funk pattern to complement Michael's beat, his ass's head bobbing.

They let the song develop and grow in volume as fog machines began to throw out mist colored by the stage lighting, through which there was sudden movement: the Voice stepping forward to the front of the stage, visible only as an emptiness within the fog. His powerful vocals throbbed from the speakers as he began to sing "Lamentation," the title song from their latest album:

> Rivers etch the stones and die in sand
> Spires carved by unknown hands cannot stand
> A storm cloud stalks the sky alone and emptied
> From a place where nothing goes and nothing ever comes

Even as the group kicked hard into the chorus of the tune, Michael could feel the dissatisfaction of the audience. Increasingly over the years, their audiences had only wanted to hear the old hits from their first three or four albums. They seemed to tolerate the new tunes, but the crowd only screamed their approval when they played the old stuff. The walls of the sound system hurled their music out over the crowd, and the front rows danced, but there was a sense that they were mostly waiting for the song to be over and hoping that the next would be one that they recognized.

Frustration made Michael pound all the harder on himself as he prowled the edge of the stage, as Shivers' guitars shrieked in a blindingly fast solo, as they came back into the chorus once more, as the song thundered into the crescendo of the climax. Applause and a few cheers answered them, and someone near the front of the stage bellowed out "DB! Play 'Fool'! Play 'Incidental Music'!" Both were songs from their first number one album.

Michael grimaced and flexed his six arms and the scrolling landscape of complex tattoos crawled over his naked torso. He shrugged to the others. "Sure," he said into his throat mics. "Whatever you fuckers want. That's why we're here."

A roar of delight answered him as Shivers began the intro to "Self-

Fulfilling Fool," finally hitting the power chord with S'Live that kicked the first verse. Michael began to play, his hands waving as he struck himself with the drumsticks, his insistent drumbeat booming, his throat openings moving like extra mouths as he shaped the sound. He walked to the east side of the stage, playing to the crowd there, who lifted hands toward him as if in supplication. The Voice began to sing:

You want to believe them
You don't want them to be cruel
But when you look in the mirror
What looks back is a self-fulfilling fool

The blast came on the word "fool."

The sound thundered louder than the band. The concussion tore into Michael, lifting him off his feet and tossing him from the stage in a barrage of stage equipment, tumbling PA speakers, and shrapnel.

The world went dark and silent around him for a long time afterward.

♥

The light was intense, so much so that he had to shut his eyes again. His ears were roaring with white noise. He could barely hear the voice speaking to him over it. "Mr. Vogali, glad to see you're back with us."

He managed to crack open one eyelid. In the slit of reality that revealed, a face was peering down at him: a dark-haired woman with a gauze mask over her mouth and nose and a large plastic shield over her eyes. At least from what he could see, she was a nat. Not a joker. So this wasn't Dr. Finn's Jokertown Clinic. "Where . . . ?" he started to say, but his throat burned and the word emerged strangled and hoarse.

"You're in Bellevue Hospital's ER, Mr. Vogali. I'm Dr. Levin. Do you remember what happened to you?"

"The others . . ." he managed to croak out. He tried to grab at Dr. Levin's arm with his middle left hand, but the motion nearly made him scream from pain. The doctor shook her head. "Please don't move," she said to him. "You've a badly injured arm, broken bones that we need to set, and we're still assessing any other possible injuries. We're taking good care of you, but . . . please don't move."

"The others," he insisted. "You have to tell me."

Dr. Levin glanced away, as if trying to see through the curtains around them. "I'll check and see if they've been brought here," she said. "Right now, I'm only worried about you and what we need to do . . ."

♣

He still didn't remember, a week later.

Michael sat at the window of his penthouse apartment on Grand Street, a specially designed, six-sleeved terrycloth robe wrapped around him. His right ankle was locked in an immobility boot, his left leg casted to mid-thigh. Two of the left sleeves were empty, the cast on the middle arm taped to his body underneath the robe. The left lower arm . . . well, that arm was missing to above the elbow; too badly mangled to save, they'd told him.

That loss was something he would feel forever. The doctors had talked about a prosthetic down the road, but . . . He could still *feel* the arm and the hand. It even ached. Phantom limb syndrome, they called it. A fucking disaster, it felt like to him. *All of it, a fucking disaster . . .*

The rips and cuts from the flying wreckage and the ball bearings the bomber had packed into his bombs were beginning to heal, but his face and his body were still marred by blackened scabs and the lines of stitches. His left ear was ripped and scabbed from where its several piercings had been forcibly torn out. Three of the six tympanic membranes on his chest—his drums—had been rent open. The surgeon at Bellevue who'd sewn the fleshy strips back together and taped them said he was "fairly sure" they'd heal, but didn't know how potential scarring might affect their sound. His left tibia had been fractured, resting now on a footstool in front of his chair; his right knee's patella had been cracked after he'd been thrown from the stage and landed on blacktop; his face and his arms—five of them, not six now—looked as if someone had taken a belt sander to his skin. His hearing was still overlaid with the rumbling tinnitus that was the legacy of the explosion, though thankfully the in-ear monitors he'd been wearing had blocked most of the permanent damage that might have occurred.

He was alive. That, at least, was something. That's what they kept telling him, over and over, during those first days in the hospital.

S'Live had also been brought to Bellevue; he'd succumbed to his injuries while in surgery. Shivers had been DOA on arrival. They hadn't even attempted to revive the Voice, who had been nearest the explosion; regrettably for those responsible for cleanup, his invisibility hadn't survived his death, either. Bottom was still alive, taken to another hospital, though he'd lost his right arm, right leg, and right eye, among other less severe injuries.

Thirty other people nearest the stage had also died, with more than a hundred wounded, some in critical condition, which meant that the final death count would be higher.

"This is all over the news," their long-time manager, Grady Cohen, had said in an almost cheery voice back in the hospital. "It's been twenty-four hours non-stop on all the channels all day. No one's talking about anything else. All this has the label planning a new Joker Plague retrospective double album; they're hoping to release it in the next few weeks, to take advantage of the publicity." At which point DB had told him to get the fuck out of his room.

No one had yet claimed responsibility for the blast. Fox News was openly speculating that it was most likely Islamic terrorism, citing Michael's involvement in the Committee interventions in the Middle East a decade ago and talking about how this might be retaliation; CNN was less certain, but certainly dwelled a lot on Michael's time with the Committee, flashing old footage over and over. The FBI, SCARE, and Homeland Security were heavily involved in the investigation, supposedly.

But the explosion was no longer the front page–featured story. A week later, other events had pushed it aside, and after all, most of the dead and injured had only been jokers.

Only jokers. The marginalized ones.

In another week, Michael knew, the entire episode would all be old news, only revived if something new and provocative was uncovered or if they caught the bomber. Already, the requests for interviews were beginning to dry up, judging by the thin stack of notes his hired caregiver had given him this morning, and coverage on the news networks had dwindled to a few minutes' update on the hour, and then only if there was some small new development.

A cup of tea steamed on the table alongside his chair, near the closed MacBook Air there. Michael reached over with his upper right hand to grab it; the motion pulled at the healing scars and muscles in his chest, and he grimaced, groaning involuntarily. That caused his caregiver for this shift—a nat Latino man named Marcos—to poke his head around the corner. "You OK there, Mr. Vogali?"

"Yeah. Fine," Michael told him.

"OK. Give me a few minutes and I'll be in with your meds." The head withdrew.

Michael sipped at the tea and stared out the window over the roofs of Jokertown, the ghetto of Manhattan where most of the jokers lived, just to the east. He knew that if he went to the window, he'd see, a few stories below on the street, a nondescript black car parked in the NO PARKING zone. Since the bombing, it was always there, with two tired-looking plainclothes cops inside from the Jokertown precinct, Fort Freak, watching his building.

Michael had caretakers he'd hired—people who would take care of him because he paid them. He had a few groupies—people who came to see him because he was still marginally famous and they hoped some of that glamor might rub off on them. He had this apartment and a London flat that he rented out. He had Grady Cohen, whose living was largely dependent on Joker Plague concerts and memorabilia sales. He had the cops who'd been assigned to watch him in the wake of the bombing. But beyond that . . .

He had no family. No wife. No girlfriend. No children, at least none that he knew of. He couldn't even call the other members of Joker Plague true friends, though he'd inhabited the same studios and same stages with them for years. He nearly laughed bitterly at that thought: *all of them dead now except for Bottom.*

That still hadn't sunk in. Bottom, Shivers, S'Live, the Voice: these were the people with whom he'd spent nearly all his time for the last two decades. At least Bottom had family: a wife (Bethany? Brittany? Michael wasn't sure) and two kids Michael had seen in pictures but also couldn't name, somewhere in Ohio in a suburb of one of the C-cities (Columbus? Cincinnati? Cleveland?). Bottom had called Michael four or five times in the last week—at least Michael had seen his number on the missed calls list of his cell phone. He hadn't returned any of the calls. He wasn't sure what to say. It was easier just to pretend he hadn't seen the calls.

The only person (other than the well-paid Grady Cohen) who'd visited him after the explosion, who had actually come to see him while he'd been in the hospital, was Rusty: Wally Gunderson, or Rustbelt, the joker-ace who had been on the Committee with Michael, and who had been with him for the disaster in the Middle East that had led to DB's angry resignation. No one else from his old *American Hero* days had bothered to do more than send a card or useless bouquets of flowers. Not Curveball. Not Earth Witch. Not Lohengrin or Babel or Bubbles or John Fortune or any of the other Committee aces or *American Hero* alumnae. That, if nothing else, showed DB how he was considered by them: somebody they knew, not somebody they loved.

It was 4:00 P.M. Michael snatched the TV remote with his middle right hand. CNN flickered into life, with Wolf Blitzer's sagging, white-bearded face filling the screen. ". . . latest on the bomber's letter—a manifesto is perhaps the best description of this long, rambling missive—that was evidently delivered to the *Jokertown Cry* the day after the explosion, but not released by the authorities until just this morning. The writer claims responsibility for the Wild Card Day blast in Roosevelt Park, and also claims that he intended to die in the blast himself." A reproduction of the letter filled the green screen behind Blitzer, with some of the text highlighted. Michael turned up the volume. "Let me read just a portion of this communication allegedly from the bomber. 'The bleeding heart liberal scum of America, who are best exemplified by Joker Plague's Drummer Boy, who preach that we must tolerate and accept those who bear God's marks of sin, can no longer be tolerated, not if we are ever to cleanse the earth of their filth. The wild card virus is God's punishment on the human race and all jokers will inevitably be purified in the cleansing fires of hell. I will purify myself with them. What I have done with my action is to set God's plan in motion.'"

Blitzer paused as the letter vanished from the screen to be replaced by footage taken after the blast. *So the bomber died in the blast—but who was the fucker?* Michael saw blast victims being treated by EMTs and jokers staggering around with blood running down their misshapen faces—video he'd seen a hundred times already. "If this unsigned manifesto is indeed from the bomber, then we are, according to the experts I've spoken with, in all likelihood dealing with a homegrown terrorist. Let's bring in the head of the UN Committee on Extraordinary Interventions, Barbara Baden, to talk about this . . ."

"Bitch." Michael flicked off the TV. He scowled, looking out through the window once more at the Jokertown landscape. *A "homegrown terrorist." A joker hater. Someone who specifically hates me. And he's killed himself too, the bastard.*

I want to know who this son of a bitch was, and I want to know if someone helped him with this.

All five of his hands curled into fists, but he thought he could feel the missing sixth hand do the same.

♠

"Thanks for meeting me, man," Michael said to the imposing joker across the table from him at Twisted Dragon, a restaurant set in the indefinable border between Jokertown and Chinatown, a once-famous place to meet now clinging desperately to vestiges of its fame under the latest in a long sequence of hopeful owners. Rusty had brought back two massive plates heaped with offerings from the lunch buffet; Michael had settled on chicken fried rice and a bowl of wonton soup.

Michael's plainclothes shadows had followed him in, taking a table near the door. One was Beastie: seven feet tall with bright red fur and clawed hands, about as unobtrusive as a velociraptor dressed in a tutu. Beastie's partner was Chey Moleka, an Asian nat, her black hair pulled back into a tight bun under a knitted black beanie hat with the Brooklyn Dodgers logo stitched in front. Despite being in regular clothing for this assignment, her appearance still screamed "cop."

Rusty shrugged metallic shoulders, and with one hand rubbed at the bolts that seemingly held his jaw in place; his other hand held a fork hovering over a mound of Hunan Shrimp. His skin was buffed and polished; not a trace of rust anywhere, which told Michael that Rusty had spent some time with steel wool that morning. "Hey, I was happy to do it," Rusty said. "After all, we're friends, right?" Michael saw Rusty glance at Michael's torso, uncharacteristically covered by a heavily modified T-shirt to accommodate his too-large chest and arms, the middle left hand bound underneath with an elastic bandage, the bandaged stub of his lower left hand sticking awkwardly out from its sleeve. Most of the time, DB went bare-chested so that his natural drumheads were accessible, and yes, because his muscled and tattooed torso was often admired. "Cripes, how are you doing, fella?" Rusty asked Michael. "You healing up OK? Y'know, those drums and all?" Michael saw his gaze travel quickly over the missing arm. Rusty tapped his own chest with a finger; it sounded like two hammers clanking together. "Your arms . . ." he began, and stopped. "Your leg's still in a cast, but you're getting along with those crutches," he finished.

"It's coming along slowly," Michael answered. "I'm mobile, and my arm's getting better quicker than the docs expected. The missing one . . ." He attempted a shrug. "It really hurts to play right now, but the docs think it'll all come back in time. Most of it, anyway."

Rusty nodded his great iron head. "That's good to hear. Ghost—Yerodin, that's her real name, but hey, she doesn't like me to call her that—said to say 'howdy' to you." He managed to look sheepish and he plopped a forkful of shrimp in his mouth, chewed a few moments, then swallowed. "She remembers you coming to the Institute, and I've told her about your band and all, but I haven't let her listen to many of your songs yet. She's so young and the lyrics, well . . ."

Michael waved away the apology. "No worries. Show me what she looks like now."

Rusty pulled out his smartphone, tapping at the screen with his fingers, then turning it around so Michael could see the screen. There was a myriad of tiny scratches on the glass screen—Michael wondered how often Rusty had to replace his phone—and underneath the scratches a young black girl stared up at Michael, her hair woven into several long braids capped with brightly-colored beads. Michael couldn't imagine Rusty managing that with his thick, clumsy fingers; he wondered who'd done the braids; as far as he knew, Rusty was still mourning for Jerusha—the ace called Gardener—who'd died during a Committee incursion into Africa, a year or so after Michael had resigned. "She's a pretty one," he said, and Rusty beamed.

"She sure is. You oughta come see her again soon. She'd love that."

"I will, I promise," Michael said. He took a slow spoonful of his soup with his middle right hand, feeling the pull on the bandaged wounds. His right hands drummed on the tabletop as he set the spoon down. It was hard to resist the temptation to tap on the T-shirt covered drumheads—a nervous habit he'd had ever since the virus had changed him—but he knew how that would hurt. It would hurt more if, once the sutures were out and the tears healed, the natural drums didn't work as they had. And the missing arm—that would be part of him forever, now. "I take it you've heard about the letter the bomber sent to the J-town precinct station?"

"Yeah. Holy cow, that fella had to've been nuts. Anyone who'd set a bomb just to kill jokers, and boy, the nasty way he talked about you, and then to blow himself up . . ." Rusty's hand tightened around his fork; Michael watched it bend. Rusty noticed as well; he clumsily tried to straighten it and set it down with a rueful glance. "I'll have to pay them for that," he said, then looked back at Michael. Rusty shook his head, his neck groaning metallically with the motion. "The other guy in your band who survived—what was his name? Bottom?—how's he doing? It must be tough, you guys losing your friends and so many of your fans like that."

Michael felt a surge of guilt. He hadn't seen Bottom since the first week, and there were still all the unreturned calls. He hadn't attended the funerals of S'Live, the Voice, or Shivers, though he'd sent—that is, he'd had Grady send—cards and flowers, saying he was still too ill to be there even though his doctor had told him he'd give Michael permission to travel as long as he promised to be careful. He hadn't personally visited the victims who'd been hospitalized, though Grady had insisted on him recording a video from his bed, later posted on YouTube, spouting all the expected platitudes and clichés.

Friends? I don't have friends, just a lot of bridges left broken and smoking behind me . . .

But he couldn't say that to Rusty. Not to those huge, empathetic, and simple eyes. "Bottom's doing as well as can be expected," he answered. "And I'll tell you, I need . . . I *want* to know more about this bomber: who he was and what he was thinking, and whether he was part of a group. I'd want to know who he is—and I'm tired of waiting for the FBI and the cops to figure it out." The last sentence sounded too eager and too harsh, and Michael regretted letting it slip out, even to Rusty.

"After he called you 'scum' and said you were the one he most wanted dead, I understand," Rusty said. Rusty didn't seem to have noticed Michael's escorts at their table. "Hey, you want to find him? Why don't we figure out who this guy was together? I could help you. I've kinda been a detective myself. I had to find Ghost's teacher when he got snatched . . ."

Michael was already shaking his head, and Rusty's excited voice trailed off. *You can't, because if I find out there are other bastards involved, I'm going to kill them the way I'd've killed that bomber asshole if he hadn't offed himself. I won't involve you in that.* "This is something I gotta do myself," Michael told him. "You can understand that, right?"

"Yeah, sure," Rusty answered, but Michael could see the disappointment in his eyes.

"Look," Michael told him, "there is something you *can* do to help. You still have contacts in the Committee, right? Could you talk to someone there, someone you trust? See if you can find out if the Committee was involved, and let me know. Could you do that for me?"

"Sure can," Rusty enthused. "I'll make a few calls as soon as I get back. Hey, why don'tcha come with me? You could see Ghost."

He should have. Michael knew that; it's what a true friend would have done. But he shook his head. "I can't right now. I have to see someone. You know how it is." He signaled to the waiter for the check with his upper right hand. "Let me get this," he told Rusty. "You've been a great help, Rusty. Thanks. Give Ghost a hug for me, huh?"

"Sure. You'll come by some other time, OK?"

"Yeah, I will. I promise."

Meaningless words and an empty promise, but Rusty beamed.

On his way out, Michael crutched over to the cops' table. "Just so you know, I'm heading over to Fort Freak, so why don't you two give me a ride so I don't have to call an Uber. It ain't like I'm gonna run the whole way . . ."

♦

Beastie and Chey accompanied Michael into the station: New York's Fifth Precinct, better known as Fort Freak. Sergeant Homer Taylor, called Wingman, was at the front desk. He glanced up as Michael slowly approached.

"Hey, DB," he said, his drooping wings lifting a bit with the motion. Beastie and Chey moved on into the precinct's depths. "Good to see you're up and moving around, even on crutches. How can I help you?"

"Hey, Wingman. Can you let Detective Black know I want to see him?" Michael asked.

"He's out at the moment," Taylor grunted. "Lunch."

"Mind if I wait? I'd hate to have you send out my two shadows again so quickly."

Taylor shrugged, the wings lifting and falling with the motion. "Whatever. Help yourself to a chair. But hey, would you mind giving an autograph? My wife's a big fan . . ." Taylor held out a pen and a piece of paper.

Michael repressed the sigh that threatened as he took the pen in his lower right hand, leaning heavily on the crutches. "Sure," he said. "What's your wife's name?"

Detective Black entered the station a few minutes later. Michael had met Black before, during the investigation into the joker disappearances a year or so ago, then again after the bombing. Black—Detective Francis Xavier Black, according to the card he'd handed Michael when he'd interviewed him in the hospital, and called "Franny" according to Beastie and Chey, which struck Michael as an oddly feminine nickname for a dark-haired, burly nat in a cheap, rumpled gray suit, who looked like he hadn't slept in days. He hadn't shaved this morning, either. Black rubbed at the stubble on his chin as he saw Michael sitting in one of the chairs to the side of Taylor's desk. He inclined his head to Michael. "Come on back, Mr. Vogali," he said in a soft, quiet voice, and led Michael into a tiny office crammed in the rear of the precinct first floor.

As Michael lowered himself into a heavy wooden chair on the other side of a paper-stacked desk, leaning his crutches against the scarred and scratched arms, Black sat in the battered office chair there, pushing aside folders so that there was a clear space in which he could fold his hands. "I take it you've heard the reports about the letter." It was a statement, not a question.

"Yeah. So this guy sent his letter to the *Cry*, and blew himself up in the explosion. Is that what you people are claiming?"

"That's what the letter claims, yes."

"So someone found the body? The remnants of the guy's suicide vest, maybe?"

"You know I can't talk to you about an active case, Mr. Vogali."

"It's not that hard a question. And if the fucker's dead, what's it matter?"

"It's still an active case," Black persisted. "Look, I have to keep my nose clean right now. Frankly, my bosses would love to find an excuse to push me out of here." Something in his tone made Michael narrow his eyes.

"So are you still handling the case?" Michael interrupted the platitudes. "Or not?"

Black seemed to wince. "You already know that the FBI and Homeland Security are involved, as they have to be and should be. They have resources we don't have here. I'm still in the loop and still working any local angles, but if you're asking, no, I'm not in charge. That control's been passed further up the chain."

"So you guys don't have a name yet? You haven't identified the bomber."

Black's dead stare impaled him. "How many times do you want me to give you the same line, Mr. Vogali? I can't talk . . ."

". . . about an open case. Yeah, I get it. But the letter came to the *Cry*— where was it sent from? Was it local?"

"Even if it were—and I'm not saying that's the case—what would that mean? The guy had to be here to set off the bomb anyway. Look, I understand how you must feel, but . . ."

"But it's been kicked upstairs," Michael interrupted loudly, "and because it's just ugly jokers who were killed and injured, because it was just a Joker Plague concert in lousy Jokertown, it's not exactly high priority. If the bomber had set off the bomb at Yankee Stadium and killed a bunch of high-rolling nats, then they'd already have figured out who he is and his face would be plastered all over the news. Yeah, I get it."

Michael grabbed his crutches and pushed himself off the chair like a wounded spider. Black's stare had gentled, but his lips were pressed together in a thin, almost angry line. Michael wondered who the man was pissed at; the emotions coming from Black didn't seem to be directed toward Michael. "Mr. Vogali, I assure you that this *isn't* low priority for me. Jokertown is my district. I knew people who died in that blast, too, and I want the person or persons who murdered them to be identified just as much as you do. But y'know what, I drank a lot of iced tea at lunch and I really need to take a piss. I hope you don't mind if I do that." Black shuffled through the files on his desk and plucked out a slim file folder, placing it down carefully on top of the stack of files nearest Michael. "I'll be gone, oh, five minutes or so, then I'm going to come back and . . ." He paused momentarily, giving emphasis to his next words. ". . . look through that file. Thanks for stopping by, Mr. Vogali. I really hope we both find what we're looking for in the end."

Black pushed back his chair and moved past Michael to the door. Ostentatiously, he closed the blinds over the glass there, and shut the door behind him.

Michael watched the blinds sway, then settle. Leaning on his crutches, he reached out with his lower right hand and took the file folder from the stack. The brown, thick cover was stamped with both the Homeland Security and FBI emblems, and was labeled *Roosevelt Park Bombing, 9/15*.

Michael looked again at the closed door. He sat once more, then opened the file and started reading.

♥

Michael's brief look at the file did little to ease his mind, nor did it give him much more information. Yes, the FBI had swarmed in the day of the blast, according to Franny Black's notes. There were three bodies near the location of the explosion that—like the poor Voice—were so badly mutilated that identification had been very difficult and slow. There were sub-files for each one; none had yet been definitely ruled to be the bomber, but two were jokers local to Jokertown, none of whom had ever done anything suspicious, according to Black's notes. The other body was a male nat who was identified through dental records as Bryan Fisher—particular attention was being paid to that investigation, especially since Fisher was former military. Fisher lived in Reading, Pennsylvania; from the reports in the file, he had given no outward indication of being someone who hated jokers. His wife claimed he was a long-time fan of Joker Plague, who had once played a show at his army base in Germany. Yes, she knew Bryan had gone to New York for the show, and she hadn't accompanied him because she was eight months pregnant and didn't think it would be good for the baby or her to be exposed to the decibels or the crowds. No, the letter that was sent to the *Cry* didn't sound like anything her husband had ever said or written; she couldn't believe it was from him.

The bomb had been placed under the front of the stage, probably the night before the concert—there was a separate investigation looking into the crew who had been charged with assembling the stage and providing security before the concert. The explosive had been military grade C4 (another reason to keep Fisher on the suspect list), set off with a homemade short-range detonator—the report noted that it was indeed very likely that the bomber had been caught in his own blast.

The file had included the full text of the letter sent to the *Jokertown Cry*, though the original and the envelope in which it had been sent were in the hands of the FBI. Michael scanned it, his stomach roiling as he read the hateful, ugly words there.

The file only fueled his anger. The file only made him feel more frustrated and useless. He felt he understood Detective Black's irritation.

♣

Two days later, Michael found himself lying bare-chested on an examination table in the Jokertown Clinic as Dr. Finn removed the stitches from the torn membranes that were the natural drumheads in Michael's body. The tattoos covering his arms, chest, and back were stark against his flesh. "There, that's the last of them," Dr. Finn said. The doctor's centaur-like body stepped back, the sound of his hooves muffled against the tile by elastic booties. "Whoever stitched you up at Bellevue did a nice job. Everything looks good and it's healing up nicely so far—better and faster than I'd expect, in fact—but I don't know how bad the scarring might be or how that might change the sound. That's something you'll find out, but I wouldn't advise banging away on them just yet. Give them another few weeks."

Michael shook his head. "Jesus, doc, you don't understand . . ."

Finn laughed. "Oh, I think I do. Just take it easy, OK? Nothing too strenuous, or you're going to be back here looking for more stitches, or worse, picking up an infection." He pointed at the computer monitor on the desk in the room, where several X-rays were up. "Those are from your leg and your arms. They're all healing faster than I'd expect, too—one good trait the wild card seems to have given you is the ability to recover more quickly than normal. I think we can move you to a walking cast on the leg as long as you promise to be careful, and splints for the broken arm to replace the casts. The amputation is pretty much healed; we can start looking into a prosthetic for you soon. Sound good? You're going to need some extensive PT afterward to get full range of motion back everywhere in general, I expect."

Michael grunted. With his lower right hand, he tapped the bass membrane and flexed the throat opening on that side. A low, resonant *doom* answered, reverberating in the room. "Ouch," Michael said, grimacing. "That fucking hurts."

"Good," Finn told him. "That'll keep you from using them too much. Sounded decent, though."

"I guess," Michael said. "Hurt like a sonofabitch, though." Michael rubbed carefully around the ridged outline of the membrane, sliding a finger over the knobby ridge of healing skin. The remnants of his missing left arm flexed, as if it wanted to strike the drumhead closest to it, though it was far too short for that.

"All right," Finn said. "Let me get Troll to fit you in the walking cast and splint. And I'll see you again in a week."

"Whatever you say, doc."

Finn walked out of the examining room, his tail sweeping around as he turned. Michael's phone buzzed; he fished it from his pants pocket and looked at the screen, staring at the name there for several seconds before he stabbed the Accept Call button with a forefinger. "Babel?"

"No, this is Juliette," a woman's voice answered. "Ink. I'm Barbara's assistant now."

"Hey, Ink," Michael said. "Good to hear your voice again. What's up? Let me talk to Babel."

There was a dry laugh from the other side of the receiver. "Mizz Baden asked me to call you," she said. "She said Rusty told her that the two of you are playing detective."

"Rusty's the one who wants to play detective, not me," Michael answered. "I just want to make sure the bastard's dead, that we know who it is, and that if he had help, we get those assholes too. So I take it that the Committee's been involved in the investigation?"

"It landed on Mizz Baden's desk, briefly. She and Jayewardene decided it wasn't in the Committee's purview."

"What?" Michael's voice rose. "Why'd the Committee pass on the bombing?"

Michael could hear Ink take another breath, as if she were deciding how much to say. "It's a matter of priorities and importance, DB. Mizz Baden said you wouldn't understand that. She's sorry about what happened with your band. But you've no idea of what we've . . ."

"Are you telling me that the bombing in Jokertown isn't *important* enough, Ink? Is that what you're saying? People *died*. People I've known for decades." Michael wondered at his own careful choice of words: "people," not friends.

There was a sigh from the other end of the line. "You don't understand, DB. You can't. I've given you all I was told. Mizz Baden thought that since Rusty asked, you deserved that much, but I don't have any more information than that. Sorry. I hope your recovery's going well. I'll tell her I talked to you."

"No, no. Hang on, Ink. Give me some help here. Jesus . . ."

"DB, the bombing was a local issue," Ink said, "not an international one."

Michael couldn't quite decipher what he was hearing in that statement, what Ink was saying or not saying. "OK . . . So the person responsible's here in the States? I already figured that out."

Another pause. "Mizz Baden . . . she believes the bomber was even more local than that. That's really all I can tell you."

"Are you saying the guy's here in New York?"

There was nothing but silence on the other side of the line. Then: "Mizz Baden wanted me to call you because Rusty asked and she cares very much for him and all he's done. He's a good person, a kind one. I did, though, as Mizz Baden's assistant, see the files on the bombing. Let me ask you a hypothetical question, DB. What if the person who did this isn't so different from you? How many people have we hurt in the pursuit of what we think's right? For that matter, what is 'right'? Who has the most reason to hate jokers, DB? Who?"

"Riddles and questions? That's all you got for me? Damn it, Ink . . ."

"I've told you all I can," she answered. "Mizz Baden said to tell you she wishes you luck. Now, I have other work I need to do. Goodbye, DB." And with that, Ink was gone.

"Yeah? Well, fuck you too!" Michael shouted into the dead phone, startling Troll, the nurse, who was walking into the examination room with an assortment of equipment in his arms. The giant's eyes widened.

"Not you, Troll," Michael said. "Just the world in general."

♠

The scene at the Jerusha Carter Childhood Development Institute was chaotic. Once past the courtyard with its huge, spreading baobab tree, looking like someone had planted a tree upside down, Michael entered a large, open room. The armless, legless trunk of an infant floated past Michael's face as he opened the door, the eyes in a mouthless head large and plaintive, with dark pupils that moved to track on Michael's own gaze as it floated silently past him; the slits that served as nostrils flexed, as if

the child were sniffing him. There were joker children seemingly everywhere in the single large room, of all conceivable twisted and distorted
shapes, with an army of attendants, mostly jokers themselves, moving
among them.

One was a young boy who looked perfectly normal except that he
seemed to have the hiccups; with each spasm, he exhaled a blast of flame.
An attendant stood alongside him with an asbestos blanket and a fire ex-
tinguisher, but otherwise didn't touch the boy.

A slug-like body with a human head tracked a slimy path over the tiles,
pulling itself along with rail-thin arms. One young girl's body was covered in putrescent boils, the smell coming from her like that of days-dead
animal. A boy who looked to be about five started to cry, then suddenly
dissolved into a puddle of brown sludge, his clothing lying on top of the
pile; one of the attendants came over with a bucket, a snow shovel, and a
broom and began scooping up the mess. "Sorry," she said. "He does that
when he gets upset . . ."

"Hey, fella!" Rusty's boisterous voice called out, and a metallic hand
clapped him hard on his upper shoulders. Michael staggered forward
under the blow. "Sorry—didn't mean to hit yah so hard. But look, you're
outta your cast and into a boot, and your arms, too . . . That's great. Betcha
feel a lot better."

"Yeah, I do," Michael told him. "I thought I'd let you know that Ink,
Babel's assistant, called me, so thanks for reaching out to her."

Rusty grinned, his steam-shovel jaw opening. "So did she have anything good to tell us?"

Michael heard the "us" and ignored it; he wasn't going to encourage
Rusty to keep playing detective. "Not really. The Committee passed on the
investigation. Otherwise, she just talked in circles without saying much."
Michael shook his head. "Thanks for trying, anyway. So this is where you
spend all your time now instead of running around with the Committee?
These are all orphans like Ghost?"

Rusty grunted. "You betcha. These are the kids nobody wants. Me and
you—we both saw what happens to kids like this in Iraq, and I saw lots
worse than that in Africa when me and Jerusha were there. Cripes, the
same thing happens here, too—it's just that no one ever wants to talk
about it. There are parents can't handle a kid once their card turns, or
maybe they died too, or . . ." Rusty's voice trailed off again as Ghost came
running toward them. "Hey, Uncle DB," she said. Her voice still had the
lilt of Africa in it. "You came to visit?"

"Yeah," Michael said, wrapping his good left arm and two right ones around her and lifting her up. The scars on his chest protested; he ignored that beyond a grimace. "I haven't seen you in way too long. Look at you—you're getting so big."

"I'll be bigger than you or Wally one day."

"Maybe you will," Michael told her, laughing. "But not if I squeeze you real tight." He started to tighten his arms around her; Ghost simply went insubstantial and dropped away from him. She grinned up at him, and glided off toward the rear of the room. "She's growing up fast," he told Rusty. "Is she still . . . ?"

"The episodes? Yeah, they come and go. Most of the time she's just a little girl, but she still has problems being with the other kids, especially if she gets frustrated. And sometimes the dreams and memories get to her, and she's the child soldier who wanted to kill me. But it's getting better."

Michael looked around the room, at all the joker kids. "Do any of them ever get adopted?"

"Not enough. We've had a few of 'em adopted, mostly by other jokers. Cripes, these kids are the really damaged ones, the ones that are the most difficult to handle, sometimes even dangerous. That poor kid over there . . ." Rusty pointed his chin to the boy who hiccuped flame. "That's Moto; the kid's already been bounced from four foster homes, and he's nearly burnt down this place a few times besides. Who wants a child who can set his bed on fire because he has an upset tummy, or gets too excited or frightened?" Rusty shook his large head dolefully. "Hopefully he'll eventually learn to control the response, but maybe he won't. Some of these kids will just . . . well, age out of the Institute at eighteen. Or die before then. The virus ain't kind to most of 'em. Not like it was to us. But I'll tell you what; we really appreciate the money you've sent us every year. That means a lot."

"It's the least I can do," Michael answered. *And that's true. All I've done is the very least, and that's all I've done for a long time . . .*

Then change that, he thought, but it was a resolution he'd had a few thousand times before, and one he'd never kept. *Change that.*

Michael noticed that Rusty was looking down at the floor. The legless slug-child had dragged himself over to Rusty; he was crying, and Rusty crouched down to pat him, ribbons of slime clinging to Rusty's fingers and pulling away from the kid as he did so. "Y'know, fella, some of these kids hate themselves, hate what they've been turned into. They can't stand the pain or the abuse they've received. What kind of way is that for anyone to live? How do they get through it? That's what I worry about with them all. I wish there was more I could do, but . . ."

Rusty was still talking, but Michael had stopped listening.

Some of the kids hate themselves . . . Who has the most reason to hate jokers, DB . . . ? All jokers will inevitably be purified in the cleansing fires of hell, and I will purify myself with them . . .

The words Rusty had just spoken, the question Ink had asked him, the bomber's manifesto . . .

As he left the Institute later, Michael pulled his smartphone from his pants pocket and hit a button. The call went nearly immediately to voice mail. "Hey, Grady," he said after the beep. "It's DB. Look, I know you've always kept this shit away from us, but could you send me any nasty mail—either email or snail mail—that came in for me just prior to the Roosevelt Park show? Maybe up to three days beforehand? Send it to me, would you?—envelopes and all if it was snail mail, and with the full headers if they're email. I appreciate it. I'll touch base with you later, man."

◆

Grady ended up sending a couple dozen pieces to Michael: mostly emails and a few actual letters.

Michael read and re-read the missives over the next day, pondering what to do with them. It was a depressing read. As manager, Grady had always passed along to the band the complimentary fan mail they received; he held back "the crazy stuff." The vitriol, the anger, the insanity that Michael glimpsed in the missives was saddening. Some of it was simply former fans ranting that the band's new music sucked, that they'd lost their edge—those were the least offensive. However, even with the nastier notes, most didn't use the language that had been in the bomber's manifesto. The tone might be ugly and mean, but there were no threats against life.

Except for four: three emails and one letter.

Those four were far more visceral and ugly: written by people who claimed to hate them for the jokers they were and the people they represented, who believed (as the bomber evidently had) that they were somehow cursed by God, that they were abominations or sinners being punished or symbols of humankind's downfall, that they should all be purged and eliminated: "smears of ugly shit that need to be wiped off the ass of the Earth forever," as one of the writers put it.

Michael had experienced, viscerally at times, the hatred and bigotry toward jokers elsewhere in the world, but had been rather more insulated from it in the countries where Joker Plague had been popular. This was a blatant reminder that here, too, there were many people who shared the bomber's view of those who'd been altered by the wild card virus, who believed that those infected had somehow made a choice about how the virus had affected them, and that the deformities given them were a reflection of inward flaws or sins.

For those people, jokerhood was a divine punishment. For them, that punishment alone didn't seem to be enough. Michael forced himself to read the words, but they burned inside him.

> You deserve to die. God has placed the irrevocable sign of your sins and your parents' sins on your very body. I'll force you to crawl on your belly with those arms of yours, like a wretched spider, then I'll rip off each one of your spider arms, slowly, and listen to you screaming and begging for me to stop. I'll take your drumsticks and ram them like stakes into those drums on your chest. I'll watch you writhe and bleed and curl up and die. Satan will come and take your soul to hell and eternal torment and I'll laugh . . .

The unsigned letter had been posted from the Jokertown post office. Michael passed on the emails to the tech who maintained the Joker Plague website, asking him to see if he could figure out from the IP addresses in the header whether any of them came from New York City and especially from Jokertown: one did, and his tech had tracked down the street address.

Michael decided it was time to ditch his Fort Freak shadows. That was easy enough to accomplish; Beastie and Sal, as well as the other teams assigned to the task, habitually stationed themselves near the front entrance to Michael's apartment building. There was a dock entrance to the rear of the building which led out onto another street. It was simple enough to call for an Uber cab to meet him there. He gave the somewhat startled Uber driver the address and sat back in the seat, wondering what he was going to say if someone was there. He tapped one of his healing drums gently, the slow and painful beat stoking the anger.

The address was an apartment building just off Chatham Square; Michael watched the garish, unlit neon sign of a naked, four-breasted joker slide by: the facade of Freakers nightclub, now long past its prime (if it had ever had one). The entire neighborhood had seen better days; the Uber driver, a nat, was distinctly uncomfortable with Michael's request to wait for him, but a fifty-dollar bill elicited a promise that he'd stay for fifteen minutes. Michael got out and walked up the cracked concrete steps to the front door; it opened when he turned the knob—not locked. The address the tech had discovered gave the apartment number as 2B; Michael took the stairs up and found the door of 2B at the rear of the building.

He stood outside for a moment, taking a long breath. The hallway smelled like a stale diaper, and the walls appeared to have been last painted back in Jetboy's day. Michael knocked on the door, holding the thumb of another hand over the glass peephole.

"Who is it?" a thin, high voice called from inside.

"Drummer Boy," Michael answered.

"Yeah, sure," the muffled voice answered, "and I'm Curveball." The door cracked open, and Michael was staring at a hairless face that appeared to have been molded from wet beach sand by clumsy fingers. Pebbly eyes widened in the gritty face, and small crystalline specks drifted down like tan, sparkling dandruff.

"Oh, fuck," the joker said. The door started to close, and Michael pushed it open again with three hands. The door crashed hard against its hinges, and Michael entered the apartment to see the sandy, naked, and evidently male figure starting to run toward a back room. Michael lunged forward, stiff-legged in the walking cast, and grabbed at the joker's arm with his good left one. His fingers closed around the joker's arm.

The arm crumbled and broke like a dry sandcastle where Michael had clutched at it. Sand crystals drizzled through Michael's fingers; the hand and forearm hit the wooden floor and shattered. "Shit!" Michael shouted as the joker clutched at the remnants of the arm. A thin liquid—not blood, but clear—dripped sluggishly from where the arm had broken off. Behind him, Michael could see another room illuminated by the glow of a computer monitor. He also noticed that the floor everywhere in the apartment was gritty with sand crystals, drifted into piles in the corners.

"Fuck!" the joker screamed. "Look what you've done. It'll take me a week to grow that back. You asshole sonofabitch! Damn, that hurt!"

"I just wanted to talk to you . . ." Michael began, but then the anger surged again, and with it a sense of despair. *Not dead. The bomber said he was going to blow himself up. The concussion of a blast would destroy this guy.* Michael pulled out the folded paper on which he'd printed out the email and shoved it close to the joker's face. "Did you write this?"

The joker glanced at the paper. "Yeah. So what? All I did was tell you what half of your old fans are thinking. You're a washed-up hack and your new music sucks. Deal with it." He spoke without bravado or heat, his high-pitched voice sounding more apologetic than angry.

"Did you set the bomb at Roosevelt Park?"

"What?" The joker's voice was a piercing shriek. "You think I did that? I . . . God, are you insane?"

Michael shook the email at him. "This says you want me to die."

"That's *hyperbole*, dude. I was trying to make the point that you're already dead creatively. It don't mean I went and killed a whole bunch of jokers because I think you're a poser. I wasn't there; I wouldn't do that." The joker continued to rub at his broken arm. Michael could see the broken ends knitting together already, the sandy skin there darkening as the fluid leaked out. "Damn, you really don't like people telling you the truth about yourself, do you?"

Michael swung away from the joker, moving past him into the next room. The joker followed him as he prowled the room, not knowing what he was looking for: electronic wiring, packets of C4, even a ticket stub from the concert, anything that could indicate this guy was somehow involved in the bombing, even as he argued with himself internally. *He's not the one. Not the one . . .*

There was nothing incriminating in the room. Nothing to indicate that this person could have been the bomber. Everything about this screamed that the joker was just one of the sad people who could talk aggressively and puff himself up online but was nothing but bluster in real life.

This was a dead end.

Michael put the copy of the email on the joker's desk. "What's your name?" he said.

"They call me Sandy," he said, then to Michael's shake of his head, "Yeah, I know. I'm just a big fucking joke."

"OK, Sandy. Listen to me: if you say anything about me being here, I'll have you arrested for making death threats—and I can guarantee that if I do that, the FBI will be looking at you for the bombing, too. Send me or anyone I know anything else like this crap, and you'll have the feds at your door."

"I didn't do it," Sandy said again. His voice was sullen. The black pebbles of his eyes were downcast.

"Then all you have to do is make sure you keep your mouth shut," Michael told him. "I don't ever want to hear from you again." With that, he headed toward the door, passing the dried-out husk of the joker's arm in the front room. "Sorry about that," Michael said as he left, his shoes scraping against the glistening sand grains on the floorboards.

When Michael reached the street, he found that the Uber driver had left.

♥

Michael swung by the Carter Institute a few days later, finding Rusty standing under the baobab tree in the courtyard. It was misting, and streaks of rust were beginning to run down Rusty's arms. Wally saw Michael approaching and waved to him over the joker kids running around the courtyard, most of whom he'd met the other day. He could see Ghost among the ones closest to Rusty. She also waved to him; he waved back. "Hey, DB!" Rusty bellowed. "Good to see ya, fella."

Under the leaves of the baobab, the mist turned into large, random drops. Michael pulled up the hood of his jacket. "You too." Michael hesitated, and Rusty jumped into the conversational lacuna.

"So, we still have to find the bomber, huh?"

"Yeah, I do." Michael figured Rusty wouldn't catch the emphasis he put on the "I," but thought he'd try anyway.

"Maybe we could put up a post on Facebook—we've got a page there—saying 'If anyone knows anything about the bombing in Roosevelt, please contact us.' And we could do the same thing on Twitter. You have a Twitter account, right? Hashtag #bomber . . ."

Michael was already shaking his head, and Rusty slowly ground to a halt. "Look, Rusty, you know as much as anyone about what goes on here in Jokertown. Can I run something past you?"

That brightened Rusty's expression. "Sure. Anything."

"Good. Tell me if you've heard someone talking like this . . ."

Michael handed Rusty a copy of the unsigned letter that Grady had sent him. The joker's thick, clumsy fingers took the paper and unfolded it. Drops fell on the paper from the leaves; Rusty ignored them, scanned the letter, his breath sounding like steam as he read. He snorted nasally as he looked up at Michael with large sad eyes. "This is one sick fella," he said. "You think the bomber, the guy who sent the manifesto, is the same person who wrote this?"

"I don't know. Maybe. It's a hunch. The thing is . . . you're in Jokertown more than me. Have you heard of anyone around here saying these kind of things, especially directed toward me or Joker Plague? A joker like us. Maybe someone new to the area."

Rusty scraped at the brownish-orange stains on his arm with a finger, leaving a trail of bright metal. "A joker? Saying those kind of things . . . ?"

"I gotta know," Michael said. "I gotta know who did this, and I gotta know he's dead, and I gotta know if anyone helped him. I lost . . . I lost . . ." Michael stopped himself, bottling up the grief and fury that was threatening to spill out suddenly. He was grateful for the dripping leaves as he took the paper back from Rusty.

Rusty's hand touched Michael's top shoulder gently. "Hey, fella, I understand," he said. "Look, I have another idea. You ever hear about that Sleeper fella? He's been around since Jetboy, they say. No one knows Jokertown like him. If you can find him—"

♣

Spread enough cash around and you can find anybody. Croyd Crenson, according to the walrus-faced joker at the newsstand on Hester, could be found in the back room at Freakers. "Look for someone who looks like he's been swimming in an oil spill," the walrus told him. "And don't touch him. He's sticky."

Pushing in through the double doors between the legs of the giant neon stripper that marked the entrance to Freakers, Michael was immediately assaulted by the smells of stale beer, urine, and cigarette smoke. He forced himself not to take a step back. The faces of the joker patrons inside turned to him, and the bartender—a tentacled joker as wide as he was tall, with eyes as big as saucers—blinked and spat. "Hey, looky, a celebrity," he announced in a booming voice. "Didn't you used to be important?"

"I'm looking for the Sleeper," Michael said.

The bartender waved a tentacle vaguely toward the back. "In our *champagne* parlor. For VIPs only."

Michael pulled out his wallet. "How much to be a VIP?"

"One Benjamin. Fifty for the champagne, fifty for the girl."

He tossed down a hundred. "Here. Hold the champagne. Hold the girl."

The champagne parlor was lit by a single overhead fluorescent tube, giving off both a cold, pale light and an annoying loud hum from the ballast. Along the walls were shadowed booths where horseshoe-shaped couches upholstered in Naugahyde wrapped around small tables.

Only two of them were occupied at the moment. A busty teenaged stripper was squirming in the lap of a well-dressed nat in one. In the other, a greasy-looking joker sat alone behind a small table, the fluorescent sparking highlights from the glossy skin. He was nursing a beer.

"You Croyd Crenson?" Michael asked him.

"Who wants to know?" The man looked up from his beer. "Fucking Drummer Boy." He nearly spat the name. "Your music's total crap, you know? Tommy Dorsey, the big bands, Sinatra . . . now that was music. Everything since . . . noise."

As Michael's eyes adjusted to the dimness, he could see that there were various small objects stuck to Croyd's body like the dark spots of flies on a strip of fly paper: napkins, paperclips, two Bic pens, what looked like a torn strip of a band poster—not for Joker Plague—half a coffee mug upside down on his right bicep, and, disturbingly, what looked like someone's toupee on his chest.

"Everyone's a critic," Michael responded.

Croyd laughed. "Yeah." Eyes the color of old ivory moved in the oily face, tracking down to Michael's missing arm, then coming back up. "I'm Crenson. Why do you care? What do you want from me? It ain't like we're old friends."

"I'm looking for someone."

"Do I look like the missing persons bureau? Go talk to the fucking cops. Leave me the hell alone."

"I don't want Fort Freak involved in this."

Croyd laughed at that. He took a sip of beer from the heavy glass mug in his hand. Michael noticed that he didn't have to close his fingers around the glass; it was already well-stuck to his palm. Strands of viscous black pulled away from Croyd's lips and snapped as he brought the mug back down hard on the table. It shattered, leaving broken glass glued to Croyd's hand. The Sleeper stood up, the heavy wooden chair on which he was sitting adhering for a few seconds to his butt before dropping back down with a bang. "I don't give a rat's ass what you want. I said leave me the hell alone." He held up his hand with its glittering shards. "Unless you want this smashed across that ugly face of yours."

Michael didn't move. "You don't like my music. Fine. I think that big band crap sucks dog turds myself. But no one ever blew up Glenn Fucking Miller. And no one seems to care who blew up my bandmates and my fans."

Croyd snarled. "I read the *Cry*. The fucker blew himself up. End of story."

Michael shook his head. "Maybe. Maybe not. Damn it, I *need to know who this guy was*." The words quavered in the air, the emotion raw and tearing at Michael's throat. "Over the years, the things you've done . . .

had to do . . . you *have* to understand how I feel." All five of Michael's hands lifted, the stub of his missing one moving in sympathy. "I gotta do *something*. I can't just sit and wait."

Croyd lowered his hand a few inches. He was still standing, but he didn't move toward Michael. "And you think I might help you find the bomber?"

"They say you know Jokertown like the back of your hand."

That made him laugh again. "The back of my hand changes every time I go to sleep. Your bomber is probably dead."

Michael shrugged. "Probably. I want to know for sure. And I want to know that he didn't have other people helping him."

"You looking for revenge, Drummer Boy? You going vigilante?" Under the rubbery, slick surface of his face, his mouth turned up in a smirk. "Fuck it. What've you got?"

"Here," Michael said. He took the copy of the unsigned letter that Grady had sent him from his pocket, unfolded it, and carefully put it on the table in front of Croyd. The joker squinted down at it but didn't touch it. Michael could see his gaze scanning the writing. Croyd sniffed. "That's one sick, angry fucker," he said. "He's right about your music, though."

Michael ignored that. "All I want from you is this: have you heard anyone around here saying these kind of things, especially directed toward me or Joker Plague. A joker like us. Most likely someone new to J-town."

"And if I have? You taking this to the cops?"

Michael shook his head. "No cops. Just me. And I won't be telling anyone where I got the information."

Croyd sniffed again. His hands closed around the glass shards; it didn't seem to bother him. He sat again.

"I might be able to help. I haven't seen this guy in a few weeks, but there was a joker whose card had just turned who came in here. He was . . . angry about what had happened to him. Raving about God and sin and all the rest of the pious garbage that's in here." He pressed a pudgy forefinger on the letter. When he lifted the finger, the paper came with it. He looked annoyed and slapped the paper against the side of the table a few times; it ripped and left a corner on Croyd's forefinger. "The bouncer threw him out. Real gently."

"What was his name, Croyd?"

"Don't know, but . . . he had more arms than you. At least twelve, I think. A head like a praying mantis, fringed with purple hair around the neck. Just a long tube for a body: red with iridescent blue spots all over it. He walks on those hands like a centipede, and lifts up the front of his body a little to use the front ones—one of those was holding a stupid bible. Ask around. Someone else maybe knows his name and where he lived."

Michael felt his stomach knot. *Maybe . . . maybe he's the one . . .* "Thanks, Croyd," he said. "I appreciate, more than you know. I'll have them send you back another couple beers." He turned to leave the room, and heard the Sleeper chuckle behind his back.

"You think it's going to help you to know for sure?" Croyd asked him. "It won't. Nothing makes that kind of pain go away. Nothing."

♠

It took two days of discreet inquiries, but the Sleeper was right; the description was solid enough that Michael eventually had a name and an address for the joker: a rundown apartment building on Allen Street near Canal.

The super was a joker whose handless arms were tentacles covered in octopus-like suckers, and whose face was shaped like a rubbery, upright shovel, the eyes squashed together at the apex. "Whoa!" he said when Michael knocked. "You're DB!"

"Yeah. I'm looking for a guy named Robert Krieg—red with blue spots, a dozen hands or so? He lives here, I'm told."

The super grunted assent. "You mean Catapreacher? Yeah, he lives here. Or he did."

"Look," Michael told the super, "you have keys to his apartment, right? Mind if I have a look inside?"

The spade-face squinched up. "Not supposed to do that." His voice trailed off hopefully; the tentacle arms swayed. But he didn't have any issue handling the envelope Michael passed to him, manipulating it easily as he opened it and scanned the bills inside. He grunted, a tentacle snaking the envelope into a pants pocket.

"I suppose it wouldn't matter much. God knows how Catapreacher's left the place. Come on—he's on the first floor."

The apartment smelled of moldering food and stale air. The super gave a short laugh. "Look at this crap. This is the kind of shit I have to deal with all day, every day." He waved a hand at the cluttered, messy apartment, strewn with clothes and paper. "Krieg—he don't appreciate the name I gave him—just moved in here, what, fuckin' two months ago. Didn't get his garbage out last Tuesday. I had ta fuckin' do it. None of my renters like him. Always going on about how awful the place is, how he hates jokers and Jokertown—like he had a lotta room to talk—and spouting all kinds of religious shit."

Michael wandered around the small apartment as the super talked. Roaches scattered as Michael approached. There was a bible on the coffee table, a streak of something black, oily, and sticky on the cover. The bible was surrounded by half-empty Styrofoam cups of to-go coffee and paper plates with hard slices of frozen pizza curled on them. Flies buzzed around the remnants, with maggots writhing on the cheese. Next to a CD player on the floor, there was a stack of Joker Plague CDs. Michael picked them up, shuffling through them. The super laughed as Michael glanced at the covers.

"Hey, he mighta had your CDs, but Catapreacher didn't like your band, I can tell you," he said. "I heard him going on about that once myself, so it beats me why he decided to go hear you guys at Roosevelt Park. I was gonna go myself . . ."

Michael's breath caught in his throat as he set the CDs back down. "He was at Roosevelt Park?"

"Yeah. The guy's really fucked up—in more ways than one."

Michael moved into the bedroom: no actual bed, just a nest of rumpled blankets. On the floor next to it was a framed photograph of a rail-thin young man in a black suit, standing alongside a lectern and holding aloft what could have been the same bible that was in the front room. An out-of-focus cross was prominent on the wall behind him. Michael assumed he was looking at a photograph of Robert Krieg before the wild card virus.

It's him. It has to be. A disgruntled joker who hated what he'd turned into, a religious fanatic missing since the bombing and with an admitted hatred for Joker Plague. It had to be him.

Michael was certain when he looked into the bedroom closet. There were no clothes there at all, only a table with the legs sawed off so it was no higher than a few inches off the floor. The surface of the table was strewn with bits of wire, a soldering iron, the remnants of two disassembled clocks, and several olive-colored Mylar wrappers. Staring at the mess, Michael shivered involuntarily.

It's him. I've found him. He thought he should be feeling a surge of vindication, of triumph at the revelation, but instead he only felt empty. He remembered what Croyd had said. The anger, the rage he'd been holding in; it was replaced by . . . nothing. He stared at the evidence as his several fists clenched and unclenched. He tapped at his chest, and a soft *doom* filled the apartment as his throat opening flexed to shape the note.

A funereal, low, and solitary beat.

Voice, S'Live, Shivers, all dead because of this guy. Bottom disfigured. And me, the one he hated most of all, on my way back to normalcy—whatever the fuck that is . . . All the innocent jokers who'd come to watch us dead or hurt.

And no one to punish. No one on whom to wreak vengeance. It isn't fair. It isn't right.

Nothing left to do except call Detective Black and tell him where to come find the evidence.

"Did you know anything about what Krieg did before he came here?" he called out to the super. "Did he have any friends, people he might've been working with?"

"Dunno what he did. And he don't have any damn friends: a total loner. Nobody gives a flying shit about the little bastard and his preachifying. All I know is that if he don't hand me his rent on Wednesday, maybe I'll just toss all this crap in here out on the sidewalk. Especially now that I see how he's keeping the place."

Michael gave a brief, dry laugh. "I hate to tell you this, but Krieg's dead."

"Huh?" The super's voice sounded genuinely startled. "When did that happen? Hell, he called yesterday to tell me that he was finally getting out of the hospital on Wednesday."

The statement stole Michael's breath momentarily. The room seemed to lurch around him once. "Getting out—?" He closed the closet door and went back into the front room. The super was standing at the door, tentacles waving, one of the sucker pads holding a smoking cigarette.

"Yeah. The bastard was one of the people hurt when that bomb went off. They took him to the Jokertown WIC Center on Grand. Been there ever since, not that he ever contacted me to tell me until that call yesterday. I thought that was why you was here. Doing that sympathetic good-guy thing for a fan, even if Catapreacher—God, he hates it when I call him that—ain't really a fan. Kinda ironic, I guess."

"Yeah, kinda," Michael told him. His stomach had knotted again, tighter than ever. "Look, thanks for letting me poke around. I guess my manager gave me the wrong info. Sorry to have bothered you."

"No problem," the super said, tapping the pocket with Michael's envelope. "No bother a'tall, DB. Hey, you want to leave a note or something for Krieg? In case he actually pays the goddamn rent?"

"No," Michael answered. "I'll stop by and see him in person sometime."

◆

Michael heard the door open, then close, followed by the patter of several hands slapping the floorboards. When he heard the snap of a switch and saw the wash of yellow light fill the front room, he stepped out of the bedroom where he'd been waiting.

"Krieg," he said. "I know it was you. You're the bomber."

Michael didn't know what he'd expected as a reaction. Surprise, certainly, and perhaps fright as well. Or perhaps anger. He got none of those, and felt a wash of brief disappointment. The centipede-like body was heavily bandaged; the two rear hands were booted, not unlike Michael's own leg. The joker's mantis head swiveled toward him. Round and pupil-less dark eyes stared as the fingers of its several hands flexed and unflexed on the floorboards. The insect mouth opened, and the voice that emerged sounded cartoon-high and thin. "You were supposed to be dead," Krieg said.

"So were you." Michael was bare-chested, his injuries visible: the scars, the splint still on his middle left arm, the stub of his lower left arm sticking out uselessly. He thumped hard on the bass membrane with his right hand, ignoring the pain. He shaped and tightened the sound, focusing it on Krieg's body. The concussive blast hit the joker, knocking him over and sending him tumbling against the wall of the room. The joker squealed and struggled to right himself. The front of his body lifted, his front two hands outstretched toward Michael.

"My Lord God . . ." Krieg began, then seemed to choke on the word as Michael brought his hand up again, fisted as if ready to strike the drums of his chest again. Michael saw Krieg swallow hard. The mantis eyes blinked; his front two hands were clasped together now, as if in supplication or prayer. "Yes, my own death is what I wanted as well," he continued, "but the Lord saw fit to intervene. I was ready for that, but just as I pushed the button, another joker shoved between me and the stage. It . . . whatever it was . . . had a hard carapace, and that shielded me from the blast. It wasn't until I woke up in the hospital that I heard on the news that you'd survived too." The face scrunched in a scowl. "I suppose . . . I suppose this is what the Lord wanted of me. It was His hand that saved me. Like Isaac, who Abraham was ordered to kill, I was spared. As for you, you only lost an arm and broke a few bones. Hardly the punishment you deserved."

Michael struggled to keep his voice calm. He wanted to beat on his chest, wanted to pummel the joker with a fatal barrage of percussion: as he'd once done with the Righteous Djinn in Egypt, as he'd done to others in Iraq. His missing left arm throbbed, as if it heard his thoughts. "God had *nothing* to do with it, you fucking idiot!" The words were hoarse and loud, ripped from his throat as he shouted. "God didn't want dozens of jokers to die. God didn't want Shivers and S'Live and the Voice to die. *You* did, you bastard! You did!"

Blink. The mantis head looking briefly toward the ceiling as if searching for words there. "Leviticus 21:18—'No man who has any defect may come near the Lord's altar: no man who is blind or lame, disfigured or deformed.' Look at us, Drummer Boy. We are cursed for our sins. Psalm 37:38—'But all sinners will be destroyed; there will be no future for the wicked.' Don't you see? There you were, you and your fellow abominations, making a mockery of the Lord with your celebration of your disfigurements, with all the other sinners and cursed ones shouting your praises and buying your records. And you . . . you especially, pretending that you were doing good in the world: the great DB, raising money for charity with one set of hands and raking in more money with the other. Accepting the idolatry of the cursed ones. The aces—they've been raised up by the Lord God, gifted by Him for their goodness in their souls. But you . . . you're just a joker like the rest of the cursed ones."

"Just a joker?" Michael raged at the man. "You think that's all I am?" Again, he beat on his chest: two strikes, this time, directed right at the man, the low pounding reverberating. He saw Krieg's body respond, ripples moving down the long tube of its body. *It will be easy. Quick. That body's fragile and soft . . .*

Krieg cowered, and Michael stopped. The joker raised its front hands again. "You must know you're a sinner like the rest," he said, "even as you pretend to be as good as the believers, even as you prance on your stages. You, more than any of the others, are a symbol of all . . . of all that is wicked in this world . . . and the Lord spoke to me. He said . . . He said . . ."

Krieg was weeping now, whether from pain or from fear, Michael didn't know. Tears flowed from the bulging eyes. The bandages on his body were showing spreading splotches of red: the concussion of Michael's drums had torn open the wounds underneath. "He said that as penance for my sins . . . for the awful curse that He placed on my body as the sign of my corruption." The rows of hands underneath Krieg's body were now impotent fists, curled up on the scratched wooden floor. "My task, He told me, was to cast you screaming with torment into Hell, so that all can see His order, so that others would follow my path and purge all the joker abominations from the earth."

"You're a sick, sick bastard, Krieg. You know that?"

The joker sucked in air. "You can't understand. You don't even believe in God or in His truth. But you will—you'll scream for His forgiveness as you writhe in agony for eternity in the afterlife that awaits you. While I was in the hospital, I prayed and I prayed. I asked the Lord why He let you live, and I could hear Him telling me that His will would be revealed. Now I know why. He had a task for you. You intend to kill me, don't you?"

Michael nodded. "You don't think that's what you deserve for what you've done?"

"For what I did to jokers?" He gave a laugh that sounded like chitin rubbing together. "No, I don't—that was only what the Lord demanded of me, to demonstrate to Him I had repented." Michael's hands curled, all of them, and he took a step toward the joker, ready to end this. "Listen," Krieg said imploringly. "I failed the Lord in my past, back when I was normal, when I was preaching His word. I wasn't a good man then. I was prideful. I gave in to lust and envy and greed, and the Lord saw each of my transgressions. Look at me now; anyone can see the mark of sin He's placed on me. No, for you to kill me will be a sign of His blessing and forgiveness. He'll take my soul from this wretched, horrible body, and clasp me in His arms to carry me to Heaven. So go ahead," he told Michael. "Do it. Do what the Lord God commands. Kill me, and show the world what you and the other jokers really are."

Michael ached to obey. He imagined S'Live and Shivers and the Voice calling out to him to avenge them, imagined he heard all of those Krieg had killed and wounded screaming for the man's blood. Seeing this creature shattered, broken, and gone would assuage the sense of impotence that haunted him, the sense of being adrift without purpose.

It would. It must.

The mantis watched him, waiting. Blood had spread further on his bandages. *So easy.* Michael's fists opened, closed again. He brought them down on his chest, all at once, and the sound shook the walls of the apartment, rattling everything around them.

But the thundering roar was unfocused, his neck throats yawning wide open. Krieg cowered on the floor as if waiting for the blow to strike, his round, bug-like eyes closing. Slowly, they opened once more.

Michael slid his phone from his pocket. Still watching Krieg, he tapped a few buttons. "Detective Black," he said to the voice that answered, "I have someone you've been looking for . . ."

♥

He could hear the sound of someone playing bass inside the house in Cincinnati . . . *No*, he decided, *not a string bass, but a synth keyboard bass.* The bass line continued as he knocked, as the door opened. A woman looked out at him—she could have been taken for a nat if it weren't for a spray of glowing, iridescent freckles across her cheeks and nose. Her lips curled into a moue of distaste.

"DB," she said. "I didn't expect to see you here."

"Bethany," he said. "Hey, is that him playing? How is he?"

"You're a little late asking." She hadn't moved, still holding the door half-open.

Michael nodded. "I am, and I'm sorry. I won't make any excuses. Just . . . I'm sorry. I should have come by weeks ago. If you want me to leave, I will."

There was a distinct pause, giving Michael time enough to wonder whether she'd just shut the door on him before she stepped back and held it open for him. "Come in," she told him. "He'll want to see you." *Even if I don't.* The appended clause was silent, but he heard it.

She led him to a room at the back of the house—he remembered it from previous visits: a little studio that Bottom had built in a spare bedroom, where Joker Plague had put down demo tracks for their first album. Bethany opened the door and the bass line swelled in volume. "You have a visitor, love," she said, and left quickly.

Bottom was sitting behind a Korg keyboard wearing a Joker Plague tee, his left hand on the keys, the right sleeve hanging entirely empty, not even a truncated remnant like his own hanging out. The entire right side of his donkey-like face was scarred, the fur of his muzzle burned off to reveal pink, wrinkled skin. He wore a patch over the missing eye, the elastic weaving around his huge ears. Michael couldn't see the missing leg, hidden behind the Korg's stand.

Bottom's thick-lipped and toothy mouth creased into a smile as he looked up. "DB! Michael! Man, it's good to see you!"

"You too. Honest. Look, I should've come by before—"

Bottom held up his hand. "Stop right there," he said. "I know what Bethany thinks, but I don't hold it against you. It's been rough for everyone, and hey, I hear you found the little bastard who did it. Hard to believe that he was a joker . . ." Bottom stopped, and Michael saw a tear race down from his remaining eye. "Sorry. I still get choked up and emotional, thinking about that day. Poor Jim, Rick, and Ted . . ."

It took a moment, but Michael realized Bottom was referring to the Voice, S'Live, and Shivers by their given names. *As if they were just people. As if they weren't defined only by their appearance and what the wild card virus did to them.* Michael had nearly forgotten their real names. ". . . all those people in the audience, our fans . . ." Bottom's body shivered as he shook his head.

"I know, Bott . . ." Michael stopped. *Niall. Bottom's actual name is Niall . . .* "I know," he repeated. "I know, Niall." His own voice quavered in sympathy.

"Yeah, I'm sure you do." Niall gave a long sigh, a sniff through the huge nostrils at the end of his muzzle, then tapped out a line on the keyboard. "Can't change what's happened, though. I'll never play bass guitar again, but I still have an eye to see and one good hand, and I can sit down at a keyboard, so I don't need the leg. I figure with the Korg and its bass patch . . ."

"What I heard sounded pretty good."

Niall grinned. "I've been practicing. How's the drums? The arms?"

"Healing," Michael told him. "I've been practicing, too."

"Excellent. Tell you what, let me kick up the studio track for 'Self-Fulfilling Fool' on the computer. I'll just silence the drum tracks and the bass . . ." He paused and glanced back at Michael. "That is, if you have the time, and if you want to."

Michael unbuttoned his shirt, pulling it back to reveal the drum membranes. "Let's do it," he said.

Niall grinned again, then turned back to the computer hooked up to the studio speakers. "Here we go, then. You ready?"

"I don't know," Michael answered. "We'll find out."

The click track counted off the beats, then Ted's—Shivers'—guitar started in with the introductory, gritty power chords. The familiar sound of his guitar made the room shimmer in Michael's eyes, remembering being on the stage as they played this song a few hundred times. He blinked, feeling moisture running down his cheeks. He counted off four measures, tapping the snare on his chest and looking at Niall, ready at his keyboard.

Then Rick kicked in with the keyboard, Niall's synth bass boomed, and Jim's voice launched into the melody. Michael loosed an explosive crescendo down the toms. He could feel his missing arm moving from habit, leaving a single, empty beat in the run.

It didn't matter.

For the next few minutes at least, he could almost believe that his world was whole again.

Prompt. Professional. *Pop!*

by Walter Jon Williams

AT ONE IN THE morning I'm still driving around Culver City in a stolen car, with a satchel of hundred-dollar bills on the seat next to me and one of Hollywood's most powerful producer-directors locked naked in his own trunk.

Time is ticking by, and I'm completely at a loss what to do next. There's only one thing I'm sure of.

It's Jack's fault. It's Golden Boy who's responsible for all this.

He's the one who's wrecked my life. He's the one who invited me to Toluca Lake, only a few weeks ago, and began the cascade of events that led to this moment, this stolen car, this satchel of money, this kidnapping.

All his fault.

♣

The Toluca Lake home is mission style, with white stucco and red roof tiles and carob trees. It looks no more than 2500 square feet, hardly the sort of place I'd expect for someone with his kind of money—but then he lives alone, poor man.

So far as I know, he's been alone for a long time. Maybe he needs companionship. I'm thinking that maybe that's why he's called me.

For the meeting I'm wearing a halter dress by J. Mendel and open-toed sandals by Louboutin. It's a beautiful soft Southern California evening, and there's no reason to hide my assets. I've had my hair and nails done and I'm wearing tasteful jewelry as glossy and gold as my mane.

I park the SLK Roadster on the curb and trot up to the house; Jack opens the door before I can ring the bell. He's wearing a cream-colored open-necked shirt and soft open-front khakis, and it's all somehow Old Hollywood, which of course Jack is, because he's immortal.

I have to say that immortality suits him. He'll be young forever, tall and fit and blond and handsome. He looks just as he did that first season of *American Hero*, and he'll look that way long after *American Hero* is forgotten.

And he's supposed to be very rich. Which doesn't hurt the eyes, either, if you know what I mean.

We say hello and kiss each other on the cheeks. He asks if I'd like coffee or a drink, and I say a drink would be nice, but I don't want to drink alone.

"I have a nice bottle of zinfandel from my winery," he says, and leads me into the house. My shoes clack on the deep red floor tiles, the color of old blood.

"Jack honey, you have a winery?"

"I have several, but they're more like a hobby. On good years I break even."

I look around at the furniture, which is heavy Spanish mission style. It's all old and dark but in good condition. There is abstract art on the walls, but nothing from his days as a movie star, though I see some photos of Jack with people I assume were famous back in the day. I recognize one peppery older man with round glasses, I think maybe one of the presidents from way back when.

We go to a back room with a bar and a view through French windows of the lake, a sagging old pier, and a canoe. Jack pulls out a chair—it's bull hide slung on an iron frame—and seats me at a table covered with lovely Mexican tiles. The room has an aeronautical theme: there's a big wooden propeller over the bar, and there are photos of aircraft, and of Jack standing by old-timey planes, and a bronze bust of a pilot from back in the days when they wore leather helmets. Strangely enough the pilot is black. I didn't know they had black pilots in those days.

Jack goes to the bar, gets a bottle of wine, puts in the corkscrew, and pulls the cork as easily as you might flick a postage stamp with a thumbnail. Because he's one of the strongest aces in the world, maybe even the strongest of all time.

It's really sort of thrilling to see him use his power so naturally, even in such a casual setting.

"When you called, sweetie," I say, "you mentioned a possible project."

I haven't actually seen Jack Braun in person since the end of the first season of *American Hero*, and I didn't get to know him well because he was only a guest star. I've been busy managing my career since, of course, and he's been doing whatever it is he does when he's not judging a reality show.

Making wine, apparently.

I hardly ever see him mentioned in the entertainment news. It's almost as if he dodges publicity.

"The project?" Jack says. "Yes. But first, let's just catch up, shall we?"

He brings the bottle and a couple of glasses to the table, and sits. His old-school manners are really quite fetching.

He lets the wine breathe a bit while I talk about my career. Things aren't going as well as I'd hoped, but I'm working steadily. My last three movies were direct-to-video, not that this was my fault—terrible scripts, terrible productions. I fired the agent who brought me the projects.

The movies may have flopped, but I continue to appear as myself in sitcoms, as if I'm given to wandering into the kitchens of ordinary families to help them solve their problems. I'm a guest judge on various reality programs. I give beauty tips on afternoon television.

Sometimes I'm hired as a kind of special effect. My wild card can make things appear and disappear, and I'm cheaper than CGI or spending a whole afternoon gaffing some kind of stunt. You want a car to fall out of the sky or an elephant to vanish in front of an audience, I'm the one you call.

I always try to stay positive, but I'm afraid I show my annoyance when I talk about Cleo, my perfume. "Perfume yourself in the mystery of the Nile," said the ads, but what people know about the Nile now is the battles and massacres that took place when the Committee went there. Dab yourself behind the ears with the burnt remains of joker babies?

No, Cleo didn't sell. I blame the advertising.

Not that I express this in so frank a manner to Jack. I live by the Three P's. In front of other people, I prefer to be Prompt, Perky, and Professional.

I emphasize the projects I hope to add soon to my resume. I happen to know my photo is on a lot of desks right now.

I sip the zinfandel, which has a floral taste, very pleasant in the nose.

"So Jack," I ask finally, "what's your project? Are you developing it yourself, sweetie?" I put a hand on his arm. "That must be exciting."

He smiles and scrubs his blond hair with his free hand. "Well," he says, "I was sort of hoping some more people would—"

Suddenly there's a bang on the front door, and then the sound of the door opening and someone coming down the hall.

"Mr. Braun?" says a woman's voice. "Are you—? Oh."

And Rachel steps into the room.

I haven't seen Dragon Girl since that first season of *American Hero*, where we didn't get along. I really didn't think she should have been there at all—she was far too young for the sorts of action and danger to which we were exposed. Maybe I was a little too outspoken, but honestly, all I wanted was to *protect* her.

She's all grown up now, of course—nineteen, maybe? But she's no prettier now than she was then, poor thing, with her frizzy hair and eyeglasses in a style that was hip maybe five years ago. The *American Hero* producers, the same ones who dressed me up as Cleopatra, put her in a red leather flying suit that looked just horrible on her. Now she's wearing a tee-shirt and worn jeans, which don't look horrible but aren't attractive either, and of course the backpack with all the stuffed animals.

I understand she's going to college now, but like me she moonlights as a special effects ace. Not only can she make her stuffed animals come alive, they become giant-sized. Having a *real* dragon in your picture, one that not only flies but follows direction, is immensely better, and far cheaper, than using CGI.

Cheap enough that there's a glut of giant monster films right now. Dragons, ants, centipedes, burrowing badgers, swimming turtles, carnivorous dolphins, whatever. I don't know why anyone would watch them, or if in fact they do.

Of course, Rachel doesn't go in *front* of the camera. She's no actress, and she isn't pretty enough to be a star. But for some reason people in the industry seem to like her. Maybe she's less opinionated than when she was a kid.

"Rachel!" I say. "Hello, darling!" I rise from my chair, hug her, and air-kiss her cheeks. In the meantime I'm wondering if Jack has in mind some special-effects extravaganza that will require both our talents. If I don't get an acting job out of this, I'm going to be really annoyed.

Jack rises as well and offers Rachel a glass of wine. "I'd rather have fruit juice, if you have any," Rachel says, and Jack goes to the fridge for some kind of cranberry-mango thing.

Jack and Rachel chat for a bit, catching up—like me, he hasn't seen her since *American Hero* marched off to Egypt. I get a little impatient, because they could do this on their own time. I wait for a break in the conversation before speaking up.

"So, Jack, what's this project you have in mind?"

Jack and Rachel look at each other. "Do you think anyone else is coming?" he asks.

"I doubt it," Rachel says.

"Well." He glances at me, then looks down at his hands. "This is a little awkward, because we'd hoped to have some more of the *American Heroes* cast here."

I'm confused. "Is this some kind of reunion?"

"No. You see, we don't know your friends, so we don't know who else should be here."

"Be here for what?"

"It's an intervention!" Rachel blurts, in her usual awkward fashion.

I look at her in deep surprise. Then I look at my wine glass. "You think I'm an alcoholic?" I say. "Or a drug addict?"

"Cleonie," Jack says, "it's about the stealing."

My mouth drops open and I just gape at him. My heart is beating so loudly that I can barely hear myself when I finally manage to speak.

"Stealing?" I ask. "What in the world are you—"

"Things keep disappearing," Rachel blurts again. She blurts so much that she always sounds as if she's accusing me of something, even when she *isn't* accusing me of something.

I start to get angry. I clench the stem of my wineglass. "I'm a *public figure*," I say. "I can't use my ace power to steal! Everyone would notice!"

"Umm," Rachel begins.

"Even if I disguised myself," I say, "people would see it was me. What am I going to do—put on a dark wig? Then I'd just look like Cleopatra from *American Hero*!"

"Jack," says Rachel, "maybe you'd just better show the video."

Jack obediently takes an electronic tablet from a table overflowing with magazines and presses the touch screen a few times and then there's a video, a poor-quality feed, with garish color, clearly taken from a surveillance camera.

My blood runs cold. There's a parking lot with a truck in it, then suddenly there's woman in a jumpsuit who just *appears* in the frame. She touches the truck on the front fender, the truck completely disappears, and then the woman disappears, too.

"See, it's always trucks with a cargo of high-fashion designs," Rachel says. "Brunello Cucinelli, Stella McCartney, Michael Kors. Sometimes just accessories that are easy to fence."

"I'm not the only ace who can teleport," I point out. "There's Popinjay in New York. Not that I'm accusing him," I add quickly, when Jack gives me a look. "I'm just pointing out that there's more than one of us. There could be a teleporter we don't know about."

"And whoever's doing this is wearing a mask and a hood," Jack points out. "We never see the face."

"Right!" I say.

"But then," Rachel adds, "there's the Alexander McQueen jumpsuit. And the Valentino boots with the strap over the instep. They both just say *Cleo* to me."

"Those are the same boots you wore on *American Hero*," Jack points out.

Oh, I could just spit. But I remember the Three P's and I refrain.

"The police brought this video to me," Jack said. "They asked me if I recognized the perpetrator. They mentioned you by name."

I freeze. I'm so wrought up that I'm beyond speech.

"I said I couldn't swear to your identity," Jack says. "And I can't, not without seeing your face. But honestly, Cleo, it's *you*. It's so clearly you."

"I—" I begin. "I can't believe—"

Rachel looks at me. "You've got to stop," she says. "They're onto you. They're only waiting for you to make a mistake. Then your career will be over, and you'll hurt all the wild cards, and . . ."

It's the pitying look on her face that sets me off. As if I should be pitied by some stupid girl who flies around the sky on stuffed animals.

"This is outrageous!" I say. "I can't believe you're making these accusations!" I push my seat back. "I'm not going to stay here and listen to this!"

Jack puts a hand on my arm. He doesn't clamp down or anything, but suddenly I'm very aware that this is the strongest man in the world, and that he's barely touching me but I can't stand up.

And because I can't stand up, I just huff and glare at him. And you know, I don't even *think* of teleporting away. Even though I could.

"Cleonie," he says. He's looking not at me but *through* me somehow, as if he's focusing on something a hundred miles away. "I know you're ambitious," he says. "I know that you think there are certain things you need, and certain things you deserve. I know you think you need it all *right now*. But let me tell you that what you want—" He hesitates. "It's not whether it's worth having or not, it's that it doesn't *exist*. Not really." He cocks his head and actually looks at me now, his eyes focusing on my face and not on whatever he was looking at before. "I've been a hero," he says. "The greatest hero in the world. And I've been a villain—pretty much the worst ever, according to some people. And now—" He offers a sort of grin. "Now I'm just a clown on reality TV. But that's okay." He shrugs. "I have a long perspective. And what I've learned is that it isn't worth it to compromise yourself this way. Not in the long run. That sort of thing never ends."

Honest to God, I have no idea what this man is talking about.

Suddenly a ringtone booms out—it's a riff of Drummer Boy's, I recognize it, and when Rachel digs in a pocket for her phone I remember the cute little crush she had on Drummer Boy during *American Hero*—when I was sleeping with him—and I realize that maybe she's still into him, which is just so, so pathetic . . .

She answers. "Yes. Yes. Okay, text me the coordinates." She stands up and tosses her rucksack over her shoulder. "There's a distress call from a yacht foundering down by Cape Esposito. They've asked me to check it out."

Oh, did I mention that little Rachel does rescues? Pulls people out of burning buildings, off mountains hit by blizzards, from oil tankers breaking up off Big Sur . . . ? And they all get a free ride to safety on a stuffed animal. The Highway Patrol and the Coast Guard and the Forest Service probably all have her on speed dial.

I could do rescues. *I* could pop people right out of danger, easy as anything. But nobody ever calls *me*.

Rachel dashes out of the house and all the lights in the room go dim as energy is sucked into turning a stuffed animal into a giant flying lizard. After which there's a roar, and a great ponderous flapping of wings as Puffy labors into the sky with Rachel as his passenger.

I look at Jack, then down at the hand that's still resting on my arm. I have to admit that this hadn't exactly been the skin-on-skin contact I might have wanted. "So much for your intervention," I say.

He takes his hand off my arm. "It could have gone better," he says.

I try to reassemble my tattered dignity. "I think I'll be leaving now."

He shrugs. "I won't stop you."

I stand and begin to clack my way across the blood-colored tiles. Jack rises to walk me out, but I ignore him.

"One more thing," he says. I give him a look over my shoulder.

"That thing you do," Jack says. "Where you leave your picture and portfolio on the desks of producers who might be casting, I don't know, Meryl Streep or someone . . . ?"

My rage boils over. I spin to confront him.

"I would *never* compete with Meryl Streep for a part!" I tell him. "She's *far* too old!"

He seems a little taken aback. "I stand corrected," he says. As I turn to stalk to the front door, he adds, "Just wanted to let you know that you're being talked about, and not in a way you'd like."

Which puts the topper on my day, as you can imagine.

Anger propels me out the door and to my SLK roadster. There are people standing on the street looking at the dragon still flapping its way into the sky, and I make them jump aside as I burn rubber out of Toluca Lake as fast as I can.

Damned stupid town. Stupid lake. Stupid dragon.

I don't calm down till I get out of the Valley and into Hollywood, where I feel more at home. By then the anger has turned to depression.

They've caught onto my little trick of teleporting into people's offices along with my portfolio. I'd thought that was pretty clever.

But worse, I think as I drive, I'm going to have to call up Tomás, and tell him that our plan to hijack a truck full of Versace just isn't going to happen.

♠

I blame an inability to resist Latin men. That smooth skin, the soulful brown eyes, the attention to grooming . . . And of course, when they take you to clubs and you feel the way their hips move against you when doing the merengue or bachata or whatever, you know that they're going to be able to please you later.

Tomás is a masseur at a spa, and I met him when I stopped by for a tune-up. I knew as soon as I saw him that our souls were intertwined. We got to talking as he worked, and I relaxed maybe a little too much and started to complain about the high cost of being Cleo. My fans expect me to be perfectly turned out on all occasions, and to have the latest fashions and accessories, and how with my movies having flopped I was beginning to feel a financial pinch. And he said, "But can't you just teleport what you want?" And I told him what I told Jack, that if things just vanished from the stores, everyone would know it was me. And Tomás said, well, maybe not from the *stores* . . .

So that's where my adventure with hijacking began, only to end in the miserable botched intervention in Toluca Lake. I didn't keep anything from the trucks we disappeared, because it might be traced from the robbery. Instead the contents of the trucks were sold, and I bought new clothes and kept the receipts. Because, in my business, that's all deductible.

I didn't make as much money out of crime as you might expect, since there was Tomás' share as well as the fence, but I was able to keep the lifestyle my followers expect.

And now it had to end. I was going to have to go into my condo and get rid of that jumpsuit, and those Valentino boots that I've had forever and that I really love. And it's all Jack's fault. And the stupid police. And stupid Rachel.

When I call Tomás he tries to talk me out of it, but I'm firm. He begs to see me, but I tell him I'm busy. I get in the convertible and drive to Rodeo Drive and go shopping, because that's what I do to make myself feel better.

Which is how things stand for the next two weeks. I keep busy with my projects, and I shop a lot, and I don't see Tomás, because I'm afraid I won't be able to resist him when he pleads for another hijacking or two. I have a fling with a competitive bodybuilder from Bolivia in hopes of forgetting Tomás, and it works, at least a little.

And that's where things stand when I get a call from Chas. Thatcher, one of the hottest producer-directors in the business. He calls me at home, not going through my agent at all, and tells me he'd like to have lunch the next day and talk about a project. Which has me practically jumping with delight right out of my Blahnik suede pumps, because top directors don't call you personally if they just want you for some kind of special effect, like dropping a piano on somebody.

We meet on the terrace at Mama Marais, and we get to look down on all the people jammed bumper-to-bumper on Sunset Boulevard. On a hill right behind the restaurant is a huge billboard for Chas.'s new movie, *The Underground*.

I'm in a sleeveless black mini dress by Balenciaga, gold Neuwirth drop earrings, and Louboutin spikes that make satisfying clicking sounds as I cross the tiles. I can tell that Chas. is deeply impressed by my appearance. He sort of half-rises from his seat, then drops back into it as the waiter draws my chair back. He bobs up again as I kiss him on both cheeks and we both settle down with our menus in front of us.

"I know you're from the South," he says, "so I thought I'd see if I could find some Southern food."

I tell him he's very thoughtful; I don't mention that Southern and Cajun aren't the same thing. He's from Manitoba or someplace where all they have to eat is moose meat and cheese curds, you have to make allowances.

Chas.—he insists on the period, it's the way he stands out from the other Chatsworths or Chastitys or whatever Chas. is supposed to be short for—is a fortyish guy in a worn black tee and bib overalls pulled up over a vast stomach. He hasn't shaved over the last four or five days, and his black-rimmed glasses are tilted on his face. It's all I can do to restrain my-self from reaching across the glass-topped table and adjusting his specs.

I have sweet tea and a shrimp salad, and he orders gumbo and barbe-cued alligator tail.

"You ever have gator?" he asks.

"Not a lot of those in Montgomery, darling," I say. "Not even in the suburbs."

I'm beginning to suspect that all he knows about the South is reality shows about people who live in swamps and pursue reptiles.

"Sweetie, I'm excited about *The Underground*," I tell him. "It's such a different approach."

In fact it's not that original an idea, it's just the anti-*mACE*. *mACE* was about a group of aces who band together to fight evil, specifically an alien invasion. It's based on the Committee, clearly enough, and the movie was a huge hit and has now spawned *mACE II*.

Chas.'s picture *The Underground* is about a bunch of aces hidden from public view who band together to fight an invasion, I think from a differ-ent dimension or something.

It's all ridiculous, anyway. Aces haven't fought aliens since before I was born.

So I tell Chas. how brilliant he is, and he agrees with me. Which makes it a typical show business conversation so far.

"Do you know what you'll be doing as a follow-up?" I ask. Because I'm hoping he called me here to offer me a part.

"Balzac's *Pere Goriot*," he says. "Except set in an American high school."

Normally I'd say, "Is there a part for me?", but *Pere Goriot*, whatever that is, has me a little startled and throws me off my game, leaving me with no response at all. I decide to change the topic. "Honey, you must be really looking forward to the opening," I say.

"I was," he says. "But have you heard what that rat-bastard Dag Ringqvist has done?"

Dag Ringqvist is the creator of the mACE movies. A stunning, beauti-ful man, blond and tall, with a charming accent from whatever Scandi-navian country he hails from.

"No," I say.

"Announced just yesterday. He's opening *mACE II* the same weekend as *The Underground*."

"Oh my gosh!" I say.

"Two big ace movies going head-to-head, and *his* movie's the sequel to the biggest ace movie ever." He rubs his unshaven cheek with one plump hand. "He *says* it's just a business decision to take advantage of the Fourth of July weekend, but it's clear that he's declaring war on me. And he's got all the big guns."

"You poor man!" I tell him. "Can you move your opening?"

He gestures at the huge billboard behind him. "We've been advertising our opening date for sixteen months."

"It's all so terrible," I say. "I wish there was something I could do to help."

I say this because I'm beginning to wonder what I'm doing here. I have a feeling it's not to be offered a part in *Pere Goriot*. (I am wonderfully youthful, with glowing, flawless elastic skin for which I give equal credit to my DNA and my dermatologist, but I'm over thirty, just barely, and I don't think I can play a teenager anymore.)

An expression of cunning forms behind Chas.'s tilted spectacles. "Well," he says. "Maybe you can be of service."

A little warning shimmer goes up my spine, a warning that is only confirmed when Chas. grins and nods. "Your ace," he says, "may come in useful."

I sit back in my chair and frown at him. "What do you mean?" I ask.

Chas. summons a bit of indignation. "Remember," he says, "that Ringqvist declared war on *me*."

"Okay." Cautiously.

"He tried to wreck my opening weekend." He raises a hand and flips it slowly from one side to the other. "So I wreck his instead."

I blink. "And I can help you . . . how?"

He flashes a snarling Mad Scientist grin and leans forward, his fingers twining. "*mACE II* is going through post-production up at Kenyon," he says. "What if a copy of the movie just . . . disappeared . . . and showed up for free download on every pirate site in the world?"

I think about this for a moment. It strikes me as a brilliant and totally evil idea.

"And of course," Chas. goes on, "because the movie hasn't finished post-production, it will *suck*. Rough edit, music not properly synched, lines inaudible, sound effects absent because they haven't been Foleyed yet, guns firing blanks and sounding like cap pistols instead of real weapons." He flashes his toothy grin. "They'll *hate* it. The buzz will be *dismal*. And come the opening weekend, *The Underground* will just *kill* it."

Well, you know I can see that this could certainly work. Though I am lacking incentive for the part that Chas. intends for me.

I cross my arms. "Mister Thatcher," I say, "are you asking me to break the law?"

"I'll pay," he says. "A quarter-million dollars. In cash, and you can teleport it straight to whatever tax haven you want."

He's rather overestimating my powers here, but he has made his point.

I am never averse to a rich man who is willing to share.

♦

Two nights later I find myself at Kenyon Studios, which is in Valley Village just off the 101. It's a small independent studio that hasn't made its own features in decades, but rents its facilities and offices to other companies.

There are guards at the gate, of course, but I don't have to use the gate. There's another guard patrolling the grounds on an electric cart, but I can hear him coming. And there are cameras over the doors, but I don't have to go through the doors.

It's a measure of Chas.'s smarts that he thought of me.

The post-production facilities are in the Jobyna Ralston Building, which is on the northeast corner of the lot. I need to get to the third floor—no problem—and there I have to plant "keystroke readers," which will record the passwords on the editing machine.

Once the passwords have been recorded, I will return the following night to do the actual job.

Chas. has given me ten thousand in advance, and I've used it to buy an all-cotton Yohji Yamamoto jumpsuit that looks like something worn by an exceptionally stylish member of a World War II bomber crew. I'm wearing boots by Fiorentini + Baker that have the same vintage look as the jumpsuit, and I'm wrapping a Botto Giuseppe scarf around my head and face so I won't be recognized if I'm caught on any cameras. And of course I'm wearing gloves so I won't leave fingerprints. They're pastel blue surgical gloves, and they don't go with anything.

Still, blue gloves and all, it's a really good look for a criminal. It's a pity that no one will know it's me.

I'm excited, like I always am when I do crime. I'm never scared, at least not in a bad way. I just picture myself on the screen, thirty feet tall and beautiful, and I know that I'm a star and that nothing nasty can touch me, because the star always gets a happy ending.

I pop in at one o'clock in the morning, first to the very top of the twelve-foot brick wall that surrounds the property, and from there right through the windows of the Ralston Building to the third floor. I end up in a room lit only by light from the hall outside and the eerie glow of a dozen flatscreens, all scrolling through the same screensaver sequence of a horde of ugly trolls, or whatever, fighting an army of pointy-eared elves. It's a demonstration of special-effects wizardry, particularly with regards to blood spray.

I think it's stupid, typical geek crap. I think they should advertise something beautiful.

I'm the only person in the building at this hour. All the computers are running even though no one is logged in, so all I have to do is plug in the thumb drive and click the file that will load the keystroke monitor. There's enough light from the flatscreens to do my work, and I install the software and pop myself right out of there.

Afterward I feel a letdown, because it all went so fast and easy. I'm still overstimulated. So I get in the SLK and put the top down and take Sunset all the way to the Pacific, where I park by the beach and listen to the surf crashing in and look at the lights on the pier, and I think about how wonderful it will be when everyone realizes how talented I am and all my dreams come true.

♥

Next night I'm back in Valley Village, but this time I'm not alone. Chas. doesn't trust me to do the file transfer without somehow getting it wrong, so I have to bring a tech along with me, one familiar with the equipment.

He's a little guy, mid-twenties, somebody's assistant. Chas. calls him "Greektown," but his actual name is Aristotle Dimitropoulos. He wears a hoodie and huge shades to hide his face. I tell him not to worry. Nobody's going to see him.

We walk along the outside of the fence, and we hear the guard approaching in his electric cart. I can tell that Aristotle is nervous. We wait on the far side of the wall for the cart to go by, then I pop to the top of the wall to make sure no one's around.

Nobody is. I pop back down to the sidewalk, touch Aristotle on the shoulder, and pop him to the top of the wall.

He's clearly not used to teleporting, so even though he's lying atop the wall perfectly safe he begins to flail, and I quickly pop up next to him, gain a line of sight on the target, touch Aristotle on the leg, and send him into the Jobyna Ralston Building. Then I follow, and find Aristotle flopping on the floor like a spastic cockroach. He's clipped a table on his way to his landing, and seems out of his mind with terror.

"Breathe, honey," I tell him. "You're all right."

"Hurts!" he says.

"Just breathe, sweetie. You'll be fine."

He stops flopping and breathes for a while, then slowly gets up, clutching his side and moaning, and makes his way to a terminal. I don't find Aristotle's dramatics entertaining, so I look around the office for something interesting, only to find the endless battle between the elves and trolls as it was before.

Aristotle checks the keystroke monitor, finds a password, and get into the system on the first try. He's brought some portable hard drives with him, and he starts downloading stuff. This takes quite a while, because he downloads *everything*—not just the rough cut, but all the outtakes, and the alts, and the sound files.

I find a comfortable chair and daydream about what my life will be like when I'm a star, and the houses I'm going to live in, and the clothes I'm going to wear, and all the beautiful men who are going to be in love with me. Then Aristotle signals that it's time to go.

He's still clutching his side, the little drama queen.

"Can't we just go out the door?" he asks.

"The doors have cameras," I point out.

"All they'll see is the back of my hood."

I'm out of patience, so I just look out the window to gain line-of-sight on the top of the wall, touch Aristotle's arm, and pop him out. I'm right on his heels, and before he can yell or flail from his new position atop the wall, I pop him to the sidewalk below. He makes another bad landing and I get to watch some more squashed-cockroach action before he picks himself up.

"Let's get to the car," I say.

"I *hate* that."

"The car, sweetie."

We walk to my car, which I've left a couple streets away, and Aristotle surprises me by telling me to drive him to the Chateau Élysée, which is this enormous castle that dwarfs the one at Disneyland, with turrets and many pitched roofs and colorful awnings on every window, that sits on Franklin just above Hollywood Boulevard and dates from the olden days of the picture business.

"Do you live there?" I say in surprise. Because part of it is offices and so on, but it's also a very expensive apartment building.

"No. That's where I'll be working on *mACE II*. There's a post-production facility at the Chateau."

"I thought you were just going to upload the rough cut to pirate sites."

"No. I'm going to mess with it first." He gives a diabolical little grin. "I'm going to make sure it's a real turd before I send it out. Re-edit it to use the least effective shots and the worst acting. Add a lot of boring stuff. Make sure the action scenes fall flat, and if any of it's been color-corrected, I'm going to undo that. And I'll also fuck with the sound to produce the muddiest dialog and the most boring soundtrack in the history of modern cinema."

I'm impressed by the scope of Chas.'s revenge. He might actually succeed in killing the summer's biggest movie.

I drop Aristotle off at the Chateau, then head for home. I'm not happy about destroying someone's film, which after all represents so many hopes and dreams; but then I think about the money and what I can buy with it, and I feel fine.

♣

I don't get to see Chas. until the next evening, because he doesn't want to give me a sack of money where people will see me. I'm his last appointment, and his secretaries and assistants have gone home by the time I arrive.

He has a corner office on the fourth floor of the Marie Dressler Building at the Sony Pictures lot, which used to be MGM back in olden times. It has a view of Culver City, which is no doubt why the windows are shaded and the office filled with NBA memorabilia. Jerseys in frames, signed basketballs under glass, posters, autographed photos of players. Framed tickets to significant games. Even a pair of wilted-looking signed Nikes under a glass dome.

I'm glad for the dome, because I'd prefer not to have to smell someone's used basketball shoes.

Chas. is in a great mood. He's got a big smile on his unshaven face, and he's wearing a Lakers cap over his unkempt hair.

I'm in an Alexander Wang V-neck dress and Balenciaga wedges. Not too formal, not too evening, but dressy, in case Chas. decides to take me to dinner. It's an outfit that's completely Professional, and I enhance it by being Prompt and Perky.

"Beautiful, baby!" he says. "You've saved my opening weekend!"

"Oh honey, I'm so happy I was able to help."

"Care for a drink?" He walks to a bar installed along one wall.

"I'll have a chardonnay."

He pours himself a whiskey and gets out a bottle of wine, then struggles for a while with a corkscrew as he tries to pull the cork. I can't help but compare the superb ease with which Jack Braun pulled the wine cork on that otherwise regrettable visit.

Other comparisons float through my mind as I look at the photo above the bar—last year's Lakers, grinning over their signatures. I remember being with one of the players in his bungalow at the Beverly Hills Hotel, where I completely realized that our souls were entwined. I popped all over the room, pretending to run away before finally letting him catch me. I also recall being with two other players in a hot tub in Vegas, which led to one of the five most memorable nights in my life.

There's something especially exciting about being with really large men, particularly if they're athletic and in perfect physical condition.

If there's more than one of them, of course, that just adds to all the possibilities.

And Chas. is such a fan. I wonder if he'd envy me if he knew about how his beloved players have played with me.

"Your drink?" I realize I've been daydreaming, and I take the wine he's finally managed to pour. There are bits of cork floating on the surface, and I pick them out with a fingernail. "Are you a fan?" he asks.

"Oh yes." Not of basketball, particularly, but the players, certainly. Which I don't tell Chas.

"Have a seat?"

We make ourselves comfortable on the sofa. Chas. talks about the Lakers and I pretend to be interested. He's still in a very bouncy, excited mood, and I congratulate myself on my good deed in boosting his opening weekend's gross.

He finishes his whiskey. "Well," he says, "I've got a meeting down in Marina del Rey, so I should push on."

I'm a little disappointed that we won't be having dinner, but I remember that I'm about to get a quarter-million dollars, and that I can buy a lot of dinners with that—dinners with men who will pay more attention to me than to a basketball team.

"We should have lunch again sometime," I say, and he agrees.

We stand, and he goes to his desk, opens a drawer, removes a small satchel with a zip, and hands it to me.

"Here's what I owe you," he says.

I'm instantly suspicious. My flirtation with criminality has given me experience in dealing with bundles of cash, and this one isn't nearly big or heavy enough. A quarter-million in hundreds should weigh twenty-five or thirty pounds, and take up as much space and weight as a phone directory might, from back in the day when there were phone directories.

"This seems a little light," I say, hefting the bag.

"No," he says quickly, "it's what I owe you. Minus the ten thousand I already gave you."

I unzip the bag. There are nice little bundles of hundreds wrapped in pink tape, but there are only fifteen of them.

"There's only fifteen here," I say.

He blinks at me. "That's what I owe you. Fifteen, for a total of twenty-five thousand."

He's a really terrible liar. Insincerity shines off him like the sweat that's just appeared on his upper lip.

I can feel rage boil up just below my surface, but I try to stay cool and Professional. I'm afraid that by this point I've pretty much lost all my Perky.

"You said a quarter-mil, sweetie," I tell him.

"No," he says, "I said—" And then he gives up on the lying, because he sees there's no point. It's just the two of us, it's not like he's trying to convince a jury.

"Look," he says. "Twenty-five grand is a pretty good payday for a couple hours' work."

"And you'll make millions," I point out. "All for what I did for you. And you won't share?"

"Twenty-five is fair," Chas. says. A sneer twitches the corner of his mouth. "And you can hardly go to the cops about this, can you? Plus I've got a meeting, so I really need to—"

He tries to brush past me, so I don't even have to reach out and touch him to pop him up into the air.

It's only three feet or so, but he lands badly and crumples on his carpet with a crash that seems to shake the whole Marie Dressler Building. He looks at me with wide eyes.

"*Cops?*" I tell him. "Why would I go to the *cops* about this, sugar, when I have my lovely wild card power?"

He heaves himself to his feet, then makes a run for the door. I pop the sofa in his path and he piles into it, knocking the couch over as he goes sprawling once again. I walk over to the desk, touch it, and pop it so that it blocks the door.

"Sweetie," I say, "I think we need to talk about what you owe me, and how you're going to pay it *right now*."

He thrashes around in the wreckage of his sofa. "You're crazy!" he shouts. "You're out of your mind!"

"*You're* crazy if you think I'm going to sit still for this!" I tell him. I walk to one of the basketballs and pop the glass case into the air. It falls eight feet and crashes to the ground with an enormous noise. Chas.'s whole body jerks at the sound, and he puts his hands over his ears.

"You might want to listen to this next part, sugar," I say. I pick up the basketball and see the signatures written across its bright orange surface. NBA Champions, 2001.

I hold out the basketball so Chas. can see it. "How much am I bid for this?" I ask. "Maybe . . . *a quarter-million?*" Chas. just gobbles at me. "No bids?" I say. "Okay, sugar . . . however you want it."

I look far, far out through the window, up into the darkening sky, and pop the basketball into the wild blue yonder. My range is awesome when there's nothing in view but air.

Chas. gives a little shriek.

"Sugar, I bet that made it all the way to Long Beach," I say. "You don't know how much pleasure it's going to give to whatever kid picks it up."

I walked over to the plinth and pop away the dome covering the sneakers. I pop it right over the bar, and it falls in an enormous crash, taking wine glasses, decanters, and expensive whiskeys with it.

"Now what am I bid—" I begin, then turn to see Chas. in the act of heaving himself up to charge at me. His face is bright red with rage. My heart gives a lurch—he might be obese, but he's really, really large, and I see murder and desperation in his eyes.

But he's not very good at moving his bulk in anything but a straight line, and at the last second, I step aside, and I brush his shoulder with my fingertips, and suddenly he's five feet above the floor, his legs and arms still pumping like Wile E. Coyote suspended above a canyon . . . and then he comes crashing down.

He has a bloody nose this time, and I guess that he's torqued a knee, because he clutches it and moans.

"*Help!*" he shouts. "*Help!*"

"Oh, shut up for heaven's sake," I say. "There's a reason you met me after working hours. Nobody's going to hear you."

Which, after he shouts a few more times, he finally figures out on his own. I approach the plinth again and twirl a shoelace around a finger. "Now what am I bid for this?" I ask him.

The fall and the shouting have left him breathless. "Those shoes aren't worth a quarter mil," he says. "A few thousand, maybe. Nothing in here is worth anything like what you want."

"Sweetie, I'm only getting *started*," I tell him. "I can make your whole *house* disappear, piece by piece."

I don't want to mention the fact that I could pop him two hundred feet straight up. But if he's thinking straight, he already knows that.

Pain twitches across Chas.'s face. He clutches his knee. "I don't have it," he says. "I don't have that much."

I laugh at him. "Why don't I believe that? You're the most successful young director in town. You did *Hard Stand*. You did *Consumer Reports*. You did *Freak Weather*."

Tears are shining in his eyes. "And I had two divorces. My exes took practically everything I'd made up till then. And then *The Underground* ran into so much trouble and went seventy million over budget, and I put everything into it. I took a second mortgage on my house, I put in all my cash into it. I even raided my *daughter's trust fund!*"

By now I'm beginning to get this horrid feeling that he's telling the truth. But I really don't want to believe it. "You put your *own money in your movie?*" I scream.

Because that's just a *horrible* idea. Motion pictures are nearly the worst investment in the world. George Lucas, who has two of the most successful film franchises of all time, nearly lost every penny because he financed *Howard the Duck* with his own savings.

"I did," Chas. sobs. "That's exactly what I did. That's why I need the good opening weekend so badly."

I'm simply furious. I'm furious at Chas. for being so stupid, I'm furious at Chas. for tricking me, I'm furious at Chas. for being so weepy and useless and unable to give me what I need right now, which is a quarter-million in cash.

Doesn't he understand that I have *commitments?*

I pop the signed, limited-edition basketball shoes out over Santa Monica somewhere. Not because I think it will do any good, but just because I'm angry.

Chas. just moans and shakes. Clearly I'm not going to get anything out of him now, not here in his office. But I can't let him go—I've already committed felonies, and there's no telling what he'd do if I let him loose.

I've got to keep control of him until I can get my money. Maybe I can demand a ransom from the studio or his friends or somebody.

I'm shaking as badly as Chas. is, but from rage. I stalk my way to the window and look down at the parking lot. There aren't many cars left, but I see a deep blue Maserati Quattroporte parked right in front of the building. It's the only car left in a line of reserved parking spots, and that means it belongs to Chas.

I turn to Chas. and snap my fingers. "Give me your car keys," I say. He doesn't do anything but clutch his knee and moan, so I walk up to him, touch his bib overalls, and pop them off his body. His legs are pale and hairy. I dig around in his pockets till I find his car keys and his cell phone, which I confiscate.

There's CCTV cameras on the roofs of some of the buildings, so I pop over to them and make sure they're pointed away from the parking lot, or I make them go somewhere else. Then I return to Chas.'s office, where he's begun to look hopeful as he realizes I've left the building. He sees me reappear and his face falls.

I pop a windowpane out of place—more crashing in the office, more shrieks from Chas.—and I point the key fob into the parking lot and press the button that will open the trunk. I look carefully to make sure no one's looking my way—no one is—then I pop him to the parking lot, pop myself right after him, open the trunk, and pop him in. While he's still stunned and disoriented, I pop off all his clothing, including his shoes—I don't want him trying to kick his way out. Then I slam the trunk on him and drive his car off the Sony lot.

The car's interior reeks of rich leather and handcrafted luxury, but I can't help wondering who the hell would buy a Maserati *sedan*, as opposed to the sports cars that made their reputation. Does Ferrari make sedans? Does Lamborghini? It makes no sense.

Maybe Chas. uses the Quattroporte to take his kid's soccer team to practice. There's no other use for it that I can see. But still, the windows are smoked, and the guard at the gate doesn't pay attention to anyone *leaving*—he's only interested in the people trying to get *in*.

I'm cooling down just a little by this point, and I realize that the guards in the Marie Dressler Building lobby know I came in. I was on Chas.'s schedule for the evening. That means that if Chas. goes missing, I'm going to be a suspect.

But I can't let Chas. or his car go. I've *already* kidnapped him, there's no point in letting him walk away now.

So I get out of the car and pop it to the roof of a medical supply building on Venice Boulevard. That way no one will hear Chas. if he screams or tries to bash his way out. I pop myself along the rooftops till I'm across the street from Sony, then teleport myself straight into Chas.'s office.

Which is an appalling mess. The air reeks of spilled whisky. I'm a little shocked at how far I went in destroying things.

It seems clear to me that the best thing is to make it look as if *someone else* destroyed the office.

I lay out more glasses on the coffee table, and I pour whisky and brandy into them. I throw pillows around. I'm trying to suggest a drunken orgy with half a dozen people.

I clean up my own wine glass. I scrub fingerprints from anything I might have touched.

I step into his private bathroom and freshen up for a moment before letting myself out. I don't forget the fifteen thousand in the little bag.

I'm glad that I've had a little practice at criminality before having to do all this. If it hadn't been for Tomás and his lessons in crime, I'm sure I would have made a real mess by now.

I'm charming to the guard in the downstairs lobby, then I get in my car and leave the lot, waving cheerfully to the guard on the gate so that he knows I've left on my own.

By now it's quite dark. I return to Chas.'s car, pop it down to the road, and drive off.

♠

Which is how I find myself driving around Culver City in the early hours of the morning, with a naked producer-director in the trunk, a bag of cash on the seat, and time ticking by. I'm trying to decide whether or not to call Tomás and ask him if I can stash Chas. with him until I can arrange a ransom. But something holds me back—I'm not sure that the jump from grand theft to kidnapping is a good fit for my beautiful soulful-eyed masseur. It might make him far too nervous.

I pull over on a side street, dig out Chas.'s phone, and start flipping through the directory. I'm trying to figure out who should get the ransom demand.

Of course he's got the private numbers of the elite of the industry. Why wouldn't he?—he's one of them himself. But who among these people is going to pay money for his safe return?

His agent maybe?

Then one name scrolls by. *Dag Ringqvist.*

Dag Ringqvist, the tall, blond, gorgeous, incredibly successful, rich, and talented creator of *mACE* and *mACE II*, the latter of which Chas. has schemed to ruin.

Ringqvist, it suddenly occurs to me, is the anti-Chas. *mACE* is an immensely successful ace movie; *The Underground* was designed as a reverse of *mACE*. Chas. is a social misfit living out his fantasies through his films; but Dag is the fantasy Chas. wants to live. Chas. lives among NBA memorabilia; but Dag's house is filled with paintings and sculpture and a series of girlfriends who are almost as attractive as I am.

Dag is a blond Norse god. Chas. is a swarthy troll.

I wonder how grateful Dag Ringqvist would be to the person who let him know that Chas. has stolen his movie with the intention of sabotaging it.

Wait a minute . . . What would he do for someone who got his picture *back?*

◆

"Thank you, sugar," I say. "You'll be hearing from my agent."

I'm amazed at how well Dag and I got along over the phone, especially considering that I was calling him at one in the morning with bad news. But he was extremely gracious, even after I told him that I'd met Chas. at a drunken party, and he'd boasted to me of stealing Dag's movie, and of how he was going to ruin it by releasing a bad cut on every pirate channel in the world.

I explained that the police wouldn't be able to prevent his work from being desecrated, because all that Chas.'s editor needed to do was upload *one* copy to *one* site, and then it would spawn practically everywhere else. So *someone* had to get into the Chateau Élysée, get Aristotle's portable drives, and make sure all copies were accounted for or destroyed.

I graciously mentioned that I was willing to try to do this.

"Hell, Cleo, the Élysée is a damn Norman castle," Dag said. (Everyone calls it that. Norman must have been the architect.)

"Walls can't keep me out."

"This is very generous, Cleo. Are you sure there isn't anything I can do for *you?*"

My first thought is the missing quarter-million, but then I think of something better.

"You know," I said, "I've always wanted to work with you."

Then the conversation gets a bit serious, and in the end he's agreed that if I aid in retrieving any hypothetically lost intellectual property, et cetera, Dag will cast me in *mACE III*, if it's ever made (which it will be), and that my part will get at least fifteen minutes of screen time. Which doesn't seem like a lot, except that it will be an ensemble film with a big cast, so fifteen minutes for a new character is actually very good. I'll be noticed.

"What sort of part are you considering?" he asked. "A teleporter?"

"Teleporter or not, hero or villain," I tell him. "You're the genius, sugar. I know you'll make my part interesting."

I call my agent, who is surprised to be awakened this early in the morning, but he's *very* interested when I give him an outline of what's happened and give him Dag's fax number. I am told that a rough agreement will be faxed to Dag in a few minutes.

I hang up and cackle. Then I look over my shoulder and shout at Chas., hoping my voice will reach him in the trunk. "Did you hear any of that, Chas? I've been talking to Dag Ringqvist, and telling him how you're trying to fuck with him!"

From the answering groan, I know he's heard me.

While I wait to hear from my agent, I drive to my apartment in Hollywood and change out of my dress and into the Yamamoto jumpsuit, the cute Fiorentini + Baker boots, and the rest of my ninja gear. Then I drive past the Chateau Élysée. At this hour the streets are almost deserted, except for a line of kids camping out at a multiplex, waiting for opening day tickets for *mACE II*, which won't be released for a couple months.

The chateau is *huge*, bigger than I remembered—it's brightly lit, and surrounded by a wall. Neither the wall nor the lighting will cause difficulties for me, but the size of the place is worrisome in view of the fact that I don't know where in this giant building I can find the post-production offices.

Something whips by me so fast I barely recognize the skinny little butt in the orange latex body suit as it rapidly recedes from me; and before my instant of recognition is over, the skater is gone.

Blrr. Who I've seen here and there since *American Hero*, mostly at auditions.

Blrr's Hollywood career has been unusual. It should have been handicapped by the fact that there aren't a lot of acting parts calling for a roller blader who skates faster than the cameras can properly record, even at 48fps—and without the skating, she would have been just another actress wannabee with spiky hair and a tattoo.

But somehow she managed to parlay her *American Hero* experience into a starring role in a sitcom, *Who's That Grrl?*, in which she basically played herself and which ran for several seasons. Which was downright odd, because sitcom stages are tiny and she had no real opportunity to use her power.

If I were making a TV series with Blrr, it would have been an action series, with lots of chases. Foot chases, car chases, motorcycle chases, helicopter chases . . . anything that would let Blrr use her power. But instead she was cast in a sitcom.

I don't understand it. *I* can be funny. Why didn't *I* get a sitcom? I can use my power right onstage.

Blrr's career has been on hiatus since then, but Blrr's punk stylings were perfect for the outsider aces in *The Underground*, and Chas. cast her. Which would have set me to wailing and gnashing my teeth, if I weren't so Perky and Professional that it would never have occurred to me to complain.

Now it looks as if Blrr's been set to guarding the treasure Chas. is hiding in the castle. I wonder if she knows what it is she's guarding.

But it's her career at stake, so my guess is that she won't care. I certainly wouldn't.

She zips past me again when I'm stopped at a light but I turn off Franklin and find a place to park in the hills behind the chateau, on Foothill Drive. I'm not worried about Blrr so much—I can just pop around her—but I'm starting to get worried that there might be other aces guarding the treasure. Maybe it's my turn to call in some reinforcements just in case I run into trouble.

But who do I know that I can call at this hour of the morning?

I call Jack Braun anyway. Because this is all his fault, somehow.

He sounds sleepy when he answers the phone. "There's this weird situation," I tell him. "I'm wondering if you can help."

I explain as quickly as I can. When I finish, there's this long silence, then Jack says, "You want me to help you steal something."

"Yes."

Another long pause. "Isn't this what we talked about?"

"No," I say, "this is *different*. I'm not stealing anything, I'm rescuing it from the people who stole it in the first place."

"I think it's still a felony, Cleonie."

"All I'm asking for," I tell him, "is a little backup. In case I run into trouble."

"Cleonie," he says, "they'll *recognize* me."

"You can disguise yourself."

"I *glow gold* when I use my ace powers. Nothing can disguise that." There's another long pause, then he sighs and says, "All right. Tell me where I can meet you."

Suddenly I'm overwhelmed with gratitude. "Thank you, honey!" I say. "I'll make sure you won't regret this!"

"Yeah," he says. "Because no one has ever said that to me before."

While I wait, I think about who else I can call. There's Drummer Boy, but his band is touring Asia. Of the other competitors on the show, I've lost touch with all of them except the ones that stayed in L.A., and most of those sort of hate me . . . which is hurtful, because they don't understand that it was a *game*, we were *supposed* to try to win, and all those things I said about them on camera were just a part of the scenario and not malicious in any way . . .

I'm frustrated, I can't think of anyone else, so I call her.

"Rachel?" I say. "Sweetie, you're not busy, are you?"

♥

Half an hour later, my agent tells me there's a signed preliminary agreement with Dag, and Jack and Rachel are meeting me on Foothill Drive a couple blocks from the Maserati, because I don't think they'd react well if they found out that I'd made them accessories to kidnapping.

I'm trying to spare them the knowledge of something bad, though I'm afraid they'll never know or appreciate how much I'm trying to protect them.

But it isn't long before I'm thinking I might as well not have called them at all, because they're *useless*. Jack won't do anything because his glow will give him away. And Rachel won't help because her powers are too recognizable.

"If the cops see a sixty-foot penguin attacking the castle," she says, "they're gonna know who to call."

"Look," Jack says finally. "Keep your phone on speaker so we can hear what's going on. And if you run into trouble, we'll try to pull you out."

Well, that's about all I can hope for. So I wrap the Botto Giuseppe scarf around my face and set out.

I scout the castle from the roofs of the surrounding buildings. I see Blrr zooming along far below, moving so fast that I'm sure she can't see me.

At this hour most of the windows are unlit. I look for a row of windows all lit up, particularly if they're otherwise dark but lit with the blue shimmer of video monitors. I see nothing like that from my limited perspective, but there's a line of windows lit on the fourth floor, east side, so I jump into a corner, where I hope I can find cover if I need to.

I don't need to. I'm in a series of law offices, and I hear a vacuum cleaner a few offices away, which tells me that cleaners are here. I find the nearest exit and walk through it, to find myself in a corridor.

I wish I could just go to the lobby and look at the directory that's bound to be there. But the lobby is also guaranteed to have security, and that would be bad news.

I'm wandering randomly on the fourth floor when I feel my cellphone throb in my pocket. I look at it and see that Rachel's sent me a text message.

"Argyll Productions," it says. "Map on web page says 5th fl E side." Fifth floor, east side. Only one floor up from where I am right now.

I'm sure I would have thought of checking online myself if I hadn't been so frazzled. But still, it's nice that Rachel's paying attention instead of just playing with her stuffed animals and being useless.

"Thx," I text back—because I am Prompt and Professional—and find an elevator.

Which turns out not to be the best idea, because when the elevator doors open on the fifth floor, there's Rosa Loteria sitting in a chair, obviously guarding the place. And she's looking right at me—but while she might not recognize me, I'm sure she knows a very fashionable ninja when she sees one.

I'm as surprised as she is, so I pop over next to her and say, "Hi, Rosa."

Which gives her a jolt, and me a great deal of satisfaction.

Rosa and I have a history, and it's not a nice one. In fact she's one of the very few people on the planet that I hate. We were both on *American Hero*, where I was convinced that my soul was entwined with that of Drummer Boy, and he and I were doing fine until Rosa started shaking her tits at him. And she was always saying nasty things about me, and I was tempted to reciprocate—though I didn't, because she lied about me and I only told the truth about her.

Since then I've seen her at auditions, where I'm pleased to say she hasn't been doing all that well.

Rosa can't use her ace power on camera, because it's all tied up with her antique deck of Spanish cards, and she can only turn into the character that she draws randomly, and there are something like a hundred cards in a lotería deck. Though some of her characters are enormously powerful, she can't keep a whole film crew standing by while she shuffles through her deck time after time trying to come up with the right card for the scene.

And she hasn't been doing all that well playing non-ace characters. I'm guessing that's because there aren't a lot of speaking roles for skanky Chicana whores.

Oh—was that less than Professional? Like I care.

Rosa gives a jump and stares at where I've just materialized on her right side, so I pop to her left side and say, "Chas. didn't tell me you were a part of this."

She jumps again and starts to get pissed off.

"Chas. and I go way back," she hisses at me. "I'm in his damn movie, which is more than I can say about *you*."

It must be a pretty minor part. I hadn't heard she was in it at all.

And I bet she had to fuck him first, while he fantasized about the Lakers. Because hanging onto another guy's sneakers is totally a symptom of sexual health, right?

I pop right in front of her, just inches away. She controls her reaction better this time, but still, I see the flinch. She's toying with her cards, and I know I've got to get rid of her before she tries to draw one.

Of course, I could touch the cards and pop them out the nearest window, which would mean she has no ace powers at all. But I think that might just turn her from a whore ace into a non-ace whore who is enraged, violent, and murderous, so I think that's not the best idea.

"Do you know what you're guarding here?" I ask. "Or do I have to tell you?"

She thrusts her lower lip at me. "'*Course* I know," she says. "Chas. and I are tight, you know."

"Okay," I say. "I'm here to tell you that word's got out, and the cops are on their way as soon as they can get a, a what-do-you-call-it, a subpoena."

"You mean a *warrant*, bitch?" Sneering.

"Yeah, a warrant. They're on their way, and I'm supposed to pop the disks off to where they can't be found. And *you* just need to leave before you're recognized."

She falls for it, the stupid bimbo. She walks right past me to the elevator and presses the button, and I'm cackling behind the scarf that's wrapping my lower face.

I wait for Rosa to leave, then call Jack.

"Rosa Lotería was here," I tell him. "I told her the cops were coming and talked her into leaving, but see if you can make sure she doesn't have any second thoughts."

"Okay." There's a pause. "Maybe I can send one of Rachel's pets on a scout."

"Inconspicuous, okay?"

"If that's possible." Given that all her toys are the size of King Kong.

I hang up and walk to the front doors of the Argyll offices. They're big, heavy, pretentious carved wooden doors, completely opaque, so I can't pop myself through them. They're unlocked, however, so I just walk through.

I walk past the reception desk and there's a big, long room full of monitors, and I see Aristotle staring into one of several flat screens that are arrayed in a semicircle around him. There's a hot coffee smell in the air and blaring, discordant music. His workspace is half-buried in snack food wrappers, empty cans of energy drink, and foam coffee cups.

I undo the top buttons of the jumpsuit to show some of my assets. I've noticed that men generally seem less intelligent when I do that.

Aristotle looks up at the sound of my cute Fiorentini + Baker boots on the tile entryway. He's still wearing his hoodie, but the hood is pulled down to show a surprisingly tiny head, with spiky hair and sharp features.

I pull the scarf down around my neck so he can see my face. "We're in trouble," I tell him. I walk briskly, I speak briskly, as if there's no time.

"Police will be here as soon as they get a, a—a warrant. You've got to get *mACE II* off the computers. Off so completely that even experts won't be able to find it. And the same with the cloud and the servers or whatever."

I have only a vague idea of what *the cloud* and *servers* might be, but Aristotle seems to understand.

"Put everything you've got onto as few disks as possible," I say. "Then give them to me, and I'll pop out of here along with them. You can just walk out, and if the police stop you, they won't find anything on you."

I'm very proud of my little plan. If I hadn't found Aristotle here, or someone like him, I would have been at a loss to manage this all by myself.

After all, Aristotle knows I'm part of Chas.'s conspiracy. He has no reason to doubt what I'm telling him.

And apparently he doesn't. He bends over his keyboard and starts calling up files. "It'll take a bit of time to erase these thoroughly," he says. "Even if I zero out the file, there are forensic tools now that can reverse it. So now I have to overwrite the damn thing a zillion times—" He flashes me a jittery grin over his shoulder. "Fortunately I wrote a utility for that."

He goes on speed-babbling this sort of nonsense as he works at his keyboard, his voice raised to carry over the blaring music. Clearly the poor child has swallowed far too much caffeine.

"Do we have to listen to that music?" I ask. I don't want to interrupt the music if it's vital to his process, but its blaring chords are giving me a headache. It's like the soundtrack to every bad Biblical epic of the 1950s, all of which I had to watch when I was growing up in Alabama and all of which I hated.

I mean, *Victor Mature?* Who thought *he* could be a star?

Aristotle cackles and turns the music off. "Horrible, isn't it? It's generic music from old B movies. You can download it for cheap. I was putting it on all Lars' big dramatic scenes, so they'd seem as low-end and corny as the music."

I shudder. I think that's punishing viewers far too much.

Aristotle detaches the cables from his portable drives, then hesitates. Then he pull a flip-phone from his shirt pocket and calls up the speed dial.

A warning sizzles through my nerves. "Who are you calling?"

"Chas. I need to know if he wants me to erase the software, too. I don't think they can trace it to me, and it'll take twenty or thirty minutes to overwrite those tracks enough times to make sure they can't reconstitute it . . ."

"If it can't be traced, just leave it." But then I realize that it doesn't matter, because Chas. is in my trunk and won't be answering his phone.

Which promptly begins to sound its ringtone, Lil Wayne's "Rich as Fuck," which is a problem because the phone is in my jumpsuit pocket. I'd forgotten I had it with me.

Aristotle looks at my pocket, and the raucous ring tone booms out into the big room. I reach into my pocket and pull out the phone, and I try to figure out some way to refuse the call, but I have to jab it several times, each jab more frantic than the last, before it finally turns off.

Aristotle narrows his eyes. "That's Chas.'s phone?"

"Yeah," I say. "There must have been some kind of mix-up."

I try to look cute and confused and adorable. I bend over a little bit to show my assets under the jumpsuit.

But Aristotle seems immune to my girly act. I figure he's got to be gay.

"What's going on?" he asks. Suspicion has entered his tone.

I'm really terrible at improvisation. It took me some time to come up with the plan I'm following, and now that it's falling apart, I don't know how to respond.

"It doesn't *matter!*" I say. "We're going to get *busted* if we don't get out of here!"

He puts a protective hand on his portable disk drives. "Maybe I'd better hang onto these," he says.

"That's not what Chas.—"

"I don't *know* what Chas. wants," he says, almost snarling.

"I *told* you . . . "

"There's something weird here," says Aristotle. "And I'm not letting go of these until I hear from Chas. himself."

All I have to do, really, is lean over, touch the drives, and pop them across the room. Then pop myself to the same place, pick up the drives, and get my shapely butt out of the Chateau Élysée.

And really, I'm out of ideas, and the more I talk, the less Aristotle believes me. So I lean over, touch the drives, and pop them twenty feet down the room, in the direction of the exit.

And I'm about to follow them when Aristotle bolts out of his chair. And because I'm so surprised, he beats me to the drives and scoops them up.

He doesn't run like anyone I've ever seen. He moves with incredible speed, but instead of being visible along his entire path he seems to skip from one point to the next, as if his path was being illuminated by the flashes of a strobe. Behind him he trails a series of afterimages along his path, each of which shows him frozen in the act of running.

It's as if he's on a strip of film, but only every tenth or twentieth frame is projected, so that he seems to teleport about a yard, flash into existence, then teleport again, and again, and again.

And when he teleports, the images show him in the act of running. Which isn't how I do it—when I teleport, I arrive in the same posture as when I left. I don't have to dash around, I just *go* there. He has to actually transit the space between himself and his target, and that takes time—not much time, but a little.

He stops, the portable drives in his hands. The afterimages he's left behind fade away, one after the next, as if he's sucked them into himself. He looks at me and laughs at the baffled expression on my face.

"Oh?" he says. "Nobody mentioned I was an ace?"

"Chas. stiffed me," I tell him. "He didn't pay what he owed. And he's not going to pay you either."

He sneers. "He's *already* paid me, Pop Tart. I'm in his *movie*. Right now I'm just trying to make sure the movie's a big hit."

I don't like being called Pop Tart, and anyway I'm starting to get really angry—and the last time I got angry, I wrecked an office and teleported a pair of limited-edition basketball shoes off to Santa Monica.

I don't remember reading about any ace named Aristotle in Chas.'s movie, but then maybe Aristotle Dimitropoulos isn't the best name for an aspiring movie star, at least outside Athens or wherever, so he's picked a new one.

Or maybe he's just an exceptionally loyal film editor. Who knows?

It doesn't matter anyway. I pop next to him and reach for the disk drives. He spins away—flash-flash-flash—but I grab his hoodie and I manage to pop it, with Aristotle in it, into the air over his workstation. He comes down with a satisfying crash in a blizzard of crushed coffee cups and cardboard fast-food containers, but then there's that blinding speed again, and I see, flash-flash-flash, like a strobe light, as he picks himself up and begins a race for the exit.

I pop a chair in his path and he piles right into it, knocking himself and the chair sprawling . . . the portable drives skitter across the carpet as they spill from his fingers. I pop to the drives and grab them, and he jumps to his feet with completely unnatural speed and swings at me with a fist. My heart gives a leap, and with a fraction of a second to spare I pop clean to the other side of the room and watch his fist flail the air.

Then there are the swift series of strobes as he comes at me, as he picks up the fallen chair and slings it through the air right at my head . . .

I pop away but I don't have time to spot my landing properly, so one leg twists under me and I fall. I feel a jolt of pain as I bang my shoulder on the corner of a table, and though I'm half-stunned I know that Aristotle is on his way, so I give a desperate glance under the table toward the far side of the long room and pop myself as far as I can see, which is about halfway before my view is blocked by a long planter full of ferns.

I'm still lying on the floor, but at least I'm not where Aristotle thinks I am, and I have a chance to lurch to my feet before he can take another run at me. Pain shoots through my twisted ankle as I rise, and I clench my teeth. I am trying to work out how to escape.

The big wooden office doors are opaque, so I can't pop through them, and if I just run through them Aristotle will catch me. My other option is suggested by the big windows looking out onto Hollywood, but the problem is that it's dark, and I can't spot my landing. I'd have to pop high up into the air, then hope to spot a safe landing and teleport to it *as I fell tumbling through the sky*, and if I got it wrong I could impale myself on someone's picket fence, crash through the roof of a car, or just turn into a bloody splotch on the pavement somewhere.

Still, I'm desperate and on the verge of trying exactly that. But then I realize I have a third option, which is *to kick the living crap out of Aristotle.*

Or not *kick*, exactly. I could teleport him up just below the twelve-foot ceiling and let gravity do my kicking for me while I preserve my ladylike composure.

Prompt. Professional. *Pop.*

All this rushes through my head in the second or two it takes for Aristotle to realize I'm not where he thought I was. He looks at me and I see anger twitch across his tiny little face, and now here he comes, flash-flash-flash.

I teleport out of his path and he races past me. I reach out to snag him so that I can pop him into the air, but my bad ankle folds under me and I stagger, barely able to keep my feet. He stops dead, turns, rushes again with his arms thrown out to catch me. I do my little side-pop again, reach out, and this time I catch one of his outthrust arms.

So I pop him up to the ceiling. And this time he actually does his flash-flash-flash strobe action all the way down, except he hits just as hard as if he fell normally and then splays like Wile E. Coyote on the ground.

I've seen a *lot* of Wile E. in the last few hours.

"Had enough?" I ask.

He heaves himself to his feet. There's blood on his face, but his expression has hardened somehow, and hatred blazes in his eyes.

"Oh no, bitch," he says. "We're not done at all."

His eyes half-close and his face hardens. His fists clench by his side. He's nearly vibrating with concentration. And suddenly there's two of him, then *four.*

He's not running, he's splitting himself up somehow, and the different versions of himself aren't fading away like they did before. Suddenly they *all* look at me with the same malign expression, and one of them comes after me.

I pop away, but then a second Aristotle charges, and I teleport only to see a third Aristotle come flashing toward me . . . Between them all they're covering the big room very thoroughly, and I realize that I can't outrun all four of them, that one of them is bound to catch me sooner or later.

Panic seizes my heart. I pop again, and I decide to take a blind jump out the window, into the sky over Hollywood, and hope I can make a safe landing. Except that as I glance outside, I see something *move* out there, something huge and viscous and gleaming, and for an unsettled moment I freeze in my place and Aristotle Number Four almost overruns me . . . I pop away, desperate, my head swimming . . . A fist belonging to another Aristotle swishes within an inch of my face . . .

Suddenly the windows burst in, and a bundle of huge gleaming purple tentacles lunge into the room.

Oh great, I think. Chas. has *another* ace working for him.

One of the tentacles wraps around me and I scream at the slimy touch. Then I see the Aristotles yelling, all four of them, as they're swept up by the purple leviathan, and I wonder dazedly who the monster is actually working for, Chas. or Dag Ringqvist or maybe even a third producer come crashing the party.

The tentacles withdraw, and suddenly I'm outside and I realize that I am the captive of a giant purple octopus that is oozing, like a great squishy balloon filled with sea water, across South Yucca and into an area filled with large apartment buildings.

In the battle of Giant Octopus vs. Norman Castle, I realize, the castle doesn't stand a chance. Or Norman, either.

I also realize, after my initial moment of terror, that I can pop to safety whenever I want to, but what I really want to do is catch my breath, and since Aristotle can't hurt me right now, that's exactly what I do.

But then there's a blur, and there's Blrr, who's just rocketed up South Yucca in her orange jumpsuit, and discovered the octopus retreating with me and the Aristotles . . . and she stops dead in the middle of the street and stares.

Because what can she do, exactly? Her ace power is to skate really fast, which isn't of much use when Godzilla, or the Empire State Ape, or any other giant critter turns up. She can run *away*, sure, but Jack the Octopus Killer she is not.

After a moment's thought, she zips away to a safe distance, then gets out her cell phone. After which Chas.'s phone, still in my pocket, begins to play "Rich as Fuck" all over again. Which makes me laugh.

The octopus oozes along, then pauses in a passage between two apartment buildings. Three of the Aristotles have faded away, leaving only the one I presume is the original sagging and panting in the grip of a purple tentacle. Dividing himself into four seems to have taken a lot out of him, and he's a long way from his stack of energy drinks.

The octopus draws me close to one of its huge yellow eyes, and I hear a voice come from the direction of its beak. (Did you know that octopuses have beaks? I didn't.)

"Did you get what you came for?" Rachel's voice.

"Yes."

"Can you pop where you need to go?"

"Yes."

"Then do that. I'll take care of what's-his-name here."

"*Strobe!*" Aristotle has revived enough to shout. "I'm called *Strobe!*"

"He's called Greektown," I say, before spotting the roof of the apartment building and popping myself there. I look around, and I listen for the sound of sirens, and it seems that at this hour of the morning, even Hollywood hasn't noticed a giant purple octopus mooching around. I pop a couple more times till I'm standing next to Jack, who's leaning on his car, and I hand him the disk drives.

"Can you take care of these?" I say. "Greektown comes after you, you can knock his block off."

"Who?" he asks.

"You'll know him if you see him."

I glance down to where Rachel is sitting on the curb. She's a little abstracted because she's controlling her octopus telepathically. Poor dear, at this hour, and with her wiry hair sticking up all over the place, she looks even less attractive than usual. A few minutes later the octopus itself comes slouching down the street, pauses between a couple of palm trees, then turns into a stuffed animal. The streetlights give an extra flare at the released energy. Half a block away, one of the streetlights explodes.

Rachel hops up from the curb, picks up the stuffie, and puts it in her rucksack.

I run up to her and give her a big hug. "Thank you, sugar," I say. "You saved me from that, that *person*."

"Greektown? I dropped him off on top of a building."

"Let's hope that slows him down."

Rachel's phone gives a beep, and she fishes it out of her jacket and looks at the text. "Gotta go," she says. "There's a boat gone missing."

"Thanks again, sweetie!" I tell her. "Let's have lunch some time!"

But she's already getting out the stuffed dragon, and within only a few seconds she's flapping into the sky.

"That should help her establish her alibi," Jack says. "And we should establish ours."

"Rich as Fuck" begins to play again. I take out Chas.'s phone and offer it to Jack.

"Can you crush this?" I ask. Jack obliges, and Lil Wayne's rap comes to an end in a strangled squawk. Dust and crushed electronics spill from Jack's hand, and a thrill goes through me at this demonstration of his power, and for a minute I forget how everything is his fault.

"Sweetie," I say. "Could you do me one more favor?"

He gives me a look.

"I am not going to like this, am I?" he asks.

♣

But in fact this is where Jack shines—or maybe I should say *glows*—as the peacemaker who settles everything just the way it should be settled. He offers to let Dag Ringqvist and Chas. meet in his Toluca Lake home to mend fences. I call Dag, and he agrees once I tell him that Jack has the disks of *mACE II* in his possession.

I guarantee that Chas. will show up, but even so maybe Jack and Dag are a little surprised when I back Chas.'s Quattroporte into Jack's driveway and pop the trunk to reveal one of Hollywood's most powerful men naked and lying like a beached white whale in the belly of his own Maserati.

Dag just stands and watches with considerable interest as Jack helps Chas. out of the trunk and supports him as he limps inside. I'm limping myself as I walk up to Dag and smile. As I believe I may have mentioned, Dag is tall and blond and handsome, with an oversized nose that makes his face interesting, and he's dressed in what I recognize as Bruno Cucinelli flannel trousers and a chambray shirt from Alexander Olch. He looks magnificent.

On my way to Toluca Lake, I've given myself a few moments to freshen up, and I've tried to remove any evidence of the night's proceedings. I've brushed my hair till it has exactly the right amount of bounce, and I've kept the military-style jumpsuit and boots even though they're marked with octopus slime, because I think that makes me look a little more authentic. Dag should know what I've gone through on his behalf.

Besides, the outfit is just so dashing and perfectly criminal.

"I think everything's worked out," I tell Dag, and I take his arm and walk with him into Jack's living room, with its mission-style furniture, abstract art, and photographs of people who are dead, and those blood-red tiles he has in his bar. There are roses of an interesting mauve shade in a tall vase, presumably picked from Jack's garden out back.

"Are you all right?" Dag asks. "You're limping."

"I twisted an ankle," I tell him, "but I'll be all right." I wince a little, just to let him know I'm putting on a gallant show after being injured on his behalf.

I sit with Dag on a sofa. The scent of roses drifts gently through the room. Jack appears with Chas., who has been given a bathrobe that doesn't come close to fitting him. Chas. sits on an easy chair, and Jack takes his place in a brown leather armchair at the head of the room. He puts his fingertips together, and holds the silence for a long time.

"This stops *now*," he says finally. "I don't know exactly what's going on, or why or how, but it needs to stop." He points at Chas. "You're not allowed to steal someone else's movie and release it."

He squirms. I can tell he's on the verge of claiming he never did that, but his courage fails him at the last second and finally he just stares at the floor and nods.

Jack turns his finger to Dag. "No retaliation," he says. "This has gone far enough. There's been violence, there's been property damage, there's been some kind of abduction." His eyes turn to me in an accusing way.

"It appears no harm was done to me," Dag says, with his thrilling Scandinavian accent. "I have no grudges against anyone."

Which was nobly said, I thought. I squeeze his arm to show him my support.

"And one last thing," Jack says. "*Nobody talks.* Nobody talks about this to *anyone*. Because if word gets out, everyone in this room gets fucked."

We all nod.

"We're all agreed, then?" Jack says. He's speaking with perfect authority, as if he were some Mafia don instead of a washed-up actor. And the others are respecting him, which makes me think he might be a better actor than I thought.

"Well then," Jack says. "Why don't we all go home?"

We all get up, and I run over to Jack and give him a peck on the cheek. "That was just perfect!" I tell him.

"Cleo," he says. "Next time you're in trouble, I'd be thankful if you find someone else to call."

"I don't plan to be in trouble ever again!" I tell him, Perky as you please, and I ignore his skeptical look and bounce back to Dag Ringqvist. I take his arm.

"Could you give me a ride back to my car?" I ask. I don't tell him it's all the way down in Culver City.

He looks at me with stunning blue eyes. "It would be my pleasure," he says.

And right away, I know we have a connection. It's as if our souls are already singing in harmony with each other.

I'm going to get to know Dag better, I realize. I'm going to be in his next big picture, and I'm going to need to see a lot of him in order to talk about my character and her situation and how I should portray her.

It's going to be a very fruitful partnership, I think.

We walk through the front door into a morning that smells of desert flowers, and I see Chas.'s car in the driveway with the trunk still hanging open. "Oh, wait a minute," I say. "I forgot my bag."

Which is the little satchel with the fifteen thousand in it, which I take. Dag looks at me over the Maserati's roof.

"Ready?" he asks.

"Of course!" I tell him.

He's got an Audi R8 Spyder in a deep gunmetal color. The interior smells of leather and money and power.

He reaches across the console to make sure my safety harness is in place. I put my hand on his arm. He starts the engine and hundreds of horsepower split the air with their song. The eastern sky is just beginning to lighten.

I'm ready, I think. I'm ready for Dag, I'm ready for stardom, I'm ready for my close-up.

Acceleration punches me back into the seat.

Fade, I think. *Roll titles.*

Dag and I roar off into the dawn.

Happy Ending.

How to Move Spheres and Influence People

by Marko Kloos

CARD, TURNING

THE FIRST TIME IT happens, she's in PE class, because of course it has to be PE.

It's fashionable to hate PE, and most of the other girls at Mapletree Academy claim they do, but T.K. really doesn't mind it. It's only twice a week, and they mostly stick to sports she can do with her one working arm. She knows she could easily get out of PE by pulling the Cripple Card (although she never calls it that; her parents and teachers would flinch in horror at her own insensitivity toward *herself*, go figure), but she doesn't because she likes to run around even if she's not very good at it. She also doesn't want to give her stuck-up classmates the satisfaction of being able to shoot her pitying glances as she sits on the sidelines and eats Goldfish crackers while doing her math homework. Truth be told, it's the only time during the week when T.K. doesn't feel like everyone's pussyfooting around her disability.

They're playing dodgeball that day, at the end of the class. T.K. is pretty good at it considering she can only use one arm, even if she gets nailed by the ball a little more than the other girls. But this session is a shooting gallery, with her as the target. Again. It's just two girls who are targeting her specifically—and her left side, too, where she can't block—but they're stealthy about it so Mrs. Williams, the PE teacher, doesn't come down on them. For some reason, Brooke MacAllister has decided that if T.K. wants to play with the varsity, she can take the hits too. And for this week, she seems to have recruited Alison Keller to be her wingman, because T.K. is getting targeted fire from two angles. Mapletree has a special version of dodgeball where you have to crank out five push-ups on the spot if you get hit. Mrs. Williams wanted to give her a waiver on the push-ups, but T.K. refused the special treatment. She's not strong enough for one-armed pushups, but she can do crunches just fine, so she does those instead. And today, she's doing a lot of crunches courtesy of Brooke and Alison. In the middle of her fifth set, a ball comes in and beans her on the left side of the head just as she is coming up from a crunch.

"Ow!"

T.K. glares in the direction of the ball's origin and spots Brooke, who gives her a curt and jock-like "Sorry!" without even the slightest tone of apology in her voice. T.K. doesn't want to make anything of it, so she doesn't even look for Mrs. Williams, but she has her limits, and Brooke's attention is starting to poke at the edges of them. She finishes her crunches and gets back up to rejoin the ranks. Another ball shoots past her face, so close that she can practically smell the rubber, and she ducks and flinches. This one came from the other side of the court, from Alison's direction, but Alison pretends to not notice T.K.'s glare as she conspicuously picks another target. T.K. grabs a ricochet off the gym floor and chucks it at Alison, but it misses her by a foot and smacks into the mats lining the wall behind her. Alison looks over to T.K. and smirks, which only serves to crank up the dial of T.K.'s Pissed-Off-O-Meter another notch. She can't really complain about them throwing balls at her, because that's what the game is about. But getting singled out for no good reason takes the fun out of it.

"One minute," Mrs. Williams shouts from the sideline. "Wrap it up, ladies!" Then she turns around and checks her cell phone. T.K. groans.

"Don't you—" she calls over to Brooke, but Brooke does, and so does Alison. Of course they were waiting for the opportunity for one last cheap shot. Alison's shot hits T.K.'s right thigh and bounces off. Brooke's ball comes in a flat arc, and T.K. knows that she'll take the stupid thing right on the bridge of her nose.

That's when the thing happens.

Later, she'll puzzle about what triggered it. She's hot and sweaty, angry at Brooke and Alison, hurting from the shot to the bare skin of her leg, and the muscles on her left side, the one with the paralysis, are taut enough to snap, which is what happens when she overexerts herself. But she knows that she feels a swell of fresh anger, and something goes snap in her brain. There's a hot, trickling sensation, like someone just opened the top of her skull and poured a cup of coffee directly on the back side of her brain and down her spinal column. T.K. raises her hand to keep the ball from hitting her in the face, even though she knows it's too late for that. But then the strangest sensation follows the hot trickle. She can feel the ball not three feet in front of her face—its roundness, the way it displaces the air around it—and she gives it a tiny little shunt with her mind, and it's the best feeling she's ever had, like finally scratching an itch you couldn't get to for an hour, only a hundred times better. The ball—the one that was about to give her a nosebleed—hooks ever so slightly to the left and whizzes past her left side, close enough to her ear that she can hear it whistling through the air.

Nobody notices. T.K. isn't even sure that Brooke saw the ball didn't fly true, that it made a little skip at the end of its arc. There are still half a dozen other balls in the air, and there's a lot of movement and yelling, kids paying attention to throwing or not getting hit. But she is dead sure that she caused that little skip, because she knows that for just that half second, the ball was in her control, and that it went precisely where she had wanted it to go.

♠

They hit the showers and get dressed, and T.K. is too amazed and shaken to seek out Brooke and Alison to bitch at them. Now that PE is over, nobody pays attention to her anymore. In the first few weeks after she joined the class, her awkward-looking one-handed maneuver to get back into her bra and shirt got some interest from the other girls in the locker room, but that's old hat now, and she finishes up and leaves as quickly as she can.

PE was the last class of the day, and now they have an hour of library time before dinner. But T.K. doesn't feel much like going to the library. Instead, she unloads her backpack at the dorm and then goes back to the gym.

She had figured the place to be empty by now, because Mrs. Williams usually leaves on time. But when she walks back in, Mrs. Williams is still there, walking toward the door with a bag on each shoulder.

"Tilly," Mrs. Williams says, and T.K. tries not to frown. Most of the teachers address her by her chosen name instead of Tilly, which she hates almost as much as its proper long form, Lintilla. She knows she's named for a great-grandmother she never even knew, but "Lintilla" sounds like a species of exotic rodent to her. So she was Tilly until she was thirteen, at which point she decided that "T.K." was edgier than "Tilly Kendall." Like she's a New York City spray tagger or a skateboarder instead of a skinny fifteen-year-old redhead from rural Vermont with freckles and left-side hemiparesis. But Mrs. Williams insists on using her actual name, which strikes T.K. as slightly disrespectful.

"Mrs. W," she replies. "I, uh, forgot something in the locker room."

It's a quick and shoddy lie, but Mrs. Williams, loaded down with bags as she is and clearly in a hurry, buys it without trouble. Besides, the gym is always open for the students anyway—there's a keypad at the door and everyone knows the code, and what kind of trouble can you get into in a school gym?

"Well, go get it. But make sure the door is latched when you leave, okay? The latch sticks sometimes if you don't push it shut all the way."

"Will do, Mrs. W," T.K. says. "Have a good evening."

"See you tomorrow, Tilly."

T.K. heads toward the girls' locker room and pauses in the doorway to wait for the "click" of the sticky door latch. Then she turns and goes to the door that leads into the gym. That feeling she had just a little while ago, when she moved that ball away from her face, had been the most wicked rush of her life, and she wants to see if she can repeat it.

The balls in the gym are neatly stashed away in nets hanging from the wall on the back of the gym, right next to the equipment lockers. T.K. walks over to one of the nets and pulls it open. She fishes out a ball and tosses it into the middle of the gym, where it bounces a few times and rolls to a stop.

"Here goes nothing," T.K. says to herself. Her voice echoes a little in the empty gym.

She's afraid that the moment of total control during the game was a fluke, a one-time thing, some momentary and non-recurring phenomenon, maybe a glitch in her brain. That she'll stand here in the gym and stare at that ball like an idiot for a bit while nothing happens. But when she concentrates, that control comes back with absurd ease. It's like looking at the curve of the sphere throws a switch in her mind, one that wasn't there before. It's not as strong as it was the first time around, but when she feels the curvature of the ball with whatever new sense her brain has flipped on with that switch, that feeling of deep satisfaction comes back, and she knows that it wasn't a momentary thing. It feels like she's holding that sphere in the palm of an invisible hand, one that's much more strong and limber and precise than her own.

T.K. laughs with relief. Then she picks up the ball with her mind and flicks it halfway across the court to the basketball rim on the far end. The ball hits the rim and bounces off. Before it can hit the gym floor, she picks it up again without effort, raises it slowly, and dumps it straight through the hoop.

"Holy shit," she says and laughs again.

She has superpowers. She's a damn *ace*.

◆

For the next hour, well into dinnertime, T.K. practices in the empty gym. She pitches the ball all over the place, and every time she does, she gets more accurate with it. It's like her new talent is a muscle that can be made stronger with practice. When she tries to manipulate other things, other shapes, that feeling of control evaporates, almost like the angles on the thing poke through whatever force she uses on the spheres and pops the bubble. But if it's round, she is in full control of it. She tries one of the heavy medicine balls out of the equipment locker, the ones she can't even lift with her own physical strength, but with the new power she just turned on, it's just as easy to throw those as it is to pitch a basketball. She throws the medicine ball around until she gets a little too giddy and tries to slam-dunk it onto the hoop rim. It smacks against the backboard hard enough to make the nearby windows shake, and the crash from the heavy ball on the board is so loud that she's sure they'll hear it all the way up in the library. She quickly picks up the medicine ball and moves it back to the equipment shack, before someone can come in and wonder how the partially paralyzed girl managed to move a twenty-five-pound ball ten feet up in the air by herself. Then T.K. tidies up and leaves the gym to head back up the hill to the dorm, with some reluctance.

SODA CANS AND BRICK WALLS

THE NEXT DAY, T.K. can barely muster the patience to sit through her classes. She was up until three in the morning, playing with tennis balls and marbles in her room, experimenting and chasing that euphoric feeling of control. The tiredness makes the day even longer and more unbearable. She has an idea for the afternoon, and she can't wait for the clock to hit 3 P.M.

When classes are finally over for the day, she rushes back to the dorm to dump her backpack and her books. Then she leaves the school property to go to the mixed-use building that sits just a quarter mile away from campus on the rural road. There's a country store here and a pizza joint, and the back of the building houses a little post office and a hardware store that's much bigger than it looks from the outside. T.K. usually comes here to get snacks, just like lots of other Mapletree students, but today the stuff she wants is in the hardware store.

The store has quarter-inch ball bearings at seventy cents apiece, individually bagged. She cleans off the whole peg, a dozen bags, and carries them to the register. T.K. has an alibi handy if they want to know why she needs a dozen ball bearings—school science experiments—but she must not look particularly shady, because the clerk rings her up without comment. Then she spots little plastic containers of BBs on the shelf behind the clerk and asks for one of those too, fully expecting to be treated like an aspiring terrorist any second. But the clerk just adds the total to the bill—eight bucks—and bags her stuff for her. She reads the label on the pellet container right before he bags it: 2,400 BBs.

Well, I wanted to know if I can do multiple spheres at once, she thinks. *Guess I'll find out.*

♥

There's an old abandoned factory half a mile away from Mapletree Academy, dilapidating away on the bank of the Connecticut River. A few of the juniors and seniors sometimes go there to drink, but the place isn't much of a hangout, littered as it is with old factory debris and broken glass. But it's away from people, and there's nothing T.K. can break here that's not already broken.

She brought a twelve-pack of soda from the country store, and for her first experiment, she lines up three cans on a crumbling brick wall in the central yard between the buildings. Then she walks back fifty yards and unbags her ball bearings. They feel weighty and serious, both in her hand and in her mind, when she lifts them one at a time with her power. T.K. expects the first one to drop to the ground when she lifts the second one, but it doesn't. She grins as she repeats the process, and three quarter-inch ball bearings are floating in the air in front of her.

She gives the first one a push, about as much as she pushed the basketball yesterday. It shoots off and knocks the first can off its perch. It lands on the pock-marked concrete with a huge dent in the center. T.K. finds that even at fifty yards, aiming the spheres isn't difficult at all. She pushes the second ball bearing a little harder than the first. This one streaks across the yard in a blur and punches into the second can dead-center, sending soda spraying everywhere.

T.K. concentrates on the last floating ball bearing and pushes it as hard as she can.

The third can disintegrates in a spray of soda and aluminum shrapnel. She knows the ball bearing went through the can and into the brick wall of the building twenty yards behind because she can see the puff of brick dust and hear the shattering brick as the bearing cracks it.

"Whoa," she murmurs, awed by the power she just unleashed with nothing more than half a second of concentration. She could seriously hurt somebody with this ability, even kill them.

T.K. steps up to the brick wall of the building she just shot with her ball bearing. Several of the bricks are cracked from the impact, and one of them is almost completely gone. She can see the hole the bearing made as it passed through. It went right through four inches of brick, and she suspects it also went through the back wall of that building, because that quarter-inch ball of steel was moving fast.

She spends half an hour experimenting with the rest of the ball bearings. She target-shoots the rest of the soda cans and finds that she can modulate her power very precisely, right down to the point where she can send a sphere right into a can with just enough power to knock it down without even denting it. Used like this, she can retrieve her ammunition and reuse it instead of having to dig it out of holes in broken bricks.

Then T.K. opens the container of BBs. They're so much tinier and lighter than the ball bearings that it hardly seems she'll be able to do much with them, no matter how fast she pushes them. So she pours them out on the ground in a pile and then tries to lift as many as she can at once.

They all rise like a little silver cloud in front of her—all 2,400 of them.

"No way!" T.K. laughs.

Then she starts playing with them like they're a flock of birds, moving them in one direction, then another, sideways, up, down. It's weird—she can feel each individual BB in her mind, but she can move them all as a mass, and it feels almost like she's manipulating a liquid made of thousands of perfectly spherical little drops. A hundred of those BBs don't weigh what one of the ball bearings did, but with so many of them in front of her at the same time, she realizes that not much can get through to her if she keeps them moving quickly. She directs the BB cloud into a stream around herself, around and up, then down and up again until it looks like she's the vortex of a metallic tornado. The BBs move so fast that she can't make them out individually anymore. They're just a blur of flashing silver.

It's like armor, she thinks. *Like a suit of armor you can carry around in your pocket.*

And then, on a whim, she wants to see if her power is divided among all those BBs evenly, or if each of them pushes off with the same speed as the ball bearing before, regardless of the number of spheres. And these BBs are tiny and lightweight, and *how much damage can they possibly do?* So she focuses on the cloud of spheres swirling all around her and pushes out with all her might, shoves them in all directions. They explode out from around her in a flashing ring of polished steel.

The result is instant and terrifying. T.K. hears glass breaking and brick cracking all around her, and for a moment she thinks she killed herself with her new powers, like a complete idiot. There's brick dust in the air, and as she stands there, cowering with her right arm over her head, it settles on her clothing and the ground in front of her.

She looks up and takes a sharp breath. All the way around the yard, the walls look like someone just blasted them with the world's largest shotgun, thousands of little holes bored into the brickwork, whatever glass was remaining in the window frames blown out and pulverized.

"Let's not try that again," she murmurs to herself.

It's kind of sobering to know that she can turn herself into a living shrapnel grenade with nothing but an eight-dollar container of BBs. That's more easy destructive power than she—than *anyone*—should be allowed to control.

But still, even as cowed as she is by her own display of sphere mayhem, she takes two of the quarter-inch ball bearings and sticks them into the pocket of her jeans as she packs up to go back to Mapletree. After all, you never know when you might need a sphere-shaped object handy in an emergency, and she won't always have a hardware store nearby when she needs one.

PE, RELOADED

THE NEXT DAY IS a Thursday, which means PE again.

T.K. goes into the inevitable round of dodgeball at the end with a live-and-let-live attitude. If it hadn't been for Brooke trying to cream her with a ball two days ago, she wouldn't have discovered what she can do. Or maybe it would have come out of her at some other time. But she's willing to forgive and forget, if Brooke and Alison don't pick her for target practice again.

But whatever chip Brooke has on her shoulder this week, it's still there today. T.K. makes it three minutes until Mrs. W has to take a call on her cell. And sure enough—five seconds after Mrs. W turns her back, a ball comes zooming at T.K. from where Brooke and Alison are playing side by side today. Brooke isn't even hiding that she took that shot. She grins at T.K., who gets smacked on her bare thigh again, in almost exactly the spot the other ball landed two days ago.

T.K. doesn't shout at them to cut it the hell out. She just drops for her five crunches. But even as she does, she keeps an eye on Alison, because she knows that Alison isn't the sharpest crayon in the box and probably thinks she can plant another one while T.K. is crunching away.

Alison takes her shot right as T.K. finishes the last crunch. T.K. knows that both girls are watching her, and that she can't pull the same sort of last-ditch save she performed on Tuesday. So she takes the ball to the side of her head on purpose. It's just a glancing blow, but it clips her ear and hurts, and she yelps involuntarily. Alison and Brooke, satisfied with their strafing run, turn their attention away again.

"All right then," T.K. says. She picks up the ball that bounced off her head. Then she chucks it at the spot where Alison and Brooke are standing, and gives it more push and a more precise direction with her new power.

The gym is noisy, and there's lots of crossfire, so nobody notices the utterly perfect path the ball takes. It flies a foot or more past Brooke's head, who whips her head around and smirks at her as if to congratulate her for the missed shot. But as soon as the ball has passed Brooke's peripheral vision, T.K. accelerates it and makes it bounce off the wall right behind her head. The deflection is implausible for the angle of the throw, but not impossible, and nobody notices anyway. The ball smacks into the back of Brooke's head, and it's just the right angle and momentum to bounce off her skull and hit Alison in the side of the head as well.

Brooke takes the brunt of that hit. T.K. swears she can hear her teeth slam together from the impact even across the noisy gym. Brooke goes to her knees. Next to her, Alison just lets out an indignant "*Ooowww!*" and then looks at Brooke, pissed off, as if her friend had chucked that ball from half a foot away.

T.K. almost laughs. She can do this over and over until both of them are tired of the game and leave her alone. But she can't help but feel a little bit of concern for Brooke, who's still on her knees and looking dazed, even though T.K. knows that she calibrated the pitch enough to not rattle that girl's cage too hard.

I could have knocked her unconscious, T.K. thinks and looks away.

And then a small voice in her head chimes in.

You could have knocked her head into the next zip code, it says, and it chills her to the bone.

And right then and there she resolves to only use that power on people when she absolutely needs to. It's too much, and it's not right to use it for frivolities like a high school tiff with a stuck-up rich girl who will have forgotten T.K.'s name two days after graduation. And then, despite it all or maybe because of it, she walks over to Brooke to make sure she's all right.

EDINBURGH

HERE'S THE THING ABOUT Mapletree: everyone who goes there is pretty much by definition a rich kid. The tuition is fifty grand a year, and there are no scholarships. But T.K. doesn't consider herself one of the rich girls because her allowance is small, and her parents didn't send her to boarding school with a wallet full of credit cards. At the beginning of the holiday break, however, there's no denying that she's from a loaded family. The parking lot in front of the gym looks like an exotic car dealership on pick-up day as all the parents are trying to out-Porsche and out-Benz each other.

Her mom and dad come by precisely twice a year—when they come to pick T.K. up for the summer break, and when they take her home for the holidays. That's when the big ceremonies for the parents take place. It's graduation in June, and the holiday concert in December, everyone dressed up and watching all the grades perform. T.K. supposes that when you shell out that much tuition money, you want to see caps and gowns and hear some uplifting display of liberal arts education at least twice a year. Mapletree doesn't teach any one-handed instruments, so T.K. sings in the choir, which is much more fun than she had expected. The grades do their performances to lightning storms of camera flashlights, a darkened gym full of middle-aged parents all holding up phones like they're at a concert. Then there's the milling and hand-shaking at the end, and then they are released for the holiday break, a whole week sandwiched between two long weekends.

"How was your trimester, sweetie?" her mom asks from the front seat as they are driving the fifty miles back home to Casa Kendall.

For a moment, T.K. thinks about answering truthfully. *Oh, it was awesome, Mom. I learned how to move round objects with my mind, and now I could wreck our house with a bowling ball just by thinking hard.* She tries to suppress a grin when she imagines that scenario and mostly fails, which her mother takes entirely the wrong way.

"That well, huh?" her mom says and winks knowingly. "Is he a junior or senior?"

T.K. only catches on after a second. Her mom thinks she's smiling about a *boy*. As if the whole school didn't have only two hundred students, less than half of them boys, none of whom are exactly falling over themselves to romance the only girl on campus with an obvious handicap. Not when all the other girls are well-bred, pretty, and with left arms that don't hang by their sides like recently broken wings.

"Neither, Mom," T.K. answers. It's not exactly a lie, after all, and her mom takes the evasiveness as cute embarrassment.

"Playing your cards close, I see. Well, I'm glad the trimester was fun for you."

"Where are we going for the holidays?" T.K. asks, mostly to change the subject. Dad always takes them out of the country for the holiday week as a treat. Last year it was Montreal, and the year before they went on a cruise and then stayed in Puerto Rico for three days.

"Edinburgh," her father says from the driver's seat. "Do some Christmas shopping in the old town, see the lights, have some good food. What do you think?"

"Sounds awesome," she says and gives her dad a thumbs-up. Then she sits back in her seat and thinks about the upcoming holidays. If she does the job while her parents aren't watching, hanging all the ornaments on the tree should be super easy this year.

♣

They head to Edinburgh for their usual holiday week fun rituals: shopping, restaurant meals, and enough sightseeing to fill the memory card on her dad's camera even though they've been here half a dozen times at least already. Edinburgh is pretty, especially the old town, which is aglow with Christmas lights everywhere, and it takes T.K. no time at all to get into the holiday spirit when snow starts falling on the evening of their first stay.

On the morning of their second day in Edinburgh, T.K. is out by herself to get Christmas presents for her mom and dad, who are off doing their own thing. Dad's having brunch with an old medical school buddy of his, and mom is getting a massage back at the hotel spa. There's a huge Christmas market set up on George Street, a rustic village of hundreds of booths and vendor stalls. T.K. spends the morning browsing the rows of merchants and taking in the sights and sounds. By lunchtime, she has converted most of her pocket money into gifts and trinkets for her friends. It's not bitingly cold, but the two hot chocolates from the beverage stalls

have worn off, and T.K. is ready to head back to the hotel to stash her pur-
chases and get some lunch.

At the end of George Street, there's a big, park-like square. It's a wide
expanse of grass surrounded by a perimeter of trees and a high wrought-
iron fence. T.K. is about to cross the street and walk through the park to get
to the hotel when she hears a commotion on the other side of the square,
screeching tires and then a loud metallic crash. The pigeons on that end
of the park take to the sky seemingly all at once. T.K.'s first thought is that
someone just had a bad traffic accident. Around her, heads are turning toward the noise. Then there's a second crash, louder than the first one, and
then she spots the source of the commotion. A delivery truck has knocked
down a section of the iron fence on that side of the park. As T.K. watches,
the truck drags part of the fence with it into the park square. There are
people walking on the garden pathways of the park, and they are dashing
out of the way of the truck now, shouting in alarm.

Everything happened so quickly that T.K. hasn't even had time to get
scared yet. After a morning of Christmas lights and warm drinks and
cheery holiday mood, the scene unfolding just a hundred yards in front
of her seems surreal and out of place. T.K. stands rooted to the sidewalk
at the end of George Street, transfixed by the sight of the delivery truck
bulling its way across the neatly manicured park, while people around
her gape or shout or rush to get out of the street. The truck swerves to
avoid the huge statue standing right in the center of the park. As it does,
the piece of fencing it was dragging comes loose and clatters against the
statue's plinth with a thunderous racket that reverberates across the park.

Three police officers come dashing down George Street and past T.K.,
shouting at people to get out of the way. They run toward the edge of the
park and the approaching truck. Now the crowd really starts moving, as if
the appearance of the police makes the danger official and concrete. T.K.
glances back down George Street, which is still packed with holiday shop-
pers. The end of the street is blocked off to traffic, but the barriers are just
orange-and-white plastic blocks with hip-high metal fencing at the top.

Two of the police officers try to block the truck as it approaches the gap
in the park's perimeter fence where the walkway lets out onto the street
where T.K. is standing. They wave their arms and shout at the driver, who
pays them no mind. The officers jump out of the way when the truck
reaches the gap, which isn't quite wide enough. The front of the truck,
already dented and scraped from the previous collision, smashes into
the iron fencing and knocks it aside. The truck's forward momentum is

slowed down briefly by the barrier, but the truck's driver revs the engine and starts to push through.

Up until now, T.K. thought it may have been an accident, or maybe a medical emergency. But then she sees the face of the driver through the windshield of the truck. He doesn't look like he's scared or in distress. His face is all wide-eyed focus, so devoid of obvious emotion that it almost looks like there's a department store mannequin behind the wheel. He steers the truck slightly to the right, then to the left again, to shunt the sections of fencing aside that are scraping along the side of the truck's cabin. One of the policemen jumps up onto the running board on the driver's side and hammers a baton against the window. The driver opens the door abruptly and forcefully, and the police officer goes flying and lands on the sidewalk.

T.K. doesn't consciously decide to act. She just looks at the people crowding the street behind her and the truck that's about to drive right into them in a few moments, and there's no way for her to get all those people out of the way, no way to stop that truck in its tracks. But there are hundreds of decorated Christmas trees all the way down George Street, and almost every stall and vendor booth is festooned with decorations as well. And so many of them are globe-shaped ornaments.

Without thinking about it, T.K. drops her shopping bags, reaches out with her good hand, and lets that newly awakened part of her mind pull every round holiday ornament in sight toward her.

It sounds like a thousand birds taking off all at once. All the way down the street, people shout and yell as trees rustle and sway, and a multicolored swarm of glass and plastic spheres rises into the cold winter air and speeds toward the truck just as the driver has managed to break all the way through the fence. The ornaments are bigger and much lighter than the ball bearings she has been using for practice. T.K. tries to keep control of them all, but they are so light, and there are so many of them, that the light breeze blowing over George Street is enough to make her lose her grip on many of them. It's like trying to hold on to a handful of powdery sand. Dozens of the ornaments fall out of the swarm and bounce or shatter on the street, career off vendor stall roofs, or bop people in the head. But she manages to hold on to most of them, and there are a lot, many hundreds, maybe thousands. T.K. hurls the stream of colored orbs against the front of the truck, where they start to shatter in little silver-bright explosions.

The ornaments have almost no mass, and they burst against the front of the truck and its windshield without doing damage, spraying glittering fragments of glass and plastic. But the cloud of ornaments T.K. has yanked loose from their trees and light chains has so much volume that dozens of them smash into the windshield every second, a flurry of green and red and silver shards that envelops the front of the truck like a cloud and obscures the driver's vision completely. The truck starts swerving. For a heart-stopping moment, it heads right for T.K., who redoubles her mental efforts. Then the driver swerves back to the right, over-corrects, and clips one of the traffic control barriers. The left front wheel of the delivery truck hits the corner of the barrier, and the truck jolts with the shock of the impact. It careens further to the right, bounces onto the sidewalk, and crashes into the front of the house on the other side of the street.

T.K. releases her hold on all the spheres that are still in the air. They fall to the ground, once again beholden only to gravity, and for a few moments, it's raining Christmas ornaments all over George Street. Maybe five seconds have passed since she started pulling the spheres with her mind and steering them toward the truck, but she feels like she has just run a track relay all by herself.

The policemen run up to the truck's cabin. One of them jumps up on the sideboard again and yanks on the door handle. The door flies open with a bang, so forcefully that one of the hinges pops off. The policeman jumps out of the way at the last instant, and the weight of the door bends the other hinge as well and makes the door flip forward and hit the ground with a shriek of tortured metal. The driver jumps out of the cab and onto the sidewalk, and T.K. lets out a shocked gasp. He's a joker—or whatever they call those in this country. Taller than the biggest of the policemen by at least a head, he is bare-chested, and a set of leathery wings is protruding from his back. But that's not even the most joker-like thing about him. Out of his chest, T.K. sees two extra vestigial arms protruding, each with three long fingers that end in sharp-looking claws. He grabs the nearest policeman by the front of his bulletproof vest, lifts him off his feet, and throws him backwards. The second policeman swings his baton and hits the joker on the side of the head. The joker almost goes to his knees. Then he whips his arm around and returns the blow with a backhand from his left arm. He's much stronger than the policeman, who takes the hit to the side of his head and bounces off the delivery truck's cabin only to crumple to the pavement.

The joker looks around, fury in his face. He yells something, but his Scottish accent is so thick that T.K. can't make out what he's saying. Then his gaze locks on her, and the fury turns to naked hatred in his expression. He gets up from the half-crouch the cop had beaten him into with his baton, and strides toward her. The wings on his back unfold with a little shudder and then pop out to their full extension. They are leathery like a bat's, and they make him look like a gargoyle or a demon from a comic book. She freezes in wide-eyed fear.

Then it's the joker's turn to get wide-eyed. He bellows a strangled scream and falls to his knees. Behind him, the last standing police officer is aiming a small black gun-looking thing at the back of the joker. She can see two little wires coming from the device and reaching all the way to the joker's back, to a spot right between his wings. Whatever the policeman is doing to him must hurt, but it doesn't seem to hurt enough to keep him down. He twitches a bit and rolls around, and his big leathery wings make an awful soft scraping sound on the pavement of the sidewalk. Then he reaches back and yanks the little wires right out of his back. The policeman fumbles with his little black taser thingie, but the joker is getting to his feet again, and T.K. can see that whatever the cop is doing won't be done in time.

She only realizes that she took her two ball bearings out of her pocket when they are floating above her palm and in front of her eyes already. The joker has his back turned to her as he is advancing on the remaining police officer, who is retreating and yelling into his radio.

T.K. doesn't want to kill the guy. She doesn't even want to hurt him. But she does want to keep him from hurting anyone else, and this is the only thing she has right now that will make a difference in time. She focuses on the ball bearings above her palm.

Easy, she reminds herself, remembering the holes she bored clean through bricks with these things not too long ago. *Pretend you want to bop Brooke with a basketball.*

She lets the first one go, but even as it flies toward the joker, she knows that she went a little too light on this shot. The ball bearing hits the joker square in the back of the head. He stumbles and goes to one knee, but catches himself and gets up just as the police officer tries to take advantage of the situation. The policeman tries to use his baton again, but the joker snatches it away from him and throws it aside. Then he grabs the policeman and flings him backwards. The officer crashes into the wall of the house behind him and slumps to the ground.

The joker turns around and glares at T.K. He bares his teeth and tenses his body like someone about to launch into a fifty-yard dash. She doesn't take the time to think about how to calibrate her next shot. She only has one ball bearing left, and there's no time to look around to see where the other one bounced. So she gives it a harder push than before and lets it fly.

The little silver steel orb hits the joker right in the middle of his forehead. This time, she can hear the dull thud of the impact from twenty yards away. And this time, the joker doesn't just go to his knees. He collapses to the pavement like T.K. has just turned off his main power switch. His wings splay out on the sidewalk, and then he lies still.

Sounds come rushing back to her brain like an aural flood. There are sirens everywhere now, and people are shouting and talking all around her. Three more police cars come screaming around the corner, sirens blaring and lights flashing. T.K.'s knees are shaking. She feels like all her energy has drained from her in the last few minutes.

There are police converging on this intersection from all directions now. Someone grabs her shoulder and shouts something at her, but it's like her brain has temporarily lost the ability to understand English. She can't take her eyes off the joker who's lying motionless on the pavement twenty yards in front of her, his wings draped over his body like a shroud.

Then one of the wings twitches a little. She sees a hand rising, then an arm. The joker tries to push himself up or roll on his side, but he doesn't get far because at least half a dozen police officers descend on him and pin him down. But he's alive. She knocked him out, maybe cracked his skull, but she didn't kill him.

T.K.'s legs give out, and she sits down hard on the cold pavement. Then she bursts into tears.

AFTERMATH

WHAT WAS SUPPOSED TO be a three-day trip to Scotland ends up turning into a week-long event. After Edinburgh, it seems like everyone in the country with a badge or a government ID wants to talk to T.K. Everyone is super nice to her, but she's still having to go to various places guarded by men in uniform who are carrying guns, and she never once has the feeling that all these talks are optional.

Her parents are dumbfounded to find out that their handicapped daughter is basically a superhero now. At first, T.K. is worried that her dad is going to ground her until college. But when he sees that everyone seems grateful for T.K.'s intervention and amazed at her ability, T.K. can tell that he enjoys basking in the positive attention by proxy a little.

After a few days of interviews and unceasing attention, T.K. is kind of over the whole thing. She's tired, both in mind and body. Whatever she did in Edinburgh took as much out of her as finals week in school. And when they spend the last day before their return home in London, she gets nervous every time she hears a car horn or the squealing of tires. The cops tell her that she just knocked the joker terrorist out—only they call him a "knave" instead of a joker here—and she is glad to know that she didn't hurt him permanently or end his life because then she knows she'd never use her ability again. But when she falls asleep in her hotel bed in the evening before the return flight, she sees the angry grimace of the truck's driver in her dreams, that twisted expression of fury directed at her, and she wakes up with her heart pounding in her chest and doesn't close her eyes again for the rest of the night.

♠

Her first inkling that life at home isn't going to be normal again comes when they arrive back in Boston. Before they even get to the immigrations check, three uniformed police officers and two men in dark suits wait for T.K. and her parents on the jetway right outside the plane's door. There's some hushed commotion behind them because the flight attendants are making everyone wait until T.K. and her folks have deplaned first. She feels uncomfortable with this unexpected attention, and when they grab their carry-on bags and leave the plane, she feels like she has done something wrong. But everyone is cordial and professional. They lead the Kendalls into a quiet room away from all the bustle, and all they want is to have a chat with her about what happened in Scotland, and for her to show them her ability again. They have donuts and coffee, and they're just as friendly as the cops in Scotland, but once again T.K. has the distinct impression that this isn't optional, that she wouldn't be able to just say "no, thank you" and walk out of the room. So she spends two hours with her parents and the cops in yet another boring conference room and retells the same story for the fiftieth time this week. Finally, the men in the dark suits thank her and let them go through immigrations and customs, and T.K. is relieved right up until the point where they walk into the international arrivals hall and see about two hundred camera lenses aimed at them. A crowd of reporters is waiting in ambush, and the flashes that go off when T.K. and her parents walk through the sliding doors leave no doubt about who they're here to see.

"Can we go back to check-in and fly somewhere else?" she says to her dad, even though she's bone-tired and wants nothing more than to go home and crash in her own room and on her own bed. "Like, Antarctica maybe?"

Her father replies with a chuckle, but from the expression on his face, she can see that he's at least considering the idea a little bit.

ACE, OUTED

"ABSOLUTELY *NOT*," HER DAD barks into the phone downstairs for what seems like the tenth time today. "She's fifteen years old, and she has to go to school on Monday."

At first, the constant barrage of calls and stream of people at the door were amusing to T.K., but the novelty has worn off very quickly. She has been holed up in her room since they got back from Scotland while her parents have been fielding reporter questions and interview requests. Every morning newscast in the country suddenly wants to talk to T.K., and so far her dad has shot down every request. But the phone hasn't stopped ringing even though Casa Kendall has an unlisted number, and T.K. has no idea how she is supposed to make it to school while there are news crews camped out on their street.

"So you basically suck for not telling me about this earlier," Ellie says over the phone. Ellie has been T.K.'s best friend since kindergarten—their families have been friends since T.K. and Ellie were toddlers—and Ellie is one of the few callers who makes it through the mom-and-dad screening vanguard today.

"I didn't know until, like, two months ago, I swear," T.K. says.

"You found out at *school?*"

"Yeah. In the middle of gym class."

T.K. gives Ellie the condensed version of the week her card turned, leaving out the part where she accidentally found out that she's basically a walking weapon of mass destruction now.

"That's insane," Ellie says. "I saw the news story. The stuff you did in Europe. You're gonna be a rock star at school. You *saved* people."

"I don't know about *rock star*. More like freak show, probably. Like I wasn't sticking out enough already."

The thought of returning to Mapletree with her new abilities known to everyone makes T.K. feel queasy. But the cat is out of the bag, and there's no stuffing it back in, not after cell phone camera footage of her from eight different angles showed up on television screens all over the world a few days ago.

"Can you come over?" T.K. asks. "I'd say let's go out to the Creamery and get some monster sundaes, but my folks won't let me within twenty feet of the front door."

"Tell you what," Ellie replies. "You show me your new superpower thing, and I'll come over with a half-gallon of Moose Tracks and two spoons."

T.K. laughs, relieved that at least some things are still the way they were last week, back when she was just a high school girl with a busted wing to everyone.

◆

Thirty minutes later, Ellie walks into T.K.'s room and plops herself down on the bed. She has a grocery bag in her hand, which she puts on T.K.'s nightstand.

"There are six news vans out in the street right in front of your house. This has gotta be the most exciting thing that has ever happened here. They practically peed themselves with excitement when my dad pulled into your driveway."

T.K. groans and drops onto the bed face-first next to Ellie.

"I'll never be able to leave the house again," she says into her pillow.

"They'll go away sooner or later. Or you could just go and talk to them, you know. It's not like you did something terrible."

T.K. sits up again and eyes the plastic bag on her nightstand.

"You saw the whole thing on TV?"

"Who didn't. It's been on the local news for days now. They kept replaying the footage."

Ellie opens the bag and takes out a half-gallon container of ice cream. She pops off the lid, fishes around in the bag for two spoons, and tosses one onto the bed in front of T.K.

"You should have seen my mom and dad when I showed them the newscast. It was the best. Like they just found out that their daughter's best friend is secretly moonlighting as a rock star."

T.K. wants to keep up the indignation, but she has to admit that Ellie's report pleases her. She was worried how her friends and family would react, but so far everyone is interested and even excited about her new ability. She feels like she just won the multi-state lottery jackpot. Even her parents, put out as they were by the sudden media siege and the disruption of their regular lives, had reacted with wide-eyed amazement when she demonstrated her powers to them. She wonders if everyone's reactions would have been the same if her card turned joker instead, but she knows the anthropological interest and slightly repulsed fascination with which her father reads the occasional features on New York City's Jokertown in *National Geographic*. No, she concludes almost instantly. Things wouldn't have felt like a lotto win if she had started sprouting tentacles or horns or something.

They make it through half the container before Ellie puts down her spoon and looks at T.K. expectantly.

"Well? I held up my end of the bargain. Now let's see what you can do."

"I thought you saw that on the news already."

"That's different," Ellie says. "Come on, don't back out now. I ran the camera gauntlet for you with that ice cream."

"Fair enough," T.K. demurs, secretly excited about having an excuse to pull the ball bearings out of the pocket of her jeans.

Ellie flinches a little when T.K. opens her hand and lets the ball bearings float above her palm. Then her friend leans in closer to look at the glossy orbs circling each other slowly, making orbits around a common center of gravity like a miniature binary star. T.K. has been practicing plenty since Edinburgh, and she has honed her fine control over the last few days. Turns out it's harder to move the balls in a slow and tightly controlled path than it is to fling them somewhere quickly or with a lot of force. Moving heavy stuff or shooting bricks requires effort, but fine control takes concentration, and the more precise she wants to be, the more she has to focus.

Ellie watches as T.K. makes the ball bearings in her hand spin around each other, first slow and then faster, until they're just a chrome blur. Then she slows them down again and sends them zooming around the room. She makes a low pass of her desk with one of the bearings, but misjudges the flight path a little. The ball bearing taps against the edge of her desk lamp's metal arm and knocks it over with a clatter.

"Whoops," T.K. says. Ellie just watches, mouth agape, as T.K. brings the errant ball bearing under control again and lets the orbs resume their formation-flying.

"You're doing that with your *mind?*"

"Yeah," T.K. replies. "Pretty awesome, huh?"

Ellie holds out a hand, and T.K. steers one of the ball bearings over and drops it gently into the center of Ellie's palm.

"Heavy," Ellie says. She bounces the ball bearing on her palm and turns it with her fingertips. "How fast can you make those things go?"

"Pretty fast," T.K. says, intentionally vague because she doesn't want to give Ellie the idea that she's dangerous now. "I still have to be able to see what I'm moving, though, so not that fast."

She's fibbing a little, of course—while she needs to be able to see the sphere to get its movement started, she can push it so fast and so hard that it instantly goes out of her control, like a bullet fired from a gun. But that's something that she will keep to herself for the moment.

"So what are you going to do now?" Ellie asks. "I mean, you're an ace. Everyone knows about it. You're going to go back to school like nothing happened?"

"Yeah. I mean, what else am I supposed to do? Put on a spandex leotard and go fight crime?"

"You're going to get your diploma. And then you're off to college. When the whole country knows your face. And what you can do." Ellie looks at her with a skeptical little smirk.

"Yeah," T.K. repeats. "And famous people go to college all the time. Actors and stuff. If they can do it, I should be fine." She scoops out a big spoon of ice cream from the now half-empty tub.

"Besides," she says around a mouthful of Norwich Creamery Moose Tracks. "It's not like they'll mob me for autographs before gym class. I'm *nobody*."

"Right." Ellie waves her own spoon vaguely in the direction of T.K.'s bedroom window. "And *nobody* has camera crews from all the major networks laying siege to her house."

Then Ellie uses her spoon like she's holding a ruler and sizing T.K.'s measurements up.

"Speaking of spandex leotards—we need to design a costume for you. And you'll need a catchy ace name. Like *Sphero*. Or *Ballistica*."

"Absolutely *not*," T.K. says and flicks a small spoonful of ice cream at her friend, who retreats with a little squeal. "Not in a million years."

RIPPLES IN THE POND

WITH THE REST OF her life so off the hinges right now, T.K. looks forward to going back to school after the holiday break, to see things return to normal. Mapletree is a private school, with controlled access to the campus and electronic keypads on every exterior door. There are kids at Mapletree whose parents have a lot of money and influence, so reporters aren't welcome there without a good reason, ace students or not.

But the day before school is about to begin again, her parents get a call from the school asking them to see the headmaster at drop-off in the morning, and the dread T.K. feels in her stomach tells her that *normal* may not be happening for her this school year.

♥

"You're *expelling* her?" T.K's dad says. He's using the same tone and facial expression he adopts whenever someone pitches an unwanted solicitation over the phone. They're sitting in the headmaster's office, and it's a cold and gloomy January morning outside, to match T.K.'s current mood.

"It's not an expulsion," the headmaster replies. He looks a little uncomfortable. "The board got together last week and decided that the school is not equipped to deal with the media fallout. And some parents have voiced concerns about safety. We don't allow students to bring weapons to school. And your daughter's, uh, abilities can certainly be used in an offensive manner. As we've all seen on TV."

T.K. doesn't like that the headmaster is speaking about her in the third person as if she wasn't sitting right in front of him.

"I've had these powers for months now," she says. "I've gone to class every day, just as always. And nobody got hurt."

"Of course we don't think you're out to hurt anyone, Tilly," the headmaster says.

"But you are kicking her out of school," her dad interjects. He still sounds like he's telling someone on the phone that no, he doesn't want or need any supplemental life insurance, thank you very much. Like he's haggling over an annoyance, not discussing whether to yank half of T.K.'s life out from under her feet.

"The board has decided to not renew the enrollment contract for this year. We feel that Tilly would be better off at a school that can take her abilities into account. But it's not an expulsion. We will send her on with a recommendation that reflects her flawless academic and disciplinary record."

It sure feels like an expulsion, T.K. thinks. *Whatever you want to call it.*

Her dad tries to argue because that's what he does. But T.K. can tell that the headmaster is done with them, and that her dad's protests and attempts at negotiation are going to extend this unpleasant business, and she is relieved when her father finally gives up and takes himself and his checkbook out of the room in a huff. T.K. trails him out of the school office and into the parking lot. Her schoolmates are going to classes, alone and in small groups, catching up with each other after the holiday break, and she has never felt so shut out in her life. She skipped right from disabled to too-abled, without getting to spend any time in between at just *abled*.

♣

"We were thinking about a different school anyway," T.K.'s dad tells her on the way home. "There are lots of great places in the area. Your mom really likes that boarding school in Quebec, the one with the houses and the school ties."

T.K. is sad and angry, and her father's forced cheerfulness doesn't help. She has no interest in thinking about a new school right now, with the sudden and complete separation from Mapletree still hurting like a razor cut. She didn't even have time to say goodbye to anyone. But she doesn't talk to her dad about her feelings. He's well-meaning, but he'd misdiagnose the problem and try to apply the wrong solution. In his world, everything can be fixed by writing a big enough check, and this isn't something money can mend. It's easy to make him think he's helping, though.

"I'll think about it," she tells him. "Do you think you could take me over to the Powerhouse and let me hang out there for an hour or two? I don't want to deal with the cameras at the house right now."

"Oh, sure, honey." From his expression, she can tell he's relieved that she is speaking in a language he understands. "I can drop you off and go see the accountant for a bit. Tax time is coming up, after all."

He gets his wallet out of the inside pocket of his sport coat and fishes out a credit card without taking his eyes off the road.

"Here. Use this one if you want to get a few things. Just don't buy a new car or anything."

"Not likely," she replies and returns his smile. But when she thinks about it, buying a little convertible and pointing it west isn't the worst plan of action she can think of right now, and if she had her license already, she knows she'd at least consider it.

♠

Their rich little town has an expensive little mall. It's a converted old powerhouse, renovated at great expense to look like something out of Victorian England, two levels of cute little shops along an indoor concourse lined with hardwood and decorated with lots of wrought iron. This early, most of the shops aren't open yet, but there's a cozy little café on the ground floor where T.K. can wait for ten o'clock to roll around.

She's halfway through her vanilla chai latte and picking at her blueberry scone when a magenta-haired girl walks into the café. The girl looks around, spots T.K., and heads straight for her table. At this time of day, most of the patrons in the café are blue-hairs from the nearby retirement village, so the girl walking T.K.'s way sticks out even more than she usually would. She stops in front of T.K.'s table, pulls out a chair, and sits down without asking. She's definitely past high school age, but that brightly colored pixie cut and her goth outfit make her look like she doesn't want to be a grown-up just yet. As she sits down and scoots the chair closer to the table, T.K. spots a golden nose stud.

"Hi," the girl says. "You are Lintilla Kendall."

T.K. makes a face.

"It's T.K. Or Tilly, if you don't do the initials thing. I haven't been *Lintilla* since preschool."

"T.K. I'm Simone. Simone Duplaix." The girl holds out her hand. She's wearing a bunch of bracelets on her wrist, and they jingle softly as T.K. accepts the handshake almost automatically.

"Nice to meet you," Simone says. Her English has a charming French accent that somehow matches her inoffensively cute appearance perfectly.

"*Vous êtes Québécois*," T.K. guesses, and Simone nods.

"*Oui, c'est vrai.* I see you took French in school. Very good."

"Wait, I think I've heard of you. You're one of the Canadian aces." T.K. looks around in the café to see if anyone's head has turned their way, but the mostly old folks are sipping their coffees and talking to each other without paying any attention to them.

"They call me *Snowblind*," Simone says, with dramatic effect in her voice on the last word. "I can blind people for a while. Like they are caught in a, how do you say, *nor'easter*? It is a good talent, but it is not quite as good as yours, I think. I watched the news footage. What you did, it was very impressive."

T.K. squirms a little in her seat, but she doesn't try to protest the compliment. It's the first time someone has said something unequivocally positive about her new talent. In truth, it pleases her a great deal, even if the memories of that day still twist her stomach.

"How did you know where to find me?" she asks.

"Oh, the place where I work, we have ways of tracking people. And you have been in the news lately quite a bit, no? It was not hard to find you."

Simone glances around the room poignantly, leans across the table, and lowers her voice a bit.

"You need to keep that in mind, after what you did in Europe, T.K. Now that everyone knows what you can do. You don't know yet what things are like for people like us in the world. There are jokers who already resent you for what you did. And there are many people who will want what you have."

T.K. looks at the café patrons again. The people sitting at their tables and drinking their coffees are still the same ones that were here before Simone walked in, but now T.K. feels anxious and a little afraid. The ball bearings in her pocket are a comforting weight, but she's still only a fifteen-year-old girl with a physical handicap and no talent or stomach for fighting. *Aces and jokers, government agencies and terrorism.* When did her life turn into a bad international mystery thriller?

"I got kicked out of school today," she says glumly. "They think I am dangerous."

"Well, of course you are," Simone says.

"But I'm *not*," T.K. protests. "I'm still the same person. I don't want to hurt anyone. I just want to go back to the way things were."

Simone looks at her with unconcealed pity and shakes her head with a little sigh.

"Oh, *chérie*. Your old life? That is over. From now on, when you meet new people and they know what you are, they will either want something from you, or they will be afraid of you."

"Really? And which kind are you?"

It comes out a little snippier than T.K. had intended, but Simone just smiles.

"Well, I am not afraid of you," she says.

"So what do you want from me?"

Simone reaches into the pocket of the leather jacket she's wearing and takes out a business card, which she puts facedown on the table right next to the plate that has the rest of T.K.'s blueberry scone on it.

"I *want* you to think about your future. About what you will do with this talent of yours. You will find that it opens a lot of doors for you. But you will have to decide which of those doors you want to step through."

T.K. picks up the business card and flips it over to read it.

"I work for the Committee," Simone says. "The Committee on Extraordinary Interventions. You may have heard of it."

"You work for the government?"

"Not for *a* government. We work for the United Nations, for all governments. People like you and me. Aces and joker-aces, keeping the peace. Helping out where we can with our talents."

"I'm *fifteen*," T.K. says. "I can't work for the United Nations yet. My parents won't even let me get a summer job at the gelato place."

"But you will be eighteen before too long, no?"

Simone nods at the business card T.K. is still holding.

"Maybe in a few years, if you decide you want to use your talent for a good cause, we can show you the sort of things we do. Until then, we just want you to know that we are around. So call me or send me a message if you need help. Or if you just want to talk. You know, with someone who knows what it's like."

"I'll think about it," T.K. says. She would laugh at the ludicrousness of the situation if she wasn't so overwhelmed by it all. If she hadn't gotten kicked out of school this morning, she'd be back in PE right now, and she's reasonably sure that Brooke and Alison wouldn't throw any balls within fifty feet of her ever again. But instead of doing crunches while thinking about lunch hour and afternoon science lab, she has the United Nations and international intrigue swirling around in her head, and that's not a leap her brain is willing to make right now. Her face must show some of the stress she's feeling, because Simone reaches across the table and squeezes her hand lightly.

"When you did what you did in Europe, it was like you threw a rock into a pond, T.K. It started making ripples. You do nothing, the water will smooth out again, eventually. But you know what you can also do?"

"What's that?"

"Start throwing in bigger rocks," Simone says. "Turn the ripples into waves."

◆

When T.K. leaves the café half an hour later, she's in a better mood. Getting expelled from school still hurts because it makes her feel like she's done something wrong, that she's being punished. But when she thinks about her future now, it's no longer indistinct and scary.

On the drive home with her dad, she imagines herself like Simone: dyed hair, nose stud, running around in some exciting foreign city like Tokyo or London, using her new ace powers in the service of the Committee. *Brooke and Alison would absolutely lose their shit*, she thinks.

♥

That evening, T.K. sits down with her parents in the living room to talk about school stuff. The way they are accommodating her right now, they must think she's devastated about getting kicked out of Mapletree. T.K.

chooses to reaffirm their parental instincts by telling them how unfair she thinks the whole thing is, which is absolutely true. She doesn't tell them about her meeting with Simone today, or about the fact that unlike them, she was never really fully in love with that school anyway. But when your parents have dropped fifty grand a year in tuition for two years running, that kind of information would probably be unwelcome, and she feels like she should keep it on a need-to-know basis for now.

While they are looking through high-gloss brochures for half a dozen other private high schools, her dad is sort of half-watching the hockey game that's playing on low volume on the living room TV. T.K. has her back to the screen, so she doesn't see what's going on in the game. She's reading through the list of offered sports at one of the interchangeable prep schools her parents have picked out—most of which require two functioning arms, naturally—when her dad lets out a suppressed cheer and pumps his fist.

"Really, honey? *Now?*" T.K.'s mom scolds him. "We're looking at schools now, dear. Can't you turn that off?"

T.K. turns to see what spiked her dad's excitement. They're showing the replay of the goal now. One of the players stops the puck with his stick and then does a sort of vertical roundhouse swing with all his force. Even at the low volume of the TV speakers, the puck shot sounds like a thunderclap, and she can barely follow its course as it rockets into the goal and makes the net twitch violently with the impact. T.K. sits up straight and follows the next replay closely with excited amusement. It looks exactly the way it did when she launched a ball bearing or a cue ball in that old factory down by the river near Mapletree: the puck, sitting at rest, then shooting off so fast that it's just a blur in the air.

"What do they call that swing?" she asks her father.

"Huh? What do you mean, sweetie?"

"When they swing the stick like that, with force. You know, *smack.*" She mimics the motion with her good arm.

"Oh, that. It's called a slap shot."

"Slap shot," she repeats with a little smile.

"Yeah. It's the hardest shot to pull off in hockey. Powerful, but not very accurate. Unless you have a lot of control." Her dad seems pleased that she's drawing on his knowledge of his favorite sport.

She returns her attention to the brochure in front of her, but her attention isn't with the nationally renowned equestrian program at St. Whatsit Academy, which she wouldn't be able to participate in anyway because she can't hold the reins of a horse with both hands. Instead, her mind is on the events of the day—the hurt and shame she felt this morning when she got kicked out of school, and then the weird excitement when she met Simone and got treated like an equal by a genuine grown-up, internationally famous ace. And right then and there she knows that her future probably won't be determined by whatever new rich-kid high school her mom and dad pick for her tonight.

♣

Later, when she's in bed and scrolling through the messages on her phone half-asleep, she shoots off a text to Ellie.

Forget Sphero or Ballistica. How about Slapshot?

The reply comes only a minute later.

OMG THAT IS PERFECT. It's so freaking regional.

Slapshot it is, then, T.K. sends back. Then she puts the phone on her nightstand and pulls up her covers.

I'm still not doing a costume, though, she thinks before the day catches up with her and she falls asleep.

Made in the USA
Middletown, DE
05 June 2024

55323783R10201